THE CUP AND THE SWORD

THE *CUP*
and THE *SWORD*

ALICE TISDALE HOBART

PUBLISHERS
THE BOBBS-MERRILL COMPANY
INDIANAPOLIS—NEW YORK

PRINTED AND BOUND BY THE
COUNTRY LIFE PRESS CORP.
GARDEN CITY, N.Y., U.S.A.

To

FLORENCE AYSCOUGH MACNAIR

Scissors cannot cut this thing;
Unraveled it joins again and clings.
It is the sorrow of separation,
And none other tastes to the heart like this.

FIR-FLOWER TABLETS
Translated from the Chinese
by Florence Ayscough
English Version
Amy Lowell

FOREWORD

ALTHOUGH the background of this book is true, the happenings in the wine industry and the places authentic, the story is fiction and the characters not drawn from actual persons. If anyone sees in the characters resemblances to friend or foe it is purely coincidental. So also is any name used except where a known business house is mentioned to place some historical event. Then the name is used as it would be in any historical account of California.

It has been necessary to dovetail and telescope years and events so that all the ups and downs which occurred in the wine industry between the two great world wars could be compressed within the covers of a novel.

I should like here to thank my many friends in the wine industry for their generous help, and especially Dr. E. A. Stokdyk for first calling my attention to this material.

Thanks go also to Houghton Mifflin Company for permission to quote in the dedication from *Fir-Flower Tablets* by Florence Ayscough and Amy Lowell; and to Woody Guthrie, author of *Dustbowl Ballads*.

THE CUP AND THE SWORD

I

JEAN-PHILIPPE RAMBEAU's eyes traveled along the vistas set out before him. The whole of the old house had been transformed into the living room where he sat. Its doorways gave glimpses of the new dining room, library and the wide timbered passage leading to his own wing. With satisfaction he surveyed the luxurious perfection which surrounded him. Although the room was darkened against the fierce California sun, the evidence of his wealth was everywhere apparent. And in his mind's eye he could see his vast vineyards lying all around him here in the San Joaquin Valley, and farther north in the state, in the dry wine country of the Napa Valley, his other vineyard.

From twenty-odd nations men had come, as he had, to these valleys sheltered between the Sierra and the coast range, seeking the pockets of mineralized earth, precious as gold, on which to grow grapes. They had brought with them every kind of vine that Europe possessed, also those of Asia Minor, Persia, and Egypt. He remembered now the music of their names—Sauvignon blanc, Muscat of Alexandria, Riesling, Gutedel.

He closed his eyes and listened to the wind blowing in great rushes through the oak outside, like wave after wave washed against a shore. For fifty autumns he had listened to the sound. He had stood leaning against the tree the day the carpenters had begun the house. It was harvest time then as now. But no wine was being made today from the loads of grapes coming in down at the winery.

Well, he would stop thinking about it. His granddaughter was to be welcomed into the family today. He took out his

11

watch. Her train was due in another hour. He wondered what she would be like. A Rambeau in looks as well as name, he hoped. But he understood she had blue eyes as her English mother had had. Again he felt the old disappointment that his son Lon had preferred to be an architect in London rather than take his part in the family business. Philippe Rambeau was a Catholic, and wine was more to him than a business. It was a symbol of communion with God. Communion with man, too, because in spite of his allegiance to America he remained proudly French. Whoever heard of a European gentleman dining without wine?

The sharp staccato of quick steps sounded on the tiles of the terrace outside, and he heard the voice of his daughter Martha as she directed the Chinese chauffeur David. "You're to go to the winery, David. Mr. Fairon will be there. You are to drive him into Fresno to meet the afternoon train. You haven't any extra time, tell Mr. Fairon. It's nearly five now. If Miss Elizabeth has too much luggage to be put into the back of the car, arrange to have it sent out."

So Martha wasn't going herself to meet Lon's girl but was sending Francis, her husband, instead. Perhaps it was just as well, thought Philippe. *Francis is both wise and gentle. He'll take care of her if she is shy.* A girl of eighteen might well be, meeting her father's family for the first time.

Philippe settled himself for a nap, paying no attention to his daughter Martha, who had entered the room and was opening the blinds, letting in the late afternoon sun.

From the back seat of the car Elizabeth Rambeau looked for the first time at the San Joaquin Valley. By sitting in the middle, she could see between the two heads in front of her—those of Francis Fairon, her Aunt Martha's husband, and David, his Chinese chauffeur. Through the countryside the road, wide and shimmering, stretched straight on without turning. Far in the distance it looked wet and black, an illusion which moved ahead as the car approached it over the shining oiled surface of the pavement. There were no winding lanes, half-hidden in trees, as in England. No tree-covered slopes to soften the light from the sky, or the light on the road. Once a windbreak of eucalyptus trees, standing tall and straight, made a line of shadows across the way. They were quickly passed. As far as Elizabeth could see, the Valley was spread out in unbroken brilliance to where, dimly against the horizon, lay the pale shapes of mountain ridges. On the Valley floor, the vineyards and orchards shone in the intense sunlight. The symmetrically pruned trees and vines cast close shadows over the bare, cultivated earth beneath. The blazing light hurt her eyes; the hot, quivering air made her dizzy. *Strange country,* thought Elizabeth.

Francis Fairon was as unfamiliar as the land. He was a man in middle age, looking to her very American indeed. Almost too well groomed, if she were to judge him by the studied casualness of the Englishmen to whom she was accustomed, and judged him she had in swift appraisal when he had met her at the train, comparing him to his disadvantage with the lean, supple, man-about-town look of William Humphreys whom she had so much admired.

The fine texture of Francis Fairon's light summer suit, his hand-woven Panama hat, the quality of his linen, all gave unmistakable evidence of wealth as did his car, its appointments, the liveried driver. *But it's only his wealth that gives him distinction,* Elizabeth decided. Such severe judgment helped to make her feel hard. She wanted to be hard. It was the only way not to break down.

I'm not making a very good start. I must, she thought, trying to rouse herself, realizing that at the first of the ride Francis Fairon had turned often to speak to her, but now was not doing so.

I've accepted his hospitality. I'm going to live in his house! She must have been mad when she allowed herself to be persuaded to make her home among strangers. Lon had talked as if his family by right would give her a home. What hold had she upon them or they upon her? She was trained to the ways of her mother's country and her mother's faith. She felt an old insecurity. She was as much adrift now as she had been ever since she was a little girl. She felt her courage running out in a last effort at conversation.

California, the place she had counted upon to bring back happiness, had added to her unhappiness by its strangeness. Loneliness and strangeness had taken hold of her as she had watched from the train window the vast country of America accumulating behind her in miles of prairies, deserts, and mountains, putting her farther and farther away from her own land. England was her own land. It held her father and it held William Humphreys. It held the places marked by the happiness of her meetings with William Humphreys and the spot where she had learned the truth—he had not been in earnest, as she had. Her lovely passionate mouth set in lines of frustration and suffering. In spite of all she could do, tears rolled down her cheeks. She did not wipe them away for fear Francis Fairon might see she was crying.

All at once something dropped in her lap. So he had seen! In mingled mortification and relief she buried her face in the man-sized handkerchief.

"This is our road. Our land at the side," she heard him say.

The car had turned into a long avenue bordered by eucalyptus trees, the bark stripped away. The light glanced from their sleek trunks, the lofty branches hung their drooping slender leaves against the sky in gray-green lances. Palms like huge poles stood among them, their tufted fan-shaped tops mingling high up with the leaves of eucalyptus. Low against the ground oleanders, pink and white, fled by in an alternate succession of color as the high-powered car rolled quickly on. The blinding light of the highway reached her now only in flickering spears.

Francis Fairon turned and smiled at her. Elizabeth was beginning to think she had been hasty in her judgment. He was really very nice.

"The Rambeau-Fairon vineyards," he explained, "extend for a mile on either side of the road."

"What use can you make of the grapes now?" asked Elizabeth, grasping at the first idea that came into her head to make conversation. "I thought you had Prohibition out here."

"We have," Francis Fairon answered. "It's a long story—what we do with our grapes—but I suggest you don't mention Prohibition before your grandfather. Your Aunt Martha thinks it better not to."

I wonder why, she thought, *but I must remember, I must see that they like me.*

"Stop here, David," Francis said to his driver, as the road began to circle a wide lawn. But when the car came to a halt he made no move to get out.

By some understanding grown up between them in the last few moments, Elizabeth realized he was giving her an instant's time to collect herself. Comforted by this slim tie with her new environment, she turned to look at the low white house set in the center of the smooth lawn.

She had seen nothing like it during the drive. Although made of perpendicular boards, battened, a type of construction she had noticed in numerous humble cottages along the way, it managed to convey the ultimate of pretension. Wing after wing led out from the main part, making a house of great size. Heavy plantings of shrubs, placed in the ells, gave it the appearance of being a series of small dwellings, but the long uninterrupted lines of the gray shingled roof belied the subterfuge. The length of the house was emphasized by the dwarfing of its height, the effect gained by an oak of tremendous spread which leaned over it. A band of iron supported the two central branches of the tree. Its scarred trunk had been reinforced with cement. The oak and the house were eloquent of the expensive care given them.

Touching the lawn at every point were the vineyards. Elizabeth had a sensation of beauty and strength as she saw the vines against the clipped green of the grass. Their knee-high, two-pronged trunks were clearly outlined—short, sturdy, more gnarled than the oak, with cinnamon-brown shredded bark. From the tops the trailing branches sprang away. Grapes hung down in purple and white clusters.

"Ready?"

"Yes."

Francis Fairon leaned forward and sounded the horn. The door of the house was instantly thrown open.

Elizabeth knew the woman who stepped out. She had seen pictures of her. The prominent, well-chiseled straight nose, the large black eyes set far apart, and the heavy hair piled on the top of the head, all were familiar. But Elizabeth had expected a tall woman. Her father had never said Aunt Martha was tall, but her strong, rather large features went with height. This woman standing waiting in front of the green paneled door was short, built with such marked compactness that she was not stout. Less well put together, she would have been so.

Glancing at Francis Fairon as he helped her out, Elizabeth felt that a change had come over him. But there was no time to analyze it. She realized that the situation demanded eagerness on her part. She walked quickly toward her aunt.

Martha Fairon waited, still not speaking. And then, just before Elizabeth reached her, she took the initiative. Stepping forward, she placed her hands on Elizabeth's shoulders, and kissed her. As her aunt's lips clung for one instant to her cheek, Elizabeth had a vivid sense of a powerful, unexpressed force seeking to bring her under control.

"Come. Your grandfather is waiting to see you." Taking Elizabeth's hand, Martha Fairon stepped through the door into a large room. At its end, near a window which reached to the rafters, stood a slight, short man with white hair and closely clipped Vandyke. The sun's rays shone horizontally across his animated face. So this was Jean-Philippe Rambeau! Elizabeth knew of course that her grandfather was very old but her first impression of him was of a man little older than her father. The flesh over his cheekbones seemed to have almost the firmness of youth. Color glowed beneath his olive skin.

He held out his hand and offered his cheeks to be kissed. Elizabeth was conscious then of his age. The skin under her lips was soft and dry.

"Sit down, child," he said, "and tell me about yourself and my son." There was a courtly air about his speech that was very engaging. She knew now where Lon's charm came from, but there was a quality in her grandfather that was not in her father. Something about him was more like Aunt Martha.

"Father sent you his love," said Elizabeth. "I've a package for you, too," she added impetuously.

She was about to sit down by his side when Aunt Martha broke in. "You must be tired. You'll want to freshen up before dinner. I'll take you to your room."

Elizabeth looked from one to the other, wondering what to do, feeling slightly embarrassed, for she realized a contest was going on between them. All at once it seemed to be over.

"So Lon sent me a present, did he?" her grandfather was saying. "May I have two guesses?"

"No, only one." She was seated beside him now, and she had forgotten that he had been a stranger to her a moment ago, so natural did it seem to be talking to him.

"Then I won't guess."

"I'll tell you."

"No."

"Then I'll show you. It's right here in one of my bags. Lon made me carry it like that so it wouldn't get broken." Elizabeth moved quickly across the room to where a spare, old Chinaman stood, her luggage piled around him.

"Just a moment," said her grandfather. "I want you first to know Chu. Chu, this is Miss Elizabeth. I've told you about her. And Elizabeth, this is Chu Rambeau. Your father has undoubtedly told you about Chu."

But Lon hadn't. Her father had told her very little about his old home. Chu Rambeau. Evidently a servant in the house, but why was he called Rambeau? Whoever he was, she saw he regarded himself as an important member of the family. He bowed gravely, saying, "Missie very pretty."

"Thank you," said Elizabeth, not knowing what else to say.

"Now the small bag, Chu," said her grandfather.

"And you can carry the rest of Miss Elizabeth's luggage to her room," Aunt Martha commanded, then preceded Chu down a long passageway.

Elizabeth felt more comfortable now that her aunt was not there. Hunting among a quantity of soft things in her bag, she felt at last the hard package she was seeking. She could hear her grandfather jingling the coins in his pocket. It made her smile to herself. Lon had told her how Philippe Rambeau always carried gold pieces in his pocket. Gold was the only currency he dealt in. "The one currency for a California gentleman," he insisted. The habit of letting one gold piece fall against another, he resorted to when he was very happy.

In all except her eyes she is pure Rambeau. Philippe looked at her with delight. She had risen from her knees and was coming toward him. *She is beautiful. She has grace and she knows how to carry herself. Lon would see to that,* he thought with satisfaction.

"Here it is, Grandfather. Lon bought it in France, for your collection."

Out of the cotton wool in which it was wrapped Philippe Rambeau took a goblet. His fingers lay against the glass as he held it to the light. Elizabeth noticed that his hands in spite of care showed the marks of hard work—the cuticle around the nails was thick, the skin under them was pushed far down showing how the earth of his vineyards had once pressed in.

"Very fine," he said at last. "A rare piece." He was seeing it in a special niche in his secluded sampling room built into the great stone winery. Arranged on shelves were the beautiful old goblets of kings and peasants—French, German, Egyptian and Greek, they stood side by side, too precious now to hold wine.

"What have you there?" Martha had come back into the room. She stood looking over his shoulder. "I see. Another piece of glass. Lon spent a good deal for that. Come, Elizabeth, you've just time to get some rest before dinner."

II

THE next afternoon Elizabeth was lying in a long chair in the great living room. Martha had placed books and magazines at her side, telling her to make herself comfortable—meaning, stay out of the way. All the afternoon her aunt had been moving in and out with a look of concentrated, worried pleasure. She had brought in a tray filled with wineglasses to polish, a dish of fruit to arrange. She moved flowers about, rang for Chu, directed him in details of the family dinner she was giving this evening.

In the corner of the room where Martha had her desk, the middle-aged servant placed himself so that he could look out the window. During the interview he maintained his careful gaze on things outside, giving little grunts of pleasure or distaste, his only answer to his mistress' commands.

"It's the way he maintains what he considers his dignity," Martha told Elizabeth after Chu had gone. "You see his family has been in America as long as ours. He never lets me forget he considers himself my equal."

"And you, what do you think?" Elizabeth had asked.

"Well, isn't he? Doesn't the Constitution make him so?"

Elizabeth felt a little confused, remembering that the evening before Martha had addressed David, Chu's son, distinctly as an inferior. Elizabeth would have liked to learn more about Chu but obviously her aunt was too preoccupied to talk.

At last everything seemed to be done to Martha's satisfaction and she came and sat down. *She looks as if she'd be off again any moment, though,* thought Elizabeth.

20

"Pretty soon, my dear," said her aunt, "the family will be here. I've kept them off for twenty-four hours and that's a feat in itself. You'd better be getting dressed."

Elizabeth scrambled to her feet. "Of course. What would you like me to wear, Aunt Martha?" Elizabeth knew that her aunt would have a definite idea in the matter.

"The best you have," Martha Fairon replied. "They're expecting a good deal of your father's daughter. The Rambeaus expect a great deal of every member of the family."

As Martha spoke the name Rambeau, Elizabeth thought, *I've never known anyone so proud, nor so separate. Even if she does bear the Fairon name it does not hold in her mind the proud place of Rambeau.* Not trained to undue deference for her elders, Elizabeth said somewhat airily, "Do you expect more of the Rambeaus than of other people?"

Seeing the quick displeasure in Martha Fairon's face, she hastened to add in a tone as humble as she could make it, "You see, I don't know as much as I'd like to about the Rambeaus."

"Poor child, I suppose not, Lon going off as he did." Her aunt was as quickly mollified as she had been aroused. In short, clipped sentences, with obvious delight in her chance to inform her niece, she told her about the family—facts some of which Elizabeth had known, but to which she had not attached especial importance. Marriages, deaths, money, the great tracts of land they owned, the extent of their vineyards, hundreds of acres—counting in the Fairon land—two marriages into the Fairons, Martha's and her sister Isobel's.

"Your Aunt Maria married into a Spanish line. Titled, you know." Martha gave a short, sharp laugh. "Maria of all Father's children to have brought home a title! Maria is— well, you'll see Maria tonight. The young Don, she calls her son. He's not her son, really. She's only his stepmother. His name is Enrique, but I've insisted that we call him Henri after the French. Your uncle André also married into a Spanish line. No title there, though. Spanish is the only blood in the family not French, except yours. English blood is what's given you your height, I suppose. Possibly a little too tall and rangy. But you carry it off fairly well."

Her aunt scrutinized her in silence before she went on. "I've never understood why you weren't sent to me way back in nineteen fourteen when both your father and mother went to France and left you alone in an English school. That would have been the time for you to come to America."

"I think Mother wanted me where she could see me sometimes. She did have one leave from the hospital," Elizabeth answered, wondering for what information her aunt was probing.

"Well, then after your mother died, why weren't you sent?"

Made uneasy by her aunt's persistent questions, Elizabeth hastened to say, "I think Lon wanted me near him, just as Mother had."

"Why do you call your father Lon? It doesn't sound very respectful."

"Because he asked me to. We did everything together after he came back from the war." Elizabeth felt a kind of desperation as her aunt pressed closer to the reason for her leaving England.

"You were rather a young girl to be much of a companion to a man of the world like Lon, weren't you?"

"Yes," said Elizabeth, "I suppose so."

"You would have been much better off here," her aunt continued. "I urged Lon often enough to give you to me and he wouldn't. And then quite suddenly he sent you. I wonder why?"

It was the question Elizabeth had been dreading to have asked. It was after she had told Lon about William Humphreys that he had wanted her to come to America. "Hasn't living with me taught you how to manage an affair of that sort?" he had asked her. "How was it, my little, you didn't know that a man like Humphreys is never in earnest? . . . I am evidently not the one to care for you," he had added. "I expect I've been selfish, but I wanted to keep you to myself."

"And now you don't?" she had asked. He had never understood how he had hurt her by suggesting she go to his own people. . . .

"Well, let's look at what you have to wear." Martha changed the subject as Elizabeth did not answer her last question. "I can tell you what the family will like." She preceded her niece down the long corridor to the bedroom wing of the house.

Elizabeth took down the dresses she had hung in the closet that morning and laid them on the bed for her aunt's inspection. Martha's dark eyes went back to the closet.

"What's that peacock-blue thing? Evening dress?"

"Yes, but it's a costume affair. I hardly think it would do."

"Just the thing. I like its *bouffant* skirt and its small puffed sleeves." Martha Fairon spoke without hesitation, unaware that her niece must have some reason for not wearing it as she had not shown it to her.

Elizabeth had not meant to wear it ever again.

"It looks French to me. The others are more English. Besides, it's good with your blue eyes," her aunt added. "I'll leave you now."

Elizabeth went about her dressing determined, in spite of the necessity to wear this dress, to hold herself, as she had all day, above her difficult emotions. But it was like walking on thin ice; the surface might break and strong currents carry her under. If only she did not have to wear this dress. Slowly she picked it up.

"The curve is the exact curve of your breasts, my darling," William Humphreys had said. And afterward, when he had put her cape around her. . . .

There was an emphatic tap at her door. Knowing already her aunt's special tap, and that she would hardly wait for consent to enter, so quickly would she act upon it, hastily Elizabeth slipped the dress over her head. She was trying, while she was submerged in its folds, to regain composure. "I'm caught," came from her in a muffled tone.

"Bend over," said her aunt, parting the voluminous folds of blue which held Elizabeth entrapped. "Why, you're not caught," she exclaimed in some surprise, pushing the dress down over Elizabeth's shoulders. "You can't be. There aren't any hooks to be caught on! There."

She stood off, surveying Elizabeth, scrutinizing her carefully, taking due note of her full passionate under lip and the sensitive willful lift to the upper, the stubborn chin, the broad forehead, the intense blueness of the eyes.

Umph. The expression about the eyes was not entirely youthful.

Lon said to mold her. . . . It's been done, was her final conclusion. The suspicion that the girl had had some kind of love affair had been growing in Martha's mind all day. Her sudden fits of inattention, a kind of restless irritation about her. Now she felt almost certain of it. *Why else, after all, would Lon suddenly send her? He's always refused before. Why did he give in now, unless it was because he couldn't manage her himself?*

Martha felt a bitter disappointment. She had plans for the girl's marriage. Martha Fairon was a woman who could not bear failure in anything she undertook. *But I'm going to have trouble this time; it will be a battle,* she said to herself.

She doesn't like me, thought Elizabeth. She stood withdrawn into herself with watchful eyes. Then the moment of mutual suspicion was over, almost without either of them realizing the antagonism which had sprung up between them.

"My dear, you're pretty in that dress," said her aunt, the self the world knew stepping into the foreground, hiding her intuitive self that did not like Elizabeth. "Whoever selected it knew what she was about. I must go," she added. Voices outside had brought Martha into immediate action. "Come as soon as you're ready." She went swiftly out of the room.

Elizabeth lingered, smoothing her hair, touching her cheeks with a little more color. She wished she had her aunt's hard finish. It seemed to guarantee control of emotions.

As she stood irresolute, unsure of herself, at one of the open doors which served as the windows of her room, she felt the soft touch of the half-tropic, half-desert night on her skin, and her mind seemed all at once to step over emotion, eager, curious, reaching for new experiences. By training and heritage, active and sensitive, it now shook off the hold of her emotionally driven spirit.

When she entered the hall in the main part of the house she saw that a door at its farther end, which she had not noticed before, had been thrown open. Through it, she looked straight into a garden enclosed on three sides by the house. A long table was set in the middle. Groups of men and women were standing about. *Am I related to them all?* She hesitated.

"Here she is. Come out here," Martha called, taking her hand as she came through the open door.

Elizabeth had no very clear impression of any one person, but the whole company seemed suddenly ludicrous to her. *As if Lon and I had been dismembered for the party, our features sprinkled through the crowd. There's Father's nose! That man's walking around with it just as if it belonged to him. A magnificent nose, really. And there's my mouth on that young man over there. I don't know that I like him to be wearing it. It's especially mine.* She felt an hysterical desire to laugh.

"I'm your Aunt Isobel, your Aunt Martha's sister, you know," a middle-aged, kindly-looking woman was saying. "I met your mother in England before you were born. But you're not like her, my dear. More Rambeau." Without any effort to disguise it, the older woman looked Elizabeth over. "It's surprising," she went on, "how the Rambeau strain always predominates. It does in my children, even though they bear the name of Fairon. Andrew"—she turned to her son standing near—"come and meet your new cousin." The young man who came toward them was a little older than Elizabeth. He did have the Rambeau features, as his mother said, but they were oddly softened. The chin seemed rounder, the eyes sunnier.

Before Elizabeth could speak to him Aunt Martha had taken her hand again, leading her across the grass to one group after another, introducing her, then taking her to the table saying, "Here, next your Uncle Francis. On his right. It's your party, you know."

"Good looking, *and* a Rambeau," Francis' brother, Ronald Fairon, the man at Martha's right, said leaning toward her. *She may not prove so difficult after all*, Martha thought. Looking down the table at Elizabeth, in gracious conversation with Fran, she was better pleased with the girl. Fran liked her. Martha had feared he might not, for he hadn't wanted another member to his family. Because she was a Rambeau, Martha inwardly had accused him.

Elizabeth had not seen Francis Fairon all day, and now as he turned to her with a little smile, she felt that sense of companionship of yesterday.

"Everything all right?" he asked.

"Yes."

"No more need for handkerchiefs?" He smiled at her.

"No. No more need."

"That's fine." Without more ado he gave himself to the business of eating his soup.

Elizabeth turned to speak to the man on her right, but he was obscured for the moment by David's white-clad arm reaching between them to pour wine into her glass. Elizabeth waited.

"All clear." She turned, facing her cousin Jean. "I thought you were never going to talk to me," he said. "After all, you'll see a lot of Uncle Fran. John Rambeau. Your Uncle André's eldest son. You remember?" Martha had pronounced it "Jean."

"Oh, it's you," she said.

He bowed. "I'm flattered that you remember me."

"It's your mouth," said Elizabeth.

"What about it?"

"Nothing. Only it's mine."

He laughed. "Yours! Oh, you mean you've got the Rambeau mouth. That's nothing. A lot of them in the family. There's another one over there." He nodded toward a girl sitting on the opposite side of the table. "Monica, my sister."

"No, it's not the same," Elizabeth answered. "Hers is serene and—quiet."

"You're right," he agreed. He looked boldly at Elizabeth. "Ours *are* different. They get us into trouble."

Elizabeth flushed. *She's prettier than ever when she flushes,* John said to himself. *I'll have to make her do it often.* He felt a growing excitement in watching her. Striking, the combination of black hair, faintly olive skin and blue eyes. She had a temper. He'd seen that when she flushed. He'd like to see her really roused.

"Look," she said. "Everybody has black hair except Grandfather." Against the night that hugged the lighted table, the dark masses of their blue-black hair made a definite dado.

"Does that strike you as strange? After all, we're all French. No towheads among us, and we turn gray very slowly. We're tough and long-lived."

Elizabeth detected that same proud note that had been in her aunt's voice when she spoke of the family. "French? Not American?"

"I was in the war. I guess that makes me an American," he answered. "Ran away to get in. Lied about my age."

Five years since the Armistice. He must be, at least, twenty-three, she thought. "You are all very beautiful, anyway," she said aloud. The light from the hurricane lamps, set at intervals down the long table, rose into their handsome faces. Their hands, holding the heavy silver forks, grasping the stems of wineglasses, were well-shaped, acquisitive hands.

The dinner was over, the table cleared except for a single glass by each place and a tall urn of blue-black grapes in the center, used by Martha for decoration instead of flowers. Elizabeth noticed her grandfather had paused in his conversation. As if he had given a signal, silence fell upon his family. Elizabeth watched, curious to see what would happen.

With considerable ceremony, the old man took from a basket at his side a bottle covered with dust, handed it to Chu who went the rounds of the table, filling the glasses.

Grandfather Rambeau got to his feet and there was the sound of chairs scraping the tiled surface of the court as the others followed his example.

"The circle of my family is all but complete," he began, "in the return of my granddaughter. It is a great Rambeau occasion. England has given up at least part of what belongs to us. To honor this member of my family, I have chosen a fine old wine sent out from France long ago."

He clasped the stem of his glass, raised it, paused a moment holding it to the light. "To Elizabeth Rambeau, my granddaughter," he said at last.

Elizabeth saw the glasses touch, heard the murmur of her name circle the table. She bowed slightly in acknowledgment as she had once seen Lon do in response to a toast.

John Rambeau had been watching her carefully. *She's not going to let anyone rattle her, that kid. By gad, I'm going to try. She can't be as contained as all that.* Maybe he could make her blush again.

"Speech, speech!" he demanded. His voice, low but insistent, reached his brother farther down the table.

"Speech!" echoed the fifteen-year-old Charles.

Soon the younger members of the party were chanting in unison, "Speech, speech!"

Elizabeth stood up with no idea what she would say, only the determination to get through the ordeal somehow without calling down censure or ridicule upon herself. She mustn't step into the trap John had set for her. She wasn't going to offend Grandfather or her Aunt Martha, either, by saying flippant things that came to her tongue which would undoubtedly delight John. And she mustn't say anything that would show that she was moved by her grandfather's recognition of her. John might twit her about it afterward. But what should she say? Oh, now she had it. She dropped her eyes, knowing that in her costume frock she made a lovely picture standing before the tribunal of her family.

"I would like to give you a toast," she said. Her modulated English voice though low was distinct. "My father. And may he return to us soon."

She looked at her grandfather. His eyes, shrewd and quizzical like Lon's, gave their approval. Then they changed suddenly to somber, unhumorous eyes.

"André," he said to his eldest son sitting across the table from him, "how is the wine? No one has said. You have the best palate of us all. Tell me, is it good?"

"It has flavor, bouquet, and brilliance," answered André. "Only the French can do it so well."

He says it, thought Elizabeth, *like a parrot.*

The old man reached in the inside pocket of his coat and drew out some folded papers worn at the edges, held together by an elastic band. "I'd like to say one thing to my family"— he did not stand this time, but his voice rang with authority— "before I relinquish the business completely to my sons, which I plan to do when the harvest is in."

Elizabeth leaned forward not to miss a word, her mind alert, forgetful of all but the important statement the head of the family had just made, watching to see the effect of his words. From all at the table there was a polite protest. "Not yet," they murmured. *They're taking such an important announcement calmly enough*, thought Elizabeth.

"I have something more to say to you all," Grandfather Rambeau went on, ignoring their protest. "You do not have to send to France for wine like this. You are drinking your own!" With a flourish he threw the papers across to his son André Rambeau.

Elizabeth felt the dramatic quality of the moment. She

watched the others. *Why don't they clap?* she wondered. She was indignant that they did not. *Grandfather is really a sport.*

"There are the bills of lading," the old man went on. "I've traced the wine from the time it left our vineyards. New York, then France, and back again. Only the label is different, to satisfy the American public," he said with scorn. "I've kept my secret until tonight. Now that the time comes to hand over the business to you, I want you to have pride. No more nonsense about not being able to produce the best. No more cringing because the Government has made wine illegal, classing it with hard liquor. Ours is the business of gentlemen. We have reason to be proud of what we have wrought for America."

Now everyone did clap. Elizabeth, carried away with enthusiasm for her grandfather, clapped with all her might, forgetting to hide her emotion until she caught John Rambeau surveying her with a sardonic grin. She realized then that her aunt had risen, was already moving away, the other women following her. She hurriedly picked up her beaded bag from the table and followed them to settees set out under the great oak.

"Well, Elizabeth," Martha said, once she had seen that everyone was seated and had coffee, "Grandfather rather stole the show from you, didn't he?" She laughed lightly with acrid amusement that confused and angered Elizabeth.

"Oh, but I was so excited at Grandfather's news," Elizabeth protested, "I forgot all about my part. It was wonderful, wasn't it? I forgot all about everything else."

As she looked around the group she had the uneasy feeling that there was some point she was missing. Aunt Maria seemed about to speak, then catching Martha's eye evidently thought better of it. Aunt Isobel hastily changed the subject. Looking at the three Rambeau sisters, Martha, Isobel, and Maria, sitting side by side, Elizabeth had the unpleasant feeling that they thought her naïve. She bit her lip, wondering what she had done to make them think so.

Monica, John Rambeau's sister, sitting on the settee beside her, put down her coffee cup and laid her hand over Elizabeth's, saying under cover of the general conversation, "You mustn't mind Aunt Martha. Grandfather didn't really steal the show."

"It wasn't that," Elizabeth answered. "It's that you act as if I shouldn't be interested in what Grandfather said."

"He's given us that news five times now," Monica told her quietly.

"You mean——"

"Yes, shown us the papers. Told us about the wine. It's only kind to show surprise. See him now. He's thrown his shoulders back and he looks almost young and he's laughing."

He was standing just outside the door to the living room, a handsome old man, a cigar in his hand, his son, grandsons, and sons-in-law around him. The strong rich aroma of their tobacco floated on the small breeze springing up.

"Just after Prohibition came in," Monica explained, "he did it the first time. It was a surprise then. You should have seen the commotion in the family that time!"

"Now?"

"Now we try not to let him suspect he's told us the same story before. Grandfather's over eighty. I guess he forgets. He didn't, until his wines became illegal."

Why, thought Elizabeth, *do they all hark back to Prohibition? Uncle Fran did yesterday, and John when he was talking to me at the table, and now Monica.* "Prohibition was a shock to all of us," Monica went on, "but especially to Grandfather. Winemaking had been an honorable occupation until this happened. It bothers him that his business is under a cloud. Urging us all to have pride seems to take away his humiliation for a time."

Elizabeth had a sudden realization of some deep hurt to the family. Then her attention was caught by a young man coming toward her, the cousin with the sunny eyes. He smiled as he raised his hand in a half salute. *Let's see,* thought Elizabeth, *he's Aunt Isobel's son. Andrew.* Andrew Fairon, for Aunt Isobel had married Ronald Fairon, Francis Fairon's brother. *He looks nice,* she thought.

Then her attention shifted to her cousin John Rambeau. He was standing in front of them. He was frowning.

"Monny, why don't you explain to Elizabeth, while you're about it, that Grandfather has told us five times he was going to retire?" he asked.

Monica did not answer.

"You needn't get mad about it, Monny. You're a girl and it's all right for you. But I want my chance."

"Oh, forget it, John." Andrew Fairon spoke with quiet determination. "Why don't we go swimming over at your house? I'd like to see the new floodlight you've put in."

"I bet you look swell in a bathing suit, Elizabeth," Charles, John's younger brother, anxious to say something to the new cousin, put in.

"How will Aunt Martha take it?" Elizabeth asked doubtfully.

"We often do after dinner," Monny explained, "when it is as hot as it is tonight." The breeze that blew through the branches of the oak scarcely fluttered its leaves. The air lay against their skins like a dry, powdery substance.

"Anyway it will be all right, if Henri puts it up to her. Go over and ask him to, Charles," commanded John. "I'll keep guard here." Elizabeth felt the settee settle under his weight.

"Doesn't he look like something come out of a castle?" John asked in a voice of mock admiration, pointing to a young man Elizabeth had scarcely noticed before who was now leaning over Martha. So that was the Don Swanaña. He was tall, slender, and very dapper. *Almost foppish,* was her quick judgment.

"A gentleman, every inch," John said in a mincing tone.

"Stop it, John," Monica commanded in a low voice. "It isn't fair."

"Why should I want to be fair to Henri?" John asked. "Have you ever known *him* to be fair?"

"She's said yes. I saw her nod." Andrew, sitting on the grass directly in front of Elizabeth, whistled three notes. A tall girl about Charles' age sitting among the older women looked up. He beckoned to her. "Suzanne's my sister," he told Elizabeth, "and those two girls sitting on the grass near Mother are, too. I don't suppose you have us all placed yet. Leli is the oldest of us, Françoise comes next, then I—Suzanne is the youngest one in the Ronald Fairon family."

A few moments later Elizabeth found herself crowded into the front seat of a car between her cousins John Rambeau and Andrew Fairon. John drove at a furious speed along the highway, and turned up another avenue of trees to a house, two-storied, rising abruptly out of its gardens—the André Rambeau residence. Upstairs, across the front, the lights blazed.

"That's Mother's room," Monica told her. Then Elizabeth remembered the tone of scorn with which Aunt Martha had said, "André Rambeau's wife is an invalid." She wondered why Aunt Martha had used that tone. "Shan't we disturb her?" she asked.

"She doesn't sleep until late and she likes to hear us," Monica said simply as she and Elizabeth went toward the bath house.

The pool was wide and deep. It seemed to Elizabeth her skin sucked at the water, so much in need of moisture was it after the long stretch of the day's heat. Lying on her back, she looked up at the light streaming out from the end window upstairs. It made her hurt to think of the occupant of that room. It wasn't the pain which this unknown woman had to endure that bothered Elizabeth. She had never known physical pain and could not imagine it. It was the separation from activity that seemed terrible. She began thrashing her arms about, doing any kind of trick that put her into action. She noticed John was doing tricks too.

"Henri's planning the cousins' party for you," he said,

bobbing up in the water beside her, his dark head sleek and dripping. "A fine affair in a new café."

Monica, sitting on the edge of the pool, was watching her brother John. She was pleased to see that he liked the new cousin. She hadn't seen him so happy for a long time. The fit of restlessness which had held him in its clutches for days now seemed completely to have disappeared.

She had come to dread these fits of restlessness that came upon John. When he was a boy, Charles' age, she had known how to help him. But since his return from the war she had often been at a loss. Sometimes he seemed to want her near him; at other times she only irritated him. In all the five years she had never found a sure approach. Sometimes, in a day or two, she could quiet him down. Sometimes it took infinite patience, days, weeks, when perversely he side-stepped every approach she made.

After their mother's sickness and until he went away to the war they had hardly ever been separated, although she liked gentle, quiet things to do and John, from a child, had wanted hard games, competition. Their great delight was to ride together. John, who from the time he was fourteen had taken part in every rodeo for miles around, admired her horsemanship. She admired his showmanship. On their first ride after their separation Monica had seen him hit his horse. She loved horses too much to let the matter pass and she was really angry. "John Rambeau!" she had cried. "What on earth has got into you?"

And there had been shame in his eyes. He had apologized instantly.

Monica was thinking of this little scene now as she watched him, trying to marshal her forces for the struggle she knew was ahead of her. What she had been hearing made it necessary to reach the decent John. He mustn't have anything to do with the night riders.

III

Long after the house had settled to sleep Elizabeth lay between sleeping and waking, the family tramping through her mind, moving toward some objective unknown and mysterious to her but taking her along.

At last she slept, but it seemed to her she was almost immediately conscious that it was daylight, that the sun had pushed itself vigorously above the shoulder of the distant mountains. It was shining directly into her eyes. Her eyelids seemed paper-thin and of little protection against the fierce light. As sleep made her defenseless to the impact of light, so also it made her defenseless to the impact of loss. Her senses ached in their futile reaching for something denied them. Slowly, through the layers of the last year's happenings, she groped her way to the surface of the day. She sat up in bed. *My third day in this house*, she thought. She looked at her watch. It was only six o'clock. A long day. Even now it was very hot. Leaning on her elbow she looked at the expanse of green lawn outside her windows and the grapevines along its edge. She could see men and women, even children, working among the vines.

The harvest everyone was talking about last evening. If I could slip out, before Aunt Martha is up, perhaps I could go for a walk before breakfast. She still hoped to outdistance her aching sense of loss in spite of the fact that she had not done so in her dash across half the globe.

As she came into the long hall leading to the main part of the house Martha Fairon entered it from the other end. She wore a blue linen dress and was carrying a basket and shears.

35

"What on earth!" she exclaimed, catching sight of Elizabeth. "I didn't expect to see you before noon."

"The sun waked me and I thought maybe I could look around this morning. I like to walk."

Martha felt an instant irritation that at the very beginning of the day Elizabeth should upset her plans. She had a series of telephone calls which she didn't want Elizabeth to hear, plans to make which her niece might not enter into if she knew about them. She had not liked John Rambeau's interest in Elizabeth the night before—the last thing she had expected. She had seated the two together only to disguise her real intentions of mating Elizabeth with Henri. Why, Elizabeth and John were cousins, but if John took a fancy to Elizabeth he would not think of that. She must nip this thing in the bud. Well, she'd have to get the girl out of the house, so she could make her arrangements.

"You'd better come and have breakfast," she said aloud, and, as a masterly afterthought, she added, "Why not go with Fran and see the first of the vintage? It's bound to interest you. Come along. Grandfather and Fran will be starting in a few minutes. I've no plans for you until afternoon."

The sun blazed up in its full summer fury as Francis Fairon turned the car to the east out of a lane bordered by olive trees. Their way, now, led across the unbroken brilliance of the vineyards to a huge stone building.

"I built the winery in the early eighties." It was the first time this morning that Grandfather Rambeau had spoken to her. "Your grandmother and I used every penny we had to do it." They had drawn up in front of the building now. "I'm going to take a look around before coming in," he said to his son-in-law, "if you don't need me right away."

"Take your time, Father." Francis was hoping the old man would find something wrong outside that would keep him busy until today's shipment of grapes was arranged for. It would only make him unhappy to know what was being done. *I've*

not a minute to waste though, he thought, striding ahead of
Elizabeth into the winery.

Old Philippe Rambeau walked along outside until he came
to the unloading platform. No mounds of grapes traveling
along the narrow thoroughfare to the crushers. No sound of
their steady revolving. He stepped inside and with some difficulty climbed the stairs to look down into the redwood vats.
No mass of broken and crushed grapes, bubbles bursting from
the purple mass in the mystery of the living process of growth.
Instead lime-crusted water filled the vats—mimicry and
mockery from which Philippe turned away.

He heard splashing and commotion in a vat at the farther
end of the room. "Hello. What you doing down there,
Hugo? Where's your helper?" he asked as he saw his winemaker at the bottom of the vat, scrubbing at the boards.

The man looked up. "*Ach,*" he spread his hands in a motion
of despair. "Too long de vater be here." He climbed up
the ladder. "Meester Rambeau, vhen vill ve make wine again?"

"Your guess is as good as mine, Hugo."

"I tink then I go back to Alsace."

"What for?" growled Philippe. "I'm paying you just the
same."

The man on the ladder looked down into the vat. "Dis I
cannot stand. I am a winemaker. In France I can work."

"You're crazy," said Philippe. "What do you know about
France? All your family are dead. You're as old as I am,
Hugo."

"Just the same, I go."

Philippe felt his heart contracting—not to have his cellar-
master about to bully and talk to! Philippe resorted to pleading. "We're two old men, Hugo. We came over together.
Let's go the last lap together."

The stubborn old man on the ladder looked at the stubborn old man on the narrow walk. "If you'll take me north
to make altar wine."

"You know I can't do that, Hugo. Diener is up there. You two would scrap like the devil. If it's that or go, it's go." Hugo backed down the ladder.

Philippe went to his office.

I wish Aunt Martha hadn't made me come along, thought Elizabeth as she followed her uncle into the winery. This Francis Fairon was a different Francis Fairon from the man she had known so far. She felt the hard core of detachment beneath his politeness.

"What about those cars on the siding?" she heard him say to André Rambeau as he stepped into the next room. "You mean that we've got to use unrefrigerated cars? We're down to shipping in open cars? Better not let your father know."

"Unless some of us use our pull with the railroad again. You're right, though, about keeping it from Father. He'd let the grapes rot on the vine before he'd ship them east in that shape," André Rambeau answered.

Elizabeth felt sure now she was in the way, but she didn't see what she could do about it. Not wanting to eavesdrop on their conversation, she walked to the other side of the room and studied a relief map of California fastened to the wall. How beautifully the mountains enclosed the valleys! The uptilted ridges made the valleys into great bowls. In the San Joaquin Valley, a large space not far from the center was stamped in red letters, *Rambeau-Fairon Vineyards.* Farther north a small, deep valley, looking on the map no larger than the hollow of a man's hand, was marked Napa Valley and stamped at the very foot of the mountains were the words, *Rambeau Vineyards.*

She heard a step behind her.

"Well! Who built a fire under you this morning?"

She turned to face John. "I did," she answered. "But Aunt Martha set it going."

John looked at her quizzically. "She throw you out?"

Elizabeth nodded. "She's busy and I'm no help."

"I'm a sort of fifth wheel around here, too," he explained. "Little late getting in on the business."

His words were like an echo come out of England. All the young men in England, back from the war, had talked like that. They were disillusioned, some of them, like William Humphreys, cynical. She had thought it was because they had no jobs. But John had one. She had heard her uncle consulting him the night before about a raisin deal.

"I suppose I might as well take you the regular rounds like all visitors. That's part of my job. If you get bored it won't do you any good." As he talked he had taken her arm and guided her toward a low wooden building. "Here we're packing grapes. A new department put in since Prohibition."

A long row of girls were working at the packing tables. All at once a grape spun through the air, landing on John's sleeve. "Little devil," Elizabeth heard John say under his breath. She noticed that he looked both amused and interested, an expression that turned into a sheepish grin when he realized that she had noticed. The missile had evidently been thrown by one of the packers, she guessed by the pretty girl at the end of the line, now suspiciously absorbed in her work. Elizabeth marveled at the camaraderie between worker and master here in America.

"Who is she?" she asked.

"Daughter of a small grower down the road. Dietrick's the name. Buz Dietrick, christened Ethel." He moved toward the door. "That's her father," he said, as they walked along the crushed-stone driveway. "I guess he's looking for me. I'll have to leave you for a moment."

Dietrick, a tall spare man with pale blue eyes and sun-bleached sandy hair, leaned down from the high seat of his truck. "You wanted to see me, Mr. Rambeau?" Elizabeth heard him say.

John dropped his voice, glancing around as if to make certain that no one in the winery overheard.

"Yes. Don't fail us, Dietrick. We're going to ride tonight."

"Sure thing; I'll be there." A light flared momentarily in Dietrick's pale eyes. He gave a belligerent hunch to his shoulders. "Them goddam Eyetalians," he muttered.

"We'll count on you."

John strolled back to Elizabeth. "Want to see the cellars?" he asked her. "They're really something."

"You seem to have a great deal on your mind," she said, adding after a pause, "for a fifth wheel."

The stone-lined room into which he took her was cool and dark. "This is where Grandfather has always aged his wines. Some of these puncheons came over from Spain, some from France," John explained. "Oak is the only thing to age wine in. Wine, Grandfather says, is alive. In oak it can breathe."

"Oh, perfect," said Elizabeth. "I fancy you impress tourists no end."

He stared at her in surprise. "Doesn't it interest you?"

She saw she had missed his mood, that he wasn't cynical now.

"I'm talking the way a good vintner talks. I could have been one. I've the feeling, like Grandfather. I've got it more than anybody else in the family." He leaned against a cask, looking suave and handsome in his blue trousers and white linen shirt.

"You mean," said Elizabeth, "you'd like to work at it?"

"Of course, I'd like to. But there's no use doing it, now the reformers have put the screws on. Instead I'm to be a raisin expert." He laughed. It sounded reckless and a little hard. He took her familiarly by the arm. "If you're to be a good member of the family, you must see Grandfather's redwood tanks."

The room they entered was a huge one filled with barrel-like tanks as tall as the room. In the narrow shaft of light cast by the open door, the long row of tanks to the left and the long row to the right, bound about with hoops of iron, were tall columns of reddish-brown staves rhythmically repeated down the room.

"How lovely!" exclaimed Elizabeth.

"Lovely maybe, but useless."

"Are they empty?" Elizabeth asked.

"No, not empty," said John, "but they're bonded. They can't be opened or the wine used." The door slammed shut behind them. "How do you like them now?" John asked.

For a moment Elizabeth could see nothing. Then close above her in the dim light she saw John's face. Violently he brought his lips down on hers. She struggled for a moment, then made no protest, getting the sensation of unusual animal strength from his hard, firm body. With cold and reckless determination to end one passionate longing by creating another, she leaned against him in a kind of destructive delight, feeling her senses stir under his touch.

Our two violences match, she thought bitterly, finally releasing herself.

IV

DIETRICK had driven along to the packing shed, waiting for the girls to file out at noon. Today was Saturday and a half day. He believed he would take Buz to town.

"Hi!" he said as she came running toward him. "Want to come along with me?"

"If you're going to do what you said you would."

"I reckon so. But you quit before the grapes were all picked."

"Now look, you old tightwad"—Buz grinned at him as she climbed up to the high seat of the truck—"you told me to take this here job."

"Bargain's a bargain. Supposin' I take you home and you work for me this afternoon. That'ud make it straight between us."

"You try that on! You just try it."

Nelson Dietrick smiled covertly. He drove out of the enclosure and toward his own place down the road, but he did not turn in when he reached the gate.

Buz hitched her proud little self forward on the seat so that her feet would touch the floor of the car, her child's mouth set in a firm line. She was going to see that he did what he said he'd do. A bargain was a bargain. He'd got to get her new clothes and he'd got to let her go to work in town next week just as he had promised. She had kept her part of the bargain, stuck by him all summer, and she meant he should get her the clothes today.

Buz had her father's realistic attitude toward life, with no means of escape into a make-believe world. Her escape came

42

only when promises were made real to her in things she could touch with her hands.

"I guess you don't need shoes, do you, Buz? Them I got for you last spring still pretty good, ain't they?" he asked hopefully.

"You said shoes," said Buz firmly. "I ain't going to give in, Pa."

"Well, I don't know as I blame you," Dietrick answered. "You done good by me. Better a whole lot than Pork did. That Porkfat, he moves hisself only once and a while."

They fell silent.

Dietrick had passed his own land now. "There's that Eyetalian." He sniffed. "Yep. They're the kind we goin' to git. Petucci!"

Petucci's land joined his. Each regarded the other's methods of grape culture with scorn. "He ain't doing them raisins right. Shouldn't lay his raisin papers that way. Dirt all bumpy under 'em. Raisins'll fall off."

"Nice name, Petucci." Buz's blue, rather prominent eyes mirrored her father's contempt. Dietrick felt contempt for all "furriners." His own northern European origins were too remote to have any meaning for him. Pioneers first in the Middle West and then in the Far West, his family was identified in his mind with America. To a stark and bitter clan spirit he had been raised, and in turn raised Buz.

"Hi, there!" called Dietrick, stopping his truck.

Petucci came to the edge of the road. He held out his hand. In the hard-calloused palm lay a dead bird. Its head hung down, pulling the feathers of its throat apart, making them look rough and untidy. Petucci shifted the bird, letting its head rest against his fingers, smoothing the feathers gently with the blunt, nail-broken forefinger of his other hand.

"What you doin', Petucci—goin' around killin' sparrers?"

"Must-a hit-a da car," said Petucci reproachfully. "Poor little fallo. One-a them wild cannery, ain't it?"

"Canary," corrected Buz, trying not to look at the bird.

Dietrick leaned across Buz. "You going to sign that contract?"

Petucci's dark skin was immediately suffused with heavy red. His eyes, soft and liquid with pity a moment before, were hot with rage. Violence spoke from every taut muscle.

"I no change-a da mind."

"It's my advice to you to sign up," Dietrick answered, starting the car.

"Look back," he told Buz. "See what he's doing."

Buz wriggled herself round in the seat. She knew her father didn't mean her to look out of the window, thus letting Petucci know they were impressed with his anger.

"He's standing in the road shaking his fist and talkin' at us," Buz reported.

"Crazy. Half crazy. All of 'em crazy." Dietrick leaned out, spat.

V

ANDRÉ RAMBEAU'S house, built in the period of cupola and porte-cochère, had not the simplicity of the older Rambeau dwelling. The verandas were made in wide curves that formed circular outdoor rooms. Inside, the house had heavy ornate moldings and carved woodwork. Its one beauty was a wide circular stairway which ascended in balanced and graceful curves to a square upstairs hall. It was evening now, and the crystal chandelier which decorated the ceiling was a blaze of light.

Monica came out of her mother's room, crossed the hall to John's, hesitated a moment, then knocked lightly on his closed door. There was no answer, but she could hear voices within.

"It's Monny, John," she called out, rapping again.

"Well, come on in," he answered, not too graciously.

The room she entered was over the porte-cochère, half-circular in shape, with big, full-paned windows. Charles was lounging on the window ledge; John was sitting on the side of the bed pulling on his riding boots.

Monica seated herself beside Charles. "How did you like Elizabeth, John?" She asked the question idly, seemingly occupied with the task of improving Charles' disheveled appearance, smoothing his hair, buttoning the open cuff of his shirt sleeve. In reality she was watching John's restless movements. He had his boots on now and was pacing back and forth.

"You don't have to ask him that question, do you? A fellow with half an eye could tell he liked her." Charles gave his brother a wink.

"I suppose you're wanting me to add my two cents to the

family gossip." John, ignoring Charles and his wink, spoke directly to Monica. "The whole family's been hashing her over, I suppose."

Monica saw she was on the wrong track. Hastily she shifted the talk to business. "How's the raisin setup going?" she asked.

"What are you nosing around for, Monny? Come out and say what you want." John stopped his pacing, came and stood before her, his feet spread apart, his hands on his slender hips. The army had certainly perfected what nature had well started, she thought, admiring his splendid physique. He had come through the months in France without injury, returned home physically sound, his flesh hard. The tunic of his uniform, expanded to full capacity, fitted him like his skin.

"Yes, I do want something," Monica answered. "I've been hearing stories, of how they intend to get the Armenians and Italians to sign the contracts. Are you in on it, John? Is that why you're dressed for riding?" Fearlessly she challenged him.

An angry flush spread over John's face. "I'm not a lap dog, Monny, least of all yours. And I'll run my affairs my own way."

"But, John, you'll ruin yourself in the community if you have anything to do with that kind of thing. And if Grandfather ever found out——"

John's face darkened. "If this is a threat, Monica, you can take it from me it would get you nowhere to go tattling to Grandfather."

"Why, John Rambeau!" exclaimed Monica. "I'd never do a thing like that!" It shocked Monny that even in his anger he should say such a thing.

"Well, see you don't. —Come on, Charles."

"No," said Monica, firmly, stepping between the brothers. "That, John, you can't do."

"If you'd give me credit for a little sense we'd get on better. Charles is going to bring my horse around." John followed his younger brother out of the room and down the stairs.

Monica walked across the hall to her own room and stood by the window where she could watch him ride down the drive. She had failed again to reach him.

VI

John was pressing his horse to a faster and faster pace. He didn't want to be late. *I wish Monica would get married,* he thought angrily. *Take her mind off me.* Gradually his anger gave way to excitement. The Armenians and German Russians in the valley were getting just a little above themselves. They'd fix them tonight. John, in the arrogance of his thoughts, did not allow himself to remember that most of the Armenians had co-operated. The few that hadn't condemned the whole lot as far as he was concerned.

John had taken it upon himself to represent his family. His father, André Rambeau, the next in point of authority to his grandfather, had called him into his office a few days before. "Handle the raisin business in your own way," he had said. John had interpreted that remark as license to join the night riders.

He turned off the road onto the dry crumpled earth of vineyard land. Back of a deserted winery he found the crowd gathered. A half-dozen young fellows of the neighborhood— four of them had been overseas together—were riding thoroughbreds. A few men like Dietrick, small growers and several big landowners, had come in their cars. The horses were restless. They felt the excitement of the men. John's pedigreed mare lifted her delicate hoofs and stepped away as far as John's close holding of the bridle would allow.

"Hello, Rambeau. Began to think you weren't coming."

"Where do we start?" asked John.

"Petucci'ud be my choice." Dietrick saw the evening's work purely in terms of Petucci.

"Let's start in with the Armenians," turning to the whole

group, old Judge Hueber, called so by the community because of his pompousness, put in. "They're the ones who are really blocking all the reform in this valley. There's Mamoulian. He's fought everything we've wanted to do. We've got to get him and his outfit signed up, or we haven't a monopoly. I'd say he was the one to begin on, or——"

"Well, let's get going," John broke in. He was impatient of the older man's explanations and his effort to make the expedition look orderly. Everybody knew it was lawless. Why not say so—among themselves?

They rode silently through the vineyards, keeping their horses to the aisle between the vines, neighbors well disguised against recognition. Already the perilous quest for order and freedom which had cost the world so much suffering was being abandoned. The Ku Klux Klan again was riding in Illinois, and vigilantes in California.

Joe Mamoulian was trying to understand what his neighbors had said to him that afternoon. Sign a paper, giving up his rights. He had struggled hard for his rights, come to this country to get them.

He was staying up late to work it out, had sent his woman to bed so she would not bother him. Clad only in his trousers, he sat by the table.

Slowly, patiently, he thought into Armenian the English words they had used. *Contract,* contract means . . . Could it mean that great and powerful thing, the association of men? If so, then it was good. But why didn't they go to our Little Father who brought us here to America? Tell him. Let him instruct us.

Contract . . . What was a contract? Did it mean he couldn't bargain any more with a man who would come to buy from him, spend an afternoon talking it over? In the end, getting a cent more on a box? He liked that bargaining. It made him feel a big man. But *association* . . . that was a big thing, too.

He heard the sudden soft tread of horses' hoofs, the stealthy sound of men moving into position around his house. This was something he did not have to translate into Armenian—fear needed no words to be made real to him. Persecuted for centuries, an Armenian knows the stealthy approach of his enemy. His neighbors had told him this afternoon they'd give him only until this evening to sign. So what they had said had been a threat. Mamoulian drew in his breath with a click, moved toward the bedroom along the board that he knew did not creak. He must get to his woman, not let her cry out. Sitting down on the side of the bed, he placed his hand over her mouth, whispered to her, "You keep quiet."

There was a heavy peremptory knock on the outside door. Joe Mamoulian did not speak.

"We'll come in after you, Joe. We know where you are."

"Better come out and talk to us, or we'll come and get you."

Joe started to get up. His woman tried to hold him, but his warm sweaty shoulders slid from her hands. He opened the door a crack.

"Come on out," the men commanded.

As soon as he was beyond the door they thrust a paper in his hands. "Here's where you sign. No fooling now."

"I no sign." Mamoulian planted his bare feet firmly on the rough boards of the veranda floor, flexed his big hands.

"We've had enough of your Ma-mulishness." A general guffaw greeted this sally.

"No sign." Mamoulian spoke the words very loud in his terror and anger.

"All right. We've given you your chance. Tie him up, boys," he heard them say.

Then there was the swish of a rope through the air, and a lasso fell neatly over Mamoulian's shoulders. With quick, deft movements men wound the heavy cord round him a dozen times, binding his arms to his sides.

"Tie him to the back of his car," a voice, deep and obviously disguised, commanded. "Then get going."

"Give him another chance first," someone called out.

"How about it?" He could feel the warm breath of the speaker on his face.

"I no sign."

The car gave a jerk. Mamoulian, ill-balanced as a man is without arms, swayed, tottered, then righted himself.

"You sign, Mamoulian?"

"No."

"Speed her up, boys."

Along the aisle between two rows of his vines over his drying raisins, the car moved, Mamoulian stumbling behind. Some of the men ran along beside, some brought up the rear on their horses.

"Sign, Mamoulian?" they kept shouting at him.

"No," he shouted back.

"Speed her up." The car moved faster, too fast. Mamoulian, armless, helpless, went down.

"Sign?"

No answer.

"Ain't them goddam Armenians stubborn!" Dietrick forgot to disguise his voice.

"Another quarter mile'll do it." Hueber spoke grimly, but with careful disguise.

They moved still faster now, Mamoulian bumping along like a log, his eyes, his mouth full of dirt, and his own dirt-covered raisins, his body shaken and bruised, his nose bleeding.

The car stopped.

"Ready now?" John Rambeau leaned over him.

"I sign," Joe muttered sullenly.

"Let him go, boys."

Mamoulian could feel the blood pulse in his body and the pains shoot through his arms as they loosened the rope. He was dizzy and, most of all, cowed. It was like this in Armenia.

"Here. Put your cross on this line, Mamoulian. I don't suppose you can write."

Joe's hand, calloused from work, red welts on it from the

rope, took the pen they handed him. In the glare of the car's headlights, he made his mark.

"Now this will teach you," came from the man leaning over him, "teach you to be a good citizen. Teach you how to co-operate."

"Better explain to your neighbors. It will save them a lot of trouble. We don't want to be any harder on them than we have to be," the Judge told him, saying it all in a judicial tone of voice.

"There, get along home. And mind you don't break that contract," John Rambeau called out, and feeling a sudden contempt for the cowering Mamoulian, gave him a kick from behind.

The men rode rapidly toward a couple of small ranch houses, little more than shacks, the homes of some Russians from the Ukraine. The lights were on in one and there was singing.

John jumped from his horse and went close, looking in the window. "It's only a family party. Mostly children," he reported coming back to the rest of the men. They guided their horses and cars into a semicircle around the dooryard. "See your masks are well in place," Hueber cautioned. "Ready?" He walked up to the door and banged on it. "We're here with the contract," he called out, then stepped back among the waiting horses, cars and men.

There was no hesitation this time. A strong and powerfully built man came out on the porch. It shook under his tread. Yakowitz looked down at the masked men, then pulled his shirt off, showing a strong and lean body. "I don't want to sign this what-you-call contract. All right. I fight any man you say. He win, I sign. I win, I don't sign."

"Close in on him, boys." The lasso fell neatly over his shoulders. They ducked him in his irrigation ditch. Ducked him twice before they had the desired signature.

The men's blood was up now. "It's Petucci's turn!" shouted Dietrick.

Petucci had been listening for them. News travels fast in times of trouble. When he heard them coming, he ran around the house, climbed on the roof of the lean-to, then with catlike agility scrambled up the roof of the main part of his house to the gallery that circled the water tower at the top. "You wanta da Petucci, you come take-a da Petucci," he shouted.

"We'll come after you all right," shouted the men, placing a ladder against the house.

Petucci ripped the railing from the gallery and hurled it down upon them. The men stood off. They were angry now. Dietrick stepped from among them, shouting, "We're going to shoot, Petucci, if you don't come down."

Laughing like a maniac, Petucci with deadly accuracy dropped another stick of wood in their midst.

There was the crack of a pistol, then an angry shout from Petucci, then silence.

The door of the house opened, and Mrs. Petucci stepped out. Her short black hair was pinned severely back from her face. She looked with scorn at the group of men. Second-generation Italian, she spoke clearly and with dignity. "If Mr. Petucci signs the contract, will you promise not to shoot again?"

"Yes," Hueber answered.

With the white slip of paper, she climbed the ladder, lifted it after her in strong arms, laid it on the roof, and ascended to the water tower. In another moment the signed contract fluttered at their feet.

It was midnight when they had made their rounds. Picking as they had the strongest men in the opposition, they believed there would be no more trouble. "Everyone will make money on raisins this year, for we'll control the price and we'll boost it. Everyone, that is, will make money except the lordly Westbrook and his kind," they all agreed. With Westbrook they had dealt hardly, making no excuses for a man of wealth and education who refused to come in with them. They had sent a crowd of men out to destroy his rows of drying raisins. There were a number of men like him who had made their fortunes in the Valley—Americans who had come here poor and now lived in San Francisco or Los Angeles, absentee landlords who underbid their neighbors. They were the ones who had been the first to break the contracts in the past.

John Rambeau rode at the head of the party. Hueber drove up beside him. "A fine night's work, eh, John? Sometimes that's the only way to make good Americans out of foreigners. They don't understand anything but force," he called out.

"My road here," said John. "Good night, sir." He put his horse into a gallop. *The old fuddy-duddy,* he said scornfully to himself. *Trying to justify the night's activities.* Why hide from yourself the sensuous pleasure in violence?

There was the happening of the morning, too. That had put him somewhere with the new cousin. She was as reckless as he. Life was picking up. It didn't seem so dull as it had forty-eight hours earlier. He would not have been interested had he known that his grandfather sometimes speculated as to whether or not civilization depends on the ability of men to live on monotony.

VII

THE sun, which had blazed down upon the valleys without intermission since March, had built up a reservoir of heat and light. Moisture, gone from the surface of the earth, had receded far into its depths. The air was thin and dry. Each morning the sun, coming up in a burst of light, undimmed by any cloud, tightened Elizabeth's nerves, giving her a sense of physical vigor. Going down at night in brilliance, it left her with unsatisfied, hungry energy.

The family, too, gave off powerful currents of almost passionate energy. They were in the midst of changing their not inconsiderable fortune into great wealth. Elizabeth felt the excitement of success mounting around her. Aunt Martha by means of the telephone kept herself in constant touch with the men of the family down at the winery. Elizabeth realized, from fragments of conversations unavoidably overheard, that her aunt was directing every member of the family toward the one great purpose of making money. Elizabeth felt herself carried along like a leaf in a gale.

Each day there was an increasing demand for grapes. The idea of making wine had seized hold of the imagination of countless little men all over the country. Wine had become to them the symbol of freedom. With rebellious determination they meant to tread out the wine of their democracy in homemade presses. They stampeded the market for grapes to make homemade wine.

The grapegrowers, who had found it advantageous to force men into a contract on raisins, found it to their advantage to make no contract on wine grapes. This wasn't a falling market but a rising one. Let each man get what he could out of it.

The available refrigerator cars were soon used up just as Francis Fairon had foreseen that first morning. Although more and more, since Prohibition, old Philippe had turned over the running of the business in the San Joaquin Valley to the younger men, giving his attention to the northern winery where he made wine for sacramental purposes, still the men felt that should he learn they intended to take no responsibility as to what condition the grapes arrived on the Eastern coast, he might take matters into his own hands. He might refuse to let them ship at all. That would mean that the highest-priced harvest they had ever had would be wasted.

They saw no reason to concern themselves about the condition in which the grapes arrived. In whatever shape the grapes were shipped, the quality of wine made undoubtedly would be very poor. Winemaking was an art and the layman could not hope to master its delicate technique overnight. However, if they gave this reason to old Philippe it would only make him the more determined not to ship his grapes.

It was Martha who made the practical arrangements which gave the men a free hand. If old Philippe could be induced to visit his northern vineyards, he would know nothing of what was going on here. Calling Diener, the wine-master at Philippe's northern winery, Martha learned that picking would begin in another week. A succession of good ripening days, he said, had raised the sugar content of the grapes with unusual rapidity. Immediately Martha maneuvered to shift old Philippe's anxiety over the quality of grapes shipped to anxiety over the quality of his own wine.

"It's a waste, Father," she told him, "for you to be concerned about shipments when your special knowledge is needed in creating the finest altar wine. Suppose something goes wrong, and you are not there."

Philippe knew nothing could go wrong with Diener watching over the wine, but he liked to feel that he alone could contribute the final delicate touch. A letter from his friend Father Flanigan, from Kansas City, saying he was thinking of coming west a little earlier this year to buy his wines, decided Philippe. He would go up in time to meet the father and to help Diener.

Martha had written the priest that her father was failing and they would like to get him away from the anxieties of the shipping season, asking if he could not aid them by coming a little earlier than usual this year. Her father would let nothing keep him from being on hand when his guest arrived. Father Flanigan's response had been so prompt that Martha had had to wire him asking him to postpone his visit for a couple of days as matters had arisen delaying Philippe. Martha found it suddenly necessary, before Philippe left, to get his approval to a plan she had worked out since Elizabeth's arrival.

"Can't we, Fran," she had said to her husband, "get Father to send John east to look after men who are handling our sacramental wine?"

"But why," asked Francis, "when John is just well started in raisins, take him away to do an unnecessary job somewhere else?"

"And have him here to be arraigned before the court over that night-riding affair?"

"Who said there was to be any dust-up over that?" Francis asked her. "Where did you get any such idea?"

"I understand that the Armenians mean to press their case."

"Do you mind telling me the source of your information, Martha?"

"Chu."

"Damn Chu!"

"You'll have to own he's rarely ill-informed," Martha answered. "He tells me there is considerable indignation among some of the influential men of the Valley. John is hotheaded, you know. We can manage much better with him away."

"I doubt if I can make the need for John to go very convincing to your father," said, Francis, but he was really alarmed over the turn things were taking.

"Isn't there some logical job for him which would satisfy

Father? If you could sell directly to the dealers in New York, wouldn't it perhaps net us a better price on our shipments and in Father's eyes be a more respectable way to ship? Couldn't John do that?"

"I'll have to see what I can make of it, Martha. I'll talk to André. Then if we can work something out, we can take it up with your father." Francis was puzzled over Martha's sudden interest in John's welfare. *There is something behind this which she is not telling me*, he thought. Aloud he said, "We'll have to make it extremely plausible or your father will suspect something. He always knows more than you think he does. Besides, if Chu told you about the raids, what's to hinder him telling your father? In such a case there would be no object in sending John off."

"I don't think Chu will have told Father. Not right now at least." A quiet little smile played around Martha's lips. Francis was pretty certain, then, that Martha had not told him her real object in wanting John sent east.

Martha was playing her cards carefully. She meant to increase their wealth by taking advantage of this unprecedented rise in grape prices and also by marrying Elizabeth to Henri, thus uniting the two fortunes. Getting Philippe away would insure the first and John off would help accomplish the second.

VIII

JOHN had had no opportunity to see Elizabeth in the few days that lay between their meeting at the winery and the sudden decision of the older men to send him east. Elizabeth's time had been well arranged for by Martha and those arrangements did not include him. Purposely, John was certain. That Martha would have plans for Elizabeth's marriage was a foregone conclusion in John's mind. Probably she intended to marry her to Henri. John had meant to have some fun at Aunt Martha's expense if he had been on hand this winter. His going away changed everything.

But he was determined to see Elizabeth alone before he went. He was interested in her, although he hardly acknowledged it to himself. Maybe when he came back he might like to think about marrying her. Anyway she was his girl now, and he did not intend to have Henri take her away from him. From a child John had been used to getting what he wanted. All the cousins understood that. Well, he would see her at the cousins' party that evening.

Toward noon he drove into town on some final business concerning his raisins. Immediately he caught the note of excitement in the city. Passing the station he saw a steady line of men coming out of the freight office, bills of lading in their hands. They did not get ten feet before they were accosted. Sometimes there were half a dozen men trying to talk to the same grapegrower at once. Buyers from the East, was John's quick conclusion.

He saw Dietrick emerge from a group of men and come

59

toward him. His pale blue eyes looked like shining beads. He kept running his hand through his unkempt hair, putting his hat on, taking it off, again combing his hair back from his forehead with his hand.

"What's up, Dietrick?" John called out.

"Just sold my grapes for seventy the ton."

John whistled.

Dietrick grinned. "Sold 'em first for fifty. Bought 'em back when they went to sixty. Now I've got seventy."

"Figure they'll go any higher, Dietrick?"

"Maybe they will, maybe they won't. Some's talking they will. A sure seventy's good enough for me."

John decided to hunt up his father. Undoubtedly he would be dealing with the more exclusive buyers usually hanging around the hotel lobby. They were sharp fellows and would fleece his father if they could. John thought of his father as conservative, not taking risks of any kind and thus losing out.

As John came into the hotel he saw André going into the dining room. "Hello there, Dad. Everybody seems to be feeling pretty good. How'd you make out?"

"Suppose we have some lunch," André replied.

He's not to be drawn, thought John. *Bet he sold too low and now he's regretting it. I'll have to wangle it a bit to find out what he's done.* He waited until his father had given the order, then he asked, "Did you get as much as fifty? We'd do pretty well on that, wouldn't we?"

"Did better than that. Sixty the lot." André began cutting his beefsteak with an air of considerable satisfaction. It really was a good price, he told himself. They would substantially add to their fortunes if he could get cars for all the crop. John, too, had evidently not expected they would sell for more than fifty a ton. Never mind if others beat them the first day.

"I thought Dietrick was telling me a pretty big one," said John innocently. "Ran into him down at the freight yards. He talked seventy for his grapes."

"He's lying," said André, but he knew Dietrick wasn't.

He had overheard some men talking eighty just after he had sold.

"If they've gone to seventy, my bet is they go higher before night," John ventured, suspecting that his father was smarting under the knowledge that the untutored Dietrick had outdone him. Dietrick had been more or less a humble pensioner of the Rambeaus. They had bought his grapes each year for wine until Prohibition came. "Helping him out," they called it. To have Dietrick drive a better bargain than he had managed would irk his father no end.

"I've an idea, Dad, you could buy your grapes back at seventy-five."

"What should I want to do that for?" André looked at John as if he doubted his sanity.

John laughed. "Look, Dad, I've got a hunch grapes will go to a hundred before night. You'd do pretty well on that. Even Gramp might not mind Prohibition at that price."

"That's all right if we win, but suppose we lose?"

"We won't."

"You don't know, John. What do you know about the New York market?" André had no very high opinion of his son's business ability. He thought him shrewd but too hasty.

"Let me have a try at it," John coaxed. "I've a pretty strong hunch I could make us a lot of money this afternoon."

"Don't forget," his father answered, "you will be up against the shrewdest traders in the world when you go up against these buyers. Most of them are Jews, and they play their cards close."

"Shrewdest traders, my eye, Dad! There's one race that can beat them. That's the Chinese—if Chu is any example. And I wouldn't put the French down as any slouch at bargaining."

"Well, I don't know." André didn't mean to be drawn into any wildcat scheme.

"If you don't want to take a chance on the whole lot, let

me buy, say, a third back," John urged. "You would average out to a pretty good profit that way."

"There's something in that," said André. He was beginning to feel pride in this son of his. John wasn't entirely an idler as he had once thought him. He had handled the raisin business with a great deal of energy, and what he was proposing now was smart. He believed he'd give John a chance on the grapes.

"Tell you what I'll do," he said at last. "I'll let you buy back a fifth. If you make good, I'll put you on a commission on the next lot you sell. I know the others will stand by me on this, *if* you win."

His smile was enigmatic but not unfriendly. *Pretty good sport about his own failure to get a top price,* John thought. "I'll not let you down, Dad," he said. "I'll go at it cautiously."

At first John bought in small lots, increasing his amounts and his risks only after he had a neat little backlog of profit, reporting back to his father after every transaction. By five o'clock they had averaged out to an excellent profit. As they left the hotel together André was happy over the companionship he had had with his son this day, happier even than he was with the profit they had taken, although that, too, brought him no little satisfaction.

"Look here, John, suppose you stay over a day or two," he said. "There isn't any real hurry about that eastern business. Help me out with this bargaining. You're better at it than I am."

"O.K., Dad. I'll call up the railway and change my tickets."

I guess he's pleased, thought André, *but he isn't going to show it.* In reality John was delighted with the idea. It would give him a chance to cement his position with Elizabeth. When he saw her tonight he would tie her up for a few dates before Aunt Martha could interfere. He had plenty of money to spend on her. His take on the afternoon's sales was very good indeed.

IX

THE cousins had carried their point. Their dance for Elizabeth was to be held at a new restaurant in Fresno, in spite of the fact that Aunt Martha insisted the place was not exclusive enough. All of their set, they told her, were giving parties there because of the good Spanish food and the equally good orchestra, to say nothing of the floor show. Besides, they explained, if we invite all those Elizabeth should meet, none of our houses would be big enough. We want a crowd down from San Francisco and there'll be a lot coming up from Los Angeles. It was their party, they argued, and they were going to have it the way they wanted it or not at all.

Martha almost made the mistake of saying Elizabeth could not go. She drew back just in time, realizing that she might not be able to enforce her command. The realization increased her growing antagonism toward Elizabeth.

John was late. When he came into the restaurant the long table where his crowd was to sit was in disarray. Napkins thrown down, food half-eaten, chairs pushed back. Everybody except Monica was dancing; she was sitting at the end of the table facing the door. *Waiting for me, I'll bet,* he thought. He sat down in the chair next her, putting his hand over hers. He was silent, trying to think how to tell her that he was worried for fear his grandfather might find out the part he had played among the night riders. The Armenians were stirring up an awful rumpus. He believed they might go so far as to see old Philippe as they had threatened to do. Monny would be the only one who could help him

63

out with his grandfather if they did tell him. He must make peace with her somehow.

"Look, Monny," he said hurriedly, for the music had stopped and the others were coming back, "you're not angry with me, are you? You'll write to me, won't you, while I'm away?"

"Why, of course, John. Whatever put it into your head that I wouldn't?"

"Oh, you know—the other evening. Monny, if Grandfather finds out, you'll do what you can for me, won't you?"

"Yes."

She has the tenderest eyes in the world, thought John. His gaze followed hers to a tall blond fellow coming toward them. "Who invited Nate, Monny?"

"I did," she answered.

John looked at her with special attention. Monny interested in any man except himself was a new idea to him, not wholly pleasant in spite of the fact that on the night of the raid he had wished she would get married and stop bothering him. John did not want anyone poaching on his territory. Monny's devotion to him had always seemed his right, just as Elizabeth seemed to be his because he had paid her attention the first evening. The cousins always respected his claims. He had seen to it since childhood that they did. But this Nate Frostner acted as if he had a right to Monny as he led her out onto the floor—and Monny looked as if she liked it.

"Well, demureness." Nate's unruly, straw-colored hair had escaped from its careful combing and hung in a fringe well over his eyebrows. His eyes looked out, bright, alert brown eyes. The heavy bones of his face set off the tanned hollows of his cheeks.

He looked down upon Monny. "What are you thinking about?"

"You, Nate." He seemed to tuck her up under his arm and whisk her away down the length of the room. It was so lovely to be with Nate. It was like anchoring in a sunny cove after traveling a rough sea. Monny had none of the turbulent nature of her brothers.

Elizabeth had come back to the table. As she looked at John, the color rose in her cheeks. "Glad to see me?" he asked, going over to her.

"Oh, I don't know, should I be?" Her blue eyes looked squarely into his cold and knowing black ones. Whatever thought lay behind them was lost in their blackness.

John sat down next to her, giving himself to his dinner with considerable enthusiasm, not addressing her again.

"Aren't those dancers lovely?" Elizabeth turned to Henri, who had seated himself on her other side. She was watching the couple in the floor show.

"Yes. I come often just to see them," he answered.

The woman's black hair was brushed back in lines of classic severity from her long, thin, aristocratic face. She wore no mantilla or high comb to make her picturesquely Spanish. She was dressed in white with a black matador's cape, the man all in black. They danced with graceful restraint until she threw back the cape. As she flung it with bold daring, its flaming red lining cut for a minute across her partner's face. Instantly he lowered his head, charging with fury. The dance mounted in intensity. The woman flung her cape with more and more speed until it seemed like a reddened knife cutting the air. The man charged with more and more animal violence until they tangled in one swift final motion of abandoned struggle, then parted. Bowing gracefully, they left the floor. Applause broke wildly over the onlookers.

Elizabeth glanced at Henri. His long wide nostrils were pulsing. She felt repelled. With relief she turned to the healthy, normal John, who had looked up from his dinner, now and then, to watch the dance with matter-of-fact pleasure.

"Come, let's dance," he said to her, getting up. She was glad to go with him.

"There's the girl we saw picking grapes," she said, determined to keep their conversation to the casual.

"Well, if it isn't!" he exclaimed. "She's decked out, isn't she?"

"And she certainly knows how to dress. She has just the right dress on. A girl like that in England wouldn't know how to do it."

"American girls always know how," John answered her with not a little pride. "Come by it naturally. My guess would be that Buz has never had a dress that cost over three dollars before in her life. Her dad is making money like the rest of us," he added. "Dietrick is a sharp trader all right. But imagine Buz coming here the first thing she gets hold of a little dough."

"So you agree with Aunt Martha that the place is not very exclusive." Elizabeth glanced at him slyly.

John did not answer. He hated to be teased and he suspected Elizabeth was teasing him.

"I like this girl you call Buz," Elizabeth said frankly. "She doesn't quite know her way about so she's watching. She's handling herself better all the time. See, she's looking at us, John."

John grunted.

The music stopped. As they walked back toward their table, they passed Buz's crowd. "Hello, how's everything, Griffanti?" John asked and nodded at Buz, conforming to the pattern of neighborliness his family always maintained.

"Introduce me," whispered Elizabeth, knowing John had not intended to but determined to make him do it.

Buz was coolness itself. She, too, knew John had not intended to introduce them. But she was glad John Rambeau was seeing her here. She wished, though, she'd been with somebody besides Luigi Griffanti. But the same realism she had shown in her transaction with her father made her acknowledge to herself that she wouldn't be here if it weren't for Luigi. Luigi, known among the girls as a good spender, sure was swell, bringing them to a swanky place like this, not even letting Jim and Cora Patterson, the two who had come with them, pay for themselves.

"Look here," said John to Elizabeth as they moved on, "I'm going away tonight, and I don't know when I'll see you again. Nobody's going to mind if we slip out for a while. I've got my car."

"You'll be back," Elizabeth answered. "In the meantime——"

"In the meantime!"

John was beginning to feel annoyed over her mastery of the situation. Every effort he made to get on a more intimate footing with her failed. He understood she meant the evening to stay on the casual note where she had placed it. But the odd fascination she exercised over him betrayed him into a determination to see that it did not. Putting his hand under her elbow, he guided her toward one of the many entrances which led to the garden. "We can, at least, get ourselves cooled off before we go on dancing," he said with a little laugh.

Elizabeth had scarcely stepped beyond the range of the lighted windows when, with more daring than before, he kissed her, holding her close. For a moment she relaxed against him. Sensing her acquiescence, excited by the sweet scent of her skin, her hair, the softness of her clinging dress, suddenly he lowered his head to her breast. Elizabeth pushed him away. "You've made a mistake, John," she said, her voice shaking with anger.

"Oh, have I? Then why did you let me kiss you at the winery?"

"I don't know why I did. I suppose I didn't care the other morning. I was awfully unhappy."

"Is that the kind of thing you do when you're unhappy?"

"No, of course not."

They were both angry now, both humiliated. Without another word John led her back into the restaurant. He was cool, suave, and very polite as he took her to a seat next to Henri and left her. After dancing with every other girl in the party, he made his excuses to the crowd. "I've a lot to do before I get off," he told them. He meant they should all see that Elizabeth did not interest him any more.

Henri, watching him, came to his own conclusions. *Guess John has met his match for once,* he thought. Until now Henri had thought Elizabeth too northern a type to suit him. Too English. Now he began to think he would like to give her a rush just to annoy John. She was dancing with Andrew Fairon. He walked toward them.

Elizabeth, seeing him coming, said to Andrew, "Let's slip out into the garden just for a moment for a breath of air. I'm not used to your California heat."

"I believe you're tired." Andrew's voice held solicitude. "I tell you what. Let me take you for a five-minute spin in my car?"

With a sense of relief, Elizabeth accepted, glad to escape Henri, glad to forget John in the quiet presence of Andrew and the quiet night.

Andrew did not speak as he drove his open car down a side street and out into the country. Elizabeth leaned back, dropped her hand outside the car door, letting it trail in the wind as she had often trailed her hand in water. Andrew's companionship gave her a sense of harmony with this new land she had not felt before. The wide mountain-rimmed valley, the broad vault of the sky, seemed for the first time friendly.

"Ready to go back?" he asked at last.

"Yes," she answered, smiling at him.

X

JOHN, once he had left the party, began to feel the full force of Elizabeth's rebuff. He stood in the doorway of the building, smoking a cigarette. He wasn't used to being turned down. He was smarting from the experience. From some hidden unexplored center within him, like a breath of cold air, rose a sense of inadequacy in himself. As he stood there, Luigi Griffanti's party came out. Griffanti, with large-handed hospitality, was talking about another café. "One where things move faster than they do around here," he was saying to Buz.

"Mind if I come along?" asked John.

"Oh, sure, the more the merrier." Griffanti was not a little flattered.

Buz was both flattered and excited. All her life she had admired John Rambeau. Here he was leaving his own crowd and joining hers.

"Want to dance?" John asked Buz as soon as they arrived.

Dancing with him, something awoke in her which had never been awake before, something which answered the rhythmic swing of his strong body and his black eyes looking into hers. An hour ago she would have weighed carefully any hazard to her friendship with Luigi. She knew perfectly what she had ahead of her if she were to hold him in the face of his popularity with other girls. But dancing with John Rambeau, nothing existed but his swinging, dipping body and hers held in its embrace. That feet-on-the-ground attitude of hers began to leave her. Her ambition took wings. Why shouldn't John come to like her a lot? He'd always kind of picked her out.

Luigi cut in, swinging her expertly into his own arms, asking her roughly, "Who do you think brought you here anyway?"

She answered in a tone as pert as his was truculent. "Whoever it was, I didn't give him a mortgage." When the music stopped and John sat down close beside her, putting his arm across her shoulders, she looked at Luigi with an impudent grin.

Luigi came over to her. "You needn't try this kind of thing on me. Come on. We're dancing."

"Take it easy." John by now was feeling entirely reckless. "This is my dance."

Luigi neither spoke nor moved but his brows drew together, his eyelids lowered.

John enjoyed taking Buz away from Luigi. He always enjoyed rivalry. Buz's evident pleasure in his company soothed his hurt pride. What if she was just Dietrick's daughter? She was a sweet kid. The childish roundness of her body had its own appeal.

As he led her to her seat he said, "I guess your friend doesn't like me, Buz. How about letting me come to see you tomorrow evening?"

"Oh, sure," said Buz.

Both had spoken loud enough for Luigi to hear.

For the second time that evening John found himself at loose ends—still restless, still not wanting to be alone with himself. He decided he would drive around and see what was doing at the hotel—sure to be a lot of fellows wanting a good time. *Maybe I can get into a game,* he thought.

The September night seemed to hold the heat of all the preceding nights of the summer. The sun, beating hour after hour upon the pavements outside the hotel, had turned the rooms into fiery furnaces—no one could think of going to sleep.

The buyers gambling all day on the price of grapes had

their minds set for gambling in the morning. They felt the
need to bridge the excitement of today into the excitement
of tomorrow.

John found the lobby full of them still milling round, still
bragging over what they had made buying and selling. A
sale or two was still going on. Just leaving a group of buyers
was the man who had bought the last lot of John's grapes that
afternoon.

"Hello, Jacobs. Have a drink?" John asked.

"No, no more tonight," said Jacobs taking a large handkerchief out of his pocket and running it over his forehead,
then wiping the backs of his short chunky hands. "I'm getting
together a little party for poker. You want to lose a little of
that money you got from me this afternoon?" Jacobs slapped
John on the shoulder with considerable zeal.

"How about me taking a little more from you?" John
asked, feeling his cool, shrewd self uppermost again.

"We'll see about that. Go on up to room 212. Meet you
there as soon as I line up a couple more fellows."

John went along the corridor. Most of the doors stood
open but hardly a sound came from the men sitting at card
tables within. In one room John saw a middle-aged man
with a great diamond on his hand raking a pile of chips
toward him. "My God," he said, getting up, "what did the
kid bet a thousand for? It's cleaned him out."

"What do I care?" It was evidently the "kid" speaking.
"There's a lot more where that came from. Grapes is gold
this year. At Lodi they're playing craps for a thousand the
throw."

John passed out of hearing. He stopped at the next door.
"This 212?" he asked, realizing immediately that he was
wrong. A long table covered with a white cloth almost filled
the room. On it was a display of crockery and glassware. An
elderly man, evidently a traveling salesman, dozing in a chair
near by, opened his eyes and looked dully at John. "You the
fellow said he'd come around this evening?"

"Not me. A mistake. Sorry." John backed out shutting the door behind him.

In 212 three men were lounging about when John entered. "My name is Rambeau. Jacobs said he'd be along in a minute," he told them.

"You playing?"

"Yes."

"My name's Doyle," said a fat man with a loose lower lip. He looked at John in shrewd valuation. "Might have some business with you some day," he finally volunteered.

"Buying grapes?" asked John.

"No, got a better deal on. I ain't even playing poker. I'm the bank." John took out his money, bought a quantity of chips. Jacobs had come in with two more men and with hardly a word the game began.

Jacobs dealt the opening hand. John dropped out on the first round. He hadn't any cards. On the second hand, too, the betting was pretty steep and again he threw in his hand early. It just wasn't his evening for winning. Jacobs took in the chips four times running.

For a couple of hours the game continued to go against John. But by no word or look did he show his pique. Finally he got up, walked over to the banker, put down a roll of bills. The fat man had been asleep. He opened one eye saying, "Help yourself," but his round pig eyes weren't missing a trick, John noticed as he counted out his chips.

This time John drew a moderate hand. Jacobs opened for twenty-five. The man next to Jacobs bet a hundred. Two of the men threw down their cards. The next raised to two hundred, making it four hundred when it reached John. He was tired of caution. Hell! he had a chance. It was a good pot. He raised it a hundred.

He watched the group carefully figuring out who was bluffing. The man who had raised it to four hundred had drawn three cards but the two he threw down he kept his hand on longer than he needed to. *He isn't sure,* thought John.

"How many, Rambeau?"

"Two." John picked up his cards.

Jacobs drew one and started the betting low. It went the rounds, no one dropping out this time, each man raising the bet. But on the second round only John and Jacobs were left.

"Let's see what you've got, Rambeau."

John laid down his cards—a full house against Jacobs' flush. John pulled the pile of chips toward him. The hand had netted him a clean thousand.

"We gotta be getting a little sleep. Let's cash in," Jacobs said, yawning and stretching his arms over his head.

The banker woke up and counted out each man's money. John looked at him a little more closely this time. He gathered from the good-natured jibes going round that the fellow was one of the men getting rich in the Valley, bootlegging. *He had his nerve*, thought John, *thinking he would ever have any business with me.*

Even those who had won took their profits with little or no enthusiasm. The stimulus of the day was exhausted now. The muscles of the men's lips, taut during the game, suddenly seemed to sag. Their eyes were as dead as fishes' eyes, Jacobs' a little bloodshot. As the pale hot dawn came in at the window, one by one they shuffled off to their rooms dog-tired.

John did not bother to go home. Taking a room in the hotel, instead, he quickly threw off his clothes, lay down on the hot sheet. Even the fan blowing full upon him seemed to bring no air cool enough to make sleep possible. His inexhaustible energy, stimulated by the long day of excitement, contended with sleep for the victory. Going round as on a race track, neck and neck with sleep, faster than sleep, his mind dwelt on the money he had made in grapes during the day, on poker this evening. Three thousand on the two transactions. That's what he wanted—money. Another couple of days to clean up and he would go east in style. Sleep gaining . . . his thoughts slowing down . . . the sensuous pleasure in his relaxing body . . . the sensuous memory of Buz's soft childish contours.

XI

THE night of the party, Philippe Rambeau went early to his own wing of the house. He had a desire to see his winery free of the money-changers, as he called his family tonight. With the sharp knowledge of an old man too much looked after, he waited in his bedroom for the house to lose its last murmur of activity. The day had been an unhappy one. He felt himself no longer a part of the life around him. Something more real than his eighty-five years divided him from it, and they were real enough, for he no longer had any contemporaries. He was either "Father" or "Grandfather" or "sir" to the world now. No one called him Philippe—instead, "old Mr. Rambeau." Until lately, though, he had thought of his family as made in his image. Now, all at once, they seemed a different breed.

What had a man who had spent his life working with soil and vines to the end of making wine of the finest quality to do with men who saw grapes only as a business, selling them for more than they were worth, letting anyone make them into wine, not caring whether it was inferior or not?

As he had driven into town that afternoon, he had seen the cars without refrigeration standing on the siding, loaded with grapes. He could easily imagine the shape in which they would arrive at their destination, a crushed mass unfit for the making of good wine. He had not asked whether any of these cars held Rambeau-Fairon grapes. He had not found it in his heart to tell the men of his family to let the grapes rot on the vines, the good money go to their neighbors. He was caught squarely between the two horns of an old dilemma.

His thoughts drifting about in his memory came upon

the day when, in the French cathedral, he had made his resolve to come to America. He was little more than a beggar. He had no family. He had lost them all during the War of 1870. Alsace-Lorraine now belonged to Germany and he had begged or stolen for many weeks, drifting from city to city.

It was raining and he had gone into the great cathedral to escape the rain. He remembered how cold he had been and how hungry. But as he stood there he had felt himself caught up out of his squalor. He saw the gleaming altar, the seven points of candlelight on each side, setting the burnished candlesticks and the gold and silver vessels shimmering. The sight spoke to something in him which desired gold and silver and rich velvets and silks and fine linen. For a moment he coveted the very fittings of the church itself. Even now he could feel the furious desire to be rich that had come over him.

Then sweat had broken out on him as the meaning of what he desired came to him. He, son of the man who had made wine for the Holy Sacrifice of the Mass at the village church, fallen so low as to covet the very vessels upon the altar. He sank down on his knees there at the back of the cathedral in penitence. As the procession came down the aisle, the holy water fell upon his unkempt, bowed head. "Cleanse me with hyssop and I shall be clean," they chanted. All during the Mass he had remained kneeling, the sacred words coming down to him, incense drifting over him.

He had risen at last, gone out to fulfill his resolve. Like his father he would make wine for the altar. But it would be in America where all cathedrals would be rich and beautiful like this one and all men rich—he the richest of all.

Now his house was still, the last lights had gone out in the wing across the court from his own. That meant Martha was in bed.

Quietly he stepped out through the french window which opened directly on the garden. He had always insisted on this freedom for all his family. Everyone should be able to escape the house and put his feet on the earth without being asked his purpose. *Even,* he said to himself with a smile, *if like me they have to wait until midnight to do it.*

It was but a short distance to the winery, if he walked through the vineyards. His way led through the old part of the garden, French in design. In the foreground the close-cut grass was brilliant with moonlight. On its farther side, black as charcoal, lay the shadow of the balustrade that bordered a second level. Briskly he mounted the two wide steps leading to the upper terrace, followed the flagged walk across it.

In the formal flower beds white petunias seemed to float free of their stems. The path circled a figure of Bacchus trailing bunches of grapes, clumsy and ill-proportioned by daylight, re-sculptured in the moonlight to delicacy and proportion. Passing through an opening in the hedge that bordered the garden's final level, he was in the vineyard. Far away at the end of aisles of vines stood the massive stone winery, wholly functional in line, wholly beautiful whether in moonlight or daylight.

He walked easily tonight, as easily, it seemed, as in his youth, perhaps even more easily. There had been times, then, when weary with hard work he had dragged himself home through these aisles. Such exhaustion he no longer knew. Money and Martha's care made the lowered vitality of age free of the exhaustion that comes of work.

This was the oldest part of the vineyard. He had planted these vines his first year on this land which had come into his possession only after many years of toil. For seven years he had been poor and ragged here in America, even as he had been in France. But he had not begged; he had worked. The pomace, left after the wine had been drawn off from the grapes, he had bought and sold again to be put on the vineyards for fertilizer.

He had hauled for the old Don, Henri's grandfather. In payment the Don, money-poor that year, had given him a strip of land. Philippe was proud of these years of toil.

When he had married the aristocratic Marie Therese La Tou-
rette, daughter of one of the northern vineyardists, he was
well on the way to a fortune.

The vines, pruned for half a century, were knee-high trees,
shaped for bearing. Now and then he stooped to touch the
shredded bark of their sturdy trunks. Sometimes he pressed
a leaf between his fingers. By touch he knew a healthy vine.
He knew exactly what this soil and these vines would produce. They had given him his wealth. The flavor of the first
wine he had ever made was on his palate still—sweet wines,
the best produced in the irrigated regions.

North in Napa County, from the meager bunches of grapes
grown on the stony hillsides, he made his dry wines. With
unlimited patience he had aged, sampled and endlessly tested
them until he had wines fit for the connoisseur and for the
church. Wines long used now by bishops and archbishops for
the sacrament—miraculously changed into the blood of Christ.

Philippe Rambeau's own life was soon to be given back to his
God.

But not yet. Sturdy old Philippe straightened his shoulders.
Like his vines, he was built for age.

He took out his key, let himself into the winery, walked
through the rooms, clean as a creamery, where the bottled
wines lay on the pine-board racks, on through the rooms
where the small casks lay on their sides, on into the room with
the high redwood tanks.

He was in the original part of the building now, with its
cathedral-like arches upholding the roof. In the year he
built his winery the mortar for such an undertaking had
to be brought from Belgium, for no cement was made in
America then. The German who had designed the room
was an artist at his work. The Italian masons had been
artists, too. *As I am*, Philippe Rambeau said to himself proudly.

To make glad communion with men, it was not legal now
to sell these wines; only to make communion with God. Old
Philippe snorted.

He was tired when he reached the garden again and he

paused before going down the steps. With a start he realized
he was not alone. On a bench between the beds of petunias
a girl was sitting. Her hands were clasped behind her head
and her face was raised to the moon sliding now toward the
saddle between mountains. She wore a white dress. For
a moment his mind leaped the years . . . Marie, one night
after the harvest, the first year of their marriage.

"Nice, isn't it, Philippe Rambeau?" It was Elizabeth and
she spoke his name just as if they had not been divided by
more than half a century.

"What are you doing here?" he asked, surprised, almost
startled, but pleased with her use of his first name.

"What are you?" She moved over inviting him to sit down.
"I was getting lonesome, but now that there are two of
us . . ."

She was offering him a comradeship he had long craved,
not the barren substitute of deference his other grandchildren
had been trained to give him. He laid his hand over hers
where it rested on the seat between them.

She, too, felt no barrier of age as his blunt but fragile
fingers closed over hers. She fell silent, comforted by his
sympathetic handclasp. She was glad he had interrupted her
troubled thoughts. When she had returned from the party
she had stepped out into the garden, tempted by its coolness
and mystery. Suddenly she had felt a sharp regret that she
had let John go. She thought she had rebuffed him because
of her loyalty to William Humphreys, but all at once she
had known it was because John had the power to stir her
emotions. She had been hurt when they had been roused
before. A sigh escaped her that sounded half like a sob.

"Is something troubling you, *petite?*" the old man asked
her gently.

"Well, a little." She squeezed his hand.

"Didn't you enjoy the party?" he asked, probing for what
lay under her remark.

"Oh yes, very much." She smiled brightly—and then all

at once she burst out, "I'm not right for your California. If I could have come new—not brought my thoughts—Lon said it was a beginning."

"None of us come new," said Philippe. "We've brought too much with us for that." He stopped. His own consuming desire for wealth, even yet not satisfied, troubled him tonight. He wished to loosen his tenacious hold upon it, yet was unable to do so. To him, toughened by so many encounters with the world, Elizabeth seemed incredibly innocent. How could the spirit, housed in such a lovely receptacle, have been touched? He wondered what could have happened. Perhaps her trouble lay in her very beauty, he thought with sudden insight. She stirred even his old heart, sitting here in her white, shimmering, low-cut dress. Remembering the night of Martha's dinner and John's evident interest in Elizabeth, he said, "You mustn't let John upset you. You are a very pretty girl and John likes pretty girls even when they're his cousins. He means nothing."

Elizabeth felt an instant hot desire to defend John against something derogatory she felt lay in her grandfather's words. But she did not speak, suddenly conscious that she did not want to be warned against John.

I must see that she is happy, Philippe was thinking. *I must see that she has something of her own when I am gone.*

They sat there in silence for a long time, each feeling some special security in the other. Finally old Philippe rose, saying, "We had better go in, my *petite*. Suppose your Aunt Martha should find us here?"

"It wouldn't do, would it?" Elizabeth answered. Hand in hand, they stole across the grass.

XII

THE morning after the party Andrew Fairon awoke to his sister Suzanne's singing. He heard a splash as she tumbled into the tub for her morning bath. He was usually awakened in this fashion. Her windows were at right angles to his.

The house was a rambling one of no particular architecture. With little attention to anything but usefulness, rooms had been added onto the original building. The result was a house of convenience but not of privacy. Nobody in the household had ever wanted an exclusive and separate privacy. It was a family that delighted in its combined activities.

"Hi there!" called out Andrew. "Take it an octave higher, Sis. I like it better that way."

He lay back, contentedly listening to the clear effortless voice of his sister, his thoughts drifting away to last night and his ride with his new cousin. She was prettier than Leli and Françoise—as pretty as Suzanne, he thought. If he weren't going away to the northern vineyard with Grandfather, it would be fun to take her around while John was in New York.

Then his thoughts went to the matter in hand. He and his grandfather were leaving this morning for the Napa vineyards, where he was to live for a year, learning to make wine. At twenty-one he yet had not had the training his father, uncles and cousin John had had. Prohibition coming in just as he was ready for his apprenticeship may have been the reason. His grandfather had left the care of the northern vineyards almost exclusively to Diener since then.

There was the breakfast bell. He should have been dressed,

for his mother liked them all to sit down at one time. Immediately he was out of bed. By hurrying, he managed to trail his sisters into the dining room. His mother was already pouring the coffee. Promptly Andrew's father, who had been standing by the window studying something in his hand, joined them. But before he took his place he laid a specimen of rock on the table beside Andrew. "Do you know what this is?" he asked.

"Oh, Ronald," begged Isobel, "do let Andrew eat his breakfast or he'll keep Father waiting."

"True, true," Ronald Fairon murmured. Taking his seat, he unfolded his napkin and smiled across at his wife.

Ronald was a replica of his brother Francis, only done in less careful fashion. He wore loose comfortable clothes; his hair did not lie in smooth blackness as Francis' did. He ran his hand through it too often when he was perplexed about some rock formation. But his eyes like his brother's were quiet and gentle. It was a dreamy face like Francis Fairon's.

Any spare time he could gain from the wine business, he spent studying the geology of California. On week ends, almost from the time his children were born, he had packed them and his wife into a carriage or an automobile and taken them to camp in the hills. He was at his best then. At home he left everything to his wife.

Isobel was the ruler of the household even as Martha was of hers, the rule no less determined because the ruler was happy and satisfied. She was questioning her children, now, on last evening's party. She had thought Suzanne too young to go but Andrew had persuaded her on the grounds that it was his last evening at home. He had promised to look after her.

"And did you?" she asked.

"You should have had *me* watch Andrew, Mum." Suzanne looked at her brother and laughed. "He disappeared altogether and took Elizabeth with him. Snatched her right away from John."

"California was just a little too much for Elizabeth," Andrew answered. "It was awfully hot last night."

"Hear, hear!" cried Leli and Françoise.

Isobel looked at her son. He was not in the least disturbed by his sisters' banter. He knew his sisters adored him, his mother and his father too. He was the handsomest of their children.

In Andrew the round, stubborn Rambeau chin was slightly modified, lengthening his whole face, somehow sensitizing it. His black brows were more arched than those of the rest of the family. And his eyes were smiling eyes. His mouth was wide and generous, albeit passionate.

There is a good deal of his father in him, thought Isobel, smiling across at Ronald Fairon who was explaining to Andrew an expedition into the mountains he was planning. She wondered how Andrew would get along without them or they without him. But she was glad he was to have this year of responsibility.

Philippe. Yes, Elizabeth had called him Philippe, the old man was thinking as he drove north with Andrew. He wished his grandson would drop the Grandfather and call him Philippe. *Andrew would be shocked out of his skin if I proposed it.* Old Philippe chuckled to himself, thinking of his daughter Isobel, and the good training she had given her children.

Long before they reached the Napa Valley he had forgotten his dissatisfaction of yesterday over his family's money-making activities. The intimate narrow valley when they reached it pleased him too. They were passing Beaulieu Winery. He admired the Frenchman who had created it. He was the son of one of the oldest families of vintners in France—a great vintner in his own right.

The deep-verandaed, brown-shingled house where for many years he had brought his family in the summers, suited him too. So did the simple life he led here with Diener's German wife, Gerta, to care for him, and Diener, an Alsace-Lorraine man like himself, to work with. A winemaker if ever there was one. There would be the young Father Flanigan in another day.

Immediately on his arrival he dressed himself in a copy of working clothes done in blue linen and went up to the winery, a small stone building built close against the hills. Here his wine was stored in caves chipped out of the rock. He walked through them, running his dry old hands over moss the color and texture of a mouse's skin which clung to the uneven walls. That moss was a pride to him. In France they claimed that only in wineries where the wine was of the finest quality did such moss grow.

Then he went out again into the sunlight. The last load of the day was coming in. "You're picking the hill vine-yards early, aren't you?" he said to Diener who had been following him about.

"Ve test always before ve pick."

"Of course, of course. I wasn't implying they weren't ready," Philippe said a little acidly. These two delighted in argument over the work.

Two white horses pulled the wagon up to the unloading platform. It was a conceit of Philippe's to have white horses for use in the high vineyards. He walked over to examine the grapes and picked up a bunch here and there out of the lug boxes, studying the varieties. Even Diener did not know the arrangement of the vines in the fields. His own secret way of blending for his finest wines was to plant the vines in such a way that when the grapes were picked he would have the proportions of each variety as he wanted them in the finished wine. He stood there until the last box had been emptied into the moving conveyor which carried the grapes to the crusher. The fragrance of the crushed fruit filled the dry September air. It was late, almost sunset, but Philippe never allowed a load of grapes to stand overnight. Diener knew it. Never over four hours after picking should the grapes stand, Philippe contended, and Diener agreed with him.

Now Philippe followed Diener inside the winery, looking down into the full vats, getting the pungent smell of fermenting grapes.

"Goot," Diener said, "goot this year. Just right de grape. She plump out fine des year, de sugar, de acid, yust right. See how she bubble."

The deep purple mass that Philippe looked down upon foamed up in an effervescent lavender froth. The airy bubbles broke, new ones crowded up from the depths of the vat where the union of the gray bloom of the grape's skin and the juice brought about this strong ferment.

"The wine it ess restless, too. Ve go see." Diener, bent with rheumatism, grasped the rail of the stairs leading down from the vats, took the steps one by one like a child.

"If you'd sleep in a bed like a Christian at night you wouldn't be all crippled up," scolded Philippe.

"A winemaster go to bed at night when the vine ess make! *Ach,* you are a fool, Meester Rambeau. Every hour I must test."

Philippe winked at Andrew who stood at the foot of the stairs. *Evidently he's forgiven me for trying to make him rest when he first came. My eye, didn't he fly at me! I'll not try that again,* was Andrew's silent conclusion.

To Andrew this free and easy Philippe was a new manifestation. None of his family had warned him that his grandfather was a different man when he was here alone.

His mother had told him he must look after his grandfather. There was in Andrew an instinct to take care of people he loved. The idea of watching over old Philippe had given him a deep satisfaction. But he saw it wasn't going to be easy. Grandfather meant to do as he pleased up here. But he'd enjoyed writing his mother of the irritating and lovable crotchets of Philippe, knowing she would take a delight in them all.

Old Philippe, looking down on Andrew, was shrewdly trying to estimate the strength under Andrew's gentleness. Although he was almost as old as his cousin John he seemed immature in comparison. He had none of John's virile desire for combat, none of his hard ambition. That he was two years younger did not explain it. Charles was eight years younger than John, but John could not dim Charles' assertiveness. Compared with his step-cousin Henri, Andrew seemed even more immature. There was a simplicity about him which left him untouched by the more worldly attitude of his cousins with whom he had grown up.

So far Andrew had not interested Philippe greatly. John was more to his liking, although he would not own, even to himself, his preference for John. He was a little ashamed of it, for John, he sensed, was himself, unprettified by any benevolences. He remembered John here with him before the war. He had the making of a good vintner. He had the artist's touch, but he didn't have the artist's heart. The small business of making wine for the church—that wouldn't interest the ambitious John. But Andrew might choose it as a way of life. Philippe's heart was sore that so many members of his family seemed to be intensified fragments of his own acquisitiveness. Why didn't some one of them partake of the other side of his nature, the side that liked to make altar wine? Perhaps Andrew would be that one.

Down one side of the room they now entered stood casks filled with aging wine; on the other side, on racks stacked to the ceiling, lay bottles of matured wine.

"Ah," said old Philippe, forgetting Andrew, "it is true as you said, Diener. The wine stirs."

Andrew watched the two men moving about among the behemoths of barrels. The mysterious process of aging and mellowing, going on in the years the wine stood in the casks, always pricked Andrew's imagination. What was wine anyway, he asked himself, with its mystical content, and how did man come to make it? Bread, too? What was its meaning?

"The wine in these bottles, Andrew—" his grandfather laid his hand on one of the higher racks—"I want you never to forget is of the vintage I sent to Rome. Remember this shelf. Sometime when I am gone the family, for some great occasion, will want to use this wine. But I think," he added, taking down a bottle, "some of it must go this year to Father Flanigan. Remember, Andrew, when I ask for it, where you can find it."

The next afternoon the bishop of a near-by diocese was coming to select wine for his church. Old Philippe walked about his old-fashioned parlor, waiting to greet his guest. From the center table everything had been cleared. Upon it there had been placed glasses and bottles of red and white wine, but neither wine was from the shelf he had pointed out to Andrew. That wine would go only to the young father.

Just at noon the bishop came, walking across the fields from a place in the hills where he rested at times. As he entered the room he dropped his cassock which he had not changed for this informal meeting with his friend. The black folds fell to his heels. He had gathered it about him to keep it out of the wet as he had passed through the winery where men were washing the floors that no alien germ might get into the wine.

"Philippe," he said, "it is good to see you. We are two old men in everyone's eyes but our own."

Again the use of his name reached through to Philippe Rambeau's heart. "This," he replied, "is the best wine I have ever offered to you. Old, old stock, mellowing for years, waiting for this hour."

"Ah, Philippe. Suppose there had been no Prohibition—would you have offered me this old, old stock?" The bishop's eyes twinkled.

"You talk too much." Philippe moved briskly about the table. "Which one will you try first?"

Two days, and the young priest from the East had not come. Then on the third day, just as Philippe had given him up, he saw a car coming in between the stone pillars which marked the entrance. It stopped before the winery. As Father Flanigan got out, the sun picked out the cross, golden symbol of brotherhood, that lay upon his breast. The sun shone full upon his serene countenance.

Father Flanigan never hurried about selecting the wine. He waited a few days, sitting in meditation in the grape arbor at the back of the house looking out at the hills.

Old Philippe liked to sit quietly at the end of the long table which half filled the arbor, content just to be near the young priest. Looking at the father's rapt face, he had thought sometimes that if ever he had a vision it would come to him here, and at such a time. In spite of his love of all material possessions Philippe was deeply religious and longed for a vision.

It was evening and the three sat in the arbor. Gerta had cleared their supper away. She had gone to join Diener now, the two of them sitting out in front of the winery, their voices coming down to the three in the arbor. There in the California night, with the sky blue even in the darkness and set with big stars, each of the three men dreamed his separate dream, their faces no longer revealed to one another.

Philippe was conscious of rising impatience. Was he never to have his vision? He was a little vague as to what he wanted—some assurance, perhaps, that his wine had been acceptable as an offering unto God. With the suddenness of old age he dropped off to sleep. As his head fell forward he awoke with the lonely sense of mystery which, like some cold dark wind, sweeps over the spirit sometimes in the instant of waking.

"You there, Andrew?" he asked in a tone louder than necessary.

"Yes, why?" asked Andrew. "Anything I can do for you?"

"No. Why yes, my coat." A shiver had run over him as if he were making some cold passage.

After bringing the coat Andrew leaned back in his chair.

Again his hands supported his head. He was tired from the day's work. It would be pleasant to lie down on the hard-packed earth as he used to when a little boy and look up at the great vine that stood like a central pillar holding up the trellised arbor. The branches, clinging together around the old trunk, on the trellis stretched themselves free among their leaves and fruit, making an interwoven roof.

He had not been able all day to forget the new cousin. How beautiful she was with her blue eyes. Strangely sweet she had seemed as she sat beside him in his car, her head thrown back, her gaze on the stars.

Andrew brought the front legs of his chair down with a soft thud. In gently sentimental mood he wandered out into the moonlight. What had an old man or a priest to do with dreams like his?

XIII

PERHAPS for the first time in her life, Martha's power to get what she wanted was weakened because she wanted two things at once—two things diametrically opposed —Elizabeth's marriage tying Henri into the family and Elizabeth's separation from the family. That half-felt antagonism stirring in her the evening of the dinner had rapidly crystallized into a hard and bitter antagonism. It was compounded of her sense of injury that Lon had tricked her in gaining her consent to take Elizabeth, and her bitter disappointment that Elizabeth was not an unformed girl to be brought up by her. She did not want this poised young woman whom she doubted she could mold. Even if she brought about the marriage with Henri, might not Elizabeth thwart her in the use of the Swanaña lands?

Elizabeth did not know what to think in the days after old Philippe had gone. The house seemed a different place without him. At first she thought her aunt's unpleasant manner toward her was due entirely to her grandfather's absence. Martha gave much shorter shrift to everyone in the house. Chu no longer seemed a privileged member of the household. He, as well as his son David, was now treated like a servant. The gracious formality that existed between Martha and Francis seemed to have sharpened into armed neutrality. Was it not a part of the changed atmosphere that her aunt should treat her differently, too?

To all outward appearances Martha was showing her off. Almost every day she took her to meet friends, driving as far as Los Angeles and San Francisco for the purpose. She seemed especially anxious to make the evenings pleasant for her. "Too bad Andrew and John are both away," she would say. "Of course you're bored, cooped up with two old people like Francis and me. I'll call Henri and see if he can have dinner with us."

"Please don't trouble," Elizabeth would tell her. "I've always been with people older than myself."

"Nonsense," her aunt answered, "why shouldn't I go to trouble? Besides I want him to get to know you. He can give you a very good time this winter if he likes you."

But then when Henri came Aunt Martha would say sharp things that humiliated her. *If she wants him to like me, she's going about it in a funny way,* thought Elizabeth. *From the things Aunt Martha says he'll think there isn't anything right about me. Perhaps she just has no tact,* Elizabeth finally concluded, trying to be fair to her aunt. *She's too good to me in so many ways. Surely she doesn't mean to make me unhappy.*

One day in the exclusive shop where they had gone to do some shopping, Elizabeth realized with a shock that her aunt was really trying to make her unhappy. "See, we've something of a problem. Not the French figure," Martha was saying to the saleswoman. "Too—what shall I say? Elizabeth, slip off your dress, dear."

Elizabeth stood before them, her pretty arms held stiffly. In some mysterious way all the self-consciousness of adolescence suddenly seemed to have reasserted itself, its special kind of embarrassment gripping her when she walked awkwardly across the salon.

"Never mind, darling," Martha consoled her. "We'll soon have you fixed up. Madame has handled far more difficult problems. It's really just a matter of choice. Keeping away from the English look. And the shoes—that's part of it."

Tears of mortification sprang to Elizabeth's eyes as she bent her head to allow madame to slip the dress down over her shoulders.

I wonder why Aunt Martha is bullying me, she thought. *She must have a reason.*

All the way back from San Francisco Elizabeth tried to work it out. *I've been as nice as I knew how. But she doesn't like me.* She glanced at her aunt's profile. Outlined against the window of the car it looked as if it had been cut out of flint. *She intends to make me so unhappy that I'll go back to England,* Elizabeth thought. *Well, I won't. Grandfather likes me. So does Uncle Fran. I'm going to fight it out.*

She shifted her position and looked out the window. They were driving across the hills of California's coast range, hills bleached to a tawny brown in the months of unremitting sunshine. They looked savage and cruel to Elizabeth in their shining brilliance. She did not yet know how to deal with this land.

"Do stop fidgeting, Elizabeth," said her aunt.

"I didn't know I was," she answered faintly, feeling as uncomfortable as her Aunt Martha meant her to feel. When they reached home Elizabeth saw to her great relief that her grandfather was back. His car was in front of the door and Chu was taking out his luggage.

The next day Elizabeth dressed herself in English tweeds for a tea to which her aunt was taking her.

"My *dear* girl!" exclaimed Martha when Elizabeth entered the living room. "This is a *party*." She herself was wearing an afternoon dress of pale gray, hat, gloves and bag in a slightly contrasting color. "What you have on isn't suitable for an afternoon affair. Besides it's far too warm for a suit. I'll wait while you put on the frock I bought for you in San Francisco."

"I'm all right," Elizabeth answered roughly.

Grandfather Rambeau, sitting in his accustomed place in the living room, was not deaf to the note of defiance in her voice.

"What did you say, *petite?*"

"I said I was all right."

His experienced old eyes studied her, then Martha. What was Martha doing to Lon's girl? He had known servants in the house to get sullen and then leave. He'd lost his best cook that way. He wasn't going to lose this best granddaughter.

He smiled and his smile was engaging. "If my favorite granddaughter," he said, watching the effect of his words on Martha, "would do me the honor of being French this afternoon?"

Elizabeth smiled, touched him lightly on the shoulder and went to her room to change.

Old Philippe faced his daughter stern and unsmiling. "Martha, you rule us all. Elizabeth you'll rule, too, but I won't let you break her. I've made you head of my house, but I expect you to hold yourself in control."

He picked up his newspaper, ignoring Martha, so poised a moment before, now completely stricken.

"Father, I . . ."

He made no sign of hearing her.

She held a small lace handkerchief to her lips to hide their trembling, then twisted the handkerchief in her hands, heavy with rings.

Of all the human beings who walked the earth, her father was the only one to whom Martha gave allegiance. From the time she could remember, he alone had been a figure powerful enough to be respected fully. To be spoken to like that by him!

Elizabeth, coming back into the room, found the atmosphere changed. What had happened in her absence she could not guess. Grandfather was reading as usual; her aunt stood just where she had left her, but she looked pale, and for Aunt Martha, indecisive. She seemed on the point of speaking, then evidently decided against it; she seemed on the point of going, even moved a step toward the door, then evidently decided against that. Elizabeth stood waiting.

Finally Grandfather Rambeau put down his paper. "You look very nice, my dear," he said. "I'm inclined to think you're the only one in the family who looks like your grandmother. A handsome woman, your grandmother. I'll walk with you to the car," he added, getting up from his chair.

"I think Elizabeth had better drive you today," he said when they reached the car. "David is getting ready to go back to school, Martha."

Martha gave a small gasp of surprise, so sharp that it sounded almost like a squeak. Had her father intended all the time that Elizabeth should drive today? Were things going on in the household which she knew nothing about? And David, too. So Father had been planning for David's return to college. Had he guessed that she had thought to wear Chu down and prevent it? A Chinese boy going to college—it was nonsense. The thing for him to do was to learn to be a good servant.

Martha, shaken before, was doubly so now. More and more of late she had thought her father too old to bother with what went on about him. Without knowing it, she had come to have a slight scorn for his failing abilities. And now, almost in a breath, he had stepped back into her life with all his old authority.

As Elizabeth took hold of the wheel and slipped in the clutch, the mechanism under her control seemed alive and akin to her. It gave her what she craved—quick, running movement. It was going somewhere! Where, she should direct it. She gave herself over to guiding the beautiful responsive organism beneath her hand.

"Careful!"

She'd forgotten Aunt Martha!

"I don't trust your driving, Elizabeth."

"You can," Elizabeth answered coolly but she slowed down to the circumspect speed that Martha demanded of David.

Martha said no more. Tears of anger and humiliation were close to her eyes. Under the robe that lay lightly over her lap she clenched her hands, forcing herself to calmness. Not since the days when she had struggled with Fran had she cried. It devastated her to cry. If she must, it had to be postponed until she was safe from interruption. Did her father, then, not respect her as she thought he did? Had he all these years not liked the things she had done?

What can I do, she thought, *to make Father respect me ... as he always has?* ... *Yes*, she said firmly to herself, *as he always has*.

Along the avenue that led to the house of their hostess—all Aunt Martha's friends seemed to live in mansions approached by avenues—Elizabeth drove the car.

Beyond a group of eucalyptus stood the house, large and imposing. Seeing it, thinking of her friend's wealth and position and her own well-established place in society, Martha felt her poise returning. Her keen mind was capable of an instantaneous about-face when she saw a chance to change a disadvantage into advantage. Elizabeth could be her favorite niece, as she was Father Rambeau's favorite granddaughter.

Why, I can do wonders with her, with Father feeling the way he does. Martha settled back in her seat, no longer divided in her purpose toward Elizabeth. Yes, she would see that she married Henri.

"My dear," she said to her hostess with a purposeful smile, "this is Elizabeth, the daughter, you know, I've always longed for."

XIV

ARTHA and Elizabeth had scarcely left the house when Chu came tiptoeing into the living room. If the Old One were asleep he would not wake him. But the Old One was not.

"Chu. What is it?"

"My most unworthy son David leaves me now."

"And you would like——?"

"That he should tell the Honorable One good-by."

Chu, coming as he had to America when he was twenty, had never lost the polite convention of his own language. David was different. He used American slang, and the familiar *you*, even in addressing the Old One. Chu was proud that he did. David he meant should be equal to the Rambeaus in every point, especially in education—but in wealth, too. Chu had bought land in the name of David with his savings, grape land. It would bear next year. *Chu a rich man pretty soon now.*

"A little matter in the town not made known to the Honorable One," Chu said after David had left the room.

"Yes?" said Philippe.

Chu, in Philippe Rambeau's employ in one capacity or another for thirty years, managed many things for Philippe better not known to the rest of the family. He had been coolie first, then head of the coolies on the Rambeau place. By and by he had come to the house to work, taking the name of his employer according to custom, but he still lived in the head coolie's room and acted as counselor to his people. Then when the Chinese had been driven from the fields, he had taken his wife and sailed for China. But he had brought a young concubine back with him that he might have an American son. He had not meant to return. Watching his people mobbed and beaten in those years of anti-Chinese feeling, he had hated America when he went away. Perhaps it was his remembrance of his countrymen's early difficulties in America which made him bother with the affairs of this uncouth Russian, for so did the stalwart Yakowitz look to him.

"The man Yakowitz wants me to speak for him," said Chu. "He is just now sitting in the Honorable One's kitchen."

"Well, bring him in." Philippe Rambeau's white brows drew together in a scowl. Something was wrong he could tell from Chu's tone.

Yakowitz towered over the meager little Chinaman as he followed him into the room. Perhaps he seemed more handsome than he was in contrast to the gnome-like, parchment-faced Chu. Philippe Rambeau liked the looks of the man, although he had little respect for the Russians in general. He had an idea that like the Greeks they drank a horrible wine that had to be treated with resin, or something equally terrible, to give the bitter flavor that their native wines had, just because for centuries in Greece their wines had been fermented in goatskins lined with resin.

"I have come," said the man without preamble, "to voice complaint, so that you may bring my trouble before the law."

"And why do you not make your own complaint to the legal authorities?" asked Philippe Rambeau, watching with narrowed eyes this man before him. In his eighty-five years of living Philippe Rambeau had learned a good deal about men.

"Because I have no power in this community."

"Bah!" said Philippe. "You pay taxes. You've got a voice. Why don't you use it?"

"I have used it and it does me no good. Nor anyone else. Didn't I try to talk to them when they came to my house?"

"Could anybody stop you? A man of your size?"

"Yes. Your——" He hesitated. This small indomitable old man, Yakowitz held in too great awe to allow him to tell him what his grandson John Rambeau had done. "Even Yakowitz, with all his strength, could not stop twenty men," he went on. "We were celebrating my son's birthday. Right before my sons and my little children they took me and bound me. Me, *me!*" Yakowitz struck his breast. "Me, who to the big sons and the little ones am the strongest man in the country. Now I can do nothing with my children. I am no longer strong before them. My boys, they go to bad places. I cannot lick them now. I have been licked before them. I am a shamed man." Yakowitz' head sank on his breast.

"The names of these men?" asked the old man curtly.

"They hid behind black cloth."

"And what did they want of you? That, you have not told me. Perhaps you have been a nuisance in your neighborhood."

"I am a decent man," said Yakowitz, rising to his full height. "They said I must not sell raisin grapes to a neighbor for a little less."

Philippe Rambeau shot up out of his chair. Such anger as he had not known for years burned out the slow substance of age that had accumulated in his veins. The color in his cheeks which Elizabeth had noticed on their first meeting was intensified into a dull purplish hue. His lips drew back almost in a snarl. "Chu!" he called. "Get me the judge on the telephone."

He took the receiver from Chu's hand the instant he heard the distant twang of a voice. "Now, you get out!" he barked at Chu. "And take Yakowitz with you!"

Chu, listening on the other side of the door, heard the caustic remarks that Philippe Rambeau spoke into the receiver.

"Go," Chu said to the Russian. "This matter will be taken care of."

But no one heard the talk between the old man and his son and sons-in-law. That conversation was carried on in the sampling room at the winery. The heavy masonry, the oak-plank door, shut all sound within. Usually when the men of the family sat around the old tavern table in consultation, wine was served, but not today. When André asked his father what vintage he would like, Philippe Rambeau replied, "None."

Then the men knew he was angry.

"You have been telling me this contract was unanimous."

"Is it not?" asked André. "You saw the papers."

"Papers, bah!" said the old man, and he spat at their feet. "Because of this I cannot retire," he told them. "I'll see justice done if every member of my own family is among the ones convicted. Is that why you were anxious to get John away?" he asked with sudden intuition.

"Sir," said Francis Fairon, "your own daughter suggested that John should be the one to go. I think she had some other motive."

Philippe did not press his point further. This was a matter to take up with Martha. He sat in the great oak chair at the head of the table looking old and shrunken. Just over his white head on a shelf behind him stood the beautiful blue goblet his son Lon had sent him by Elizabeth.

"Why," he demanded, "did I come to this new country, leave Alsace-Lorraine? I thought to leave violence behind. I have seen plenty of it in this Valley. Is it never to end?" He rose and went out, and he seemed older by many years than when he had come into the room.

Francis Fairon followed him. "Better let me drive you home, Father."

Without protest Philippe took his seat by his son-in-law. "I'd like you to arrange for me to go up to Napa County tomorrow," he said. "Telephone Andrew to have my room ready."

"I'll attend to it," his son-in-law told him. "And Father," he added, "Martha wanted John to go east mainly, I think, to get him away from Elizabeth. John evidently found her very attractive. And Martha, I think, does not approve."

"I am in complete agreement with her there," said old Philippe. "But might there not be two reasons for John's going? Francis, we have lived in the same house for many years. We know a good deal about each other. We've been honest with each other even when we have not agreed. I trust you—are we involved in this act of coercion?"

"Not that I know of," Francis Fairon answered after a pause. He could not bring himself to put John in disfavor with the head of the family. Let the matter blow over. He felt certain the court would see the investigation came to nothing.

Francis had taken no part in the raisin deal, expressing himself neither for nor against the night riding. He had foreseen some such probing of the situation by the old man and he wanted to be at peace with him. His own place in the household had been maintained because Philippe Rambeau had given him enough recognition so that he could carry on. The year the trouble had begun between him and Martha Philippe had made a point of emphasizing his son-in-law's value to the Rambeau firm.

To fail such a friend was hard. There was a stiffness in Philippe's manner as he stepped out of the car that told Francis he had failed him. But his father-in-law was eighty-five and could not be expected to keep abreast of the times. Grape growing was a business now, not a way of life.

In the morning Philippe decided to postpone his trip to the Napa vineyards. He might be needed to press the case against the night riders. It would be a mistake to go away now, but later he would go and take Elizabeth with him.

XV

THE blue rainless skies, hard gray at the horizon, had begun to soften. Faint, wraithlike clouds flanged upward. A shower, light almost as dew, moistened the powder-dry sandy loam, but made no impression on the cement-hard, black adobe. Then once more the clear desert sky. Finally clouds, dark and stormy, blew in from the sea and rain came down steadily. The newly drenched earth sent off pungent odors long imprisoned, and in the night the earth changed over into green.

This morning the sun was shining again as Elizabeth guided her horse up a path in the foothills of the Sierra ranges. Henri was with her. How it came about that she was seeing so much of him she hardly knew. Since her grandfather's return and the new attitude of her aunt, Henri de Swanaña had been coming to the house even more often than before. Aunt Martha seemed to go out of her way to plan all kinds of outings for Elizabeth and they nearly always included Henri. Her aunt never said unpleasant things to her or about her now. Why the change, she did not know, but she enjoyed the comfort with which Aunt Martha surrounded her. A hundred little attentions. They didn't make her exactly happy but neither was she unhappy. She took the days as they came —and Henri seemed to be a part of them—glad that Aunt Martha was friendly.

She looked at Henri, now making his way up the trail ahead of her. He wore no hat and she could see how his thick black hair grew low on his neck. He had narrow shoulders and a waist more like a woman's than a man's. He stopped to point out the scene below them and let her come up beside him. His heart-shaped face gave the impression of gentleness until you looked at his thin cruel lips.

"My land over there," he said. "I've a thousand acres, cattle and vineyards. You can just see the line of palm trees leading up to the house from here if you take my glasses." He handed her his powerful binoculars.

It was odd, Elizabeth realized, that she had never been over to Aunt Maria's. Looking through the glasses she saw clearly the long avenue of palms, one of the number of such avenues crisscrossing the Valley. From where she stood by using the glasses she could see a dozen of them leading to various estates. The longest avenue of them all she knew belonged to an Englishman. Eleven miles it extended, a smooth highway lined with great trees, paralleled on one side by a bridle path and on the other by a road for carts and trucks. From the gates of the estate it led into the paved streets of Fresno. Dreams of grandeur, all right. It looked as if Henri's estate was almost as grand.

"How about riding over tomorrow and seeing the old hacienda?" Henri asked. "You can catch a glimpse of it now if you look a little to the right."

Henri put his hand over hers and turned the central screw of the binoculars. His clinging fingers woke Elizabeth with a start. She had taken Henri too much for granted—as a part of her comfort. In a revealing instant she saw now in the frequent visits of Henri to her aunt's home and in excursions like today, Martha's unmistakable touch.

She handed back the glasses. "It must be a nice place," she said briskly. "But I can't go with you tomorrow. I've promised to drive Grandfather up to his northern vineyards."

Henri looked annoyed. "You can be certain the old man has nothing so important to do that it can't wait."

"Your place has stood there a long time, hasn't it?" she asked smiling. "Couldn't it wait a week for me to see it? Besides, I want to go with Grandfather." She turned, heading her horse down toward the Valley floor.

Henri followed. She caught a glimpse of his face and it was dark with chagrin.

At the first small town he drew rein saying, "I've business here. I don't suppose you mind riding home alone?"

"Not in the least." Elizabeth hoped she had made her point plain. She perhaps would have, had Henri not turned and noticed how distinctive she looked, sitting her horse. Her blue eyes lent a piquant look to her face. She rode well, she dressed well. She had a slightly foreign air about her which added to her unusualness.

Moved by his acquisitive instinct rather than by passion, he coveted her. Henri's passions were not so sternly held down that the banked-up fires were dangerous to the point of explosion. Already there had been women in Henri's life. He prided himself that because of this he could choose his wife coolly and thus wisely.

Elizabeth took a side road leading in the direction of the Rambeau ranch. *How little I've seen since I came,* she thought. *In the car we always go through the main streets of the towns and along the big highways. Whether we drive to Los Angeles or San Francisco or Fresno, it's always the same.*

Ever since she had arrived in California, she had been impressed by the number of small houses—precarious houses, they seemed to her. She slowed her horse to a walk, studying them today. Buildings interested her, as they did her father. Some of these houses looked no larger than one room. Many of them appeared to be in a continual process of building. Many had old cars standing in the front yards, a woman and a child or two running about, a man putting on siding or shingles in a clumsy way. There were houses with one side rough-boarded, an indication that the owner hoped sometime to add a room or rooms. Almost without exception they were ugly. No architect had designed them. Unfulfilled dreams of their builders, probably.

Something happening to the autumn earth gradually claimed Elizabeth's attention. A soft green covering, like nothing she had ever seen before at this time of year, was spread over the ground under the trees in the orchards, among the brown stumplike trunks of the grapes, up the mountainside. A soft ephemeral green. Later she would learn that the verdure was simply miner's lettuce, mustard and a thousand other weeds, but today it was pure miracle. She felt happy and for the moment at peace.

It was growing dusk when she came to the Dietrick place. She could just see the house placed far back in the vineyard, built around the water tank which rose like a huge barrel from the center of the roof. A windmill stood a few rods away. She wondered about Buz. She had seen her occasionally as they shot past in the car.

From the orchard that skirted the road, smoke rose in a thin column, smoke that moved down the aisles between the trees as if walking. As it came nearer, Elizabeth saw that a fat old horse was pulling an iron basket on wheels, from which smoke trailed. The odd equippage stopped. A girl threw an armful of dead branches into the cart, pushed them down with a pitchfork. Crackling flames shot up. As the girl swung herself to the shaft and then sat down in the hollowed space on the old horse's back, Elizabeth saw it was Buz. She had her blue overalls rolled to her knees and her legs dangling from the broad cuffs were round and childish looking.

"Hello," called Elizabeth, reining in her horse.

"Hello," said Buz in a sullen tone.

I guess I haven't managed to say hello in the right way, thought Elizabeth. She was fast discarding the English terms, putting in their places the American ones, but they were still new enough to make her feel unsure of herself.

"I thought you were in town. It's nice to see you again," Elizabeth continued.

"I'm home because it's Saturday, if you have to know."

It's more than just how I said "hello." Elizabeth, embarrassed at the girl's rebuff, was about to ride on when Buz called out, "Been out riding with another boy friend?" There was effrontery in her manner of speaking.

"I haven't many friends yet," Elizabeth said quietly. "I'm a stranger, you know."

"What about John Rambeau? You ain't a stranger to him, I guess."

Elizabeth was angry now. What right had Buz to say anything so personal to her? Surely John hadn't given Buz any reason to ask such a question. She sat her horse, looking at the girl for a moment. "I think you don't want to be friendly," she said at last. "I was told you were friendly. I'm sorry."

Buz looked up and her eyes, as blue as Elizabeth's, opened wide like a child's. *How pretty she is,* thought Elizabeth with a sudden pang. Then the lids dropped over Buz's eyes.

"Who told you I'd be friends?" she asked. "Was it him?"

Elizabeth rode nearer, putting her hand on the shaggy flank of Buz's horse. "Do you mean John Rambeau?"

"You take your hand out of the way. I got to tend the fire." Buz walked along the shaft, crushing the branches down into the flames with her pitchfork. Her voice was rough and hard. "What you coming around like this for anyway? You've taken John away. What more do you want?"

"I haven't seen John for weeks. Not since the night I saw you at the dance." The minute Elizabeth had spoken she was angry with herself for answering.

"Oh, tell it to Mickey. I'm from Missouri."

Elizabeth did not know what the phrases meant, but she knew what the tone of voice meant. "I didn't take John from you," she cried. "He's gone to New York."

Buz's baby mouth dropped open. "You mean he's not here? When's he comin' back?"

"I don't know. Maybe not for months."

Two very large tears formed at the corners of Buz's wide blue eyes and rolled down either side of her sunburned nose. "What am I goin' to do?" she asked helplessly.

"What is it?" asked Elizabeth in sudden pity. "What's the matter?"

"He's got me into trouble," Buz answered quite simply. "And now he's gone."

"Oh, no!" exclaimed Elizabeth. Then she realized Buz must be telling the truth. Some knowledge of John told her that it *was* the truth. Over her swept a flame of jealousy such as she had never felt.

"Pa'd kill him if he was to find out, and me too. What am I going to do?" Buz's reticences were gone, now that at last she was in touch with some other human being. She had been so alone, trying to find some escape and knowing none. Talking about it didn't seem so bad.

"What about your mother?" Elizabeth asked, struggling to maintain her composure.

"She ain't good to tell things to. She'd think I was a bad girl and tell Pa."

"Yes, she would," agreed Elizabeth.

"You don't think I am?"

"No," said Elizabeth. But to herself she said, *You are, too.* She was trying to persuade herself that Buz was to blame. Of course Buz was to blame.

Buz brightened visibly, then drooped again. "But you'd be the only one to think I wasn't. What'll I do? I got to move on," she added. "I got to get the brush burnt, or Pa'll ask why."

The two girls walked side by side leading the horses.

"What'm I going to do?"

"I don't know."

"If John——"

"I wouldn't count on John, if I were you," Elizabeth answered with quiet cruelty.

"Maybe his father'd give me something and I could run away," Buz sighed.

"I wouldn't count on his father, either. Look, Buz, how much money would you need?"

"What for? You mean to go away?"

"Yes. Isn't that what you were thinking of?"

Buz glanced sideways at her and Elizabeth saw that her eyes were full of suspicion.

Suddenly Buz laughed. "You sure are easy. I just told you that. It's not so. I was mad at you coming and taking John when he belongs to me."

"I understand." Without speaking again Elizabeth mounted her horse, turned his head toward the road.

Once she looked back. Buz was again sitting on the old horse's back, her feet on the shafts, her chin resting on her hand. *Does she think John would marry her? She ought to know he wouldn't. Little fool. She ought to know better.* Why be angry with Buz? John was the one to be angry with. All the time then, he'd only been playing with her . . . as he had with Buz. *Oh, why bother with that?* Elizabeth drew the back of her hand across her eyes.

XVI

PHILIPPE and Elizabeth started very early the
next morning. It was a long day's drive to the northern ranch
and the old man wanted to get in before dark. The days were
short now.

A light rain had begun to fall. It made the pavements,
dry for months, oily and slippery. It was difficult, even dangerous to drive fast, and old Philippe liked to drive fast.
Elizabeth did not mean to disappoint him—or herself. Con-
centrating every faculty on her task, she held the car hour
after hour to a high speed. It kept her from thinking of yesterday.

On the early part of the drive over the straight roads of
the San Joaquin Valley Philippe was very silent, sitting back
in the seat, the rug drawn high over his knees, his gloved hands
wrapped in the top folds, his eyes closed a great deal of the
time.

He looked frail. Elizabeth had not thought of him as frail
before. He had seemed so vigorous the night of the dinner
party, when he had stood with his sons and grandsons gathered about him. Vigorous, too, that night in the garden.
Coming momentarily out of her absorption in the tale Buz
had told her, she was alarmed. Nothing must happen to
him.

But as the day wore on she lost the impression that he was
failing. The farther north they went, the more eager he
became. When they reached the pass that led down into
the valleys of Contra Costa County, he appeared to cast off
both age and frailty. Elizabeth felt a sense of relief steal

over her. Once more he was a bulwark against the long string of events which menaced her.

The hills were closer around them now, not distant as they were in the San Joaquin Valley. Elizabeth could scarcely believe that they were the savage, tawny hills which she had seen when she had driven through the country with her aunt so short a time ago. They were still bold hills but not frighteningly so, touched by the miracle of their jade-green covering, their outlines softened by the falling rain.

Then as they took the road north into the counties of Sonoma and Napa and came into country more akin to the English countryside, she relaxed her hold on the wheel, driving more slowly. Some accord between her and Philippe told her they both were at home here. The valleys were narrow, the road winding. The hills which drew down intimately around them were covered with trees. The street of the town they were passing through was shaded with great branching elms.

"Turn here," directed Philippe. They drove straight toward the hills over a road which had narrowed almost to a lane. It mounted slightly. Up the slope marched the vineyards. The short stocky trunks of the vines stood out in black wetness against the pale green earth. The rain fell in slanting driving gray sheets. The sky was gray. Long gray veils of moss hung from the oaks.

"Now turn to the right. There it is. That's the house where Marie and I used to come for the summers." Philippe was leaning forward peering into the rain. "The children loved it. . . . Marie died here. . . . It was after Lon went away. . . . Diener and his wife were here then. . . . They're here now. They'll look after us."

He went on talking, telling bits of Rambeau history—a different story from the one Martha had told about the Rambeaus. Not proud things. Homely beginnings.

Diener and Gerta came out as Elizabeth brought the car to a stop on the graveled space before the door. The parlor into which they were ushered was warm, and from the kitchen came the rich and mingled odors of spices and garlic.

"How is the land?" asked old Philippe as Diener helped him off with his great-coat.

"Goot. The rain she fall quiet and easy. And you, Meester Rambeau, you return quick."

The door opened and Andrew Fairon came in fresh from his work in the winery. "I meant to be out to meet you, but you made better time than I expected you would in this rain. I was trying some experiments in the laboratory. I'll tell you about them later, Grandfather. I hope I've fixed things the way you wanted them here at the house. Elizabeth, your room is next to Grandfather's." He gave her a shy smile.

How nice he is, thought Elizabeth, watching him move about helping Diener with the luggage, pulling up chairs for them by the fire. When she was seated he insisted on taking off her galoshes. *He has a real air of proprietorship about the place and it's very becoming to him. I suppose he is the head of the household up here when Grandfather isn't here.*

Andrew was full of delight over their coming. This living by himself was the most difficult thing he had ever had to do. The long evenings with only the Dieners in the house had often disturbed him. Never had he come so close to himself before.

Always before when he had thought of himself, it had been with the attributes of all the family. He was not just Andrew Fairon, but his grandfather, his mother, his sisters. Even his Aunt Martha, whom he didn't like, contributed something to his own personality. He had never until now felt separate from them. After these weeks alone he was eager to get quickly into communication with his grandfather and Elizabeth.

Elizabeth fell asleep that night to the fall of the rain on the roof over her head. She was at peace. Sitting that evening with her grandfather and Andrew, who made her their special care, she had been able at last to put John out of her mind.

Late the next afternoon the clouds rolled back with the suddenness of an April day in England, and California's winter spring spread its beauty before them. Under the gray green of eucalyptus and the dark green of live oak lay the light green fields shining in the sun.

"I want you to come out with me, Elizabeth. I've something to show you," said her grandfather, getting up from his chair.

Elizabeth stepped out on the little porch, not too certain she had wanted it to clear. It took away that protected feeling she had had ever since she arrived. Just then Diener came around the corner of the house leading a jet black horse. "Oh, how beautiful!" she exclaimed.

"Try him," said her grandfather. "I want to see if he suits you." Elizabeth looked at him questioningly.

"Yes, he's for you, if you like him."

"Oh, Philippe!" cried Elizabeth, throwing her arms around his neck.

"Tut, tut," said the old man. "You're mussing my hair." But he liked it and the name! Twice today she had used it.

Elizabeth came back from her ride, and tapped on the window with her crop so Philippe would come out. Then she saw he was talking to someone. It was Henri! This was just too much!

As she rode around to the dismounting block he stepped out on the porch. "Hello," he said. "Aunt Martha thought you ought to have help driving back tomorrow."

"But we are not going back for a couple of weeks," Elizabeth answered.

"Oh," he said looking a little crestfallen. "In such a case, I can't wait for you." So Henri found it too quiet here, Elizabeth thought scornfully.

XVII

Francis knew his father-in-law was unhappy over the raisin contract and that he was going to his northern home because it offered him a kind of retreat. It hurt him that Philippe should need retreat from his home.

Too, he had hated to have Philippe and Elizabeth go because of what his home would be like without them. Philippe was the master of the house and he held it to a certain calm and even happiness. Since Elizabeth's coming that tempo had been greatly accelerated. She had seemed to Francis like a rush of wings through the house.

Even Martha of late had been more satisfied. Martha had always wanted children. He watched the expression on her face when she waited on Elizabeth—and wait on her she had, as on all of them. She would rise to shut a door behind the girl, bring her a hot drink when she came in from riding if the day were cold, a cool one if hot, she would walk by her chair and smooth her hair if it were the least rumpled, all with an absorption that seemed in some mysterious way to knit together the elements in her which warred so continuously on one another. To have Elizabeth taken away from her just now seemed a catastrophe. He had seen the look of loss and frustration come over Martha's face as Philippe's car had driven away. If only they hadn't gone away today of all days! He would have liked to be certain of peace between himself and Martha just now.

All night the coming meeting with Charlotte Rambeau had troubled him. Why had Charlotte, after all these years, asked to see him? Not since her marriage to André had they met. Immediately after their wedding André and Charlotte had gone abroad, staying there until Monica, their first child, was several years old. On their return to California André had taken charge of the northern winery. Not until after Charlotte's sickness had they come back to the San Joaquin Valley.

He wanted to remember her as Charlotte Marti. When he met her he had been fumbling about in a world gone meaningless under Martha's fierce penetration of his life. Too late he had found out what love could be, known the uninvading tenderness of Charlotte's love.

In the years since, he had disciplined himself to Martha's possession of him. Only by letting his emotions atrophy had he carried on. With the crippling of Charlotte's body had come to him a kind of crippling of his spirit which he welcomed. Now to come alive again was pain. He feared, too, Martha's watchful eyes which would be centered wholly upon him this evening. And her probing intelligence.

The front of André Rambeau's house had been made into one large room for his wife's use, thus giving it three sunny exposures. The north was shut away from her by the walls of the other rooms. Charlotte Rambeau, until her sickness, had lived continually in the sun, following it in the rainy months out onto the desert. Now her bed, which moved easily on ball-bearing castors, was rolled from window to window, as each day she followed the sun over the limited space of her room.

From long habit Monica, as she entered, looked toward the great window that filled the east hall. There her mother's bed stood in the morning. In the afternoon and evening, she instinctively looked toward the west.

Never yet when she had come into her mother's presence had she been given the opportunity to ask her how she was. Never yet had her mother acknowledged by any spoken word that she was an invalid. Only by her twisted hands and her knees always raised under the bedclothes was it evident.

She had been an unusually beautiful girl and was still a very handsome woman. The bone structure of her aristocratic Spanish face was so perfect that sickness could not mar her beauty materially. Her eyes were large and black with a curious reddish tinge in the sun. She wore her abundant hair, white now with the whiteness that only black hair attains, brushed high in a cluster of curls. The upward swerve of her hair accentuated the long, lovely curve from ear to chin. Her well-modeled ears always had earrings in their delicate lobes. Her lips were always touched with red. Only the nurse who made her ready for the night knew how white they could be. Even then they were beautiful—full, long and well curved. This morning she had on a negligee of deep rose silk, set off by a ruff of fine lace.

She looks more tired than usual, Monica was thinking, sitting down by the bed. *I suppose I shouldn't talk to her about Nate.*

Only Monny of Charlotte's children knew how small was the margin of her strength. Only her husband André of all her family knew the bleak, long hours of suffering. It was André who saw her through. Charlotte studied her daughter, who was making little movements with the toe of her shoe, tracing out the pattern in the rug. "Monny dear," she said at last, "you musn't think you never can marry Nate because your father has not yet given his consent. Nothing is ever final."

Monica started. "I thought you were asleep, Mother."

Charlotte gazed steadily at her daughter as if weighing some intention she had in her mind. But all she said was, "I've asked your Uncle Francis to come and see me this morning. I have some business I want to talk over with him. He'll be here very soon now. Will you see, my dear, that we are not disturbed?"

"Why, yes, Mother." Monica spoke with no little surprise. Never in all the years her mother had lain here had Francis Fairon come to see her. The other members of the family,

yes, but not Uncle Fran. She had understood the two had
had some quarrel years ago.

"There's the bell now," said Charlotte, turning her eyes
away.

After Monica had left him, Francis stood outside Charlotte's door for a moment, steadying himself for the meeting. Then resolutely he turned the knob and stepped within.
His eyes wandered for a moment over the great room, as
bare and fresh as a California hillside. There was no mark
of the invalid about it except the white hospital bed moved
close up against an open window. A pale rift of sunlight,
come between showers, fell across the counterpane.

"I'm over here." Her low-pitched vibrant voice, tender
and careless all in the same breath, steadied him as it always
had. He walked across the room, bent and kissed her forehead.

"Sit here beside me on the bed."

He could feel the thin line of her body beneath the covers.
"You're very beautiful, my darling."

"So are you," she whispered. "We'll always be so to each
other." Then in her natural voice she added, "You may have
wondered why I've broken our long silence. It's because I've
a present for you, Francis dear."

"Yes?" It was all he could manage to say.

"Something that belongs to you and that I have kept to
myself too long. Something very nice. Guess, Francis." She
smiled—the smile he remembered.

"I can't. I can only look at you."

"Monica, Francis."

"You mean . . . ?"

"Yes. She's your daughter."

"You are sure?"

"Yes, darling." Her eyes were dancing now with amusement, the reddish spots in the iris making pin points of warm
light. Then into her face came the look of tenderness he had

once known so well. It overpowered him for the moment—
that and the knowledge that Monny was his daughter.

"Why do you tell me now?" he asked at last. "I can have
no part in her life."

"That is the reason I have told you. She is in love, Francis,
and she's going to need your help."

"Who?" was all Francis could say.

"Nate Frostner."

"I don't know him."

"They are a new family come to the Valley. They are poor
as we think of money, and they are Jews, although Nate has
agreed that the children be raised in their mother's faith. Our
family is bound to fight it. I've not been able to win André's
consent, and Martha will hate the very idea. You know that,
Francis."

"I don't think I like the idea myself," said Francis, feeling
a sudden surge of jealous pride in Monica. His daughter
ought to marry well.

"If she doesn't marry Nate she will never marry, I'm
afraid, Francis. She loves him as a woman like Monica only
loves once."

A half-conscious resentment rose in him that a daughter
he could not claim should fill the foreground of this precious
hour. "I really am opposed to it," he reiterated.

"Monica is simple, he's simple. They fit, Francis, and when
that happens the heavens open." Charlotte ended with a little
choking laugh.

"How can I help?" he asked, giving way to her pleading.
"I can't assert myself as her father."

"What you can do," she rushed on before he could say
more, "is to get your father to give Nate a place in the office.
I believe Philippe Rambeau will like the boy. If he does,
I think I can win André over."

Francis felt a slight trembling of Charlotte's thin body,
and her cheeks had gone pale beneath the rouge. He must
not stay to see her conquered by pain—for her sake and his

own. "I'll attend to it. I'll find a way." He started to rise. "Wait a moment, dear. I've something else to say. There's one other way you could help us all."

For a little time neither spoke but their eyes kept communication between them. "You and I have done Martha a great harm," Charlotte said at last. "There is one thing we can do to repair it. I am André's wife and I love him. For years he has shared my sickness. Something very real has grown up between us." Her voice dropped almost to a whisper. "Isn't there some ground on which you and Martha can meet?"

"How do you know we haven't such a ground?" he asked abruptly. The tenderness in her voice made him ashamed that he spoke so, but he winced even under her tender probing.

"No woman who is loved is . . . is like Martha, Francis."

Francis Fairon buried his head in his hands. "You don't understand. It's as if she wanted to take my heart right out with her hands, handle it, feel its flesh and blood. I can't. Don't make me."

"My dear."

He could not bear to look at her. There might be pity in her eyes, pity instead of love.

"Thank you for telling me about Monica," he said, rising. "I'll . . . I'll do all I can. . . ."

Francis telephoned Martha that he would not be home for dinner, that business would keep him in Fresno. Late in the evening as he came from the garage, entering the house from the door that gave on the court, he had to pass the dining-room windows. Just as he reached them, Chu switched on the light and he saw that the curtains had been taken down. The chairs and table had been pushed to one side and spread with sheets. Two stepladders connected by a long board stood in the middle of the bare floor. The paper had been scraped from the walls. It was as he had feared. The going of Elizabeth and Philippe had brought on one of Martha's terrible fits of energy.

He found her sitting in her accustomed place in the living room. He kissed her, then went over to the fireplace, standing with his back to the unlighted logs. The day-long rain had chilled him. He was tired. He had been working all afternoon to fend off an investigation of the night riders' attack on the Armenians and Russians. The evidence was that it had not stopped with the one night's work. There were ugly tales of men dragged through the irrigation ditches and even of whippings. He shivered a little, stood rubbing his hands together to get them warm.

"It seems cold here. Is the heat on?" he asked.

"Oh, I think so. It's only that you've just come in."

Martha had no solicitous concern for him this evening. He never knew whether he was happier with it or without it. When he had it he felt in prison; when he lacked it he felt himself in hell. There was every indication he would be there tonight.

Presently, with an angry snap-to of her book, Martha said, "I suppose there is no use asking you where you've been."

"I've been trying to straighten out that mess John got us into. I don't want our names to appear."

Ordinarily Martha would have bombarded him with questions. To tell her of what went on in the business usually made peace between them. Tonight she brushed his words aside with an impatient movement of her hands.

"Am I forever to be put off with matters of business? How do I know you've been in Fresno?"

"Because I said I was."

"I couldn't believe you once, why should I now?"

Francis was startled. He had not thought that ever again the old trouble would come up between them. They had lived now for many years without mention of it. Had she found out about his visit to Charlotte this morning, or was it a coincidence that she should have chosen this evening to bring up the past?

"I've got to know." Martha's face was grim, her figure

taut. "I can't wait any longer for you to speak. What do you think I'm made of, anyway?"

"You know that was finished years ago."

"That's the way you've always been about it, never telling me really. It must be cleared up between us once and for all."

"My dear," said Francis quietly, "I give you my word that there is nothing between Charlotte and me to make you unhappy. How could there be? Think, Martha."

"I am your wife." A spasm of pain passed over her face.

Francis gathered his forces for one final effort. "My dear, don't let's quarrel." He went over to the couch, sat down beside her, and pulled her head down to his shoulder.

She gave a sigh, almost a gulp, as if swallowing a final violent retort, then settled against him, letting her head slip down until it rested on his breast. He stroked her hair. He should take her in his arms, explain, assure her of his love. If he could, as Charlotte said, he might take her out of this torment. He might keep her from interfering with Monica's life and Elizabeth's, keep her from so many things that harmed herself and others. But he could not and she was too acute not to sense the reservations.

With a sudden irritated movement, she threw off his arm, and rose, saying, "Well, that's that," and left him.

The whole bitter day had piled up on her to this futile ending. She had stood in the rain watching Philippe and Elizabeth drive away. Why hadn't her father asked her to go with him instead of Elizabeth? *I'd have gone, even if it isn't any place to be in winter,* she told herself, but her mind kept going back to the day he had spoken so harshly to her about Elizabeth. Martha could not bear to be spoken to like that, and the troubling thoughts of that day rose up again to haunt her. Did her father then not see her as the head of his family after he died? Did he not trust her?

She had comforted herself with the thought of the things she could do during his absence. Immediately she had entered the house she had sent for Chu. "There are a great many things we must do while Mr. Rambeau is away," she told him. Chu knew these fits of energy which at times attacked her. They were a fearful manifestation of her power. At each such manifestation he told himself, "This time I go." *But who would care for old Meester Rambeau?* Tied then he was to Martha's relentless driving force.

Late in the afternoon with the rain falling, her doubts closed in on her. Her father had wanted to hurt her. Tears, which she had not shed on that other day when he had first spoken harshly to her, pressed hard against her eyeballs. It would be terrible to cry. Coming so near to it now brought back the time years ago when she had found out about Francis and Charlotte and had cried. And then had come the call from Francis saying he would be late. As often before it roused her suspicions. She had immediately made her own interpretation. *I've nobody really I can call my own*, she had thought. *I don't really possess any of them.*

When Martha had gone, Francis put a match to the carefully laid fire, pulled his chair close up before it. His hands were cold. He was cold all over. He hated himself because he made Martha suffer. But what could he do? Maybe another time he could do better but not tonight, with the memory of Charlotte so clear in his mind. That anyone so proud, so beautiful, should be so stricken. . . .

He tried to sort out the emotions of the day. Why had she really sent for him? Was she trying to break any bond that existed between them? It gave him a feeling of being utterly lost. Why did she tell him about Monica? There was little or nothing he could do to help her. He felt no reality in the new relationship to Monny; no reality in any of his relationships. Wearily he got up, walking the length of the great house to his room.

He woke in the night with one clear impression. The Charlotte he had seen yesterday was a woman infinitely fined down by suffering and the struggle to win over it, a mature woman. And Monny was his child.

XVIII

THE evening of Philippe's and Elizabeth's return, the rain was still falling in an unrelenting downpour. Even before the car had reached the house, Elizabeth saw Martha, a black raincoat over her head, hurrying along the drive toward them. She was clasping the coat tightly just below her chin. Her brilliant, black eyes peered out at them.

"Well, you're back, aren't you?" she called out before she reached the car. "And now I'm going to keep you here. You just can't go off like this again. You shouldn't be out in all this rain, Father," she said, taking his arm and steering him toward the door. "Elizabeth, run into the house as quickly as you can," she called back.

She must have been watching for us, thought Elizabeth, following behind the hooded black figure of her aunt and the small, stooped figure of her grandfather.

She remembered now how the door had flown open the moment Francis Fairon had tapped the horn the day of her arrival and how the morning after the big family party, the moment she entered the long hall, Martha had appeared at the opposite end. A hundred other incidents occurred to her mind, making her certain that all the members of the family received a like vigilant care. For care it had become recently, even toward Elizabeth herself. Elizabeth was not just sure when it had begun. Somewhere around the day when she had first driven the car, she thought. What she had done to make her aunt like her she couldn't guess.

She gave a little sigh of delight when she entered her room. It had been redecorated, in her absence, in blue, her favorite color. So Aunt Martha had noticed. A chair was drawn up to the open fire. Dressing gown and slippers had been laid out. Almost at once she heard her aunt's brisk knock.

"I've come to see if you are taking proper care of yourself. It's as I thought," she added almost before she was within the room. "You're no better than Father about looking after your health. Here, put this warm robe on while I get a bath ready for you."

It was nice to be so cared for. Not since she had been a little girl had anyone looked after her like this, Elizabeth was thinking drowsily, as she curled herself up in the big chair. Like all the rest of the family she was beginning to depend upon Aunt Martha.

The long living room looked like real shelter as Elizabeth came into it. Eucalyptus logs crackled in the fireplace. The medicinal scent of the burning wood made the room seem especially fresh and clean. Low lights were on here and there near comfortable chairs. Tea was spread on a table by the fire. *It is a beautiful room. Aunt Martha has a gift for arrangement*, Elizabeth reflected, *something Lon has, too.* Their rooms were always orderly, but never stiff. Color, too, they understood. Elizabeth's observing mind noted that new and gorgeously colored curtains had been added. As she had passed the dining room she had seen that it had been re-papered in a fine French wallpaper which Martha had looked at the last time they had been in Los Angeles.

The dark rich oak of the old French peasant table, chairs and dresser, and the matching wood in the paneling of the lower part of the walls, set off to perfection the stylized scenes of the paper, the deep brown of conventionalized trees and castles, the stiff figures. The blue background was picked up in a vase of Mexican glass on the table filled with winter marigolds. The strong rich colors curiously conveyed the personality of the room's owner.

It cost her dough, Elizabeth said to herself. "Dough" was a new word she'd heard young Charles use, and she liked it.

It seemed really to mean money, and money seemed to be synonymous with Rambeau, these days. Everybody in the family was buying something new and expensive. Even she herself had come in for a share, with the lovely black riding horse Grandfather had given her. Yes, it was nice to be here. She almost said *be home.*

"The Dietrick girl's been married," Aunt Martha was saying to old Philippe.

Her remark brought Elizabeth a sharp pang. *So that's how she solved it! But it doesn't let John out,* she thought bitterly.

"She's got herself into difficulty with her family," Martha went on, "by marrying an Italian. Decent enough fellow, I guess. One of the Griffantis. She's had to leave home. They say Nelson Dietrick threatened to kill her."

Not thinking about what Martha was saying, but of what Chu had told him—that there was talk of a grand-jury investigation of the night riders—Philippe answered, "The Griffantis are nice boys." Absent-mindedly he picked up a thin slice of bread and butter and his cup of tea. The light, shining directly on his hand, skeletonized it to bones and blue veins. The flesh seemed transparent.

"There's Fran." Martha changed the subject abruptly.

Something in Martha's tone caught Philippe's attention. Had there again been trouble between them? He turned to greet Francis with a sincerity and warmth that made his son-in-law know the breach was healed between them.

"It's good to have you back, sir," was all Francis could say in reply but he felt steadied by the old man's presence. He smiled down on Elizabeth saying, "We are glad to have you back, too. It's been dull around here without you." If this were Monny sitting here he could call her daughter, he was thinking.

Elizabeth realized there was real tenderness in the smile he gave her. This was home.

XIX

Buz had worked it out according to hard cold facts. She had to marry somebody dark. She had no doubt but the baby would be dark-haired. If she married Luigi . . . Luigi was dark. No one need ever know if she did it soon. She'd gone back to town feeling terrible after she'd talked with the Rambeau girl. *Gee, I had my nerve to talk to anyone like that,* she thought, *let alone a Rambeau. What if she tells? I guess I didn't know what I was doing.*

Buz's roommate was out that Monday night. It was raining and Buz did not like rain. Besides, she'd spoil her good shoes if she went to a movie or anything. She'd called up Luigi and asked him to come over.

They had talked for a little. Then he had wandered restlessly about the room. She had followed him, coaxing him to stay here, not to take her out to a movie as he wanted to.

He had put his arm round her and she had strained toward him, clasped her hands around his neck, drawn his head down, pressing her soft moist lips against his. In the backward swing he gave her body her firm little breasts were pressed against him.

"So," said Luigi, releasing her.

She gave a little laugh and smoothed her hair. She had found her way out.

Before the evening was over, they had arranged it. They would run off at the end of the week and get married. It was Buz who urged secrecy. Buz wasn't running any risk of her father's not letting her marry Luigi.

But she hadn't counted on her father's not liking her any more. She knew he'd be mad, but, shucks, she'd always been

123

able to get around him. This time, though, she hadn't. Nelson Dietrick, realistic and earthy in his conceptions, believed Buz's marriage to an Italian made her into a foreigner.

"We're Americans in this house," he'd told her when she brought Luigi home. "You can just get out of here. You're an Eyetalian now. You better go along over to his people." He had hunched his shoulders the way he did when he was disgusted. "Go on. Get going."

It was hard giving up her home but she would have had to give it up even if she hadn't married Luigi, seeing how things were. She was safe anyway, or so it seemed to her at first, and Dad would get over being mad. Of course he would.

Hadn't he always loved her the best? Hadn't she always made him do what she wanted him to?

But that scene in the kitchen of her father's house with her father so mad, and her mother just sitting still and saying nothing, and the kids throwing mean looks at her and Luigi, did something to Luigi. He acted mad too. "I don't give much for Germans," he had told her father. And he had been different with her afterward, brooding and sullen.

XX

WITH the rain had come that lovely thing called false spring, that sudden green which in November had run over the dry land like jade-green mercury. It had seemed ephemeral, unsubstantial, when they drove to the northern vineyards. It was a close recognizable covering over the earth when they drove back. Then came the juxtaposition of the leafless skeleton orchard trees upon the green—winter superimposed on spring. Before Elizabeth had become accustomed to this unfamiliar beauty, the grapevines, pruned of their trailing canes, startled her into new attentiveness with their two-pronged black strength thrust up out of seas of waving yellow mustard. And the earth that had been so hard and dry in September, replete now with moisture, left the rain to lie in shimmering pools in all the little and big hollows. The clouds, one hour close and gray over the sky, the next would roll back with almost Biblical grandeur. And the birds, in the sunshine after the rain, broke out into rapturous singing. Flocks of them stopped for a day or a week in the Valley on their way north. She would wake in the morning to see dainty yellow-green breasted canaries alight on twigs and flower stalks, or plump gray birds industriously picking at the green lawn. From somewhere far off she would hear the buoyant note of the lark.

This miracle of renewal on the earth brought a healing without her willing it, a healing she felt would come to a sudden stop at the slightest jarring of her carefully built defenses. But there was no such jarring, for Martha had wrapped her about with every conceivable lulling comfort. As winter drew on toward spring Elizabeth found herself settling into happiness, a little uncertain of it at first, a little afraid to trust it;

then as it held, at first for an hour, then a day, she began to believe in it.

There were only the attentions of Henri to trouble her. Yet often he made a day more interesting. It was he who took her to see the desert when it broke into bloom. With a kind of sensuous pleasure he rode his horse through the wide stretches of lupine and poppy, sometimes dashing far ahead of her, sometimes riding by her side. This was a new and more attractive Henri than she had ever known. He had brought a picnic lunch and a bottle of sauterne—"with which to wash it down," he said. His long hands he rested for a moment almost lovingly on the carpet of flowers as he set out their feast. Yes, he could be charming.

Elizabeth was riding with him today along the avenue of palms that led to his house. Henri's eyes had wandered first to his great vineyards, spreading away on each side of the drive, then back to her. A smile of satisfaction played about his lips, softening the cold surface of his eyes as he turned toward her. Had he spoken the words Elizabeth felt she could not have been more certain of his thought.

"*The Rambeau-Fairon men have given me good service. I, son of Don Ramon de Swanaña, possess this land and the Rambeau labor and soon Elizabeth Rambeau.*" So she mocked him in her thoughts. She certainly had held him from any declaration through the winter. To do so had given her the excitement she craved, helping her in her effort to push John out of her thoughts.

It was true that Henri in his pride disdained the comfortable Rambeaus. Let them think him wholly a waster, as the old man thought him. They, who lived wholly in a world of sports, money, clothes, seldom lifted their eyes above the earth they cultivated.

Of his passion for books they knew nothing, never dreamed of the hours he spent poring over the history of his own people, following their proud conquest of the Americas. In his library, carefully locked away, were rare old manuscripts of the priests and warriors, the civilizers of this land of California. What did old Rambeau have to be proud of, compared to that? You'd think he'd made the vineyards of California to hear him talk. In reality, it was the Spanish fathers, a hundred years earlier, who had brought the first vines to this country, that they might have wine for the Holy Sacrament. What of the many acres of Don Ramon de Swanaña's family? Lands of the crown. What did the old peasant, Rambeau, have to set against that?

Silently Henri rode by Elizabeth's side beneath the palms which threw their broad-leaved shadows down on the drive, watching his horse tread daintily upon the hard-surfaced road, a roadway paved deep with the crushed stems of Don Ramon's successive harvests of grapes.

Here Henri had ridden as a boy, on a huge black mare, stolid mother of the nervous lean horse his father rode. When his father first took him to survey his great holdings Henri's legs were so short they scarcely reached over the edge of the mare's sloping back.

Always there were people to serve them and early he had understood that in youth Philippe Rambeau had been in their employ. Yet now, like his father before him, Henri was in love with one of the Rambeau women. At first he had meant only to bother John courting Elizabeth, but now he really wanted her. Except for the ride on the desert, however, he had made no progress in his courtship.

The whitewashed 'dobe walls of the Don's hacienda, as Henri still called his home, rose before them. Climbing red geraniums, their stems old and woody, sprawled over the white surface. As they entered the hall he had a sudden belief that it would further his cause to show Elizabeth his library—the core of the house hidden behind massive locked doors. Enshrined there were his father's and his father's father's treasure.

Henri, sitting before his desk, watched her move about the room. Book after book she took down, handling them as he would have them handled, with mingled respect and affection. For the hour left to them before luncheon, they very nearly understood each other.

The room was lighted only by high windows. The wide stretches of vineyard outside and Henri's acquisitive pride in them seemed to have nothing to do with this quiet, almost austere place. The floor was bare. Two straight chairs and a table which did duty as desk made up the room's furnishings. The walls were completely given over to books. *If Henri created this place he loves books,* was Elizabeth's instant conclusion.

From locked cupboards Henri brought out his most precious manuscripts. She sat down on the floor, letting him pile her lap full. Finally he took from a locked tin box the rarest of all.

"Look, Elizabeth," he said kneeling beside her. "See this beautiful illumination along the edge of the pages. One of the men of my own family did this. . . . See, woven into the intricate design is a chalice. See, on every page. No one would find it if he didn't know it was there. My father gave this to me and showed me the sign." With careful fingers Henri turned the pages, leaning close over her, and for the first time Elizabeth felt no desire to draw away.

"Sign?" she asked.

"Yes. On the flyleaf is written in his own hand a kind of acrostic of four words. Two words are plain. See—you can just make them out—'chalice' and 'woman.' The others are too faint to read. They're supposed to have some symbolic meaning hidden from all except those who can understand, so my father told me."

"Did your father know it, Henri?" Elizabeth fingered the pages of the rare old book.

"I think so. He knew other documents like it, here and there over the world. There's a set of playing cards done before the Christian era. Those are in a museum. Forty in the set and they hold the mysteries."

His eyes were bright with interest and his mouth, as he talked, seemed to have lost its cruel lines. "One my father told me about—a woman changing a cup of water into wine. Wine is the spirit."

The room was very still and Elizabeth did not draw away when Henri laid his hand over hers. Had she, until now, not known the real Henri?

Down in the hall the gong sounded. Maria called up the well of the stairs for them to come to luncheon. Carefully Henri picked up his possessions, stowed them away, locked the cupboards. As Elizabeth handed him the precious manuscript he said, "Any collector would give me a fortune for this."

Greedy Henri, thought Elizabeth. *The lover of possessions—I, along with the books, if he could get me.*

XXI

NEITHER Francis Fairon nor any of the other influential men of the Valley had been able to stop the investigation of the night riders. After many delays the grand jury was called, just when the Valley was filled from rim to rim with the white blossoms of prune and apricot.

The panel, drawn from the list of voters, was the usual conglomerate group. But by the vagaries of chance Dietrick and Philippe Rambeau had been impaneled. André urged that his father ask to be excused because of his age, but Philippe pushed the suggestion aside. "Of course, I'll do my part. I want to see the men who are responsible for this punished," he told his son.

"Better be careful, then, about what you say," Ronald Fairon cautioned him. "You sound prejudiced to me."

Philippe looked at this son-in-law of his who seldom took any part in the family discussions. "Do you think," he asked him, "there is anyone in the Valley who isn't prejudiced one way or the other?"

"I dare say not," Ronald replied, "but I'd say those who do not want the night riders punished are the stronger element."

I've an idea Ronald isn't in sympathy with the violence, thought Philippe. It pleased him.

Although Philippe went early to the courthouse the morning the grand jury began their sittings, most of the panel were already there. Several of them were men he knew, one his near-by neighbor, Hueber. Unanimously they elected Philippe their foreman, and refused the suggestion of Philippe that they ask the district attorney in to interrogate the wit-

130

nesses. There was a strong feeling among them to hold this meeting behind closed doors and do their own questioning.

Philippe looked down the list of men summoned as witnesses. He saw that Petucci and Yakowitz were among them. "Call Petucci," he said to the attendant.

Almost as he entered the room Petucci began pouring out vitriolic remarks. "I am threaten!" he shouted. "I get-a dat Dietrick! He come-a, he talk-a, you no sign, you have trouble."

Philippe tapped for silence. "I want you to answer my questions. Did you see any violence done?"

"They talk-a, you no sign, you have trouble."

Another tap. "Answer my question. Did anyone attack you?"

"What you mean-a . . . da—tack?"

Philippe explained, "Someone hit you. Did anyone hit you?"

Petucci slapped his knee. "I think-a you mean-a da hammer"—he worked his arm up and down as if driving a tack—"you know, pounda-da-pound." This joke on himself turned him easily from anger which was alien to him. "No. No. Nobody hit. I run up the house."

"Then you did not see the men you say threatened you?" asked one of the panel.

"No."

"That is all you have to say?" asked Philippe.

"Yes."

"Then you may go," Philippe told him.

Petucci went out, his cap in his hands, his whole attention centered on how easy it had been to appear in court. He had been preparing for a week for this momentous appearance, practicing before his wife and children what he was going to say. It was only after he was at home again that he realized that he had given no evidence that would help in convicting anyone. "But why did you not tell them," his wife asked him, "the things they did—how they fired at you? You really knew John Rambeau and Dietrick were there." Mrs. Petucci had been fearful her husband would bungle his testimony, and she was bitter against the men of the court that they had not given him more of a chance to tell his story.

Mamoulian was the next witness.

"You say you were bound and dragged?" old Philippe asked.

"Yes, your honor."

"Did you see those who did it?"

"I think I know," Mamoulian nodded his head wisely.

"I did not ask you that," said his interrogator. "I asked if you *saw* any of them."

"They wore masks, your honor, but I heard them talk."

"Do you think you could describe anyone's voice so that we could identify the man?"

"No, your honor." Mamoulian was confused. How could anyone say anything about a voice except that it was loud or soft? You *could* say it belongs to this or that man, but he dared not say, I heard this man or that man speak. In the half-hour in which they had dragged him across his fields, he had become again the cowed peasant, no longer daring to talk.

Philippe leaned forward. "There are a few things that are not clear to me, Mamoulian. If you did not see them and cannot identify their voices how is it that when you came into this room you made the statement you knew who the men were?"

"I tell some by their horses. Some by their cars."

"Can you describe them?" someone asked him.

Mamoulian was gaining confidence now. He knew how to tell what a horse was like. Some were black and some brown, one piebald. Lots of ways to tell a horse. Accurately he described two horses. "One man drove an old truck," he went on.

Dietrick shifted in his chair looking around to see if anyone in the jury would be likely to recognize his broken-down truck. Old Mr. Rambeau would, but he showed no sign. He was making crosses on a paper lying in front of him. Philippe had no thought except for the witness' description of John's bay with the white star on his forehead, white forelock, long arching neck.

So John was one of the night riders. Philippe found it hard to listen to the rest of the testimony. His attention wavered and he was tired. He almost wished he had taken André's advice. Then he would not have known for certain that John was one of the night riders. When Yakowitz was called he left the questioning to the others on the panel.

It was the third day and the last witness had been called. A man named Jim Anderson.

A crazy little figure, he hurried into the room, hurriedly mumbled the words of the oath, "So help me God," hurriedly began his story.

"Simply answer our questions," Philippe told him, looking at the record before him. "I believe you claim you were beaten."

"Yes, your honor."

"Did you know any of them?"

"No, your honor."

"Who would like to question the witness?" Philippe asked wearily, looking around the table.

"How do you know they were not hooligans from out of town?" one of the men asked him.

"They ask me to sign the paper."

"And what did the paper say?"

"I put a cross. I cannot read." It was a humiliation to have to confess he could not read.

"Then you do not know whether it was the raisin contract you signed?" The man pressed his advantage with the confused witness.

"I know because I have to keep the price."

"Answer yes or no."

"No."

Baffled, angered, by these frustrating noes and yesses when

he wanted to talk and tell his story as he had done now for weeks to his neighbors, Anderson suddenly shook his fist in the face of Philippe. "I tell you I am an American!" he shouted. "I have rights! It's up to you to find out who beat me. I got prove!" And before the astonished men, Anderson let down his trousers, leaning over, with his back toward them. "See?" he shouted, his voice coming muffled from somewhere near the floor. Across the man's thin rump lay the marks of a whip, the flesh still scarred and discolored.

Some of the jury leaned forward, some turned away in revulsion. The next instant the court attendant acted to make the man cover himself and led him away.

But as Anderson reached the door, he jerked loose from his captor. "What you going to do about it?" he shouted. Suddenly his mouth gaped open and without any further ado he walked meekly out of the room mumbling to himself.

"What are you trying to say?" asked the court attendant.

"He was there."

"Who was there?"

"The man who beat me."

"That's a bit too thick! I guess I better put you where you won't bother anyone until this business is over."

But Anderson gave no further trouble. All the fight had gone out of him. What good for an old man, a little man, to fight? At night they beat him; in the day they judged him.

When they had sifted the testimony Philippe said, "We have no evidence that would convict anyone."

"I believe," said a young juror sitting next to Philippe, "if we wanted to carry it far enough we could find out from the description of the horses some who were on that raid. I think I know one of the owners right now."

"I don't see that we'd have any proof even then that the owners of the horses were the ones who rode them that evening. Men that would do a thing like that wouldn't stop at borrowing a horse," Judge Hueber argued.

"Our stables are too well looked after to have that happen," said Philippe dully. He was certain John had ridden his own horse and had only scorn for him but he did not want his grandson convicted.

Everybody was a little halfhearted about pressing the case further. After all it was only a skirmish among neighbors. Why bring the Valley into disrepute by trying to get an indictment against anyone? When the vote was taken there was no dissenting vote. The case was dismissed for insufficient evidence.

When he reached home old Philippe let Martha bustle around him. "You shouldn't have done it," she scolded. "Of course it's been too much for you."

"Yes, I guess it has," he acknowledged much to Martha's surprise. He'd let them think it was the long hours which had tired him out. Under that subterfuge he hid his dismay. How had it happened that from his very loins had sprung violence? He had come to this new country to escape men of violence. He'd better take that Frostner boy Francis had been talking about into the office. The time might come when John would have to be dropped from the business.

XXII

JOHN RAMBEAU had returned a few days before the grand jury had convened. Both André and Francis had written advising him to stay away until after the matter was settled and his grandfather had forgotten the affair. But he had ignored their letters. He had a plan for the future handling of Rambeau-Fairon grapes and he was impatient to talk it over with the family. He smiled knowingly when he heard the decision of the court.

"What did men like Petucci expect?" he said to his brother Charles. "They might have saved themselves the trouble of airing their grievances."

"Sure, who cares about a lot of bohunks?" Charles answered. He had caught from John the idea that these men were not important, and wanted to go him one better in belittling them.

Since John's return, Charles was his shadow. He was passing through the uncertainties of fifteen and longed to partake of his older brother's easy assurance. "Look it, John," he said, "that skiing job. I didn't get along so good. I don't know whether I'll take it next year."

"Just go up there and do it, kid, just as you did this year," John told him. "You'd be a fool to give it up. And now let's forget about it." He wanted to get on with his own business. He wanted to sit in on the councils of the Rambeau-Fairon men. "Or," he told Charles, "I'll have no part in the New York business next year. They won't want to lose me."

"Haw, haw—that's a good one," Charles kidded him. "Go and get yourself a white wig and nobody'll know you from Grandpop." Charles was convinced the family fortunes depended on John, but he wasn't going to let John know it if he wouldn't listen about the skiing job. *Gee,* thought Charles, *I need a man to talk to about it.* He began again, "John, about this skiing—"

"Cut it out, kid, you did it, didn't you? Now forget it."

Monica stopped at the open door. She had come upstairs hoping to find John alone—half hoping not to. She wanted to tell him about Nate's being taken on at the office. She wanted John to like Nate though she feared her brother might be as much against him as her father was.

She sat down on the bed beside Charles, rumpling his hair. "Aw quit!" he said, throwing her hand off and tossing his head in an attempt to get a lock out of his eyes—an unsuccessful attempt always, for the lock fell forward again, making a straight oblong shadow on his forehead. *He's just a baby yet,* Monica thought. *But he wants to feel he's as old as John.* Turning to John, she said, "Elizabeth's coming over for luncheon, today."

"Well, you can count me out." John laughed a hard laugh. "Do you think I'm going to hang around for Elizabeth when she didn't hang around for me the few weeks I was gone? I'm no second fiddle."

"Oh, go on. Try being one for awhile. You might like it," Charles broke in.

"It's Aunt Martha's doings, not Elizabeth's," Monica said. "I don't think Elizabeth cares anything for Henri."

"Well, I'm not interested anyway," John replied. "And now you two have got to get out and let me work."

After they had gone he finished a long column of figures, set it off with another. He meant, if possible, to talk to the Rambeau-Fairon men this morning and prove to them that they were going to take a licking on wine grapes shipped east this coming fall, if they didn't do something about it.

If I only had the power to act, he thought, leaning back in his chair, his hands behind his head. *I know the game. I know what we're up against. We ought to keep the total number of*

*available refrigerator cars down. Get some agreement among
the big growers. Grandfather probably wouldn't be willing
to do the finagling that it would take to keep the car allotment
down and the others probably will think it isn't necessary.
They believe that it's Prohibition that's put the price of grapes
up and that no matter how many grapes are shipped as long as
we have Prohibition the market will hold. I'll have to convince them that we might flood the market.*

*I wonder if I could do anything with Henri. His vineyards
if taken out of the pool would cramp the business. If I could
get him to see the necessity for the agreement and then get
him to say he'd withdraw from the firm if they didn't follow
my plan . . .*

The two front legs of John's chair came down to the floor
with a bang. "That's my card," he said out loud. He leaned
over his desk, picked up a paper knife, balancing it on his forefinger. "Yep, I guess that would about fix it. Yep. That's
my card, if I get him to threaten to withdraw his lands from
the firm. He's a lazy devil, but I guess he could make that
effort." John stood up, gathering his papers. "I believe I'll
not talk to anyone until I see Henri. If worse comes to worst,
Henri and I might go into business for ourselves."

He paused a moment by his mother's closed door, then went
on downstairs. He lingered on the porch for a little, looking
across the Valley. It was a good scene he gazed out upon. They
were beginning to cultivate the vineyards. He could hear the
familiar rhythmic clatter of the tractors. *That's where Dad
shows up,* he thought. *He knows soil as Grandfather knows
vines. Always catches it just right. He said yesterday the soil
wsa drying out rapidly.*

As he saddled his horse he kept thinking of Elizabeth. He
really did want to see her. He almost wished he hadn't told
Monny he wouldn't be home for luncheon. Halfway down the
drive he met her, riding the beautiful black thoroughbred he
understood Grandfather had given her.

Elizabeth did not notice John at first. She wasn't paying

attention to anything around her. She was thinking of her father. In a letter from him this morning she had learned that he had married again, a woman with a grown daughter. Elizabeth guessed she was jealous but she wasn't certain. And if so, whether it was of the daughter or the mother.

The old companionship she had had with Lon seemed very precious to her now. She forgot the little soreness she had felt because he had sent her to America, remembered only the days after he had returned from the war and wanted her always with him. How young she had felt herself on her first visit to London, how shy when he had asked her to call him Lon. Then they had shopped for her first grown-up clothes, and she had managed to call him Lon, and he had liked it. And suddenly she was enjoying Lon and he was enjoying her. The years after—her pride and happiness, knowing he needed her.

"Hello."

"Why, hello, John." Involuntarily she reined in her horse. At the sound of her rich, deep-throated voice his pulse beat more quickly than he wished it would.

"I heard you were back." Elizabeth was angry with herself, for as she looked at him she felt excitement and delight.

"You're a little early for lunch, aren't you? How about a canter? I'd like to see what your horse can do."

Elizabeth hesitated. She didn't want to have anything more to do with John, but she couldn't childishly refuse to see him, she told herself. After all, he was one of the family and she'd be meeting him constantly. "Oh, all right," she said.

"There's a bridle path here going down toward Henri's. I was on my way there. Suppose we take it." John turned, leading the way toward a narrow gully that cut through the vineyards.

The April morning was electric, tightening the nerves toward adventure. In the taut days of the long summer, the continuous unclouded sky, the dry air, stretched nerves to an almost unbearable tension. But today was the first of its kind this season and the sensation of life and strength the clear invigorating atmosphere gave them was eagerly grasped at by both Elizabeth and John.

John, pressing the sides of his horse with his knees, put him into a gallop, not stopping him until he reached the sprawled shadow of an old oak a mile away. Elizabeth was close behind him. "I tell you I wouldn't live in New York for a million dollars!" he cried stretching his arms high over his head. "You can *live* out here."

"And you can't anywhere else?" Elizabeth could never seem to resist the desire to tease John. His reaction to comfort was too perfect. "But the day does do something to you," she acknowledged, stretching her own arms up. There was some bond of energy between her and John that made her respond to him in spite of herself.

John looked at her sitting her horse. She was hot-blooded, strong and beautiful. There were deep and violent currents in her that answered such currents in him. Again the thought came to him that he would marry her. He would tell her now.

"Elizabeth, I'm not much of a talker. Let's just put it this way. You got me all wrong the night before I left. We could make something pretty good between us, I've an idea."

Elizabeth's blue eyes kindled. "What kind of a man are you, John?"

"What do you mean?"

"What about Buz?"

"Well, what about her?" Hadn't Elizabeth any sense? What had Buz to do with them?

"Do you think you can go from me to her and get away with it, John?"

"What business is it of yours?" he blazed at her.

"You've made it my business."

"What have you been doing? Spying on me the way Aunt Martha does?" he countered.

Elizabeth trembled with anger. "I don't spy."

"Buz been talking?" John's voice was hard and cold. "I'll do just as I please about Buz and about you, too. Too lily-

white is what you are. You stir a man all up. You're the
kind who do that and then go quietly home. Then you get
mad——"

"Stop it, John Rambeau! You can leave me right now!"
Elizabeth was trembling and her lips had gone white.

"Leave you? Why should I leave you?" John's anger
seemed to mount upon Elizabeth's. "You've got to answer me
first. It's no answer, the things you've been saying." He
leaned forward, taking hold of her horse's bridle, bringing the
animal around where he could look into Elizabeth's blazing
eyes. He liked her like that. She was worth fighting for.
Boldly he confronted her. "You know you care for me. You
wouldn't have been mad about Buz if you didn't."

Anger and fear and the knowledge that he was right roused
Elizabeth past control. She raised her hand and struck out
at him.

John's face went dead-white. He let her bridle go, giving
her horse a vicious cut with his whip. He watched the black
stallion gallop down the path, Elizabeth with difficulty keeping her seat. How he hated her! The blow, which had landed
on his shoulder because he had quickly swung to the side, had
left no impression on his firm, strong flesh, but it seemed to
him the spot was afire. He was angrier than he had ever
been in his life. He wanted to hurt someone; he wanted to
hurt Elizabeth.

In his ride up the avenue of palms that led to the Don's
house he began to see how he could make his anger serve him
and harm Elizabeth. He would let Henri understand that he
would not interfere with his courtship—in fact he'd further
it with Aunt Martha—if Henri would stand by him on the
grape deal. It gave him a cruel pleasure to think he might
make Elizabeth suffer. She would suffer if she had to marry
Henri.

Henri and his mother, Maria, were at breakfast when he
threw his reins over the hitching post at their side door.
Maria never, and Henri seldom, rose before noon. But both

were fond of eating and crowded the three meals of the day into the remaining hours—breakfast at twelve, a combination tea and lunch at four, and dinner in state at nine.

Maria never forgot that she had married nobility, and she shaped her days to fit the now defunct title. That, and her step-son, were her two passions. Within the walls of the rococo house which Don Ramon de Swanaña had built, years before his marriage to her, she lived in elegance and seclusion. Only in seclusion could she keep that illusion of her titled superiority, for Maria was the weakest of all Philippe's children, both physically and mentally. When she came into contact with the family, with almost pitiful haste her mind slipped back into childhood grooves of humility.

Only once in her family's midst had she been exalted. That was at the time of her engagement and marriage. Nobody had thought much about Maria's future. Everybody had taken it for granted that she would not marry. Then one day she had announced that she was engaged to Don Ramon. He had met her one day at a garden party. He was a very old man and her gentle timid ways fitted his aging desires. He fell deeply in love with her and remained so to his death.

She was sitting, this morning, at the head of the table in a tea gown of exquisite workmanship. The ecru lace and two tones of green would have enhanced the beauty of a younger woman. They enhanced the homeliness and age of Maria's small fat face, enhanced its gentleness, too.

The table was loaded with covered dishes of heavy silver. The butler, moving obsequiously about, was continually putting small spoonfuls of food on Maria's plate. One of Maria's illusions was that she ate lightly, for she fastidiously insisted that she be given the smallest possible helpings. How often those helpings were served she never counted.

Henri sat opposite her, sipping a glass of orange juice. As John entered he thought how dissipated Henri looked this morning. He despised him for it. Physical perfection was a passion with John.

"How nice, John, to see you! If I'd only known you were coming we'd have had a real luncheon for you." Maria rose, fluttering around John, too eager to serve him.

"I came over to see Henri on a little matter of business," John said, taking a seat at her right, helping himself generously to scrambled eggs and several slices of bacon. "I'll have coffee, not tea, Aunt Maria," he added, pushing away the tea which she was urging upon him.

Henri went on sipping his orange juice, saying nothing. He had no desire to see John. He knew his ways too well. He imagined his cousin had come to tell him to lay off Elizabeth. John had always had what he wanted, but he needn't think just because he had taken Elizabeth around before he went away that he had any claim on her now.

"How about it, Henri?" asked John, as they rose from the table. "Do you feel up to talking a little business?"

"Of course. If you've anything important to talk about." Henri led the way into the office, a room giving little evidence of being used.

What went on behind the closed door Maria, waiting for them to join her, could only surmise. When at last the door opened, Henri was smiling and so was John. The two in that interim seemed to have become friends, a thing she had for years anxiously desired.

After leaving Henri, John went on to the winery to talk his plan over with his father. André made no comment until his son had finished. Then he began questioning him closely.

"I can see," he said finally, "that it would be to our advantage if we could limit the number of cars, but I don't see that we have much chance of doing it."

"We could if we could get the big growers to join us and if we could contract for the cars ahead."

"How would we know that the railroads wouldn't turn loose other cars when the time came? There will be a lot of pressure brought to bear on them, especially if the smaller growers should get together."

"Couldn't we make it worth the railroads' while not to?"

André swung his swivel chair around and looked out the window. That companionship they had had in the fall had been good. He felt a special need today to draw close to this son. If he could go in with John on this scheme—but he could not.

"Let's suppose," he said, "we could influence the railroads to that extent. It would be a pretty ruthless plan and I don't think we could get your grandfather to consent to it even if the rest of the firm would. You say Henri would be for it, but how about Francis and Ronald Fairon? They're not likely to approve of it. But even suppose they did, we'd have to work it on the side as we did the raisin deal—and I doubt if your grandfather would be as blind as he was to that. The investigations didn't come to anything but I think the testimony convinced your grandfather that it had been a pretty violent business."

Suddenly André swirled his chair around to face his son. "Just what part did you have in it, John?"

Taken by surprise, for a moment John had no answer. Then he had himself in hand. "Isn't it a little late to ask that question, Father? Wouldn't it have been more to the point when we were talking it over here in this office before the raid?"

"Yes, I suppose it would, but I didn't think you'd go so far."

John was silent. It was evident he did not mean to talk. André did not know what to think of his son. Undoubtedly he had a shrewd, keen mind for business but was it one that could be trusted? Furthermore, what chance would John have if his grandfather turned against him? He did not like the old man's sudden putting of Nate Frostner into the office. Never before had there been anyone there except the family. He knew Francis had suggested it, but nevertheless he did not believe the old man would have done it if he had not distrusted John.

"John," he said at last, "for several reasons I think your

plan isn't a wise one—certainly not just now. Your grandfather is upset over a number of things, and we would only
further upset him by introducing a scheme of this kind."

So that was that, thought John. The only thing there
seemed left for him to do was to go straight to his grandfather. After all Grandfather was nobody's fool. *If I appeal
to the side of him that likes to make money I may win him
over. Wonder how long he'll stay north this time.* The day
after the trial he had left for his northern winery, taking nobody with him except David to drive.

That evening André sat for a long time in his library before going up to his wife. It was a habit of years to wait here
until the nurse had left. He would drink his port, look at his
paper, hunt out what he would read to Charlotte later on.

Tonight his port stood untasted by his side, his paper un-
read. He wanted to straighten out some things in his mind.
He had no longer any objection to the marriage of Monny to
Nate. But it was going to be a hard thing to tell Charlotte of
his changed attitude.

The great passion of his life was for his wife. He had loved
her since he was a small boy. He had courted her for years
and got nowhere until after that brief period when she and
Francis had been such close friends. Quietly observant, he
had not been fooled by her sudden turning to him. On what
terms he was marrying her he knew, for she had told him.
After the briefest of engagements they had been married.

Quite by accident he had been in the vineyard near the
house that morning when Francis had come to see Charlotte.
Immediately afterward Francis had become interested in
Nate's career. André understood then that in his stubborn
opposition to Nate because of his race he had failed Charlotte.
She had turned to Francis for help.

However much or little she had loved him when she married
him, he knew beyond any doubt that he had grown to be
essential to her, not entirely because she was ill and he was

able to help her through the worst times, but because in those many battles they had fought out together for her acceptance of pain and the prisonlike existence she led, they had seemed literally to become one. She could no more live without him than he could live without her.

He rose now and went upstairs to tell her he was giving his consent to the marriage.

XXIII

Buz and Luigi were going over to his mother's tonight. He had the car ready. He called, "You coming, Buz?"

"Soon's I get my cigarettes."

"Aw, Buz. Ma don't like 'em."

She turned, coaxing him with her smile please not to mind. How explain to him that need to assert herself when she went with him to his mother's house, the compelling urgency to strike out against the sucking tide of family?

All the conventional patterns of her upbringing were disarranged. The new pattern into which she had to fit herself held no security. The ways of Luigi's people were not the ways she was used to.

A small silence destined to be a big one possessed them as they got into the car. Then it was broken by Luigi. "You look awful cute, Buz, with that thing around your head," he said, forgetting that she had not complied with his wishes.

"You like?" It pleased her that she woke in Luigi special attention. Buz, touched to life by that brief interlude with John, refused to surrender herself to Luigi's domestic moods, so different from his moods when he courted her. She wanted him always as he was now, looking as if he couldn't keep his eyes off her. She began singing.

If she was happy Buz always sang in the car, curling herself up on the seat, singing in a cracked voice that wasn't music at all. It always amused Luigi who, like many Italians, had music in every pulsing fiber of his being, putting him as now in high good humor. Tonight quite suddenly she dropped off to sleep, her song half finished, her head resting against the car door. The little light left in the sky before the dark settled

147

down fell softly upon Buz's face. She reminded him of the women of his own people, with the kerchief tied under her chin. He laid his hand in her lap. It gave promise of being a broad lap, the kind he was accustomed to. When the baby came she would be more contented.

He turned the car into the road that led through his mother's orchards. The branches of the olive trees touched its top. "Better wake up, Buz." He pressed his hand against her thigh. Her eyes opened with the suddenness with which they had shut.

"Umm," murmured Buz, stretching herself. "I don't feel so good, Luigi. Let's go back."

"We won't stay long."

Buz did not answer, grown suddenly uncommunicative.

Luigi guided his car around the corner of the house to the Old-World outdoor living room at the back. Compact umbrella trees enclosed a space large enough for table and chairs—a densely shaded place by day, a sheltered one at night. An electric bulb hanging from a branch of a near-by pepper tree threw light down upon his family. "There they are." There was a note of pleasure in Luigi's voice.

His older brother, Antone, sat at one end of the table. He wore no shirt, and his sweat-moistened skin shone in the light. His hair was jet black and curly. On a bench facing him was the stout, strong bulk of Luigi's mother. At her side his younger brother. His pillarlike body, his large head, his aimlessly moving fingers, told their own tale. "Simp," the family called him in kindly humor. To the right of Antone were his wife and children, and to his left Luigi's two sisters. Their hair lay in heavy blackness over their thin angular shoulders, emphasizing their adolescence. Wine and bread stood in the center of the table. No one looked up until Luigi and Buz moved out of the darkness into the lighted space. Then Antone said, "Ma, it's Luigi."

The woman's handsome features, grown flabby with age and rich food, lost for an instant their heaviness, redefined by

the deep emotion of her love for Luigi. Then, as her eyes
rested on Buz, her face settled again into heaviness. She
motioned them to seats beside the two girls. "Antone, give
the wine," she commanded, turning to her eldest son.

Antone did as she bade him.

This obedience of the Griffanti boys never failed to rouse
Buz. Antone probably owned everything on the ranch. Why
did he have to obey his mother all the time? It was Luigi's
meekness that had made it necessary for them to come over
this evening. Luigi, though he no longer brought his pay
check to his mother, never failed to visit her on payday. He
would not give up the custom of making a report to her, saying without speaking, "I've done my work as you expected
me to do."

Buz, feeling the strong undertow of that wordless docility
in Luigi, hastened to resist it. "Got a match, Luigi?" she
asked, starting to take out a cigarette.

Luigi's face darkened; he shook his head.

With a little laugh, Buz shut her bag. "Oh, all right." She
felt safer now she had expressed, even so little, her indifference to the wishes of Luigi's mother.

Luigi was glad that his mother had turned to help the boy
at her side drink the wine, holding the glass for him. It took
her attention from Buz. Simp had been silent until now, but
at last it had penetrated his consciousness that someone he
knew had come and he tried to speak to Luigi.

"All right, Simp," his mother assured him.

When Mrs. Griffanti turned Buz was sitting demurely sipping her wine. The old woman's keen eyes searched the girl's
face, for she had heard what Buz said. Her lips tightened.
The girl who had married Luigi did things a married woman
shouldn't, and Mary and Theresa were beginning to want to do
them, too. But with the handkerchief tied under her chin,
she looked more like them tonight. Maybe Luigi was beginning to control her. Maybe when the baby came she'd settle
down to what a woman should be.

"I get something." Mrs. Griffanti rose, walked heavily toward the house and, returned with a bowl of spaghetti and a platter of meat spiced with garlic. The love of rich, highly-spiced food Buz held in common with her husband's people. Still a greedy child, she helped herself plentifully. It pleased Mrs. Griffanti that this daughter-in-law, so alien to her, so un-understandable in her bright aggressiveness, should share her own gusto for food.

With temporary good will established between them they munched the bread and meat, drank the sour homemade wine. Mrs. Griffanti tended the boy at her side, guiding his great peasant hands that wandered aimlessly above the food. When the family had finished eating, Luigi went over and sat down by the warm moist body of his mother. She quieted a queer new uncertainty which had been growing in him since his marriage. Food, rest, safety, all were associated with her hard-working presence.

The distinction of his nationality had never bothered him until he met Buz. From his own olive-skinned passionate people he had drawn his friends and his associates. The white ash soil on his mother's ranch, interlaced, for eight sunny months each year, with shadows cast by the serrated leaves of the vines, was the soil out of which his own roots grew. His identification with his mother's adopted country was as unconscious as his identification with his family. He had been born to both.

Such had been his happy acceptance of his family's adopted country until the night he had returned from his wedding journey expecting to be welcomed by Buz's family. He would never forget Dietrick's insulting words, which had driven deep into his consciousness. He was now acutely aware that Buz was an American in a way that he was not. It wasn't only that she had soft brown hair which grew down in a peak on her white forehead, that her hand when it lay in his accentuated her whiteness, his darkness. Differences which struck deeper he had come to know in the months since their marriage. Her folkways were different from his folkways.

A hundred things that seemed either important or unimportant to Buz were the other way around with him. The way she felt about "Simp." The Griffantis loved and petted this simple one sent them by God. Buz, efficient and practical, saw Simp for what he was, a drag on the family—someone who should be put away. Idle to explain to her that Simp would miss them and they would miss Simp, miss his secret chuckling laugh, his undisturbed happiness.

Luigi went with Buz's crowd now. But there were distinctions there, too. Luigi found a bitterness rising in him to meet Antone's bitterness, a new bitterness come to Antone, too.

"I dunno," Antone was saying, "what we're coming to. This ain't no free country. I got-a do what they tell me. Who'd dare to go against them next year?"

"What do you mean?" Luigi asked.

"I'm talking about the raisin contracts and the investigation. They say they wouldn't listen to the witnesses. Didn't pay any attention to their evidence. We haven't a show. Old Mr. Rambeau could have found out who kicked Mamoulian if he'd wanted to. Petucci could-a told 'em. Right now I know."

"Na, na," commanded Mrs. Griffanti. "You keep-a da mouth shut, Antone."

Antone's anger, as quick to flame as Luigi's, was alight now. He was looking straight at Buz.

"What you looking at me for?" she asked.

"Well, I ain't naming them all but I know John Rambeau was one of 'em."

Buz, thinking he was going to name her father, was taken back when he named John. "Suppose he was," she demanded. "You got a good price for your raisins, didn't you? John Rambeau's got sense enough to know you gotta fight for what you want."

Luigi's bitterness had a concrete object now on which he could center. Buz thought too much of John Rambeau. He remembered how Buz had treated him when Rambeau was about. Now Rambeau had made Antone unhappy. Who did Rambeau think he was, anyway, going round hurting other people?

"Stop-a da talk," commanded Mrs. Griffanti. "Buz, she gotta take-a da care of herself. Leetle baby no like-a da angry talk."

Buz flushed. Any reference to the coming baby in a mixed group seemed indecent to her, who had been brought up to think of all things connected with birth indecent. But she knew now what the pains coming more and more often the last hour meant.

"Luigi, we got to go home." She turned to him, suddenly frightened and helpless.

"I take-a da care," coaxed Mrs. Griffanti. "Luigi he call-a da doctor."

Buz was crying now. She was afraid to go and she was afraid to stay. She wanted her mother. With mixed feelings of distrust and confidence she let Luigi's mother help her into the house.

In the very early morning in Mrs. Griffanti's bedroom just off the kitchen Buz's baby was born. Buz during these hours came to know her mother-in-law in a new way. A comfortable peasant woman, familiar with the process of birth, she taught Buz how to help herself. Buz, holding on to her hand for support, felt something of the comfort Luigi felt when he sat close to his mother.

"You're awful good to me," she managed to say in a moment of interrupted labor. And when at last the baby was lying in her arms the two women smiled at each other.

Luigi tiptoed in and kissed her. Buz was content. *Things are all right,* she thought, drowsily hearing Luigi exclaiming over his baby.

"Ain't he cute, Ma? He ain't a bit like you, Buz. He's like me."

And Mrs. Griffanti, wiping the perspiration from her forehead, talked in her excitement in her native tongue. "Black hair, big black eye. A beautiful bambino. Call him Manuel," she begged of Buz. "My old man he named Manuel."

"He's got to be named after my father. John's his name. Please, Luigi." Then Buz was asleep.

John, thought Luigi. *Why does she want to name him John? That isn't her father's name. She's lying.* Suspicion awoke in his mind.

XXIV

ELIZABETH was using the turmoil stirred up over Monica's engagement to escape from Henri. For the time being Aunt Martha had little thought for anything else but her indignation over Monica.

"I'll fight it if it's the last thing I do," she told Francis. "And I suppose I'll have to, as I see you're not going to make any effort."

"On the contrary," Francis answered. "I'm all for Nate Frostner as an addition to the family. I'd like to see him taken into the firm. He's a good chemist and we could use him."

"And you don't care that your niece marries a foreigner?"

"Nate's no foreigner. He's lived in America as long as we have."

"But we are French."

"And he is . . . ?"

"Well, what is he? Just nothing. I'd call him a mongrel if we were discussing dogs," was Martha's caustic rejoinder. "A mixture of a lot of nationalities—German, Jew, and I don't know what not. It makes me sick to think of it. Our family, getting to be like that! And Monica of all people. Besides the Frostners are penniless. Monica is in a position to make a rich marriage."

"Why not look at it from the angle of Monica's happiness?" Francis suggested. "Monica, I'd say, is the monogamous kind. If she can't marry the man she's in love with, she probably won't marry anyone."

"Monogamous fiddlesticks!" Martha looked at her husband in plain disgust. "Monogamy is a state of mind *after* you're

154

married, not before. You can love any man if you make up
your mind to it. That's the best thing to do, and if she can't
she'd better stay single."

"Perhaps not as Monica thinks of love."

"Or you?" Martha's expression changed from one of anger
to bitterness.

The spring was unseasonably hot and the pool on André
Rambeau's lawn at the end of the day attracted the family.
Charlotte could hear the voices filled with the peculiar quality
of physical satisfaction that went with swimming. She could
all but feel against her own body the splash of the water as
someone dived from the springboard. With vicarious pleasure
she lay back against her pillows, feeling her body whole for
the moment, its surface touched by the soft substance of
water.

That's Monny laughing. How warm and eager her voice
had become of late. Nate must be there. Yes, she could hear
his whoop of delight and a great splash when he dived.

If Monica would only keep on expanding in the warmth of
Nate's personality. All the longings of years Charlotte poured
into her hope for Monica. She had never understood why
Monica should be so small a participator in life. It was as if
she had not enough vitality to plunge into anything, as if she
were the creation of an exhausted love instead of hers and
Francis' vital passion. Her two boys, John and Charles, come
of her sober mating with André, were so virile. Perhaps her
passion for Francis had exhausted itself in its own consumma-
tion.

But there was a stir from within Monny at last in this
coming of Nate. Charlotte, like the others, would have preferred to have Monica marry into the circle of the rich and
established, but she wanted Monica's happiness more.

" 'Bye!" Monica's voice came up to Charlotte. From where
she lay she could see the driveway where it swerved to skirt
the pool. Nate and Monny had changed into day clothes.

With a gesture of unmistakable pride Monica took her seat in Nate's rattletrap old Ford. With a spurt and a bang it shot down the drive.

Monny believed that until now she had been deprived of the sense of touch. As a blind person who has suddenly been given sight finds the world startlingly beautiful, so she was experiencing for the first time the wonders of touch. The hard twilled thread of Nate's suit was a lovely new sensation. The rough sandpaper quality of his cheek, when she laid her hand against it, brought her a curious new delight. And the backs of his hands with the soft fuzzy hair on them stirred emotions she was still unable to define.

"So the family says we can be engaged." Nate, as soon as he had his cantankerous machine well under control, pushed his hat to the back of his head and grinned at Monny.

"Oh, Nate dear!" she cried. "Suppose they'd said I couldn't have you!"

A puzzled look came over Nate's face. "But would that have made so much difference, chicken? We could have eloped."

It evidently was a new idea to him and it interested him. His eyes glowed with an adventurous light. "Eloping has points in its favor."

"But we couldn't do that!"

Nate laughed, seeing Monica's consternation. "You don't need to look so scared. It isn't as if we had to. We can just settle back and take our engagement easy. When do you think we can get married?"

"They haven't said. Maybe we'll have trouble yet. They aren't all for it. Aunt Martha is fighting it and Aunt Martha never gives up."

"And what," said Nate, pushing his cap still farther to the back of his head, "in the tarnation bowwows has Aunt Martha got to say about it?"

"A lot. She always does. Aunt Martha's terrible when she's roused."

"You don't mean to say," asked Nate, "that you're afraid of your aunt?"

"Well, not exactly afraid, but they——"

"They, they," mocked Nate. "Let's make it *us* from now on out."

Then Nate grew sober. There would be opposition in his own family when he told them, and sorrow. It was a little before sundown and his family had already begun the Sabbath. His mother would be lighting the candlesticks of burnished brass. Before his father's plate would be the two loaves of bread—the double portion of manna—and the empty cup and bottle of wine. He would not be there tonight, and when he was married to Monny he would not again share the Sabbath rite, receive the cup from his mother, hear the solemn words. *Blessed are thou our Lord, creator——*

"Nate, there's Aunt Martha's car now," said Monica excitedly. "I think she's going over to our house."

"What did you say, Monny?" Nate had heard only her voice, not her words.

"Where were you, Nate?" Monny asked. "I said there's Aunt Martha."

Nate put on a little speed, passing the beautiful car. "That for Aunt Martha," he said. Monica caught a glimpse of Henri and Elizabeth in the back seat. Aunt Martha was sitting very erect in front beside David.

"Who's that you're waving to, Elizabeth?" asked Martha, having seen out of the tail of her eye the flutter of Elizabeth's hand.

"Nate and Monny," said Elizabeth.

"I don't see what the family is about," said Henri, delicately flicking the ash from his cigarette.

"It's Monica who's marrying him, not the family," Elizabeth answered, managing to free her hand which Henri had captured.

Martha made no comment but the words were not lost on her, strengthening her determination to have this matter

straightened out. She almost never went to André's house. It
was distasteful to her to go there. But it was the surest way
to get hold of John. She knew that John and his sister were
very close, and she believed if he opposed this marriage Monica
would give it up. If she could not gain his co-operation she
would have to see Charlotte.

John was sitting on the edge of the pool when he saw Aunt
Martha, of all people, coming across the lawn. He had been
wondering just how he would bring about the conversation he
wanted to have with her. Henri was growing restive because
he was making no progress with Elizabeth. She evaded him,
and Henri, easily suspicious, believed it was because of John.
Nothing John could say would convince him to the contrary.

He rose and sauntered over to greet his aunt. "You're very
handsome in that lavender outfit, Aunt Martha."

"Thanks, John," she said a little caustically. "I came here
with the express purpose of talking to you."

"And I came to greet you with the express purpose of
talking to *you*."

They surveyed each other for a moment, each respectful of
his adversary. John placed a chair for his aunt, then stretched
himself out at her side, saying, "Go ahead. Plunge, Aunt
Martha."

"It's about Monica," Martha began. "Are you all fools over
here?"

The muscles of John's face stiffened ever so little, and the
change did not escape Martha. "You could break that up,"
she said. "Monica would believe anything you told her about
Nate."

"I hardly think so when it comes to Nate. Besides there
isn't anything to tell."

"There's bound to be with a fellow like that."

"Now it's my turn," said John. "It's about the family
business."

"Oh," said Martha, feeling a little flat at John's dismissal of
her request.

"Some of us younger men are getting a little restive having no say."

Martha's lip curled in sarcastic amusement. So John thought he could work her to get him a more important place in the business. "Your chance will come," she said, "if you behave yourself."

"But maybe too late. I learned a good deal while I was in the East." In a few concise sentences John made plain the threat to their wealth.

"Have you told this to your father?"

"Yes, but he doesn't seem to grasp it."

"Fool," said Martha. "You want me to talk to your grandfather, I take it."

"No. I want you to help bind Henri's interests closer into the family. He wants two things. The first I leave you to guess. The second, a greater control of the business. If he doesn't get it, he's going to go out on his own."

"And you with him?"

"Possibly." The two did not mince matters with each other.

"You're behind this new discontent of Henri's, John," said Martha, "but if it's to save our money, I expect we should all play along with you. I take it you want me to see he gets Elizabeth. You think then with Henri's backing you'll be in a position to handle your grandfather."

"That's it," said John.

"Suppose I tell you that Monica's unparalleled defiance in holding to this foreign fellow"—she would never dignify Nate with a name—"will jeopardize your whole scheme."

"And how?"

"Henri doesn't wish to belong to a family so demeaned."

John stiffened again. "You mean he thinks Nate beneath him?"

"Yes. As we all do," Martha replied.

"Listen," said John, "Henri can keep his hands off Nate. If Monny wants Nate I'm going to see she gets him. I think I can make Henri understand that. And you?"

Martha did not yield easily, but she saw today that if she succeeded in bringing about the one marriage she would have to give up breaking off the other.

"We might have the two marriages at once. You know, one ceremony." John took delight in his aunt's discomfiture. It gave him a warm feeling to think he was safeguarding Monny's happiness.

John was watching Charles at the other end of the pool. The sun lying close to the horizon sent a shaft of light directly into his eyes. They were sleepy, comfortable eyes this afternoon. Not frightened, the way they had been the other day. He'd got him out of that scrape in the Yosemite. The kid hadn't meant any harm taking a girl out without permission. Just testing the moonlight out a bit. But it was too bad he had not seen what was wrong with Charles the first thing. Too taken up with this scheme of his, he guessed. But everything was all right now. And he'd look after Monny, too, not let Aunt Martha get her claws into her.

His feeling of family was as strong as Martha's but much narrower, for it included only his immediate family and his grandfather—his own direct line. He felt no pity for anyone else. None for Elizabeth now that she had insulted him. He would have had none for Buz even if he had known her difficulties.

XXV

Buz had found the day almost unendurable in the cooped-up rooms over a garage where they lived. She had in her a Teutonic love of the earth. She liked to dig in it. She longed to take off her shoes and stockings today and walk barefooted in the fields as she had done since early childhood. She had not stayed long enough at Luigi's home either for her own sake or the baby's. The little boy, frail at birth, became frailer during the weeks when Buz had not been strong enough to give him the care he needed. And yet she would not allow Luigi to do for the baby. Luigi, proud at first of the child, grew indifferent to him, excluded as he was by Buz from any chance to father him, and then, finally, irritable with him, blaming him for his broken nights. Luigi, too, was not used to long hours confined to shop and house. The temperature in the shop often reached well over the hundred mark. He came home drenched with sweat to the baby's ceaseless fretful wail.

The day had exhausted them both and Buz had not wanted to go to his mother's. But it was better, thought Luigi, now they were there. Security took possession of him sitting there protected by the sleeping orchards and vineyards.

The baby woke crying. Mrs. Griffanti walked around the table and took the puny child from Buz. Reluctantly Buz surrendered him, then watched jealously as Luigi boasted to his mother about his son as he nestled the baby's tiny hand in his.

"When you going to christen the baby, Luigi?" his mother asked him in her own tongue.

"I don't know. Ask Buz," said Luigi.

161

Mrs. Griffanti repeated her question.

"I'm not going to have him christened," said Buz.

Old Mrs. Griffanti's heavy brows drew together, and she spoke harshly. "It's Luigi who's to say."

"I'll do what I want with him," snapped Buz.

Luigi saw that Buz was affronted and that his mother was too. Alert, watchful, feeling his two allegiances battling with each other, knowing it would be bad for him whichever side he took, he rose hurriedly, saying, "We got to be going, Ma."

But he was too late. Buz's remark had set off his mother's long smoldering resentment. "You should behave. You make my son ashame'. You talk like a bad girl." All her pent-up sorrow over Luigi's marriage at last found vent. She poured out her complaints in a mixture of English and Italian.

Buz looked at Luigi. So no one was going to speak up in her defense, not even Luigi. She couldn't bear it. And this old woman, of all people, calling her bad! Why, she was the one to be ashamed of the Italian woman!

"You don't know what you're talking about," she burst out. She turned to Luigi, saying in as withering a tone as she could muster, "You can come when you're ready. I'm going to sit in the car. This is my baby, and I'll do what I think's right with him."

The baby whimpered as she took him. It made Buz angry that he had been quiet in the old woman's arms and was not in hers. She gave him a little spank, saying, "You hush up, now."

Luigi jumped up, taking the child himself. "I'll not have you do that to him, Buz. He's too little to spank."

That night Luigi and Buz quarreled, quarreled over the baby, Luigi insisting he should be christened, Buz insisting he should not. Buz, brought up in strict Baptist doctrine, looked upon christening as a work of the devil. "I'll leave you, Luigi Griffanti, if you make me do it."

"Go," he told her in anger, "but you can't have the baby. I'll take him to Ma to be brought up good."

Buz lost all caution. She was beside herself with fright and anger. "You can't, Luigi! He isn't yours."

"What do you mean, he isn't mine?"

"I mean what I say. Figure it out for yourself, smart boy."

Luigi felt his strength going out of his legs. He sat down heavily. "Whose baby is he, Buz? I got to know."

Suddenly Buz was frightened. She had never seen Luigi so angry. "I was only mad, Luigi," she begged. "I didn't know what I was saying. Honest, I didn't mean it."

"You swear it," Luigi demanded, holding her wrists, twisting them a little.

"I swear it, Luigi. Honest."

XXVI

SUDDENLY Henri seemed to have taken root at Aunt Martha's. Both he and Aunt Martha assumed he was there because of his place in Elizabeth's life. Elizabeth would have known what to do if he'd ask her to marry him, but she didn't know how to combat this silent conquest. Wherever they went, he hovered around with an air of possession. Everyone seemed to take it for granted that the engagement would soon be announced. Aunt Maria began asking her over, sending Henri to get her. Once they entered the avenue of palms, Elizabeth felt her spirit darken. She thought wearily of her father's words: "America is a place to begin over." Begin! She was suffocated.

Sometimes Elizabeth told herself that she hated John. Before all the cousins he spoke as if it were a foregone conclusion that Henri and she were to marry. It infuriated her that he should torment her in this way. He knew she did not love Henri. In spite of her quarrel with John and the bitter words they had spoken to each other she had thought he would give her a chance for reconciliation. She was sorry she had struck him.

Philippe Rambeau at last returned from his northern visit. On his first day at the winery John saw to it that Henri was there, too. The old man had gone into his sampling room, as he did each day toward noon. The men of the family dropped in one by one. They always made a little ceremony out of Philippe's return. Philippe was showing his warm genial nature today as he had not since the affair of the night riders.

164

Busy as he had been these last weeks seeing through the slow process of making fine wine, he had for the time forgotten the happenings of the autumn and winter. A kind of spiritual renewal took place in him each spring when the vines put forth their fresh and delicate leaves and the wine came to life again after its winter sleep. He moved about the sampling room now, fingering his beautiful old goblets, holding them up to the light. Finally he came back to the table, seating himself at its head.

When the men had completed the ceremony of welcoming Philippe back by drinking his health, John, with deference in his voice, said, "Grandfather, I learned some interesting things when I was east. May I," he asked with a disarming smile, "give an account of the mission you sent me on?"

Philippe Rambeau looked at his tall grandson inquiringly.

André, completely taken back by John's evident intention to go over his head to enlist his grandfather's interest, twirled his glass nervously. *He'll ruin himself with his grandfather,* André kept saying to himself, appalled at the frankness with which his son was explaining the necessity of keeping down the number of carloads of grapes that went east this year.

"There is not," John explained earnestly, "an unlimited demand for grapes to make 'cellar' wine."

Philippe tapped with his fingers on the table. "Stop right there, John. Explain about this 'cellar' wine, as you call it." It was unfortunate that John had introduced the word, for it gave his grandfather too vivid a picture of the unlovely stuff thus made and consumed.

"So that is what becomes of our beautiful Rieslings and our Golden Chasselas." Philippe spoke coldly. "Go on," he added sternly.

John, who many times had rehearsed the presentation of his facts, drilling himself in just the right phrases to use in an appeal to his grandfather, plunged eagerly forward, stating his plan. "And," he ended, "we can only hold the price up in one way. Get an agreement between the big growers to create a shortage of freight cars. If necessary, it would pay us to buy cars and keep them on our sidings."

"And what," asked old Philippe in a silken tone, "will become of the small growers under such a scheme as this?"

John forgot for a moment to whom he was talking, saw only his own logical conclusion. "They'll go under anyway if the market's flooded with wine grapes."

The room was very still for a moment. The look in the old eyes was matched by the look in the young eyes. Neither pair of eyes wavered.

"Grandfather, you, like me, are a *very* good business man," John finally said. "Had I been given the opportunity I, like you, would have been a good vintner. You will not hurt your vineyards if for a few years you have to let your grapes go for homemade wine."

"Don't cloud the issue, John," said Philippe. "What you propose is to wreck every small grower in the Valley. I'll have no part in such a scheme."

"You prefer, then, sir, to take a staggering financial loss?" John's tone was the silky one now.

"Yes," said the old man quietly, "if necessary. We have been disgraced already by the treatment we have given our neighbors in the Valley. I did not found the house of Rambeau in America for the sake of a grandson who can find it advisable ever to kick a helpless man. I want no scheme of yours, John."

John turned a deep red. How had his grandfather found out? No names had come out in the grand-jury investigation. "Very well," he said sullenly. "Go broke. I'll be the first one to say, 'I told you so.'"

"No doubt," said Philippe dryly.

As John rose to leave the room, Henri rose too and stepped forward. "Sir," he said, "I am not controlled by your lack of judgment, if John is. If you take this stand, I shall withdraw my lands and the use of my name."

"Henri would take off his coat and roll up his sleeves and go to work?" the old man asked sarcastically.

Henri's face darkened, but he stood his ground, his head held high, his lips expressing disdain. "No," he said. "John is going with me."

"A waster and a bully. I wish you luck." Philippe threw back his head and laughed.

XXVII

MARTHA, hearing of the disastrous turn of events, put determined pressure on Elizabeth. She, and she alone, could draw Henri back into the family.

"Elizabeth," she said, "there is no use my beating around the bush any longer. Francis and I have given you a home for nearly a year now. And Grandfather has been very generous to you. Now we feel you should take responsibility and do your part. We've been patient with you, Elizabeth, even when you haven't respected the family's dignity."

"What do you mean, Aunt Martha?"

"I mean, leading Henri on and then not doing anything about it—as you did with John."

Elizabeth gave a gasp of dismay. "I've never led Henri on!" she began in her own defense, ignoring the reference to John.

"Why, then, have you been going around with him continually?"

"But, Aunt Martha, it's you who've planned for me to see him!"

"Because I thought you wanted to."

"But, Aunt Martha——" Elizabeth felt trapped. What could she say?

"And now," Martha went on, "Henri is exceedingly angry and talks of withdrawing entirely from the family."

"Would that be so bad?" Elizabeth could not resist asking.

"Bad! What are you thinking of, Elizabeth? Your act may cost us all our land—and even our homes—if he sets up competition against us."

"But he wouldn't do that just because of me, surely? Henri

work that hard! Really, Aunt Martha!" In spite of herself, Elizabeth had to smile.

"He and John have had some difference with your grandfather and they talk of starting up for themselves."

"But that has nothing to do with me!" said Elizabeth.

"If you married Henri, you could keep him from going off with John. It's John who's at the bottom of it. Henri couldn't possibly think of a thing like that himself. I mean," said Martha quickly, recovering herself, "I mean he is too kind to do such a thing."

"Kind!" exclaimed Elizabeth. "Henri kind?"

Elizabeth was certain once she was married to Henri she would have no power over him. But if she refused to marry him and he did set up for himself and terrible things did happen to the family . . .

She knew she had become the center of the household, loved by her grandfather, loved, she thought, according to his reserved nature, by her uncle, loved by her aunt, too, perhaps, in her odd abrupt way. Not since her mother had gone to France so suddenly in Elizabeth's childhood to help in a hospital during the war had anyone taken such care of her as Aunt Martha had. She couldn't bear to injure them all. But Henri . . .

"I'd like to have you settled when your father comes. You know, not bother him with your affairs so soon after his marriage. How carefree he'd be if we could announce your engagement when he arrives. Then he would know you were happy and he could enjoy himself to the full."

"You mean Father is coming here to America? Why didn't he tell me, Aunt Martha?"

"We had meant to surprise you. But as things are now, I thought you should know."

Elizabeth felt a new security. Lon was coming to see her. So he hadn't forgotten her in his marriage!

"But I must consult him, Aunt Martha. He would want me to. Certainly we can put off anything definite until he comes," exclaimed Elizabeth, grasping at the chance of escape.

"He placed you in my hands," her aunt persisted, determined to gain her point now, for she saw she had made some impression on Elizabeth.

Elizabeth felt a sudden sense of uncertainty. Yes, he had placed her in Aunt Martha's hands. "But I don't love Henri. I don't even like him!" she burst out.

"You can learn to. You're sitting in a draft, my dear, and you're shivering," Martha said, rising. "I'm going to ring for some hot tea for you. We'd just finished when you came in."

Deftly she moved about Elizabeth's room, hovering over Elizabeth, giving her a feeling of solid comfort and a guilty sense of ingratitude. "I must think about it, Aunt Martha," finally Elizabeth made herself say. Then, seeing the look of displeasure in her aunt's face, she added, "I'll try to do what you want."

"If you try, of course you'll succeed," said Martha dryly.

In the days that followed, Elizabeth forced herself to see a great deal of Henri, trying to satisfy Aunt Martha, although she knew that such halfway measures would never satisfy her. But Henri expanded under the greater graciousness she meted out to him.

Perhaps, she thought, *I could persuade him not to go in with John. If I could only get Henri to talk to me about John's plans, make him uncertain of John's abilities* . . . Elizabeth, who in all her life had never manipulated anyone to her own advantage, planned now to play upon Henri's cupidity.

In order that she might gauge the impression her words made upon him, she turned in her saddle to look at him as they rode together one afternoon up the avenue of palms. "How fine your vineyards look, Henri. Uncle André may be overcautious, but he's a genius at keeping vineyards healthy."

Henri gave her a searching look. Was she being employed by the old man to get him back? "My dear Elizabeth, just

what has suddenly made you so interested in healthy grapevines?" Henri asked. "Has some little bird, perhaps a bird
with a white goatee and mustache, been telling you of a
foolish Henri who knew so little of his own business that
he thought he could run it for himself?"

Elizabeth, both angry and mortified, for she saw that Henri
was making fun of her, answered coldly, "If it's Grandfather
you're talking about, you can be pretty sure he doesn't need
me to manage his business for him. But we all know what
you and John are planning and I think you're fools to try
to outwit Grandfather. I should think you would have found
by this time that he makes a better friend than enemy."

The amused look went from Henri's face. Elizabeth had
grasped the most vulnerable point in John's scheme. There
wouldn't be anything that Philippe Rambeau wouldn't do
to make ineffective his and John's competition. Henri knew
that the old man was a good hater. He and John would
have to be prepared for a bitter struggle.

But he was caught between the two Rambeau men. John
might take Elizabeth from him, even yet, if he, Henri, did not
join in John's scheme. Henri had not forgotten how all his
childhood John had taken things from him. From that past,
sometimes bitter, Henri drew his knowledge of John's power.
On the other hand, the old man might take her from him.
Henri realized the deep loyalties in Elizabeth. To her grandfather she had evidently given her loyalty. If she felt he was in
any way injuring her grandfather he knew she would turn
against him. Somehow he must keep from committing himself finally either to John or old Philippe until he had Elizabeth's promise to marry him. He had not yet dared to risk
asking her for such a promise. She had been more yielding of
late, but still he felt he must give her a little more time.

Elizabeth, chagrined that her feeble attempt to outwit John
had come to nothing, felt her inadequacy dragging her down
to commitment to Henri. When they returned from the ride
there was a wire from Lon, sent from the train, saying he

and his wife had caught an earlier boat and would be in Fresno
the next evening. No time now for an engagement before
he arrived. Aunt Martha seemingly forgot it, too, swept up
into the hasty but elaborate preparations she deemed necessary for the return of Lon and the introduction of his French
wife to the family. Even Grandfather showed anxiety that
Mathilde, Lon's wife, should feel she was in a French home.

Elizabeth went to the station to meet them, so happy over
their coming that she did not mind when Aunt Martha suggested that Henri go with her. They stood together watching
the train come in. "There they are! I see Lon way down there
at the other end of the train!" cried Elizabeth, racing ahead of
Henri. Then she saw there were two women with Lon.

Why, one must be Mathilde's daughter, Madeleine! Lon
had said nothing about bringing her with him. Both were
dressed in well-fitting simple black frocks and hats. The
younger woman was extremely chic and handsome, Elizabeth thought. She had curiously regular features which gave
the effect of a beautiful mask. Neither delight nor interest
showed in her face, only polite attentiveness. The older woman
was vividly alive. How French they both looked here in
America! Elizabeth, as she greeted them, had a sudden sense
of anxiety that the house, everything, would seem too
American.

But Lon fitted. In London she had not known any other
Rambeau with whom to compare him. Now she saw he was
a Rambeau of the Rambeaus.

"Well, hello, my little!" he exclaimed.

Elizabeth grinned at him, feeling all at once very comfortable and happy.

"And who is this most neglected young man?" asked Mathilde, turning to Henri standing a step behind Elizabeth.

"I forgot," said Elizabeth. "It's Henri. You know, Lon
—Henri."

Henri waited for no further introduction, but bowed low
over Mathilde's hand, a bow as Old-World as everything else

around Mathilde was New World. Then over Madeleine's.

"See, Lon, how he is charming! I had not expected to find such a one here." Mathilde chattered in French, speaking in an aside to Lon as the young people led the way to the car. "It is arranged between them? Your Elizabeth and the beautiful young man?"

"A cousin," said Lon with good-natured indifference.

"A cousin!"

"Well, not really. The stepson of my sister. His father was Don Ramon de Swanaña."

"It is perfect!" exclaimed Mathilde, taking for granted an engagement between Elizabeth and Henri.

XXVIII

THE return of his son made Philippe forget his growing sense of defeat in his family's distortion of the pattern he had set for their lives and his own. They had exaggerated the figures of wealth and power and had dimmed the tracery of the spirit which he had always intended, in the end, should dominate. But Lon, with his talk of rehabilitation for France, seemed to bring the family into better balance. That one of his sons should have been given the responsibility of restoring a French cathedral made Philippe very proud.

And Mathilde had pleased the old man from the moment she crossed the threshold of his house. She sat with him for hours, talking of France as it was in the past and as it had been since the war. She brought his France back to him in the French words. Conversation flowed between them like something living. French again became the language of the household and with it for Philippe came peace.

The clamor of commercialism which had risen to a din around him of late was muted for the time. Even the proper marketing of his grapes need no longer trouble him. Some of his neighbors had a scheme for clearing up the clogged transportation. Plenty of cars in which to send east the whole of the Valley output. Orderly routing, orderly distribution of grapes. Grapes arriving in good condition in refrigerator cars. No need for the wild speculating there had been last year. Philippe believed the plan would go through. There were many men who had joined the association. Any man who wished to withdraw from the pool could do so if he gave notice before the middle of July. A fair proposition.

André and the Fairons had favored it. Martha had, at least, made no objections.

Even John seemed to be falling into line. Philippe had heard no more of his starting out for himself if his ruthless plan was not adopted. Henri did not seem to intend to carry out his threat either. Philippe had never known Henri to be so anxious to please him.

The household activities shifted before Philippe's failing sight in a brilliant kaleidoscope. With satisfaction he surveyed the luxury and peace around him, the surface of life lying smooth and untroubled.

"Very well done," Lon told him, speaking of the improvements made in the house in the years he had been away. "The original part of the house has not been put out of balance by the additions." With Lon's praise sharpening his awareness of his surroundings, Philippe's eyes, as on the day he had waited for Elizabeth's coming, traveled along the vistas set out before him.

They were sitting together, he and Lon, in comfortable leisure, something André never had time for. The day was so hot, made hotter by the desert wind, that everyone moved in a sort of languor. Old Philippe liked it. It gave languor even to Martha crossing the sunlit terrace with Mathilde. Her short compact figure beside Mathilde's fragile one had its own peculiar grace. The blue and gray of their dresses mingled as the wind blew their skirts about, whipping them together in a fluttering banner.

Laughter reached him from the driveway on the other side of the house. Soon through the entrance door came his granddaughters, Elizabeth and Monny, and Mathilde's daughter Madeleine. The richly colored room, darkened at this time of the day to keep out the sun, made more noticeable the girls' slender delicacy, the crisp freshness of their summer dresses. They seemed blown into the room by their very lightness, caught in the draft of air from the opening door. It banged shut behind them and the white folds of their frocks, tossed forward by the wind, settled back into place only to foam out again as the door opened to let in John and Henri and Nate.

So Monny was to marry Nate. It pleased Philippe that there should be one in his family starting at the bottom as he had. To everyone's surprise he had been pleased over the engagement, had liked having Nate in the family.

He watched them go on into the dining room, bound for the pantry, he imagined. He saw Henri come close to Elizabeth's side, draw her apart. He did not like that idea, unless—could it be that such a marriage would make her happy? It would certainly make her very rich.

He turned, intending to ask Lon about it, but Lon had joined Mathilde and Martha on the terrace. Philippe leaned his head back against the chair, closed his eyes, and listened to the wind blowing in strong rushes through the branches of the great oaks. Like wave after wave washed against a shore.

He wished time would stand still, let him rest in a long afternoon before going on to that other world which, by its very newness, would of necessity call for new effort.

Elizabeth had Madeleine to entertain. She offered a problem not easily solved. She professed interest in the usual outdoor activities of California but Elizabeth could see she was bored.

"Aren't there some races we could go to?" Madeleine asked on the second day. "I like races."

"It's not the season but still—I'll ask Henri. He'll know." Elizabeth hoped Henri would take Madeleine off her hands.

Madeleine showed not a little curiosity about him. "And you are really to marry this Henri, this Don Swanaña?"

"I suppose so," Elizabeth answered, "but it's just because Aunt Martha wants me to."

"Elizabeth, he is so *chic*. Surely you can like him a little, and then there's the family."

Madeleine was straight from a convent. Henri was thrilling and exciting to her. She could not believe that Elizabeth was not excited too. She was only pretending not to be, for some strange American reason with which Madeleine did not sympathize. No girl in Elizabeth's position would refuse a handsome man with money and title.

"Can't you take it as a marriage of convenience?" Madeleine's tone was close to patronizing. Elizabeth knew little of the world if she refused to grasp at the advantages of such a marriage.

"I don't want to marry that way. If you knew him better you might understand." Elizabeth found some relief in expressing her objections even to a half-sympathetic listener.

"Perhaps you had better let me see something of him, then I could advise you." Madeleine's pale unexpressive face gave no hint of her quickening interest.

Henri was his most charming self. He paid Madeleine small attentions, thinking he might stir Elizabeth to jealousy. Cleverly he planned his strategy. Sometimes he neglected Elizabeth for Madeleine, oh, just a little.

A contest began between the girls, unconscious at first on Elizabeth's part, for it never occurred to her that she could be jealous over Henri. But it roused her pride to think Madeleine might take him from her. She exerted herself to win him back, but once he was attentive again the game did not interest her.

Henri, seeing he had gained and then lost, went a step farther and asked Madeleine to go with him up the Valley to a smart rodeo. After luncheon Elizabeth went to her room to rest during the heat of the day. Suppose she let Madeleine have Henri, just let it happen, Aunt Martha need never know but that Henri preferred Madeleine. Elizabeth would suffer only a passing hurt to her pride and she would be rid of him forever. She felt an almost overwhelming release.

But gradually the freight of her spirit seemed to weigh her down—her quarrel with John, the failure to establish the old companionship with her father since his arrival, the ruthless determination of John and Henri to defeat, even ruin old Philippe, and her own part in that defeat if she let Henri go.

If the family fortunes were lost, she asked herself, would it be because of her, as Aunt Martha claimed? Lon's and Mathilde's voices drifted in to her from the terrace where the two were sitting. Mathilde was the kind of person from whom she might ask advice had circumstances been different. But in Mathilde's eyes the marriage was right and good. Did Lon feel so too?

The next day Henri came straight to the point and asked her to marry him. "I won't be held off any longer, Elizabeth," he told her.

"I haven't yet talked it over with Father," she answered him slowly, "but if he approves, I'll announce our engagement when we go up to the Napa place. The family is all going to be together then. Grandfather wants a dinner for Monny and Nate. That's a good time, don't you think?"

Elizabeth had still a hope that in putting Henri off even for two days she might not need to marry him. She would find out from her father if what Aunt Martha said was true, find out if marrying Henri would save the family from ruin or whether it was a manufactured threat of Aunt Martha's to get her to marry him. "We're leaving tomorrow," she added. "Surely you can wait that long."

"I guess I'll have to," Henri answered, thinking to himself, *I can't hold John off much longer.* John was getting impatient. "If we're going to do anything this year," he kept saying, "we've got to get hold of the other big growers and buy up a lot of freight cars right away. Even now it's late to begin."

I must see Lon alone. I'm sure he will help me when he knows I don't love Henri, Elizabeth thought. *On the drive north, I'll watch for a chance to get him off by himself. At noon, perhaps, when we stop for lunch I can manage it. I'll make him walk down the street with me, pretend I want to get a present for Mathilde, or something.*

XXIX

As they started north the next morning, Lon was suddenly conscious of the strain in Elizabeth. He was sitting on the back seat of the car with Mathilde on one side of him and his father on the other. Elizabeth was driving, and at that moment had turned her head to answer some question Madeleine, seated beside her, had asked. He noticed a nervous twitch to Elizabeth's mouth.

With a renewal of his once keen observation of his daughter, Lon studied Elizabeth. She no longer had that casual grace he had so delighted in during their years together in London. Her shoulders, under her light cotton dress, he could see were tense. The naturally good balance of her head was destroyed by its too determined forward thrust; her hands gripped the steering wheel too tightly

What was wrong with Elizabeth? He had taken for granted that Martha would know what to do for her. Could it be that a home such as Martha was giving her had not made her happy? Surely she had everything to make her so. Martha hovered over her as if she were her own daughter. Obviously she was Philippe's favorite and Henri was devoted to her. Martha had told him that they were engaged. "Funny child," Martha had said. "She's planning to surprise us all, especially you, and announce it at the family gathering up north. Just as if we couldn't all see that they're crazy about each other." He had let it go at that. He had no desire to force Elizabeth's confidence.

It was not accident that he had not seen her alone. Deep in Lon was the memory of Elizabeth's last days in London. He knew that she felt he had failed her then. When she had come to him, hurt and broken over her affair with William Humphreys, he had been frightened, not knowing how far she had let the conventions go. He had taken refuge in speaking harshly to her and then sending her away from him. He understood now that she felt he had deserted her at a time when she needed him. Well, it was too late now to do anything about it.

He put from him his uneasiness over Elizabeth, devoting himself to Mathilde, determined to let matters stand as they were. He would be onlooker, as he had been ever since his arrival, satisfied to watch his daughter hurry from one engagement to another, the handsome Henri always in attendance. He knew that Madeleine envied her. The moods of his stepdaughter, these days, he read better than he did those of his own daughter.

When they entered the hotel for their luncheon, Elizabeth slipped her arm through his and pulled him aside, saying, "Lon, dear, I've got to see you. Tell Mathilde something . . . anything so we can get off by ourselves. You must let me talk to you."

He realized the moment had come when he must go beneath the surface with her and he was not ready for it. "Is it so very important that you have to tell it to me before luncheon?" he asked.

"There won't be time after. Aunt Martha will make us start immediately. Please, Lon!" Elizabeth urged.

"All right, then." He turned and said something to Mathilde that Elizabeth could not hear, but the look that passed between them added to her sense of being out of communication with him.

As they passed out of the door Elizabeth began, "Lon dear, why do you all take it for granted that I'm going to marry Henri?"

"My dear child, what have I to do with it? I thought you had learned to handle such matters for yourself. Wasn't that what you wanted to do?" Suddenly he stopped. He was

showing her that he had not forgotten their misunderstand-
ing over her affair with William Humphreys. This was the
last thing he had intended to do!

"It's Aunt Martha," Elizabeth broke out. "She says it's
for the good of the family. Is it true, Lon, what Aunt Martha
says, that if I don't marry him, he will withdraw his lands
and that will hurt Grandfather and all the rest of the family
—perhaps take away their money?"

"Why, my little," he said more gently, "I thought of course
Henri was your own choice." He was about to add, "Send
him packing," when he remembered that he couldn't very well
go against Martha. He had never, when he was with Martha,
been able to oppose her strong will. And, too, he loved comfort and peace. If he took Elizabeth's part he saw he would
disrupt his own and Mathilde's visit, for Martha would be
angry with him. He feared his sister Martha's anger. He had
never been able to endure it. He walked another block saying
nothing.

Elizabeth was watching him closely. He must not fail her
this time. "Lon," she said, so low he could barely hear her,
"I don't love him. I can't believe the family will be ruined
if I don't marry him. Can that be true? You must tell me."

"Why are you so sure," he asked, avoiding a direct answer
to the question, "that Martha isn't right? According to the
French, such a marriage as this one is safe and good."

"But we're not French any more, really," Elizabeth protested.

"Perhaps we have missed something by not holding to the
French principles," Lon continued.

"Really, Lon"—Elizabeth's voice broke into a laugh—"you
are funny."

"What's so funny, Elizabeth?"

Lon remembered that they had said these exact words before. In spite of himself they were repeating that other scene
when she had come to him for help and he had destroyed himself in Elizabeth's eyes. But he seemed powerless to help it.

"After all, my dear," he added in self-justification, "you didn't manage so well when you were left to choose for yourself."

Elizabeth drew back. To use her mistake over William Humphreys to trap her now! "Very well, Lon. We'd better be getting back. I wouldn't want to keep you from your luncheon."

"And you?" he said. "You'll come with me, won't you, my little?"

"No. Tell Aunt Martha I'll meet you at the car. I see Henri coming down the street. Take him along with you. You should know him better. You'll find a lot in common, no doubt." Angry tears rose to her eyes.

Without another word she crossed the street, wanting above all else some shelter. She felt exposed suddenly in the brilliant light of the street. There was a small park, she remembered, opposite the hotel, the trees so thick in it that they hid the sun.

Gray old benches stood before an empty bandstand hooded over with its sounding shell. Dry leaves broke to pieces under her step, leaves falling as they did in the autumn in England, falling here in the fierce dry heat of the summer. *I'll sit here for a moment on this bench,* she thought. Her two hands gripped the edge of the seat as she leaned slightly forward. After a time she rose, walked across the street and slid under the wheel of the car.

Lon, looking at her as he came out of the hotel, had an uneasy feeling that he had lost her. The channels of communication were completely closed between them. On the rest of the ride north, he tried not to look at her, but constantly in the line of his vision were her hands clasping the upper half of the steering wheel, lying there so lightly now they made him nervous.

XXX

Two evenings before, Andrew Fairon had stood on the veranda of the Rambeau's summer home looking out over the Valley. He was lonely. These long months away from his family had been hard for him. He watched a bonfire in a grove of eucalyptus, listened to the twang of the guitars and the laughter of the Mexicans making a fiesta out of the evening's rest from the day's labor. During the months that he had spent at the Napa vineyard he had learned for the first time in his life what it was to be completely separate in spirit.

Then he heard Diener calling him.

"Please, the mother at the telephone."

"Hello. Hello, Andrew. How are you, son?"

"Fine," Andrew answered.

"Are you lonesome?"

"Oh, I don't know," he replied with all a young man's reluctance to express his emotions.

"Well, anyway," his mother went on, "the family is coming up to see you day after tomorrow. Aunt Martha will be calling you. I thought I'd give you warning. You must do yourself proud and see we are all comfortable. The idea is to stay a week. Your father and I can't come up tomorrow but will be up in time for the family dinner. You can manage? Good-by, son."

He put down the receiver. He felt warm and no longer separate.

Very soon a call came through from his Aunt Martha. "Ask Gerta to come to the 'phone," she commanded. "I'd better tell her myself what I want done."

183

Afterward Andrew went the rounds with Gerta, inspecting the rooms, planning where everyone should sleep. Even the wide veranda would have to be used. "John and Henri and I can sleep here. The girls can have my room," he explained to Gerta.

When at last everything was arranged, Andrew, too excited for sleep, saddled his horse. He'd ride for a while in the moonlight, but first he drew up at the back of the dark house where the steps led down into the grape arbor.

"Diener," he called, "be sure to bring out the table and benches." He had really no need to give Diener instructions. As long as there had been a northern property and the summer gathering of the family there had been benches and table in the arbor.

Tonight the moon, though nearly at its full, could not find a single chink in the roof of leaves, but in the vineyards and on the foothills where Andrew rode it shone in white brilliance, laying a coal-black tracery of trees and vines over the earth. The pine-covered mountains blocked the valley in with a rim of blackness. Andrew, though all his life accustomed to this summer scene, was unaccountably stirred tonight. His dreams were hidden in these hills. Since autumn, when the young priest had visited them, there had come times when he thought the way to satisfy his longing was to take orders. It seemed to offer some mystic completion to his separateness. But the idea had contended in his mind with another dream. Far down in the San Joaquin Valley there was a flat-topped hill he had called his ever since childhood. He wanted to build a home there. Lately the image of the woman who would live there with him had without his realizing it resembled Elizabeth.

XXXI

IT WAS late afternoon when the Rambeaus turned into their own valley. As the hills began to close in around them, their cars were like horses racing home, urged forward by the excitement of their drivers. Old Philippe and Lon and Martha and Maria and Monny and John, and even Elizabeth, had dreams buried deep in the country. The finely plowed earth lay in dark strips between the green lines of shining vines. On the foothills, tawny colored in the daylight, the oaks stood out like black bouquets. The farthest hills were blue black.

They passed Inglenook, an old and beautiful winery, closed since Prohibition. Then Beaulieu. Like a haunting memory there clung to Beaulieu the French atmosphere. Then to the left was the Beringer winery with its high-peaked German house. Soon they would be home. Only some tangled, half-cared-for land to pass, and then they would be passing their own beautiful vineyards.

The first rift in old Philippe's happiness came when he was confronted with that neglected field close up against his vineyards. How often he had tried to buy it. He sniffed the dry, powdery summer air. A spark would set that field afire. Only the wide plowed furrows, he always maintained, would protect his vines in such an emergency. Good! Diener had done as he told him—taken out one row of grapes and widened the plowed space.

Elizabeth slowed her car to let Martha's pass. It was a ritual of the summer that Martha should be at the ranch house to greet the family even if she superseded the family's arrival by only a few minutes.

For the whole of the first day old Philippe sat in the arbor,

185

his family coming and going around him; all of them there at mealtime, then one by one dwindling away until only Lon and Mathilde were left, or Martha, or Diener or Andrew come to consult him. Toward evening Francis Fairon came to sit with him. They must make their final decision about the fall shipments soon now.

The men of the family had hoped that in the kindly setting of his beloved northern vineyards old Philippe might be won to a modification of John's plan. But here, where Philippe had dreamed his dreams of finest wine, proved no place to win his co-operation for increasing his profits by dubious methods. He had stubbornly avoided all attempts to draw him into a discussion of the matter.

In answer now to Francis' direct question he said, "I want orderly routing and distribution of our grapes. I like this plan the men of the association are working up. We've joined them. That settles it, doesn't it?"

"Not entirely," said Francis. "We have the right to withdraw if we notify them by the fifteenth of July, you know."

John skirted the edge of the arbor, sat down outside, listening to his own good arguments put forth by Francis. He hoped he and Henri would not have to act for themselves. It was a gamble, at best, to buy up a lot of cars. Even if the Rambeau-Fairon men were all with him, there'd be struggle enough to persuade the big men in the valleys to control their shipments. But with his grandfather's influence thrown in with the vineyardists who had joined the association with the idea of marketing all the harvest, the obstacles would be almost insurmountable. John's strong hands tightened at the thought. His grandfather's and his own shrewdness might balance but old Philippe's experience in a battle of wits far outweighed his.

But I'm all right, John told himself, *however things break, if we can keep Elizabeth in line. I can swing it with Henri's money. Evidently the old man isn't going to give in. Francis isn't getting anywhere with him.*

Very early before breakfast the next morning, Elizabeth passed John on her way to the stables to get her horse. The beautiful black creature had been sent up by old Philippe so that Elizabeth might accompany him on his early morning rounds of the vineyards. Philippe had seen little of her since Lon and Mathilde's arrival. He had missed her. This was to be their first ride.

"May I come along?" asked John, falling into step at her side.

"I'd rather you didn't, unless Grandfather asked you." Elizabeth had found it hard to have John so closely associated with her as he was up here. He had taken every opportunity to link her name with Henri's in conversation. She had counted on this quiet ride with her grandfather to help her through. She even had one last hope that through him she might escape marrying Henri.

"I'm afraid that won't deter me," John answered coolly. He did not intend Elizabeth should be alone with old Philippe. If Elizabeth could get her grandfather to oppose her marriage with Henri, he knew she would not go through with it. No quiet rides with Grandfather were to be allowed. John and Martha had decided that. "Why don't we make it a foursome, Elizabeth?" John had just seen Madeleine come out of the house. It would be better, he reflected, if he made himself as inconspicuous as possible on the ride. Numbers would help.

As the three of them passed the winery on their way to the stables, they saw Andrew Fairon standing in the door of the cooperage. "Hurry up, Andrew," John called. "We're all going for a ride with Grandfather." He took savage delight in tormenting Elizabeth, tormenting himself, too. Now that the moment had come when he would push Elizabeth into final, irrevocable surrender to Henri, he felt a sharp thrust of jealousy. With a kind of cruel humor he thought to collect as large a party as possible. It made more ludicrous Elizabeth's anticipated tête-à-tête with her grandfather. When

John saw Monica at the stable door just about to lead out her horse, he slapped his thigh and gave out such a loud laugh that Monica's horse whinnied sharply.

Monica stroked his neck. "You foolish. It's only John," she told him, looking curiously at John and Elizabeth who were walking together a little ahead of Madeleine and Andrew. *John seems extremely happy*, she thought, *though Elizabeth looks anything but happy.* Was there something between them still? There couldn't be now, on the very brink of Elizabeth's announcement of her engagement to Henri—unless Aunt Martha was wrong about the coming announcement——

"We're all going riding with Grandfather," John told her. "Come along."

When, instead of one, Philippe saw four of his grandchildren and one step-grandchild coming by the corner of the house where he sat on his horse waiting Elizabeth, he looked surprised, and, Elizabeth thought, annoyed. Had he, perhaps, seen what Aunt Martha was doing and meant to help her out? He must see what Aunt Martha was trying to do. Suddenly it was plain to her that John had thwarted Grandfather's attempt to talk to her. He had done it to hurt her. Everything he had done since their quarrel had been meant to hurt her. He was evil. She was frightened at the revelation of John's vindictiveness. Here, in the very strongholds of her family, she felt his cruelty like a sharp sword, ripping apart any security she had ever known. Aunt Martha and John were using her for their own purposes. They had used her ignorance of the business to force her into this marriage. Their twisted purposes she could only guess at. And somehow they had erected a wall of silence around her which she could not break through to reach any other member of the family who would honestly advise her.

Panic clutched at her heart. She was helpless against the forces closing in on her. As she put her horse into the line following old Philippe up the road skirting the hill vineyards, she saw Henri galloping after them. He was trying to ride past the others. He was riding at Madeleine's side now. Soon he'd be riding at hers!

She brought her whip down with a sharp cut on her horse's flank. The horse sprang forward, broke into a gallop, dashed past old Philippe's slow-pacing mare.

Philippe caught a glimpse of Elizabeth as she galloped past him. He was frightened, thinking that the spirited horse he had given her had taken fright and was running away. Andrew Fairon was just behind him. "Go after her, Andrew, quick!" he shouted. "He may throw her."

Andrew's horse shot out from the line. He had seen Elizabeth give that quick, vicious cut of the whip. She had wanted to escape. He half guessed the reason why. Nobody, he thought, could be blind to what Aunt Martha was about. What was Elizabeth going to do? She was impulsive and hot-headed. He had a sudden fear for her if she were forced into marriage with Henri. He must somehow protect her.

As he came round the curve of the hill he could not see her anywhere. Then from a thicket of manzanita and madrone, too rocky a bit of land to be put under cultivation, he heard her horse whinny. Tying his to a near-by tree he started to search for her. Parting the low undergrowth, he saw her leaning against her horse, crying and beating her fist against his black side.

"Elizabeth," Andrew said gently, "Grandfather sent me. I'll go back to the road and wait for you if you like, but you haven't very much time. They're sure to follow."

Elizabeth looked at him only half comprehending what he was saying. Oh, yes, he was to look after her. She had no illusions any longer over the care lavished upon her. From Grandfather down it was the same thing. No use to look to any of them for real help. A cold violence took hold of her. She would work her own way out.

"Hurry, Andrew, we can get away." Elizabeth mounted quickly as she spoke.

"But Grandfather . . . He'll be worried."

"I can't help it. Please, Andrew!" There was such pleading in her voice that Andrew would have done as she wished, but just then John and Henri appeared around the bend.

"Look," said Elizabeth hurriedly, "pretend that my horse ran away with me. Pretend I didn't do it on purpose, and Andrew, I've got to get away from Henri. You'll help me, won't you?"

As Andrew looked at the agitated girl his affection for her was surcharged with pity. "I'd do anything in the world for you, Elizabeth. What can I do?"

"Tonight," she answered him, "after everybody's asleep, I'll slip out. Can you meet me behind the winery?"

"Yes," said Andrew. "Hello," he called to John and Henri very near now. "Elizabeth's had a spill but she's all right. I've brushed her off and she looks as good as new." *That didn't go over with Henri,* Andrew said to himself. *He looks sullen, not concerned.*

Silently, in a line, Grandfather at the head, Elizabeth beside him, they now rode through the vineyards and back to the house. The sun was well over the mountaintops. It gave evidence of being a hot day—a day of good growth in the vineyards. Already the new spring shoots had hardened into canes. The leaves had thickened and grown dark in color. The grape berries were steadily growing in size.

After breakfast when John rose, meaning to slip quietly away, Philippe said, "John, you don't seem to be very busy. My view of the vineyards this morning leads me to believe we must get out a lot of the poor bearing vines. Now's the time to spot them. Suppose you begin marking them today."

"Very good, sir," replied John, determined not to show his discomfiture over the task. The one thing he must not do was to anger his grandfather at this time.

Andrew felt no such call for silence. Wasn't he more or less in charge here? "Grandfather, won't you let me show you first what tremendous stocks we have on hand?" he asked. Even Andrew felt his grandfather was being difficult, spending John's time on the perfection of the vineyards when John was needed to save the very business. He believed in John's plan in a modified form.

The old man did not answer, thrust his hands into his pockets, stuck out his lips in stubborn disagreement. But as Andrew rose to go to the winery, he flung out, "We still need wine to keep our communion with God, don't we?"

Andrew went out to the cooperage to look over empty barrels, puncheons, and casks to see what repairs needed to be made. *After all*, he said to himself, as he worked, *Grandfather should listen to the other men. He needn't treat Uncle Fran and John like children, even if he does treat me that way.* His resentment over his grandfather's treatment of John was really agitation over his own attitude to John. Loyalty to John was a part of Andrew's childhood. John would be the one to help Elizabeth. Everybody had thought he really cared for her. All of the cousins gave way when he wanted anything. Andrew had not been at home to witness the turn things had taken between Elizabeth and John. Of course Henri was Aunt Martha's choice for Elizabeth. But John had never stood back because of Aunt Martha. He always took what he wanted and got away with it. Why didn't he do it now? Had he, Andrew, the right to take John's place and help Elizabeth?

But could it be that Elizabeth did not care for John any more than she cared for Henri? If so, he, Andrew, was free to love her. Could it be that she loved him? She had chosen him to help her. Andrew's serene nature was deeply disturbed, but gradually the task in hand quieted him.

Out behind the winery, the moss trailed down from the branches of a live oak tree, making a kind of tent lighted only by the waning moon. Under its cover Andrew walked nervously back and forth. An hour. Another. Finally he threw himself on the ground. A third hour passed. The first streak of light was in the east. She wasn't coming.

He started to get up, stopped, one hand resting upon the ground, for he thought he heard a step. No, he guessed not. He got to his feet, dusting his trousers free of dry, brittle grass stems. There was Elizabeth in a white summer dress and a short red jacket to keep off the morning chill. She came running toward him, crying, "Andrew, I couldn't get away before. I came as soon as I could. I could hear Aunt Martha talking to Uncle Francis way into the night. I was afraid she would hear me." Elizabeth was trembling and her voice shook a little.

"My dear," he said, quietly, "tell me everything."

"I don't know how to, Andrew. You're the only one I can turn to. I seemed to be all alone and then, somehow, I knew I could come to you and you would help me."

Andrew's diffident love for her, until now hardly acknowledged to himself, always thought of as the kind of love he bore his three sisters, stirred into something more imperative. He put his hands on her shoulders and looked down into her eyes.

"Do you mind?" he whispered. "Is it all right if I kiss you?"

"Oh, Andrew!" Elizabeth gasped. "Do you love me? Do you really?"

"Yes," said Andrew. "I love you." His kiss was passionate but reverent. Elizabeth rested against him. She was comforted. This love was right, as John's had never been. She could come to love Andrew. She was sure she could when they were married and she was secure from the threat of Henri. Of course she would come to love so gentle and lovely a person as Andrew.

"We'll have to get married right away, Andrew; Aunt Martha has it all planned I'm to announce my engagement to Henri tomorrow night."

"Suppose we announce our engagement at dinner tonight? Wouldn't that settle it?" asked Andrew.

"I don't think so—they wouldn't let us marry, ever. They'd put obstacles in our way. Aunt Martha would manage somehow." Elizabeth was no longer leaning against him, and she was trembling again.

"I suppose we could run away." Andrew seemed to be weighing each word as he said it.

"Oh, Andrew!" Elizabeth exclaimed. "Do you think we could? Could you manage it?" She wanted to run away. She wanted to pay Aunt Martha and John back for what they had planned to do to her. Whatever advantages they had expected to gain for themselves by her marriage to Henri they'd lose, and without warning. They'd have a hard time explaining to the rest of the family why she wasn't marrying Henri, explaining to Henri too. In her anger against Martha and John she forgot to think of her grandfather.

For a long time Andrew did not answer. He hated to do a thing like that to his grandfather. It would mean leaving the work he had been given to do and without warning. Too, Grandfather would not approve of his running off with Elizabeth. It meant marrying her in civil marriage—not a holy marriage in the eyes of his grandfather or his own, either. But he must do it, he saw as he looked at the agitated girl. Elizabeth had first call upon him.

"Of course, I can manage," he said. Once having said it, his resolve strengthened. "Don't worry, dear, I'll find a way."

Elizabeth leaned her head against him murmuring, "Andrew, I need you so." It made him feel stronger than he had ever felt before. He put his arm around her, drew her close. Suddenly his whole being caught fire. She penetrated every corner of his mind and heart and body. Everything she wore, everything she had touched, took on glory. The bit of ground on which she stood seemed to him holy ground. Suddenly his lips were clinging to hers in passionate abandonment.

Elizabeth at last broke the embrace. "We must make our plans."

"I'll plan," said Andrew. "It can't be later than tomorrow afternoon. I have my roadster here. I'll get word to you. Maybe today, maybe not until tomorrow. It's light now.

You'd better get back to the house before anybody's up." He took her hand in farewell, kissing each fingertip, murmuring, "I'll be good to you, my darling." Again Elizabeth felt comforted.

As she came around the corner of the winery, she ran head on into Henri. "Why, what on earth," she exclaimed, "are you doing out this time in the morning?"

"And you?" Henri's expression was too veiled to give her any idea of his mood or his knowledge.

"Grandfather's little companion, you know," she answered airily. "We thought we'd start early this morning to avoid the crowd."

"Are you looking for him out here?" asked Henri. "I think you are more likely to find him in the arbor." Henri, too, meant to carry it off. He had seen Andrew kissing her. He didn't intend to be made a fool of. He'd keep her guessing today while he made his own arrangements.

Elizabeth found Philippe in the arbor in consultation with Uncle Francis.

"Too busy this morning, my *petite*," he called out to her.

The day dragged itself to its finish with no sign from Andrew.

XXXII

THE next morning Elizabeth woke with a sense of oppression. There was no coolness in the air. The heat seemed to have taken up where it had left off the afternoon before, and the sun was already pouring another day's brilliant light down upon the earth. As she had done yesterday, Elizabeth dressed, making no noise that might waken Andrew's sisters, the other occupants of the room. Softly she opened the door, hoping to find the house still asleep, the doors and windows still open to the night air. Instead she found the house already shuttered against the heat and the light. Aunt Martha closed the last door, turned, and raised her hand in warning. "Hush, Elizabeth," she whispered. "Your grandfather can't possibly ride in this heat. I don't want him to waken."

With a sense of frustration Elizabeth turned to go back to her room. She had forgotten about her ride with Philippe. She had meant to find Andrew, but now there was no chance.

"Elizabeth."

She had reached the door of her room when Martha spoke. "We'll have dinner late tonight after the air has cooled. It really will be nicer that way. The hot weather gives me an excuse to have it after dark. Everything will be prettier —even you, my dear. I'm making it the loveliest setting any girl could ask for."

"You don't need to go to all that trouble."

"Oh, but I want to," Martha answered her, her mind already busy with details. "The heat has taken the color out of the flowers, so I'm having some sent up from San Francisco this afternoon. The ices, too. And Grandfather's favorite fish.

Nobody knows, except you and me—and Henri, of course—
about your announcement. And I told Monny. Your grandfather thinks the dinner is entirely for Monny and Nate. I
want you to look your loveliest for Henri's sake. He'll be very
proud of you, my dear. And——"

Martha looked up to find the room empty. Elizabeth had
opened the door of her room and shut it behind her.

Andrew's sisters lay in a row on three cots put up for the
house party. They had insisted Elizabeth occupy the one bed
in the room. Elizabeth sat down upon it, looking at them
sleeping as tranquilly as if nothing were going to happen.
Perhaps nothing was. She found herself trembling. Could
anyone escape the care that Aunt Martha lavished upon them
in her arbitrary management of their lives?

The heat mounted rapidly. By nine, the world was drained
of color. The sky was a dim blue. The foothills were pale slag-
like masses. In the long stretch of the vineyards the leaves
turned their gray undersurfaces up to the fierce light.
Wherever the grapes were bared by the curling leaves they
hung like wrinkled green raisins leaving the gray-green stems
exposed. Sunburn would spoil a great many grapes today,
cut down the harvest.

All day the pool was never vacant. The incessant need to
feel moisture upon their skins sent one after another of the
family to lie under its wet surface. Even old Philippe gave
up his seat in the arbor for one where he could watch the
slim white bodies of those he had begotten trouble the waters
of the pool. His bare feet were thrust into Japanese sandals,
his collar was open at the throat. He held a palmleaf fan in
his hand.

Martha hovered near, desiring above all else that Philippe
commit himself to John's scheme before Elizabeth and Henri
announced their engagement. He must accept John's plan
this morning. Valuable as it was to get Henri into the family,
the announcement might anger the old man to the point of
refusal to enter into any business arrangement which included

Henri. Under Martha's urging, Francis made one last effort to win Philippe over.

"If you can assure me," Philippe said to Francis at last, "that when you buy up the freight cars you will divide shipments with the small fellows who are our neighbors, let them in on the take, as well as the big growers, I'll agree. But I have to know. I don't want anything like that raisin deal. If you think me stubborn," he said at the end of the interview, "my family has made me so."

He waved Francis Fairon away. "Come back when you can assure me of a fair deal for all. But you've only two days in which to do it. If we withdraw from the association I want it to be by tomorrow evening." Old Philippe was too shrewd not to see the advantage in co-operative control of shipments.

All that afternoon of heat they worked to get promises from enough of the men to satisfy Philippe that the small grower would not be left out and that the big growers would be men he respected. Francis went to see the men in the immediate neighborhood. John undertook to call a number of important vineyardists of the San Joaquin Valley on the telephone and gain their consent. Also he believed he could get Nelson Dietrick and a few other small growers to join them. The delicate matter of winning over Petucci and men like Yakowitz who had been victims of the night riders would have to be left to André.

Martha wished the announcement of Elizabeth's engagement could be put off a few more days to give the men more time to complete the list of names, but Henri was adamant. Not another day would he wait. They had Philippe's promise that they might have until tomorrow night to sign the men up. It seemed safe to go ahead with the announcement.

As the day advanced the nerves of the family tautened. Mathilde, new to the family's ways, wondered at the growing tension. As if some crisis were about to be reached, she thought. But maybe it was only the weather. Already she had learned the rhythm of the California valleys—the heat slowly mounting for three days, and mounting with it a tense alertness in everyone. Each day hotter than the day before. Then for three days the heat receding, then mounting again. This day must certainly be the apex of the cycle as this three o'clock hour was the apex of the day's heat.

The water in the pool Mathilde found too warm to refresh her. She flung herself down by the side of old Philippe, suddenly made apprehensive by the tension that lurked in the day. Suppose the old man should tonight, as when he had toasted Lon and herself in welcome, bring out his papers, attempt to surprise his family again with the transparent little ruse of the French labels on the bottles? She could not bear to have him do it again. It made him seem old and senile. Old he was, but not senile. Why did he do it? She did not believe what the others had told her, that he forgot he had gone through with the scene before.

"*Grandpère,*" she cried, "it is to quarrel with you about your wines I would like."

"My wines!" Old Philippe stiffened to attention.

"Beautiful wines," she said, patting his fist that grasped the handle of the fan, "but I think not French wines."

She saw she was making him angry, but before he could speak, she asked, dropping into her native tongue and his:

"Why should the *Grandpère* want them to be French?" she asked. "Why not give them names that would make a connoisseur remember them for themselves?"

"No. No." The old man shook his head. "Only if people cannot tell the difference between my wines and the French wines can I know mine are the best."

"The taste of new land is in your wines, *Grandpère,* as the old earth of France is in the wines of France. Your sons know that. You boast of André's palate—you may be sure he knows his own wines."

"In this, too, then," he answered bitterly, "I cannot believe what my family tell me."

Mathilde had not meant to go so far. Had she spoiled the evening for him and undermined his confidence in his family?

"*Grandpère*, this America, this beautiful California is— what shall I say? So far it has been a banquet table for you all." She broke off with a shrug, then added, "Might it not rather become the table of the Lord's supper?"

She turned to old Philippe, hoping to see in his eyes that he understood her. But his eyes were closed, his white head rested against the scarlet canvas of the chair. Where his shirt was open at the throat she could see the strong white hair clinging in tight curls to his chest. His hands, upon the palm-leaf fan in his lap, though carefully kept now, were still marked by hard work. Something that time could not obliterate. As Elizabeth once had noticed, Mathilde saw how the cuticle was pushed far down beneath his nails, showing how the earth once had pressed in under them. *Such a splendid old man to be so blind,* she thought impatiently. *As full of ferment yet as his wines.*

Lon dropped down beside her. They were silent lest they waken the old man, for the sleep he had simulated when Mathilde was talking to him was real now. Lon, like all the rest, seemed to be under strain, she thought.

Madeleine came through the oleander hedge that separated the vineyards from the garden. Madeleine had not been happy in America. That, Mathilde had known. But she was happy now. She was walking with Henri. *She wants him.* It couldn't be that Henri had shifted his allegiance and now wanted Madeleine. That could not happen without tragedy to Lon's family. Brittle as a goblet happiness seemed today.

At last it grew dark. The stars shone big and luminous, like desert stars. Only when Philippe wakened did Lon and Mathilde rise to go in. They heard a splash at the other end of the pool, then another, and Charles' voice. "Did you get 'em all to sign, John?"

"Not all, but enough so that tomorrow——"

The three went on toward the house. Chu was lighting

the Chinese lanterns swinging from the top of the arbor. Elizabeth hurried toward them from the corner of the house.

"What are you running like that for?" Lon asked, and caught her in his arms. "You ought to be getting dressed, my little. It's your party, really, you know." His voice and his words seemed to carry a hidden command.

He means I'm to accept Henri and tell them tonight, thought Elizabeth. She watched them go on into the house.

Still she had no word from Andrew. She hadn't been able to find him. What should she do? Then she heard the smooth running of a car coming up the driveway and Andrew calling, "Elizabeth, come and help me a minute. I've been to the station to get some things for Aunt Martha."

"I'm coming myself," Martha called, emerging from the arbor, but Elizabeth was there before her.

"Quick, Andrew! Tell me."

"Meet me down the road as soon as you can get there."

"Yes."

"Don't take anything, or Aunt Martha will be on. I've arranged."

"What have you arranged?" Martha asked. Could she have heard what else he had said?

"A little surprise, Aunt Martha, seeing you've done so much for a grand get-together." Andrew patted Martha's shoulder, then loaded her arms with bundles. "Here's everything. Now I've one more errand and then I'm through." His voice was steady and calm.

"Here, let me take some of your bundles, Aunt Martha," said Elizabeth, trying to show no haste.

"No. Go and get dressed."

"Just a minute. I want some oleanders for my hair." Elizabeth walked to the hedge where the blossoms showed white against the darkness.

Again the sound of a motor. In the light shining from the house Elizabeth could see Andrew's father and mother as they stepped out of the car. Nate was with them. And Monny, appearing from somewhere, ran straight into his arms. Then Elizabeth slipped through a break in the hedge. She began to run, guiding herself by the row of the vines which led down to the road. Behind her there was laughter and talk.

Andrew's three sisters took their mother away to their room. "You can dress here and we can talk. Elizabeth won't mind," they told her.

"Where *is* Elizabeth?" exclaimed Suzanne.

"I don't know. Maybe she dressed earlier."

"No, there is her dress on the bed."

"Where's Andrew?" asked their mother.

"Oh, around somewhere. Probably dressing."

"Is he all right?"

"Now, Mother," Suzanne pleaded, "don't worry about Andrew the first thing. Of course he's all right."

Slowly the family gathered. Even Martha could not prod them to haste this evening. Good she had set her dinner late! But at last, one by one, they came down the steps to the arbor. Their feet in the fine gravel set up a soft crunching sound.

Mathilde watched Philippe. As at all their gatherings, he was the pivot around which the family moved. The men were gathered in a knot around him now. The old man's eyes gleamed. She hoped she had not spoiled his evening for him. Still she was glad she had spoken.

"You say they're accepting our proposition? You see," Philippe said to John, "it can be done—the small and the big sharing." John made a bow, pleased in spite of himself at even this much recognition from his grandfather.

"We're all here now," said Martha in her clear commanding voice, "except Elizabeth and Andrew. Andrew had an errand to do. He said he'd be a little late, but what's keeping Elizabeth? Suzanne, run and see."

Henri, standing near his stepmother, suddenly began to be suspicious over the absence of the two. He had intended to humiliate Elizabeth by announcing his engagement to

Madeleine tonight. Could it be he wouldn't have the chance? He had not thought Elizabeth and Andrew would run away. But he was sure now that they had. For a moment his face was distorted with anger. Then, suddenly, he was smiling. His engagement would be the sensation. Elizabeth's and Andrew's elopement would be tame stuff after that—at least in Martha's eyes, and John's.

He moved swiftly to Madeleine's side. Taking her hand he led her to Mathilde and bowed his Old-World bow. "Your daughter," he said, "has done me the honor to say she will marry me, if you will give your consent. This I ask in the name of both of us."

Mathilde opened her mouth to speak, but no words came. She, who had been welcomed in the Rambeau family, was bringing trouble to it through her daughter. And to her husband, for he would suffer if Elizabeth suffered. He had not told her of his talk with Elizabeth.

Lon sensed her distress. "Mathilde, my dear," he said, "may we not together give our consent and our blessing?"

"Yes, Madeleine, our consent and our blessing." But when Mathilde looked at her daughter their eyes met in conflict.

For one swift moment, Martha, standing next to them, did not speak. She was too stunned. Her anger rose, as had Henri's, then, like his, it died away under a like necessity. She must mask her disappointment. Only one bitter glance at John she allowed herself. Hadn't John offered Henri enough? But that would have to wait. She must act quickly now to save the situation.

"How lovely, Henri!" she exclaimed. "Come now, at the dinner you can tell everyone." She knew the news had already spread through the group. "Let us sit down. We'll not wait for Elizabeth and Andrew. I think she must have gone with Andrew on his errand. They'll be here soon."

Old Philippe seated himself in his accustomed seat at the head of the table. He chose among his daughters each evening who should sit in the place of his wife Marie. Tonight

he motioned to Mathilde. Martha and Francis took their
places in the middle of the long table opposite each other.
His granddaughter Monica he placed on his right and Isobel
on his left. The others filled in the places between.

Martha allowed no awkward moment of silence to intervene
before congratulating Henri and Madeleine. Then she turned
to her sister. "You must be very proud of your son, Maria,"
she said.

Thankful to be spared Martha's anger, Maria overdid her
delight, crying, "It's too, too lovely! But what a surprise!"
She stopped, realizing Martha wouldn't want her to express
how great a surprise it was.

Old Philippe had paid little attention to the news. As far
as he was concerned Henri could choose anyone he wanted
for a wife as long as it wasn't Elizabeth. He only hoped Madeleine would take his daughter's stepson off to France with
her, and do it soon. Sorry for Mathilde, though. He'd not
want the boy for a son or a grandson. He hadn't liked Henri's
hanging around Elizabeth. That was over now. But where
was Elizabeth? He looked down the table, seeing her empty
place.

"Where is Elizabeth?" he asked of Monica and then a little
more urgently of Isobel. Neither answered. He asked it of
Martha.

"Suzanne found her lying down. I think it's the heat, Father," Martha answered. She, too, was becoming uneasy over
Elizabeth's absence.

Suzanne opened her mouth to protest. She hadn't said anything of the sort. But she closed it again, seeing her mother
looking at her.

Isobel was thinking, *What is wrong? Suzanne didn't find
her. And where is Andrew?*

"Father, this is your favorite fish. I had it sent down from
San Francisco," Martha was saying.

"Very thoughtful of you, Martha." The old man helped
himself but left the fish untouched on his plate. "Too warm

to eat" was his excuse when Martha chided him for neglecting the especially prepared dish. When the ices came he ate as if to satisfy thirst rather than hunger.

Chu had cleared the table except for a single glass at each place and had poured the wine for the first toast. Old Philippe reached in his pocket for his papers, then withdrew his hand empty.

Mathilde, watching, felt a surge of admiration for him. He was meeting her challenge. *If he toasts me—and he will,* she thought, *I must be ready to say something nice about his wine.*

"May we not begin by drinking the health of Henri and Madeleine?" Martha asked sweetly.

"Umph," said the old man. "Monica and Nate first."

But before Philippe could lift his glass Chu slipped to his side, saying in a low voice, "Meester Rambeau, this a messenger have bring."

John thought, *It's probably from Dad. He said if he got hold of the Armenians this afternoon he'd send word. Henri can go to hell now. I don't need him. Grandfather will kick through.* All through dinner John had said nothing, stunned at first by the turn events had taken. Just what was at the bottom of Henri's sudden shift? But if this was word from his father, everything was all right. Henri could not defeat him and deep within John was a feeling of exultant happiness. He had not lost Elizabeth to Henri.

Slowly Philippe broke the letter's seal, looked at the signature. It was from Andrew.

"I hate to do this, Grandfather," the letter read, "but something had to be done. Elizabeth didn't love Henri and was only going to marry him because Aunt Martha said she could save the family fortune that way. We'll be over the Nevada line when this reaches you. I'm marrying her, Grandfather. I love her. Please don't be angry with us. I'll be back on my job in a couple of days."

The veins on old Philippe's forehead stood out like blue welts. He lifted the glass of wine. Eagerly he drank, sucking up the last drop with his lips, then rose, his eyes fierce and angry. "I have no toast for you," he said. "Francis, help me to my room. Tell them," he commanded, pushing the note toward Isobel. "And you, Martha," he added, "I want to see you."

There was no sound in the arbor except the stiff rustle of the leaves of the grapevine moving against each other in a slight breeze and the crumpling of paper in Isobel's hand.

Martha walked toward the house. Suddenly she made a detour and stopped by Isobel. "Better give the note to me, Isobel. You seem unable to tell us what it says."

Isobel looked at her sister for a long moment. In all the years of their lives Isobel had accepted Martha's rule happily and naturally. But that was over now. "Yes, read it," she said in a low bitter tone.

"Fiddlesticks!" snapped Martha after reading what Andrew had written. "There's nothing so tragic. It's just that Andrew and Elizabeth have eloped. Why they thought they had to do such a common thing, I don't know. It could have been arranged. Father could have spoken to the bishop and they could have been married in the church. Naturally you, of course, are disappointed in your son, Isobel. And you, Lon, in your daughter."

She turned and went up the steps and into her father's room. He was lying on the bed. Never in all her life had she seen him lying down. An odd modesty about him had made him exclude his children from any such intimacy. Even in these late years he had always dismissed her at the threshold of his room, asking for Chu. Tonight, he was indifferent to his former punctilious standards. He must, indeed, be upset. For a moment she was frightened. Then seeing him in this unaccustomed position, she realized how short of stature he was—just a thin little old man.

He can't rule me now, she thought with a momentary throb

of regret. *I don't worship him any more the way I used to.
It's taken me my whole life to find out that I don't need to—
that I've always been the stronger.*

"Martha." His voice came weak, muffled, lying as he was
with two pillows under his head, which forced it forward.

Had he always slept doubled up like that? He shouldn't.

"I told you," he said, "when Elizabeth first came, that I
would not allow you to break her. Rule her you would, as
you have all of us. I asked you to hold yourself in control.
You have not. You have broken her, Martha. And you have
pushed Andrew into marrying within the third degree of
blood kinship without permission."

As she stood speechless before him, he went on: "Power is
what you've always wanted, Martha. You've broken all the
family to your will. Made Maria into a poor thing, sucked
the life out of your husband. It's why Lon went away when
he was a boy."

"I don't see why you are accusing me like this, Father,"
said Martha in a low, hard tone. "If you think I value wealth
and power too much, whose fault is it? You forget I was
old enough to watch you when you were still fighting to get
money out of these valleys. Don't think I don't know a lot
of things you pretend you have forgotten. It's time to do
penance yourself, Father. You can leave mine to me."

"You are a wicked woman, Martha. You will be punished."

"You can leave *that* to God," Martha answered him. "I've
no doubt that He'll have a better sense of proportion than
you, not send out His bolts of lightning because two cousins
have married each other under the civil law."

All at once Martha saw that the old man's hands trembled.
Her habitual care of him took precedence over everything else
in her mind. "You ought to be asleep, Father," she told him.
"I'll send Chu to you."

With Philippe and Martha gone from the table, the family
party disintegrated. Francis excused himself to call André
over the telephone. Business had to go on, whatever the

younger generation chose to do about marriage. Charles and
Suzanne and her sisters went off to the pool, uneasy and embarrassed, anxious to see no more of the unveiled emotion of
their elders. Monny and Nate took hands as they left the table
and moved off into the darkness.

Andrew's mother and father went to their room. Ronald
Fairon wanted to say some word of comfort to his wife but
he did not know what to say.

"Why did Andrew think he had to run off without telling
us?" Isobel asked him as soon as the door was closed.

"Elizabeth will make him a good wife," was all Ronald
could offer as comfort.

"She doesn't love him, Ronald, I'm sure she doesn't."

When the others had gone from the table, Henri moved
over, taking the empty chair by John. "This settles it, doesn't
it? The deal's off."

"If it's ever been on," John retorted.

"Oh, it was on, all right. Until I changed my mind. Madeleine——"

"You don't fool me, Henri. You'd have taken Elizabeth if
you could have got her."

"And you? Would you have offered her to me if you could
have had her yourself?"

"Oh, shut up." John's emotions had never been in such a
turmoil. Not only had Elizabeth slipped completely from
his grasp, but Andrew, one of the "meek" Fairons, as John
contemptuously phrased the gentleness of the Fairons, had
walked off with her.

"I'm done with this country," Henri went on blandly. "I
mean to sell every bit of land I can. Madeleine and I are going
to live in Paris."

"Why don't you make it the Riviera?" John asked. "That
is, if you really think you can sell your vineyards with the
grape business shot to hell. Who is going to buy a huge estate
like yours?"

"My dear fellow," said Henri in his most patronizing tone

"Old Rambeau is right. The day for the small fellow is coming. There are a hundred Armenians, Japs and what-not who'd jump at the chance to get a few of my acres."

"You mean cut up your estate? Bring in a lot of riffraff right next to us?"

"Us?" Henri lifted his eyebrows. "I thought you were going to break with traditional father and son stuff or rather grandfather and grandson. Or do you suddenly wish to be taken back into the fold?" mockingly he added.

As John did not reply, Henri flicked the ash from his cigarette and strolled over to Madeleine and Mathilde, who had risen and stood talking together. "My dears," he said, taking an arm of each, "Paris in another month, if we can arrange everything."

Finally only Lon and John were left at the table. Lon twirled his glass, looked down into his untouched wine. *I could have saved Elizabeth and the whole family from this. I suppose I couldn't stand up against Martha. Even after all these years, I couldn't do it.*

To hell with it, thought John, filling his glass again and drinking his wine in one gulp much as his grandfather had. *I know I can get Dietrick and a few more of the small growers in. I can make a go of it with the old man. I was a fool to defy him and take up with that rat, Henri.* He glanced at the watch on his wrist. If he started out now, he would be in Fresno in the morning.

He hunted up Francis. "I think I'll go on home, get in touch personally with the rest of the men. That is, if you want me to."

"Fine," Francis answered him. "Your father thinks he has Yakowitz and his crowd lined up. If you can get Dietrick's crowd to go in with us, we can meet your grandfather's requirements."

Elizabeth and Andrew felt their own labored breathing and the labored effort of the car as they reached the top of the mountain pass that would lead them out of California. Andrew was thinking, *The morning sun is filling the great bowls cut from the mountains by the Sacramento and San Joaquin Rivers.* These two valleys separated, yet merging into each other, had held the whole of his life until now. This was his wedding day. His heart seemed almost to stop beating. No longer separateness—instead he would be merged in the beauty that was Elizabeth. He looked down at her. She was turned toward him, her head pillowed on her arm that lay lightly across the back of the seat. She was sleeping as serenely as a child. He wished she would wake. She seemed to have left him in the remoteness of sleep.

XXXIII

THE house hardly settled down before it was astir again. Each member of the household, impelled by his own urgent affairs, felt the necessity to get away ahead of the other members of the family.

Henri meant to slough off the Rambeaus as quickly as possible, get out of the San Joaquin Valley forever, sell that part of his father's land he was free to sell. The house belonged to Maria until her death, but the vineyards were his and his alone. He had a great many things to arrange. He left immediately after breakfast, taking Madeleine with him without her mother's knowledge.

Old Philippe had given orders the night before to Chu that he wanted to start back at daylight. He meant to put through the final arrangements to market his grapes in the East through the association. He would see to every detail himself. He did not intend to be hoodwinked any longer. He understood now what Martha had hoped to accomplish through Elizabeth's marriage to Henri. The ruthlessness of the plan shocked him.

But Philippe did not start at dawn as he had hoped to do, for as he came wearily from his room he met Martha dressed and hatted for a journey. "Where are you going?" he asked.

"I imagine where you are. There's no use your hurrying, Father; Lon and Mathilde aren't up yet. They'll have to go in your car. Francis and I can't take them in the runabout."

"I didn't think they'd be going back today. I want you all to stay here as we planned, Martha. I'm going because of business."

"As we planned!" said Martha bitterly. "Nobody wants

to stay. Isobel told me last night she was taking the girls
back, and Maria asked to go with her. She said Henri needed
her help getting things ready."

"Ready for what?"

"To sell his land."

"To do what!"

"Sell his land."

"Who does he think is going to buy it?" snorted old Philippe
with something of his usual spirit. But when, later, followed
by Mathilde and Lon, he went out to his car, he walked with
uncertainty. *Why,* thought Mathilde with pity, *he is really
feeble and yet yesterday he did not seem so.*

Philippe had used his energy these last months with a pro-
fligacy which had deceived those around him into believing
that he drew from a deep reservoir of strength. Under the
strain of the shock he had received the evening before, his supposed vitality proved to be but a final spurt of energy through
the closing valves of life.

Lon and Mathilde watched him anxiously, wondering sometimes if he could possibly survive the long tedious drive.
But as they drew near his home, he rallied, seemed almost himself again.

John had the start by many hours. If he could get the names
by five o'clock his grandfather would be pledged to abide by
his promise of yesterday. But he wanted to secure them earlier
if possible, figuring that his grandfather, upset by last evening's happenings, would return home immediately so as to
be ready to act at five in favor of the association. If he had
the names by the time the old man arrived, his father and
uncles would be in a position to hold Philippe to their plan.

By noon he had them all except Dietrick's. With Dietrick
he ran into unexpected difficulties. Stubborn fool! He had
been all out for co-operation in the raisin deal and now he
refused to co-operate in a deal on wine grapes. John had left
Dietrick to the last, thinking it would be a matter of minutes

to get his approval, and that he could see him on his way to the winery where he intended to hand the completed list to his father.

Seeing Dietrick out in the field as he drove up, John stopped his car part way down the drive and, despite the noon heat, raced down a long aisle of vines to the place where Dietrick was working. "Hi, Nelson!" he called out.

Dietrick raised his head, then lowered it again as a bull might have. John saw he was catching him in a bad mood. For a moment he thought of Buz. If she were home now she could help him. She was the only one who could ever manage Dietrick. Good hard sense in that fluffy head of hers. John hadn't thought of her for months. Even now he thought of her only in connection with the business he had in hand.

"I dunno," said Dietrick when John explained the plan. "You tie up a lot of money buying up cars and then seems like you might not get away with it. Supposin' there's other cars can be got hold of? You'd be the fellow keepin' the price up for the other crowd. A lot of buyers around here already, jest the same as last year, promising good prices. I 'low as how I'll jest do my own business my own way." Nelson Dietrick was a born trader and he felt he'd rather trust his own horse sense. Last year it had netted him big returns. "Grapes are up and they'll stay up," he ended.

"How do you know they will? You've heard what that new association is trying to do?" John asked.

"Yes, they've been around to see me—" Dietrick gave his shoulders a forward thrust—"but I ain't having anything to do with them. They're fools."

"They may be," said John, "but they can spoil the market for little fellows like you." As soon as he said it John knew he had made a mistake calling Dietrick a little fellow. He should have played upon his importance. A flush had spread over Dietrick's dry leathery skin, and he kept hitching his shoulders in the peculiar way he had when he was angry.

"You might think it over," said John, realizing it was worse than futile to say more at present. "I'll go along now. Let me know by four if you change your mind."

There was no answer from Dietrick. He went on examining his vines. He had found some mildew among them. That damn wop he had hired to sulphur them had played him dirt. Since Buz had gone away—— Thinking of Buz started another line of angry thought. Buz married to a wop. Buz was a wop now. Dark thoughts circled and recircled in his mind.

John was desperate. He must get Dietrick's signature. If anybody could do anything with Nelson, Buz could, John said to himself. Let's see, her name was Griffanti now. He'd go and see her. Three hours yet to work on Dietrick. Close work, but she might bring him around. He hoped she had a telephone. That would make it easy to get her address.

In the outskirts of Fresno he stopped his car, went into the drugstore on the corner, hunted in the telephone book. Yes, here it was—Luigi Griffanti. Lucky break, the place was just around the corner. He wouldn't bother with his car. He could walk faster.

A flat over a garage. He ran up the flight of steps at the side of the building, knocked at the entrance door. He could hear a baby crying, then the soft rustle a woman makes moving about, putting things to rights before opening the door.

He hadn't any time to waste. "Buz!" he shouted. "It's John Rambeau. I'm in a hurry!"

Luigi, at work in the garage, heard the name John Rambeau and the command to open the door. The name ran through his mind like a sudden burst of lightning illuminating his suspicions. John was the name Buz had given the baby. He had been a fool not to see all the time. John Rambeau demanding to be let in just as if he owned the place. Perhaps he did own Buz.

Just as Buz opened the door John heard a voice behind him saying, "You get out of here and stay out. And don't you ever dare come near my wife again."

He turned to confront Luigi's blazing eyes. "Keep your shirt on, Griffanti. I'm not interested in your wife. I'm here on business. I want Buz to help me out with her father."

"That don't go down with me." Luigi's voice held an ominous note. "On your way—unless you want me to settle with you right now." The suspicion and uncertainty of months was turned into definite conviction. Buz had played around with Rambeau before she was married, and she was doing it now. Hot savage anger leaped up in Luigi. He wanted to kill John, he wanted to kill Buz, he wanted to kill the baby.

John, seeing the look in Luigi's eyes, seeing his hand go to his hip pocket, delivered a stinging blow on Luigi's wrist, another that sent him staggering against the stair rail. He heard Buz cry out.

Before Luigi had time to rally, John ran down the stairs and around the corner. Jealous fool. How would he line up Dietrick now? Suddenly he was conscious of the heat and his own fatigue. He hadn't eaten since dinner last night. There was a little restaurant down the street. He would get himself a cup of coffee and think what to do next. He wondered if perhaps Mrs. Dietrick could do anything with Nelson. Probably he should have tried her instead of wasting time going after Buz. Mrs. Dietrick hardly ever spoke, but sometimes women like that had a lot of influence with their husbands.

He had a feeling as he walked toward the restaurant that someone was following him. The heat, he guessed, was getting him as nervous as a girl out alone at night. Or could it be——? Certainly not. Luigi wasn't that much of an ass. *Unless he thought I was trying to mess things up for him and Buz. In such a case——*

He whirled suddenly to find himself again face to face with Luigi. Luigi's hand was raised and John could see the barrel of a small automatic gleam in the sun. He struck at the man's wrist. Luigi's hand dropped but with the weapon still in it. There was a sharp not very loud crack.

John gave a convulsive leap into the air, then collapsed in a heap on the pavement. For a second, time was a blank. But that second had set far off his once splendid animal vigor from his now wracked and tortured flesh. Agonizing pain throbbed in his back, reached down his legs into his toes and shot up to his brain.

Luigi ran back to the garage, up the stairs, his anger still burning him up. And then, when he was inside the door of his house—sudden sanity, sudden panic.

"Buz," he whispered, "I didn't know what I was doing."

"Luigi, you didn't . . . didn't hurt him, did you?"

"I . . . guess I did. Honest, Buz, I didn't know what I was doing."

"What'll we do, Luigi?"

"We got to get away. Yes, we got to get away. You and the baby and me. Quick, Buz. We got to get started in the car."

Buz was all at once the mature one. Loyalty to the man she had married sprang up in her and also the knowledge of how best to protect him. "You got to go by yourself, Luigi. They'd find you sure with me and the baby along. But I won't leave you, Luigi. In Mexico you'll be safe. Baby and me'll join you." There was something in Buz, now Luigi was in trouble, that made her stick to him.

Quickly she went about putting a few clothes into a bag. She thrust it into his hand and with it a little money she had hid from him with which to buy a new hat. "Look, a month from today you come for us to that town you took me to once over the border. Now hurry."

XXXIV

BY FAST driving Francis and Martha Fairon and Chu had reached home an hour before old Philippe. After seeing that Francis went immediately to the winery to help André with the last growers, Martha put the house in readiness. There were flowers in the vases, tea was ready to serve in the shaded ell of the house, Chu stood at the door to help his master when Lon drove up.

"Tea, Father?" Martha asked, as Philippe, leaning on Chu, entered the house.

"No, I don't want any," he said. "I'm expecting André. Send him to my room when he gets here." He leaned heavily upon Chu as he went down the hall toward his own room.

Mathilde excused herself, too. The heat, light, and anxiety had given her a headache.

"Give me something cold, Martha," said Lon. "Then I'll go and look after Mathilde." He had not seen Martha since last evening. Although he had no desire to be alone with her, he lingered a little, wanting to establish the amenities. There was no use to quarrel with her over Elizabeth. The past could not be undone.

He need not have concerned himself. Martha was too occupied with the possible outcome of the grape deal to give him more than a passing thought. "You didn't see Francis by any chance, did you, as you drove in?" she asked. "He promised to be back by the time Father got here. Oh, there he is now," she added, relief in her voice.

As Francis entered, he stopped David who was coming toward him carrying a tray full of tumblers of iced tea. "Has John called me?" he asked.

"No, sir," David answered.

"You are sure Chu hasn't taken any message? John said he would call, either here or at the winery, by four at the latest. He hasn't called the winery."

"No, sir." David showed neither by tone nor facial expression that rumor already had it John Rambeau could not be expected to call, perhaps ever again.

"Sit down, Fran," Martha commanded. "It won't help matters any for you to use up your energies walking around. You need something to eat."

Francis obeyed, picked up a sandwich from the tea tray, accepted the glass David handed him. Then he set it down and looked at his watch. The thing would go by default in another half hour. Philippe had specified that they must ask for the release of their crop before five if they were going to withdraw. Strange John hadn't at least left word where to reach him.

It was a quarter to five when the telephone at last rang. Francis, not waiting for David to answer it, hurried across the terrace and into the hall where the telephone stood.

Martha made no pretense of keeping up her conversation with Lon. She leaned forward as if to catch the voice at the other end of the wire. Why did it take John so long to explain? Finally they heard Francis saying in a flat tone, "Thank you for calling."

"Evidently we've failed," said Martha, staring at Lon accusingly. Her stout compact person sagged a little, then suddenly she was erect again. What was Francis saying?

"When did you say it happened? . . . Where is he now? . . . I'll get there as soon as I can."

"What's happened?" she cried, hurrying to Francis who was hanging up the receiver.

"John has been hurt."

"How?" demanded Martha.

"Shot," answered Francis, in the same flat tone he had used in speaking over the telephone. "Some disgruntled grapegrower, they think. You know, ever since that other affair some of the Italians and Armenians have been resentful. Probably they have worked it out among themselves that we are trying to keep them out of our deal."

"Is it fatal?" asked Lon.

"They don't know." Francis turned toward his brother-in-law. "Can you find André and tell him? He was out seeing some of the men when I left the winery. Nobody has been able to locate him. Try to find him. They want me at the hospital as they can't get hold of him."

Martha stood crumpling her napkin.

"How horrid," she said at last. "Our name mixed up with a shooting affair."

"How about Father?" Lon asked. "Shall we tell him now or wait?"

"Wait," said Martha.

Francis' first thought as he left the house was of Charlotte. The news had loosened his control of his thoughts, usually closely guarded against thinking of her. He must get hold of Monny and warn her, so she would keep the news from her mother until they knew something definite. So thinking, he turned in at the André Rambeau drive. But Monny had not yet returned. Should he tell Charlotte, rather than let her hear the news over the telephone as she might from some unwise friend? Remembering his talk with Charlotte he recalled her sense of reliance upon André. She had made plain to him the trust and comradeship which had grown up between them. Was he, then, at this moment when André might mean most to her, trying to rob André? Quickly he stepped into his car and drove off.

Francis and André reached the hospital simultaneously. "I'm so glad you're here!" Francis exclaimed. "They've been hunting you everywhere. I was going to do what I could until you came. I'll go along now."

"No, please, don't," André put his hand on his brother-

in-law's arm, a rare gesture with him. "I need you," he added
simply.

"Dr. Regis will see you now," said the nurse and she turned
to lead them toward a door at the left. The doctor was seated
at a desk writing and he did not look up at once. Then hand-
ing what he had written to the nurse, he glanced from one
to the other questioningly.

"I am John Rambeau's father," said André, "and this is
his uncle, Mr. Fairon."

"When your son," the doctor said, speaking to André, "was
brought in here several hours ago, he asked me to take charge
of his case——"

"How serious is it?" asked André, in his anxiety not waiting
for the doctor to finish.

"You know the nature of the injury?" asked Dr. Regis.

"Shot, I understand," said André.

"The bullet struck him," Dr. Regis explained, "in the side
and lodged in the spine. As the course of the bullet does not
lead either through the abdominal or chest cavity, we did not
feel justified in an immediate operation. There was considerable evidence of shock at first, but apparently your son is
rallying pretty well from that."

If he would only say how serious it is, thought André. *I
can bear anything but this uncertainty.*

Francis, noticing André's hands clenched tightly on the
chair arms, realized he found it all but impossible to ask the
things he wanted most to know. "I think," Francis said,
"we'd like it if you would not spare us, but tell us just how
bad it is. Will he be crippled?"

"I will tell you," Dr. Regis answered, "as much as I know.
The long nerve trunk to his left leg is evidently injured. On
the left side he is now paralyzed from his waist down. There
is some swelling and that may account for the paralysis. In
that case it is only temporary."

"But it could be permanent?" said André, pressing to know
the worst.

"Yes, it could be permanent," Dr. Regis answered, "but I

am not at all certain. I am a general practitioner. I should like consultation on the case. I would suggest that you call a neural surgeon from either San Francisco or Los Angeles," he added, thinking there was no need to save expense with anyone bearing the name of Rambeau.

"Call the best man you know," André answered.

"I'll arrange it," said the doctor rising. "And now would you like to see your son? He has been asking for you."

They saw John before he knew they were there. He lay in the one position allowed him, flat on his back, his head sunk in the pillow, his eyes fixed on a spot on the ceiling. Already, in the few short hours since his injury, his look of superb physique had left him. His cheeks were hollowed, his nostrils pinched, his lips were bloodless and set against his teeth in suffering. His closed eyelids looked as if they had been bruised.

"John," said his father, leaning over him, "Francis and I are here. How did it happen? Can you tell us without tiring yourself?"

John did not speak.

"Did it have to do with the grape business? Was it on account of that?"

"I went to see Buz Dietrick about her father signing. I got the other names."

"You mean it was Luigi Griffanti who shot you?" André questioned.

"Yes."

"This is the sort of violence that's got to come to an end. This time we'll get a conviction," André exclaimed. "We ought to fight this case through to the bitter end."

"Oh, let him go." John's voice rose on a note of excitement. "We don't want to air our private affairs in the courts. I'll be up and about in a little while. Forget it."

André wondered then if Luigi might have had reason for shooting. "I ought to get home to Charlotte," he said to Francis on the way out of the room. "Monny wasn't back when I telephoned the house."

"I'll stand by here if you'd like me to," Francis volunteered. "Undoubtedly you ought to be with Charlotte." At this time when both of them were needed to protect Charlotte, the two men relinquished a silent jealousy each had held for the other.

André came out of the hospital to find it was barely dark. He had thought of the time as late in the night, so much had life changed for him in the hour. He wished he could put off telling Charlotte until morning. Both of them would be better able to talk of it then.

His wife's room was brightly lighted, as usual, but the hall was dark, except for a dim square where the last of the twilight showed the window on the landing. The house was very still. Monny and Charles, then, had not returned. He swerved from his course for a moment. Charlotte would not expect him yet. Better not go up until his usual time. He longed to sit in his accustomed chair in the library, pick up his evening paper, feel its familiar surface, taste the port placed for him every evening, surrender himself for a while to the commonplace. But he kept on up the stairs, opened the door of his wife's room, shut it behind him, and stood just inside.

"André, I've been waiting for you." Charlotte's voice was both grave and tender. So she knew. Suddenly all his anxiety for her was swallowed up in his need of her. He hurried across the room, dropped down by her bed, buried his face close to her hand. Hard sobs shook him. Quietly she smoothed his hair with the short stroke left to her in the movement of her hand.

"I'm sorry, Charlotte," he said. He got up from his knees and sat down on the side of her bed. "I came home to make it easier for you. I've only made it harder."

"It's sweet, my dear, once to have you need me."

"Is it? But I always need you—you know that."

So they avoided for the moment the grief which had come to them both, held outside it by their love for each other.

Charlotte spoke finally. "Tell me, André, will he . . ." Her voice faltered. "I know he will live but will he be crippled?"

"They don't know yet. They are sending for a specialist. Even he can't say for a few days until the inflammation goes down."

"But you think he will be?"

"Yes."

"Badly? Please don't try to spare me, André."

"His left leg is now paralyzed. It may always be so."

"But he can work?"

"Yes, at any job which uses his hands and his brain."

"Just one more question, André. Will he suffer much?"

"Now, yes. But whether he will later, I don't know."

"He has always avoided suffering. That's why he's avoided me ever since he was a little boy. I don't know how he'll bear it, André."

So Charlotte realizes that it is more than thoughtlessness which has kept John away from her, thought André.

The night was warm and very dark. There was an old moon and it did not rise until late. Charlotte, long after André had left her, lay awake. She must have slept finally, for the struggle began which so often came to her in sleep. She felt the hampering of her heavy and twisted body, and then release as she climbed up out of the influence of pain, let loose in sleep, controlled by her will when awake.

As the night advanced toward dawn, light seemed slowly to be poured into the Valley. On many nights Charlotte had seen this mystery. But now the Valley seemed an unfathomable well of light, timeless, depthless, and herself a part of the timeless, depthless world.

Whether she slept or lay awake she scarcely knew, but through her mind in thin wisps of memory drifted her own and her children's lives, then events farther back—hers through the memories of another generation—the coming of her own and her husband's families to these valleys. Back still farther into the memories of the two nations of France and Spain her mind delved. Her family going from southern France to Spain, some of them to Ireland, making an Irish branch of the family, and some to America—she and her children the last of the American line.

Her memories slipped back into the cloudy recesses of her mind and she was again conscious only of John. She saw him now clearly defined. John born to her as the result of her union with André. She had found her way into loving André in loving his son—the most perfect of babies growing into the physically perfect boy. When he was ten had come the crippling of her body.

Since then she had been able to reach him only through Monica. Would she now be able to reach him herself? Charlotte, knowing the passionate nature which he inherited both from her and from the Rambeaus, guessed why he had been shot. A man like Luigi had a reason when he shot a neighbor. But would John see his injury as of his own making, or would he consider himself a victim of fate—believe her suffering had caught up with him in spite of all his efforts to hold it away?

How could she communicate with him, communicate what she had learned about suffering and limitation? That could not be transmitted to him through Monica. There was no language which would express to the uninitiated the first frantic struggle of the spirit to refuse the bitter draft of suffering and inadequacy. How warn him of the dangers of hopeless resignation? How show him the necessity to clear the mind of the opiate of that resignation? How explain to him the long day-in, day-out struggle to balance acquiescence —which must never turn back to resignation—with defiance which must never advance into rebellion?

André in his room adjoining Charlotte's was awakened by her sobbing. He was used to the stifled sounds of her restless movements when she could not sleep, stealthy efforts to rest her head on the pillow, then off it, and yet not waken him, countless movements that, in many years, had become precious to him for they meant to him the presence of his wife. Never had she communicated to him a sense of hopeless sickness, instead some peculiar power that mastered illness.

But now as he listened to her sobbing, fright took possession of him. If Charlotte acknowledged defeat, then were they all defeated. He rose and went to her. He lay down beside her, fitting his own body to the tragic curves of hers. After a little they both fell asleep.

XXXV

LATE that evening when Francis came in Martha learned what David had known as he served them in the afternoon. Luigi Griffanti had shot John. Why, Francis did not know, other than that the story was going around that it had something to do with jealousy over Buz.

"But Buz is married to Luigi!" exclaimed Martha. "Surely John——"

In the last two days Martha had glimpsed a time when the Rambeaus would no longer be richer than their neighbors. Now she had to accept the fact that the Rambeau name was being bandied about the countryside in common gossip.

"He will live," Francis told her, "but he may be crippled."

"Why didn't he die?" cried Martha. "It would be the most decent thing he could do! Living and crippled, nobody will ever be able to forget that he and a fellow like Griffanti quarreled over a common little slut."

"I think you've no right to call Buz that, nor to wish John dead." Francis hated to have Martha say such things. "Although I think John would choose death rather than to live and be a cripple. It's worse than death for him." Francis sat down and covered his eyes from the light.

"John has lost us the corner on grapes we might have had, too," Martha added in a bitter tone.

Francis gave a start. In his anxiety over John he had forgotten, as he guessed André had, that their best hope of making money this year was gone.

"Who is going to tell Father?" Martha asked after a pause. "I absolutely refuse to do it."

"Don't think he doesn't know. Chu undoubtedly has told him. I have a feeling that David knew it this afternoon."

"Father had his dinner sent to his room. And he's never done that before." Martha took comfort in the thought that it was because of John he had wanted to be alone, not because he was still angry with her.

Chu had, indeed, told his master. Before Francis had received the news Philippe had heard the story of the shooting. Until late in the night the old man had sat erect in his chair by the window, looking out at the garden and the vineyards he and his wife Marie had created. The spirit and the body, which had warred in Philippe in such constant duality ever since ambition awoke in him years ago in the cathedral, cried out now against the embodiment of himself he saw in both John and Martha. It was as if the strong fierce sunlight of this New World had developed into a lush growth qualities of his own he had always meant to keep down. He must cling to this life, set things right before he left it.

But there was a moment that evening which he could not remember. Only Chu knew what had happened. Perhaps a little stroke, Chu said to himself. For a few days Philippe kept to his bed refusing to see any of his family. When he did at last consent to see them he did not speak of John's injury.

After the first day none of the family mentioned it. They were like a tree which has been defaced and seeks to grow its bark back over the scar.

XXXVI

Philippe did not die easily. Nor did John come back to life easily. John had no wish to live and Philippe no wish to die.

Silently Philippe carried on his fight, struggled each day with Chu's help to get out of bed, sit in his straight-backed chair by the window. Only then would he allow any of his family to enter his room.

John struggled hard to die as he lay in the hospital. His mind was befogged by both pain and drugs, and yet he was conscious that each day he gained a little in strength. That splendid animal vitality in which he had always taken such pride took the matter out of his hands and decided for him that he would live.

Before the neurologist went back to San Francisco he told John that he would never regain the use of his leg. He made no attempt to soften the blow. A strong man like John Rambeau, he felt, should know just what was in store for him. That John had heretofore fought no battles except with his muscles, the doctor failed to realize. "I am going to tell you," he began, "just what the X-rays show." He explained to him, then, the cold facts of science. "You are lucky that you did not lose the use of both legs," he ended.

Monica, sitting in the waiting-room ready to go in to John when the doctor left, tried to prepare herself for the biggest struggle she had ever had with her brother. How possibly could she help him?

But when she stood by his bed looking down at him, for an instant she was deluded. Already suffering had fined down his face, giving him a new quality. Perhaps, like their mother, he would be able to meet this trouble.

Monica hesitated to speak, feeling suddenly that she was trespassing upon John's privacy, a privacy that he could not now defend. If it had been wholly her own idea to come, she believed she would have withdrawn. The intuitive understanding between herself and John told her that anything she might say just now would be an intrusion. Suffering had its own reserves. She had learned through attendance upon her mother something of this. And yet it was her mother who had begged her to penetrate any barriers John might erect. For her mother's sake she must go through with it.

"John," she said, sitting down in the chair the nurse placed for her, "the doctor has told me what he has told you. I——" her throat was tight. "It won't be so bad when once—when once you are up and about."

John did not stir or take his eyes from the ceiling. Only his mouth moved, twisting in a mixture of bitterness and pain. "Don't kid yourself. I don't." As he spoke, he pushed the button of the bell which lay under his hand.

"You called me?" The nurse trod so lightly that Monica did not hear her enter.

"Her voice jars the bed," he said, never moving his gaze from the ceiling. With this abrupt dismissal of Monica, John closed his heart against every human contact.

A long thin bar of sunlight shone at the bottom of the drawn curtain, showing him that just outside this darkened room was the hot burning day, the kind he had always loved. In it Monica could ride and swim and love Nate. It was pain for him to think of riding a horse, sitting a saddle. Pain to think of the water in the pool, its gentle slap against his skin. Every sensation was pain. A confused angry knowledge of Monica and Nate in the urgency of their love. A confused angry memory of Elizabeth and Andrew. Agony to think of Elizabeth. And yet in his fog of drugs and pain she was now sitting by his bed, she it was he had sent out of his room, she who returned, escaping nurse and doctor, her blue eyes regarding him with scorn and pity.

When Elizabeth and Andrew returned to Philippe's northern vineyards they found only Greta and Diener. Elizabeth had never been here without Philippe. His absence seemed to reproach her. She had done a cruel thing to run off with Andrew. She must write her grandfather at once.

The beginning she found difficult. But once she had explained the confused issues of her hasty marriage, she wrote easily and naturally. There was a real bond between these two.

She devoted most of her letter to Andrew. "He is very good to me, Philippe, and I think him your finest grandson. He is working very hard to make up for the days he was away. I believe he is going to be a good vintner. He says that you are his ideal."

Only after she had finished the letter and sealed it did she realize how much she had talked about her young husband. It had been like a renewed pledge of loyalty to Andrew, a guard against her thoughts of John since she had heard of his injury. She had felt a poignant grief, remembering John's vigorous animal strength.

XXXVII

Chu had news for Philippe this morning, but important as it was, he first must see that his master was dressed for the day. It was a difficult hour for both of them. Philippe found it hard to acknowledge even to his servant, almost his second self, that he needed help. It humiliated him to expose his failing strength even to Chu's fiercely loyal eyes. Chu must help him in and out of his bath because of his trembling legs. He must help him dress because of his uncertain hands, inadequate for handling the buttons on his shirt or the tying of his tie. Hard for Chu Rambeau to give these ministrations, see the proud old man humbled. They went through with Philippe's morning toilet in silence, each with his lips grimly set. There was mingled hostility and trust in Philippe's old eyes, blank acceptance of fate in Chu's scarcely younger ones.

Even when Chu had dressed Philippe in one of his summer suits with soft bow tie to match his shirt, the old Chinese turned his back in order that his master might drink his coffee with no one to witness the shaking of his hand as he lifted the cup to his lips.

At last Chu heard the clatter of Philippe's cup against the saucer. The ordeal was over for this time, and he turned, saying, "A little news this morning, Meester Rambeau. Henri, the what you call Don, would sell his father's land."

"So I have heard, but who is rich enough around here to buy it?" asked Philippe with some scorn.

"Big man not necessary. Plenty small man. Japan man, Armenian man, plenty man." Chu said nothing of his own desire to buy a few acres in David's name. He must wait first

230

and see what the head of his family, Philippe Rambeau, wished about the land. Wait even though David urged him to take his chance and buy now while he had the opportunity. "What do you owe to this family?" David had demanded. "Think how America has treated you. Think how it is treating me, an American by birth. Think how our people die shut up to that small strip of land in San Francisco. The girl I want to marry lives there and is not well. I want to study medicine and return to my own people."

"What does he ask for it, Chu?" Philippe's words struck across Chu's thoughts of David.

"He talk big price."

"If I know Henri, he'll tuck on the price," snorted Philippe.

Chu looked at his master. He was alive again as he had not been for days. Every feature was clearly defined once more.

Land! Philippe Rambeau's life these last months had shrunk to smaller and smaller circumference as one after another of his family had withdrawn their wills from his. His son and sons-in-law made business decisions of their own. Martha schemed and planned on her own. John tried to outwit him. Elizabeth and Andrew had taken matters into their own hands. It was as if layer after layer of himself had been peeled away. But land! He had not bought land for many years. If he could not live on in his family, it suddenly seemed to him he could live on in the land. Whatever his sons and grandsons might do, there would be the land. Some day this region he had developed might be the greatest wine-producing district of the world, his name immortalized in the Rambeau vineyards, an indestructible Philippe Rambeau.

"Chu, Chu, where are you?"

"I come." Chu made a feint of crossing the room. He had been standing very near. Could it be Meester Rambeau could not see him?

"Chu, speak to Mr. Fairon before he goes out. Tell him I want to see him on important business."

To Francis Fairon when he came Philippe issued instructions, the first he had given in days. "I want to see all the men of the family," he told him, "here as soon as you can gather them."

Before noon they filed into Philippe's office, a small room off his bedroom. They sat in a row on the straight chairs Chu placed for them—Ronald and Francis Fairon, André, even Lon Rambeau although he had nothing to do with the business. But Philippe had said *all* the men. Only John and Andrew were absent.

"I have a proposition to make to you," he began. "You have no doubt heard that Henri is trying to sell his land. The ground directly around the house belongs to Maria. She will be entirely shut in by Armenians and Japs if he does what he intends to do. I propose to buy the Don's estate."

A gasp of astonishment came from the throats of the men sitting before him. Lon Rambeau looked in admiration at his father. *Up to the end he'll do things on the grand pattern,* he thought. André, cautious though he was, after he recovered from his first astonishment thought perhaps it was not a bad idea. He, like his father, had the peasant's greedy hunger for land. It would mean hard work to put back into the ground what Henri had taken out of it. The grapevines, although still bearing to full capacity, must nearly have exhausted the earth on which they grew. Henri was a fool to think the earth would continue to yield iron and potash forever.

"It'll take a vast amount of fertilizer, Father, the next few years," he said aloud, "to keep the vines bearing as they are now. That will mean money. In the end, of course, the vines will repay all we put into them."

"It will take a lot of money *right now* to buy the estate," said Francis Fairon. "If we could hope that grapes would reach the price they were last season——"

"Why shouldn't they?" Philippe did not like to have his judgment questioned.

"Perhaps they will," Francis conceded. Anyway, he thought, the old man could probably afford it. Philippe Rambeau was too shrewd, he told himself, to overbid his hand.

Had John Rambeau been there, whether his grandfather liked it or not he would have cried out against the foolishness of the undertaking, the tremendous risk to put available capital into more vineyards when a glut of the Eastern market was almost a certainty. Now that the association had arranged to ship the bumper crop, the price might drop to the point where they would actually be paying money into the association instead of receiving money from it. They might be struggling just to live next year. But these older men would not have believed in such disaster even if he had shouted it in their ears. They were accustomed to think of themselves as rich men. Rocked as they had always been in a cradle of security, they were not easily wakened to the new conditions threatening them, and they had not been east recently as John had been.

Philippe felt a warm delight over the admiration he had aroused in his family. Again he stood among them as the boldest and most daring of them all.

"Well, then, if you're all agreed it's a good idea, I'll go ahead," he said. "Get hold of Henri for me and see what terms we can come to. Lon here," he added, turning to his eldest son, "ought to be able to get a little family consideration for us. Henri will soon be your son-in-law, won't he?" It was the first reference old Philippe had made to the engagement of Mathilde's daughter to Henri.

When André carried the news to John at the hospital, John groaned, then grew angry with his father. "Can't you see," he said wearily, "that you're wrecking the business? If I had had my way we might be in a position to buy up half the county."

Your way, André thought bitterly. But he checked himself before he spoke the words. Life had disciplined him to withhold judgment. But he was unable entirely to hold back the bitterness in his heart.

André rose from his seat by his son's bed saying, "If you're going to be any help to us, John, it'll not be by criticizing what's done. Get well and take a place in the office." He spoke the words gently, too familiar with suffering through his association with Charlotte to ignore the suffering in John's face.

He withheld from his son, too, the bitter truth of the harm John had already done them. There was a good deal of feeling against them among their poorer neighbors. Dietrick, he understood, was spreading the story about that the Rambeaus had tried to squeeze the small growers out of the market. John Rambeau had come to him offering him a chance at the kill, but he, Dietrick, had refused because his neighbors were not included.

Of course it was not true, but Dietrick, maddened beyond all reason over the connection of Buz's name with the shooting, was hitting back with every weapon at his disposal. He meant, if he could, to make trouble. He had already let the story carry the implication that John Rambeau had intended to get him to sign by frightening Buz. Good thing Luigi was at home, he said.

Upon André had fallen the task of seeing the Griffantis and explaining to them that no case would be brought against Luigi. Let him move to another part of the state and they would not prosecute him. But André had found no ground upon which he and Mrs. Griffanti could meet. Afraid of the law and suspicious of Mr. Rambeau's purpose, she would not talk, fearful that she might give him a clue to Luigi's whereabouts. She knew Luigi had run away.

On the day of the shooting he had come running across the vineyard where she was working. "Ma, Ma, I gotta get outta town," he had cried. "I gotta have some money." She had given it to him. He had not told her where he was going. She was afraid of the rich-looking Mr. Rambeau. He was not there to help her or Luigi. She always knew trouble would come from Luigi's marriage. Buz was a bad girl, and John

Rambeau was bad. But her Luigi was good and she wasn't going to have them find him.

Had she known it, Luigi was already across the border in Mexico beyond reach of the law. Neither he nor Buz kept touch with their families. They were afraid to write for fear they could be traced. Luigi was certain he had killed John. Neither of them understood the Rambeaus well enough to realize that they would not press the case against Luigi whether John lived or died, that notoriety was something the Rambeaus could not bear.

Luigi in like circumstances would have cared nothing about the notoriety, but he would have paid high for a chance to revenge himself. He was certain that the Rambeaus, in their own time, would strike.

XXXVIII

ONE late afternoon in early September Monny drove John home from the hospital. Since the day he had so rudely dismissed her she had never trespassed upon his privacy. As if nothing had happened to the family or to him in the last weeks, she chatted about the details of their lives, giving particular attention to Madeleine's and Henri's wedding.

Henri had wanted it to be gorgeous and it was. The cathedral had been packed with the rich and influential. The reception had been held at his own hacienda.

"Aunt Maria outdid herself," Monny told John. "The affair would have done credit to Aunt Martha. Madeleine was beautiful. Her veil belonged to Henri. It had been worn by his mother and grandmother and great-grandmother, I guess. And the dress, too, was some relic. Both dress and veil were so old they had turned yellow but they were lovely. Madeleine is really pretty. I'd never thought so before. I guess it was because she looked so happy. Uncle Lon gave her away."

Monny was startled by a sudden sharp laugh from John. "Why are you laughing?" She turned to look at him. There was certainly no mirth in his face.

"Just thinking it would have been the same outfit if Aunt Martha had had her way. The only difference would have been the bride."

Monny hurried on. "I was maid of honor, John, and I caught her bouquet."

"Is that significant?" he asked.

236

"You know it is, John. Anyway, I wanted to tell you I'm to be married early next month. I've been waiting until you came home."

"Is that, too, significant?"

"I thought maybe it would be—to you, John."

There was no response. It was useless for her to try to reach him. It would have to be Mother.

Monica's wedding had been postponed twice; once by a secret arrangement forced on her by Aunt Martha with the hope that she and Elizabeth could be married at the same time. Then when it was no longer necessary to wait for Elizabeth, the wedding had been delayed because of John's illness.

Nate had pleaded for a quiet wedding which would not make it necessary for them to wait for John's recovery. "We could run around the corner most any day and get ourselves married," he begged.

"Oh, no! We couldn't possibly do that." Monica was a little shocked at the idea. "Why, Nate, we couldn't do that. Look how the family felt about Elizabeth and Andrew."

"That's a very different matter," Nate insisted.

But at the beginning of September all Monica's family saw that if she were to be married before Grandfather Rambeau died there was need for haste. Old Philippe himself had asked that the wedding take place soon, and that it be held not in the rectory but at the Rambeau home. It was his way of telling them how fast his strength was failing for only on the ground of his inability to make the effort to attend a wedding at the rectory would he ask for special permission to have Monny's marriage take place at home.

Martha threw herself into the preparations. Although as opposed as ever to the marriage, she had several reasons for making it a great affair. No one should suspect that the heads of the Rambeaus had been bowed in humiliation over John's unfortunate escapade. The buying of the Don's land and the magnificence of this wedding would allow them to present their usual proud front to the world.

And all the family should be there. On that Martha was determined. Whatever rifts there were in the family's solidarity, they would be shown neither to friend nor foe.

To Elizabeth and Andrew Martha wrote commanding them to appear at Monny's wedding. She had insisted that Lon and Mathilde postpone their departure so they might be there. Lon had made his plans to stay anyway when he saw how rapidly his father was failing. Even Madeleine and Henri would be back in time from their wedding journey. Henri had not been able to wind up his affairs so quickly as he expected. Furthermore, he was enjoying the figure he was cutting among the Rambeaus.

Monica and Nate were told Aunt Martha's plans and how to fit themselves in. Nate rebelled at first, asking Monica, "Whose marriage is this anyway?" Then he succumbed to the family pressure, but he was more than a little nervous on the September morning that was his wedding day.

For one moment he questioned the wisdom of his marriage. Not that he questioned Monny. He loved Monny. He questioned his marriage to her family. For he and Monica were to live at her home, not in the small cottage he had planned to build. Their plans had to be given up after John's injury. Nate realized that. It would be like quitting for Monny to leave home now, leave her mother and John when they needed her, leave her father to take the whole responsibility of two invalids.

But just now there was this wedding to be gone through with. If Monica could only have stood with him before he placed the ring upon her finger to drink the first and second cup of wine used in the ceremony he and his people knew and loved, the cup of joy and the cup of sorrow.

He and his best man had been assigned a room in Philippe Rambeau's wing of the house. Here he was to dress. From here he was to go forth to face them all, to repeat the words

of the unfamiliar marriage ceremony. He beheld himself in
the long French mirror—rawboned and awkward. His yellow
thatch of hair straggled away in an unruly pompadour, the
top of it cut off by the frame of the mirror.

Suddenly Nate did not care about his looks, his surrender
of customs, the giving up of the cottage, or even the sick,
morose John who hereafter would be his daily companion.
Through the open door, reflected in the looking glass, he saw
Monica coming from her grandfather's room, Monny in her
wedding gown and veil. Her black hair was drawn down
to the nape of her neck in a smooth black mass. Her head was
bent as if in supplication. Her bowed head, her lowered eyes,
her slightly parted lips, her whole precious self, was at last to
be his. His buoyant nature reasserted itself. He wanted to
shout.

Elizabeth and Andrew left Napa at daylight. The September day held a hint of fall, a hint so slight that only those
accustomed to the subtle approach of the California seasons
would have noticed it. A blue and gold and white day which
preceded the coming of rain. Rain still a month—two, possibly three—away. The sky had lost the thin gray look of
summer. It was deeply blue.

The first clouds in months stood along the horizon, white
and cottony. They seemed to belong more to the realm of
architecture than that of nature: sculptured, formed, unmov-
ing, set in ornament upon the blue, sometimes packed together
in a mass, sometimes separate—flat based, rounded and tufted
at the top—never far above the horizon, never high in the
dome of the heavens. Occasionally in the higher reaches there
appeared wispy white strands. After a little they would mys-
teriously disappear, leaving only the low panel of stiff white
clouds.

The level stretches of wheat and barley stubble shone in
yellow brilliance as Elizabeth and Andrew drove into the uppermost end of the wide San Joaquin Valley. The wind blew

along the ground, never reaching above the tallest roadside weed.

Andrew had not known until now how he had missed the Valley in which he had been born. He had a sudden satisfying sense of the fitness of his surroundings. An occasional vineyard cut into the stretched-out fields of golden stubble. The vineyards became more frequent. Between the rows, upon the white ash soil leveled to satiny smoothness, spread out on parchmentlike sheets of paper, lay raisin grapes, golden brown and wrinkled, drying in the still sunlight.

These ranches they were passing were for the most part small holdings. Unpretentious houses stood among umbrella trees to which the sun crept up and stopped, held back by the dense foliage.

They were passing larger vineyards, now. They were deep in the wine country. Finally the Valley floor held nothing but the dark green mass of grapevines, in luxuriant growth trailing their leaves along the ground.

The low green mass of vines was unbroken for miles. No longer the repeated clumps of umbrella trees; instead an occasional stately avenue of palms marked the way to the houses of the big growers, great houses, hidden by cyprus and eucalyptus. Roads bordered by olives and figs crossed the great vineyards, dividing them into blocks for harvesting. Such was the ample world Andrew had always known.

Elizabeth watched her young husband, marveling at his deep joy in the scene. She was a little uneasy. What was he thinking? She had found Andrew a more complicated personality than she had expected, far more delicately keyed than she had guessed, and keener, too—too keen not to detect any lack of response in her. But there was none, she hastened to tell herself. This gold and blue day she was truly happy if a little uneasy, now when it came to facing the family— especially Grandfather, for he hadn't answered her letter.

They were among the last to arrive, for along the drive

and even out into the vineyards the cars stood. They hurried through the garden, in bloom as Elizabeth had never seen it. Blue delphinium lined the walk. "See, Andrew, they are not real. They are made of paper. Aunt Martha must have had the decorators from Los Angeles do the garden, too! Can you believe it!" They heard the faint rustle of the paper cups of the flowers in the infinitesimal wind. Inside the house the voices of the crowd died away to a whisper and then to silence.

They had planned to come late so that neither of them would run the chance of personal conversation with any member of the family before the ceremony. They wanted just to appear among them casually as if they had not been away.

They slipped into the central room. In the far corner shining candles had been massed against the dark wood paneling. The glowing flames were like the triumphant notes of music, piled one upon another. Low candles in the foreground, taller and taller ones in the background, throwing their light down upon Nate who stood waiting, the rough lock of yellow hair fallen over his forehead. Monny and André were still in shadow as they came slowly through the aisle made in the ranks of the guests.

Francis' feelings were mixed seeing André with Monica on his arm. He it was who should be giving her away. By any chance did André know?

Elizabeth looked around. In the crowded room each couple stood a little apart, man and wife together, as she and Andrew were standing. Lon and Mathilde, Uncle Fran and Aunt Martha, and Andrew's father and mother. Even Henri and Madeleine. What after all was the significance of this union of two?

Outside John stood on the terrace leaning on his crutches, not a part of the gathering but looking in upon it. As he watched Elizabeth, a hard light came into his eyes and his mouth twisted in grim satisfaction. *She looks imprisoned.*

She wouldn't have looked like that if I had married her. Let her want and want and want, he told himself savagely.

Then came the pain which so often flanged upward along the left side of his spine, giving to half of his body that sense of terrible disuse. Half of him wanted nothing but to be spared pain. The other half alive, with the sensation of vigorous manhood, the muscles free and strong, made it impossible for him to forget what life could be. If only all of him could shrivel and be useless! He turned away from the sight of Monica and Nate clasping hands.

What Elizabeth wanted most was to make her peace with old Philippe. He had taken no notice of her letter. Somehow she had not expected his anger to last. She hadn't expected him to be angry at all! It was easy enough to carry it off with Lon—the light touch on her part and his. Fun to carry it off with Aunt Martha, but to have Grandfather angry hurt her. She never guessed that Martha had intercepted her letter.

The doctor had said that Philippe was not to be upset in any way and upset he would have been, Martha had thought to herself, reading Elizabeth's letter. She had had no qualms, no feeling of guilt in reading it. She had felt a cold curiosity in following Elizabeth's words. *So she's not so self-contained as she makes out to be,* thought Martha. *I see how she got around Father, but she's not to worry him now with her after-the-act regrets.* As she read her lips lifted in scorn. So Elizabeth hoped she hadn't worried him, did she? A little presumptuous of her to think she was that important.

It never occurred to Martha that Philippe had lost ground because Elizabeth had sent him no word. He thought he had crossed the barriers of age with his granddaughter and then suddenly she seemed to forget him entirely. The ties of life were dropping away quickly, and with them his strength.

As Elizabeth moved forward in the long line toward Monny she sought in vain for a glimpse of her grandfather. Then she saw him seated in his straight-back chair just out of the moving crowd. She was shocked to see how he had aged. His face was thinner and the color had gone from his cheeks. His eyes seemed set far back in his head. She would pass very near him in a moment now. Her heart gave a little leap. But when she stood before him he did not notice her. Could it be he was too angry to speak to her! Only Chu knew how his master's sight had failed these last weeks. Impulsively she spoke, "Grandfather!"

"Perhaps once again Philippe to you?" The old note of comradeship was in his voice. He smiled.

Then she was swept forward as Philippe was engulfed in a crowd of friends and relatives, but she felt happier than she had since her marriage.

XXXIX

THOSE were his final words to her, for Philippe Rambeau was very tired and leaning on Chu he went to his room before the last guests had gone. All was done now. Even the High Requiem Mass for his soul he had talked over with his friend the bishop. Bishops and archbishops would be in the solemn procession. He could see their rich robes as they came within the Sanctuary. The chalice that would be lifted to the celebrant's lips would contain the fruit of his own vineyards, from the vintage sent to the Vatican. To this he had attended on his last visit to his northern vineyards. He awaited his priest now to administer to him the last sacraments.

In the early dawn of the next day Philippe Rambeau died. He had wakened from what seemed to him a very long sleep. He was rested. Energy welled up within him again.

This was the harvest season! At his northern vineyard the presses already were turning, crushing the grapes, releasing the mysterious forces which changed the juice into wine. The great vats were stirring with life. Airy bubbles rose, broke upon the surface, new ones formed, taking on rainbow hues from the purple liquid out of which they rose. And in the old wines standing in casks and puncheons there too was movement and life.

Philippe raised himself in his bed, brushed at the film before his eyes which of late had kept him from seeing beyond the oak tree to the short, sturdy trunks of his oldest vines. Suddenly a blinding light enveloped the garden, the room, himself. With a sigh he fell back on his pillow.

From all over California friends and acquaintances came to pay Jean-Philippe Rambeau a last tribute. The great cathe-

244

dral was crowded to capacity. It was very still. Then there
was singing far off. Coming nearer. More triumphant as it
came. The choir, the ministers of the solemn function, and
the celebrant, the bishop and archbishop took their places in
the Sanctuary for the Requiem Mass of Philippe Rambeau.
The tender Mother, the Church, was making supplication for
Philippe Rambeau's soul.

At the Last Supper the Lord clothed himself in white. Sign
of peace. Then he offered to his disciples the cup saying, "Take
this and divide it amongst you." But in the halls of Pilate he
was clad in red when the soldiers placed the cloak about him.
Sign of blood, but sign also of reconciliation by blood. On
Calvary he was shrouded in black by the blackness of the sun.
Sign of grief and approaching death prophesied by the prophet
Ezekiel. "I will cover the heavens when Thou shall be put out
and I will cause darkness over the land saith the Lord God."

Black the color for the liturgy of the dead. Black were
the robes of the priests, black was Philippe's coffin standing
just within the chancel. But about the altar there was light.
The pure wax candles set gleaming the immaculate linen of
the altar and the golden chalice.

"Eternal rest give to them, O Lord; and let perpetual light
shine upon them."

"Absolve, O Lord, the souls of all the faithful departed from
every bond of sin."

So at last was the cup lifted to the lips of the priest. Philippe
Rambeau's old friend, the bishop, committed him to life in
death. "Of these ye shall partake and not die."

The sacrificial fruits, the bread and the wine. The marrow
and blood of the earth, the grain of wheat which is the fat of
the land, and the grape which ripens in the sun to renew man's
substance and to refresh his blood. By his own labor man pre-
pares his own food, for the life of man upon earth is a warfare.

The bread and the wine dedicated and offered to God withdrawn from common use. We give up all claim to these
earthly gifts and offer them to the Most High.

XL

THIS harvest season there was none of the disorder or excitement of last year. There were cars enough to carry the grapes grown in the valleys of California. Shipment after shipment went east, hurried across the country in refrigerator cars. The men who had started the association were immensely pleased, and so were the grape-growers for the most part, especially the older men. It brought the industry back to some of its old dignity. Then came the first report on prices. "Market glutted. Prices down," the wire read.

A year ago men were making money. Now the Valley was puzzled and frightened. Organization ought to work better than the haphazard methods of previous years and yet, somehow, it had not.

Among the Rambeaus there was more than a little anxiety. They could do nothing but mark time until they knew what disposition Philippe Rambeau had made of his vast holdings.

Three weeks and there had been no reading yet of old Philippe's will. His lawyer told them there had been a new will written during the last weeks of Philippe's life and Chu said he had seen it witnessed. It was not among Philippe's papers in his desk, but there was a note written in Philippe's own hand, saying he had made full arrangements for the reading of his will and that all the family were to be present.

As Martha took her seat at the breakfast table on the twenty-first day after Philippe's death, Chu handed to her a small tin box saying, "On this day and this hour the Old One say I give this to you."

"It's the will!" exclaimed Martha. "I know it is. Why," she demanded of Chu, "did you not tell us you had it? It did not belong to you."

"My master commanded me to silence."

"Chu," said Martha, "the old master is dead. Henceforth you will do as I tell you."

"Yes, Missee," said Chu. "The master is no longer my master. Today you are my missee. Tomorrow, no. I go to my own country. It is the time when your government say I must go, but this time I do not return."

"Later, Chu, we'll talk that over." Martha dismissed him with a slight motion of her hand.

"Fran," she said to her husband as soon as the door closed behind the old Chinese, "think of Father trusting the will to Chu!"

"It could scarcely be in safer hands, if that *is* the will."

"But Chu isn't a member of the family," Martha argued, still not opening the box, her mind intent on what seemed to her a traitorous act on the part of her father and Chu.

"He bears your father's name. I am not sure he wasn't closer to him than any of us." Francis felt the loss of his father-in-law with a kind of surprised hurt. He had not realized how close had been the bond until after the old man's death, or how much his ability to discipline himself during the years of his marriage had been due to old Philippe's quiet belief in him.

The days since Philippe's death had been days of self-examination for Francis. He had not met Philippe halfway in the friendship. He had accepted but had not given much. *These past months I could have made return to him for the friendship he gave me when I was most in need. I offered him no comfort during the last weeks of his journey on earth.*

This withholding the will gave Francis an inkling of how hard it had been for Philippe to die: he could not bear to feel that life was over. Until the will was read nothing would be changed. Everything in his household would still be a projection of himself. Thus old Philippe had put death off for three more weeks!

A key was fastened to the box with a bit of red cord. With

exasperated energy Martha fitted it into the lock, turned it.
She was irritated with Philippe just as she had been many
times when he was alive. *Imagine*, she thought, *giving the
will over to Chu and making us wait all this time.* But when
she threw back the lid she forgot her annoyance.

"Fran, he's put everything in my hands!" she gasped, staring down at the flat white envelope lying in the bottom of the
box. "I'm to open the will in the presence of all the family.
Here on the outside are his instructions, and *I* am to read the
will to the family."

Francis saw his wife go through a quick transformation as
if she cast off a shell which she no longer needed. Her mind
was already busy with plans for her rule.

"If Mathilde and Lon come in while I am gone," Martha
said rising, "tell them that Father has placed everything in
my hands."

Francis sat fingering the silver forks to the left of his plate,
forks he never used, for his breakfast was a simple matter of
fruit and coffee. But Martha never permitted the elaborate
pattern she had set for her household to be changed.

He could hear her telephoning Isobel. "I want you to have
Elizabeth and Andrew here by this afternoon. Father has
specified that all of the family must be here for the reading
of his will. Call Andrew at once. They will have to start
immediately. I want everyone here by six this evening."

Martha chose for the meeting the room next Philippe's bedroom which he had used as his private office. She planned to
sit behind his desk and preside as she would be doing from now
on. Mathilde and Lon came in first, and with them were Elizabeth and Andrew. They sat in a little group over by the
window that looked out upon the garden. Lon wondered why
he should be here at all. He had had his portion years ago but
his father only a few days before his death had asked Lon to
stay for the occasion. Next came André with his two sons.
John had not wanted to be present but the will could not be
read without him, so reluctantly he had consented. He seated

himself near the door where he could lay his crutch out of sight against the wall. Ronald and Isobel and the three girls were a little late. And still Maria had not arrived. At last with many apologies she entered the room with a fluttering sidewise motion as if to apologize for her presence here at all. Finally Monica and Nate.

There was no sound except the wind rising and falling as it rushed through the old oak.

" 'I, the undersigned, in good health——' " Martha slid over the phrases of the preamble, her eyes hastening down the page.

" 'To my children, Martha, André, Isobel, and Maria, to be held between them' "—now Martha no longer mumbled the phrases—" 'the San Joaquin Valley vineyards. All returns to be equally divided among them. To my eldest child, Martha, who has cared for me since the death of my wife, Marie, the homestead in the San Joaquin Valley; to my son André, who has taken from my shoulders in late years the arduous duties of the business, the San Joaquin winery. The management of all my southern properties to be in his hands.' "

For a moment Martha stopped, glancing back over what she had read as if to verify her first reading. At last she went on.

" 'As my son Alonzo received his portion years ago, but whereas that portion is not a fifth of my holdings at the present time, I bequeath to his daughter, Elizabeth, the Napa winery and the surrounding vineyards.

" 'In case of neglect the land and buildings on my two properties are to be forfeited, said property then to be given to the government of the State of California to be used for experiments in viticulture. In order that my wishes in this matter may be honorably carried out, I appoint the following board of three members to visit the properties annually to judge of the condition of the properties aforementioned. In case of the death of any of the three, one of the following men is to be chosen in his place.' "

Then followed a list of six names.

" 'The land bought recently, although belonging to my sons

and daughters, is not to be so judged. It is to be kept or sold according to the judgment of my son André. He to decide whether keeping it or selling it best benefits the original Rambeau-Fairon vineyards.

" 'After seven years, if the San Joaquin vineyards are in good condition they shall belong to my family without reservation. After fourteen years, the same to be true of the Napa vineyards. They shall then go without reservation to Elizabeth Rambeau Fairon, my granddaughter, and her heirs.

" 'To each of my other grandchildren I leave the sum of forty thousand dollars, excepting my grandson John Philippe Rambeau. To him I leave my ancient goblets never to be sold but to be handed down in the family.' "

Monny glanced anxiously at John but he did not betray by a movement of a single muscle how he felt in being cut off from both land and money.

Martha read steadily on through many minor bequests. There was a comfortable sum for Chu, something for Diener.

She had finished at last, and rising she handed the paper to André. "Will you see that it is filed as Father asks you to do at the end?"

She walked from the room.

After Martha's leaving, no one spoke, too astonished by the terms of the will to express either pleasure or disappointment. If Philippe had planned to make one last sensational appearance among his family he could not have startled them more, Francis thought. They were probably waiting for Martha to come back, but Francis, having seen her face as she left the room, was sure she had no such intention.

He knew that the terms of the will had taken her completely by surprise, and that from the elation of the morning when she had been certain her father had delegated to her his authority she had dropped suddenly to the bitterest disappointment of her life. But he did not want her to lose the respect in which the members of her family had always held her. So proud and stiff a soul as Martha must not, for one moment, lose her pride before them. She must not let them guess her humiliation. That, Francis felt, he could not bear to have happen to her. He rose saying, "Martha planned a buffet supper for you all. I imagine she has gone to see if Chu is ready. If you will excuse me, I'll go and help her."

Martha was not in the living room or dining room or the long hall. She must have run, he thought, if she has reached her room so quickly.

He found her lying across her bed crying. "Martha," he said sitting down beside her, "you must not cry. You have the home and your share of the property. Don't let them guess you wanted more."

"He said I was hard. I'm not hard, Francis. You've all done things as bad as any I've done. I never meant to do anything but help him," she sobbed. "You know that, don't you, Fran? I did help him and I cared for him all these years and now he sets me aside and chooses to give his best vineyards and the Napa Valley home to Elizabeth, a child and an interloper. And André, whose brain I wouldn't give that for when it comes to business, he's put over us all. What do I care for the house? I wanted the winery and the managership. Father knew I did. And he wouldn't give it to me. I could have kept us rich even with things as bad as they are now."

She turned over on her side, her head propped on one hand, the other picking at the threads of the spread, in a low voice going on and on, in her anger and disappointment revealing the last materialistic details of her ambitions as Philippe's successor.

Finally Francis, no longer able to bear it, rose and went quietly out of the room. He, too, found it difficult to justify the terms of the will. The actual division of property was just, except in the case of John. As to Elizabeth, if old Philippe wanted to make it up to Lon through his daughter that was fair enough, if Lon found it agreeable. The old man may have discussed it with Lon. He thought he had, for Lon had not seemed surprised.

Nevertheless, Francis was shocked at the hard and erratic conditions Philippe Rambeau had inflicted upon his family. The will was almost one of an eccentric, and yet Philippe was not an eccentric. What then had been his purpose? Why had he made it so difficult for them? In order to hold the land they would have to exhaust themselves in the care of the vineyards. In a year like this when there would be no money coming in they would have to dip into capital for labor, fertilizer, and insecticides if the vines were to be maintained at the point of perfection demanded by the will. And yet Philippe had deprived them of the capital with which to do it. Most of his ready money he had used in buying Henri's land, the remainder he had distributed among his grandchildren, exacting no promise from them that it should be invested in the business. To maintain the San Joaquin Valley vineyards not even the revenue from sacramental wines would be available. Only from the Napa vineyards was wine now made. The dry wines used by the church came only from the hill vineyards. That revenue would go to Elizabeth. Yet with all these handicaps he and André and Ronald would have to keep the vineyards in top-notch shape to satisfy the inspectors Philippe had appointed.

One thing was clear. Philippe meant to have his vineyards survive him. Francis now remembered an incident which took on significance in the light of the will. He and old Philippe had been driving together not long before Philippe's death. The old man asked to be driven past the Spellmans' neglected vineyards. "The finest vineyards in the Valley once," Philippe had said with a note of nostalgia in his voice. "A man of intellect, Spellman. You didn't know him, Francis, did you?

"Ever hear how he went to Syria, worked as a day laborer for three years to find how the Syrians controlled the disease of the white fig? Worked as hard on the Phylloxera that attacked our grapes later. His vineyards were magnificent. I have never attained quite the perfection with my vines that he reached. You'd think he had built something impossible to destroy, but look at his vineyards now—gone to Johnson grass and weeds. Drive me home, Francis," old Philippe had ended.

Now Francis saw in Philippe's will the effort to safeguard his hard work against such destruction, to keep what he had created alive for a very long time, projecting himself beyond his span of living. But why then had he not chosen Martha, the most capable member of his family, to insure the carrying out of his wishes?

Martha indeed would have been the one to manage. She would have whipped them into a concerted effort such as André never would be capable of. And yet Philippe had not seen fit to give her the power. Did he fear she would misuse it?

And why give the hill vineyards to Elizabeth? There again was contradiction. If Philippe had wanted to get the best out of his cherished northern vineyards, John would have been the one to handle them. John was right that day when he had told his grandfather, "I, like you, am a good viticulturist." John alone of them all had inherited from the old man the feeling of the artist in the making of wine. There must have been something more than the mere preservation of his vineyards old Philippe meant to accomplish by his will.

The family rose as one when Francis told them Martha was not well and had asked that they excuse her. "Chu has everything ready," Francis added. "Suppose we go out to the dining room."

Suzanne Fairon broke the spell which seemed to bind them to silence. "I'm going to take my money and go abroad to study music, Uncle André," she announced.

Looking at André, who made no reply, Francis thought, *Martha would have had them all pledged by now to invest their money in the business.* Then Francis had an inkling of Old Philippe's intention. Perhaps he wanted to preserve his vineyards, but not his wealth. Perhaps he wanted to reproduce in those he loved best in his family something of the struggle he had gone through.

Everybody began talking now as they walked along the hall and into the dining room. Isobel had taken Francis' arm and was saying over and over how nice it was that Martha was to have the old home.

Elizabeth at first felt only a wondering delight. Her grandfather not only had forgiven her, he had loved her dearly. He had given her the things he loved best. Then suddenly her delight changed to consternation. Why had Philippe given her the responsibility of his most cherished vineyards and the rambling old house? For fourteen years she must give an account of her stewardship. Fourteen years! Until that remote day she must follow the pattern Philippe had set for her. She and Andrew wanted to start new. Suddenly she felt uneasy. Was Philippe trying to rule her as had Aunt Martha over her marriage? But Diener, she told herself, could be trusted with the care of the place. With Andrew's inheritance plus the returns from her vineyards they would be free to live wherever they wanted to.

But when she spoke to Andrew about the matter, he thought they ought to make the old house their home. "And I shall need to be there to look after the vineyards." But he added, seeing her disappointment, "We could go east for a while. Perhaps you ought to see the agents who handle the wines for the church." He knew it was not necessary, but already Andrew had learned not to thwart his young wife. A coldness arose between them when he did. Already his love for Elizabeth demanded above everything else her appreciation.

It was later as they were going over to his mother's that they discussed the matter. Just now, standing with Elizabeth among his family, around Martha's table, a plate of her abundant food in his hand, Andrew had a sense of embarrassment. Philippe's gift would isolate them from the family. He wished that he and Elizabeth could say, "We want you all to come to the old home every summer, just as you always did," but it sounded presumptuous of him to invite them to a house which, until now, had been their own. He wished Elizabeth would say something, but perhaps she did not know what to say either. She looked strangely upset. How could anyone be natural, Andrew thought, with John's cold sarcastic gaze upon him.

Just then Monny grasped Elizabeth's hand exclaiming, "We'll all be around to see you, Elizabeth. You may as well get ready to entertain us."

Her words seemed to rouse everyone to the necessity of being polite. They began congratulating one another—except John who turned to Charles saying, "How about driving me home?"

XLI

I N THE Valley the momentum of optimism which had carried California along for nearly a century, from gold rush to boom time, seemed at last to have spent itself. It could be laid to a number of happenings—to the long-delayed results of a maladjustment caused by Prohibition which had made one of the state's most respected industries illegal, and sent those who had carried it on hunting for a new use for their product. It could be laid to the profiteers who, a year ago, had pushed the Valley into a greedy rush for wealth as chimerical as it was vast. It could be laid to the shortsightedness of the idealists who had planned the association without taking into account the hard facts of a limited market. It could be laid even to the ill-advised will of Philippe Rambeau who, confused between the issues of wealth and righteousness, had deprived his family of the ready money that made them a backlog of prosperity in the Valley. Yet none of these, or all of them together, were enough to account for the seeping away of the Valley's faith in its own endeavor. Its lethargy of pessimism seemed to lie deep in the marrow of the post-war world.

A new world? "Na, na," said Mamoulian and his neighbors. They had found coercion in this new world to which they had come. Why wouldn't the evil of poverty they had known in the old country be here, too? There was nothing to do but to tighten their belts, make ready to eke out an existence without money. In this country where the sun shone most of the year their women could at least raise enough to keep them from starving. They could make wine for themselves and they had their flutes and accordions. Only somehow the men must get hold of enough ready money to pay their taxes

256

and their water rights. Do road work, do anything to get it. But a new world—na, na.

There were others like Nelson Dietrick whose disappointment turned into a bitter sense of injury. *If they'd left us alone,* he told himself over and over, *we'd have got somewhere. I coulda traded my grapes off like last year. The buyers give us good prices. Or supposin' I'd gone along with John Rambeau bucking 'em, keeping the cars tied up, I'd been all right. He's smart when it comes to business, but I hate him for messin' round with Buz. Blast his hide, he got what's comin' to him in getting hurt, and the whole Rambeau outfit is catching it as bad as me, prices what they are.*

Then it occurred to him that men like the Rambeaus might be making money right now on grapes. Perhaps they were getting a big price in the association, squeezing the little fellows out of any returns. Bah! Talk about an association where folks shared alike. . . . An association like anything else was to benefit the big fellow.

Dietrick was beginning to hate all those who had more than he. He saw rich men like John Rambeau making all the trouble for poor men like himself. He began to lay all his difficulties to the fact that the Rambeaus and their kind had money and he did not.

Brooding over it day after day, Dietrick came to be sure of it. One evening he had an inspiration. Guess what was good for the goose was good for the gander, too. Wonder someone hadn't thought of it before. He slapped his knee, feeling in a pretty good humor, better than he'd felt since things went bad with Buz.

Mrs. Dietrick, sitting beside him on the back porch, looked at him with relief. "Well, it's about time you come out of the dumps, Nelson. You ain't been any sort of company since way last year."

"I haven't, eh? Well, I got myself going again. I'll put myself in a good humor finding out what's behind this licking we've been taking on our grapes. See you later, Ma."

It was indeed later when Mrs. Dietrick heard him returning, the truck coughing and spitting as he drove around by the barn. "Them top fellows won't look so chirpy when we get through with them tomorrow night," he mumbled as he undressed in the dark.

It had not been hard for Dietrick to get Mamoulian and even Petucci to help make up a gang to do a little night riding on their own. "We won't go so far as to manhandle them, but we'll put a few of their vineyards out of commission for 'em," Dietrick, as leader, commanded.

This was a violence that went a step deeper than the violence indulged in on the raisin deal. That violence had for its purpose organization and better prices. This was violence for violence' sake, a dark union of destruction and revenge.

Men, finding their vines destroyed, grew suspicious of each other. As things stood, it would be to anyone's advantage to see that his neighbor had fewer grapes to sell next year. The big growers suspected the little ones and the foreigners. *Getting back at us,* they thought a little uneasily, fearing that the Russians and Armenians who had been rolled in the irrigation ditches over the raisin contracts were now taking their revenge.

The big growers grew suspicious also of one another. Judge Hueber, who had a fine old vineyard which was completely destroyed, went over in his mind the men who had gone with him on that other raid. *They might have done it, any one of them,* he thought. *There's John Rambeau. Guess he wouldn't stop at anything. Guess he's not so crippled he couldn't get behind a thing of this sort. Just his style.*

André Rambeau had to report to the family that in one of their choicest vineyards the vines had been cut off even with the ground.

John, when he heard what had happened, was immediately suspicious of Hueber. "Why don't you track down that pious old goat, Hueber? He'd destroy his own mother if it suited his purposes."

So the cynicism grew, fed, too, by another suspicion related to a new development in the wine industry—bootlegging. It pitted races, friends, even families against one another.

The deep pride in the making of wine had gone. These men who had come out of the Old World each bringing with him, as had Philippe Rambeau, the ceremonial of his people symbolized in wine, now felt disgraced. Rich and poor alike, they were because of their business outlaws in the eyes of the Government. Outlaws in name, many became outlaws in practice. It was not difficult to sidestep the law, for each winery was allowed shrinkage on the wines in the bonded tanks. In that shrinkage the hard-pressed growers found their chance. At night trucks went through the Valley paying big prices to those men who would sell part of their wine, later to be accounted for in reports as shrinkage. No man knew whether or not his neighbor was guilty of selling to the bootleggers. Rumors went up and down the valley. Many a man reported his neighbor to the Government authorities only to find he had been reported himself.

Almost overnight the Rambeaus had become as cramped for money as many a small grower. Their resources were startlingly reduced. With the profits of the harvest, which usually financed them until the next harvest, gone, with all the grandchildren except Monny withdrawing their inheritances from the business, and the bulk of the family's capital sunk in Henri's vineyard, they found themselves land poor.

Their real danger lay in the diminution of their fighting strength. Martha, whatever her failings, had radiated energy, but now that the hard purpose of her ambition had been crushed she made no effort to help in the business, seemed unable to endure any personal sacrifice. She spent lavishly on house and garden and her own clothes, bent seemingly on the one objective of maintaining her reputation for elegance, even extravagance. The Fairon brothers were ready to use what resources they had to help hold their wives' estates but Martha drained away most of Francis' ready money.

Among them Francis, Ronald, and André took upon themselves much of the physical labor in the vineyards, finding splendid support in Nate, a worker if ever there was one, but they were handicapped by John's drag on the family. Not only did he take no interest in the business, refusing either to use his good brain in devising ways and means to help them get along, but he gave them no help in the office. And he weakened their fighting power by his persistent efforts to undermine Nate's confidence in himself.

Francis took a peculiar pleasure in Nate. They had liked each other from the start. The boy's bewildered groping for a foothold in the household into which his marriage to Monny had plunged him roused a special response in Francis. What old Philippe had done for him, he tried to do for Nate—steady him through the first bewildering months of his marriage, steady him against the disintegrating effect John had on him.

Francis, going home at night to the elaborate empty ritual of a wealth which now did not exist, longed for the comfort Monny and Nate would have brought to his home, longed for it for their sakes, too. The little he knew of what went on in André's house did not please him. But even Francis had no idea of the burden placed on the family by John's presence.

Nate and Monica had her old room across the hall from John. They went to sleep at night to the insistent knock of John's crutch against the floor as he walked back and forth. He had had the rugs, which heretofore were scattered over his floor, removed the day one of them had slipped under his crutch. That was the reason he gave, but sometimes Monica could not rid herself of the suspicion that he wanted his floor bare in order to remind them of his bitter presence.

So far he had shown no willingness to take up any kind of work. After a time his father, growing weary of his idleness, suggested he do the bookkeeping at home. John left the books untouched on his table. The letters, unanswered, he allowed to stay where his father placed them. "With Nate in my place at the office you can't expect me to fill in for you at home," he told his father. Without a word André gathered everything together and took the pile of work back with him.

"Why should I take care of the books of an organization which booted me out?" John asked Monica.

"Oh, John," pleaded Monica, "you're not booted out. Grandfather——"

John's eyes blazed with anger. "I never wanted his damned money and I didn't lick his boots to get it. All the rest of you did. I gave him the best advice he'd ever had, but what did I get for it? A lot of goblets! Trying to be funny, I suppose. Not a single grape I could make into wine. Not even a bottle of wine to put into my goblets. And a silly girl who has never done anything useful given the best vineyards. Even if he did want to ruin me, why ruin the Napa vineyards, and the winery? The best winery in the—oh, to hell with it!"

In his anger he turned upon Monica. "I wish you'd stay out of my room. When I want to see you I'll hunt you up."

But Monica stood her ground. "John," she said quietly, "I'm coming in here every day to look after you whether you like it or not. One thing you've got to do, and that's not say things like this to Mother. She can't stand it."

"Or your pretty little Nate. I suppose he can't stand straight talk, either."

Suddenly the brave front Monica was putting up crumpled. "John, please be nice to Nate," she begged. "He's new in the family. For my sake, if for nothing more, don't make him unhappy." She turned and fled, unable to control her tears. John had made Nate the constant butt of ridicule, cruel ridicule which Monica saw destroyed Nate's natural belief in himself. The sunny, gay Nate was changing into a silent, reserved man.

Monica's appeal seemed to make John more determined than ever to hurt Nate. When Nate came home from his work at the office that evening John's door was open and he hailed him as he went by. "I was waiting for you to come in."

"Anything I can do for you?" Nate asked him, but he advanced no farther than the door.

"Oh, come on in," said John. "I've a little notion I could give you some good advice."

"Very kind of you," answered Nate in the new guarded tone he used of late.

"You're making a mistake, you know, working the way you do. It is not going to net you anything. I'll tell you confidentially there's not a chance you can get yourself into the firm. Your race alone. In fact, Father——"

Nate interrupted him. "I'll tend to my own business, John, and you can tend to yours."

"Of course, if that's the way you look at it."

All evening Monica saw that Nate was watching her in uncertainty. When, at last, they were alone in their own room she put her hands on his shoulders and looked straight into his eyes. "You must tell me, dear, what's the trouble. We can't let anything grow up between us."

"I can't tell you, Monny." He took her hands from his shoulders, held them for a moment, then dropped them.

"Was it something John said to you?"

"Yes."

"What could he say, Nate, to make you uncertain of me?"

"My race."

Monny snuggled close against him. "I married you. I knew it then, didn't I?"

Later, lying close to him, she could feel the beat of his heart and the beat of her own. "Nate dear," she whispered, "if it weren't for Mother I'd go away tomorrow." Nate was first in her life and yet she was powerless to treat him as if he were.

"I know," he said; "it's all right." Both of them seemed peculiarly bereft of words.

Monica tried to make herself believe she had told Nate the whole truth. Her mother needed her, but it was not because of her mother she was staying. It was because she could not bring herself to leave John to fight his battle alone.

One morning she had found him lying across his bed. He took her hand, laid it on his forehead. Monica could feel his temples throb. A cold sweat lay wet and clammy on his brow. She went for a bowl and a cloth and bathed his face and his hands. Finally he fell into an exhausted sleep.

Just before, he had murmured something near to confession. "I oughtn't to be allowed to live."

"Hush, John," she had said. "You mustn't talk that way. If you'd only——"

"I know what you're going to say, Monny. I can't. I can't be like this always."

She had sat for a long time by his bed, wondering how he could be made to accept pain and the crippling of his body. It meant doing something which from childhood he had refused to do—accept the beautiful broken figure of his mother.

What John was doing to Charles Monica did not guess. Charles had retreated beyond the reach of anyone into a reticence consistently maintained, a reticence armored in gaiety.

"I don't believe Charles ever has a serious thought," his father said to Charlotte. "Fortunate, I expect, that he doesn't take things hard. I was afraid he'd be pretty upset over John's injury."

"Maybe he is and doesn't want us to know it," Charlotte answered him.

"Well, if he is, he covers it up well," André answered.

Later he had said to Monica, "Charles' school work is off this year. Do you think you could talk to him, Monny? I don't like to bother your mother."

"I don't know," said Monny a little doubtfully. "I can try, of course, if I can ever get hold of him. He's never home except at meal times."

"How about at night, or before he gets up in the morning?"

"I tried it once," Monica owned. "He locks his door now."

But finally Monica caught up with Charles. The long

summer of central California had lingered on into the short winter. It was a Saturday, and Charles, let down by the languor of the Indian summer day, had stretched himself out in a reclining chair on the lawn. His feet hung down over the arm, his socks dangled untidily around his ankles. His head was thrown back, and with eyes as unblinking as if he were blind, he stared up at the sun. *Off guard if ever he's going to be,* thought Monica walking toward him.

At the sound of her step he sat up saying, "Well, I got to be off."

"Come on now," said Monica, dropping down by his side. "You don't need to tell me you're that pressed for time."

"Well, I got a fellow to see over in town."

"I thought maybe this would be a good time to talk about our going skiing at Christmas vacation, if we could make plans. Perhaps Nate and I could take a party up if you wanted us to. Nate's been talking about a shack up there he and a couple of his friends put up a year or two ago."

"Honest?" asked Charles. "No kidding?" And he lay back again, forgetting his need to get away.

"Of course, I'd like to see a little better work from you in school before then," Monica went on. "What's the trouble, Charles?"

"You lay off, Monny. Sometimes a fellow don't feel like grinding."

"You grinding! I wouldn't want to wear you down to that point, Charles." Monica ran her hand along his forearm in the comfortable gesture of affection that often broke down Charles' resistance. "Mother isn't very well just now. It might help, you know."

A strange, almost furtive look came into Charles' eyes. "It's not me who makes her sick. You can't put that off on me, Monny. You better go and talk to John. The things John does—I mean not ever going to see her," he added quickly.

Monica detected a break in his voice. So Charles was not so

carefree as her father thought, nor unaffected by John's injury.

He stood up now, moving quickly away down the drive, and Monica did not try to detain him. She called after him in parting, "I mean it about the skiing."

John is the only one who could help Charles, she thought. But when she tried to talk to him about Charles he only laughed. "I can't play Galahad to him, my dear girl."

"You could make him respect you."

"And what would I do with his respect?"

Once out of sight of the house Charles sat down again, pushing his cap to the back of his head. *Gee,* he thought, *I almost gave him away, saying that about his hurting Mom. I got to be careful. Skiing would be all right, though. We'd have a crowd all the time. I'd watch so Monny didn't get me alone. And Nate's a good egg. He never asks a fellow a lot of questions he can't answer.*

Charles' days were spent in conflict. He had patterned himself since babyhood after John. He had striven for years to grow up sufficiently to be John's buddy. That's why he had made a good skier of himself, and why he had worked in school, and not done things other boys had done. But now to be like John was, he had suddenly learned, to be things he did not want to be.

John watched him with amused eyes. "Kind of soft, are you, kid?"

"Me soft!" Charles answered. "I'm the original tough guy when I get going."

"Just not showing it to me, is that it? I'm too much of a back number to be let in on it."

"Cut it out," Charles answered.

"Do you want to prove you can be tough?" asked John. "I've a little job you can help me with."

"I got a lot on just now. Got a kid waiting to see me right now."

"I see," said John.

Charles felt miserable. John wouldn't have anything more to do with him, he supposed. But he was afraid of what his brother might ask him to do.

If he just hadn't seen John unlocking the winery one night, and the big truck without lights coming in very slowly over their private road and driving straight into the winery. He had been out with a crowd of boys. He was late in getting home and he had decided he had better take a short cut through the vineyards. He didn't want to know what John was doing, so he had hurried on. *I ought to have stayed and seen what he was up to,* something within Charles kept saying. *And I ought to have told Dad.* . . . But there was his loyalty to John.

XLII

THE hot Indian summer stretched itself out this year into a warm December. The days were still and soft. Slowly the vineyards let their summer vigor go, accepting the short rest allotted them in this climate. There was neither wind nor rain nor frost to dismantle the vines of their leaves. But in the high Sierra snow had fallen, and word had come that the Christmas skiing would be good on the slides. Lower down, the snow was still soft and mushy and there was little of it.

Charles was in a fever to be off. "It's my only vacation until Easter and there won't be any snow then. Nate says the snow is good right now at that high camp. You know you promised, Monny," he begged. "I'd like it up there. Even if you'd let me skip school later to go, Nate would be too busy—you know, pruning and stuff coming on."

"Maybe you could go without me." Monica couldn't make up her mind to leave John. He seemed to need her so much. And it would take her away for Christmas. It would be a pretty dreary affair for the three left at home.

"Aw, Monny," Charles begged, "you know Nate wouldn't go without you. You got to go, Monny. You said you would. I'm going to put it up to Mom."

Hopefully he presented the matter to his mother. "Course you'd miss us at Christmas just as Monny says, but Nate and Monny haven't had any honeymoon yet. I think they ought to have one." He brightened visibly at this splendid new argument for their going.

"So do I," Charlotte agreed with a smile. "But sit down, Charles. I'd like to talk with you a little and I can't when you're roaming around like something caged."

"Well, I'm kind of busy," said Charles.

"You do seem to have a good deal on your mind."

For some time Charlotte had been aware of the guarded look in her younger son's eyes. That Charles had not been himself since John's injury did not surprise her. Undoubtedly his brother's accident had been a shock to him, but of late she felt that his trouble went deeper.

"I want to ask you about John," she began, hoping by a surprise attack to find out how it stood between the brothers.

"What do you all want to spy on John for?" Charles thrust his hands deep into his pockets, and confronted his mother angrily.

"Whom do you mean by 'all'?" asked his mother.

"Oh, Monny—and now you and Dad a little."

"Well, is there anything you don't want to tell us about John?"

At her question Charles burst into tears and before Charlotte could speak he had rushed from the room. She could hear him running down the stairs, the front door slam.

Yes, she said to herself with a sad smile, *Monny must go on her honeymoon. Charles needs it. It will certainly take a couple of weeks for him to forget that I saw him cry. Longer maybe to forget other things. Nate, too, needs that honeymoon.* She had not been blind to the change taking place in Nate, the dying out from his eyes of hope and happiness. Charlotte lay back on her pillows waiting for strength to return. She must act to save the whole household.

A year ago her children's problems had seemed simple. Wealth and opportunity had prolonged their youth. The tests of maturity had not come to them. Now John, in his ill-adjusted manhood, was sucking them all down into his own agony, seeming to take a perverse delight in destroying the order and happiness of their lives. And yet Charlotte believed he valued the things he sought to destroy—the well-ordered house, Monica's and Nate's love for each other, Charles' youthful innocence, her own disciplined meeting of what he

himself refused to meet. He must no longer be allowed the
twisted indulgence of his sick mind.

No one knew better than Charlotte the hard individual
struggle toward righteousness. Not that John would call the
struggle to win over his handicap and pain a struggle toward
righteousness. That was part of the problem. Except for
Monny, her children did not believe in the term righteousness.
Nate, too, would object to the word. But whatever he might
call his struggle, John's victories, like her own, would be hard
won. But they must be undertaken and soon.

At noon, three days before Christmas, the two carloads
which made up the skiing party left the valley. The day, like
so many which had gone before it, was still with an Indian
summer haze. The skis and poles strapped to the top of the
cars seemed oddly out of place, the warm sunlight reflected in
the high varnish. There was no sign of snow in the foothills.
The peaks of the mountains were shrouded in mist and cloud,
but where the clouds parted there the snow lay white.

Nate was driving one car, Monica the other. Charles, sitting at her side, almost deafened her with his words shouted
to the girls on the back seat. "I bet we get a chance on the
slide before dark." He turned to her. "Couldn't you speed her
up a little, Monny?"

"It's not safe to drive faster," she told him, slowing down
to make the sharp hairpin turn around the mountainside.

"Shucks on the safety! We want to get there before dark."
Charles would have enjoyed taking the curves in a reckless
dash.

Snow began to appear in sheltered places. Finally they put
on chains, for the road was glassy smooth where cars had
passed over it. In among the redwoods, blue spruce and pine,
the purple shadows were already long across white drifts.

At last Nate who was ahead stopped his car, got out and
ran back. "Here we are, kids. It's up to you to carry your
own packs the rest of the way," he called to them. By the

tone of his voice Monica could tell he was almost as excited as Charles. *And he doesn't look much older either*, she thought with a sense of relief flooding over her. He had his cap off and was pushing back his heavy yellow brush of hair.

"That it up there?" Charles pointed to a low cabin perched on the mountainside. The snow, heavy on its roof, gave it the look of a sheltered cave hewn in the rock.

"That's it," Nate answered.

"Some shack!" Charles was trying not to show his pride in the kind of party Nate was helping him to put on.

"You go along, kids. Monny and I will follow you up. Here's the key, Charles."

Charles put the key in his pocket, thinking Nate was the man to copy. He smothered the thought because it seemed disloyal to John, then turned to his friends with an air of responsibility. "Get yourselves loaded up," he told them.

The six of them trod up the incline, packs on their backs. Soon they were only a bobbing mass of red and blue—girls and boys alike clad in bright red jackets and blue ski pants. Charles, in gray, could hardly be distinguished against the snow.

"Now we can hold hands, Monny." Nate arranged his load so that his hands were free. "They won't even think to look back." Under a great pine he lowered his pack, drew Monica to him. For a long time they stood there, their backs against the tree, more completely alone than they had been since their marriage. Then Monny said, "I suppose we should be going. Charles is too excited to be trusted."

Nate did not answer, only tightened his hold on her shoulder. He was thinking something through and he had to get to the end of it. Slowly in the weeks since his marriage he had been working to a conclusion, a conclusion shaping itself clearly in his mind now. Completely to possess Monny's precious self had been his expectation the day of their marriage. His conception of marriage had altered since then. To make

Monny happy meant more than he had thought. There were things in her he had not counted upon. Hardest among them to accept was the fact that he did not fill the whole of her horizon as she did his. It had hurt him at first. He had even resented it. No doubt he was the dynamo that ran the cunning little machine that was Monny, but he ran it a great deal for the benefit of others. And the more he stoked the fires in Monny, the more would go out to others. If he wanted to keep her whole and sweet, he'd have to let her have someone to mother. But he stuck at John. The remembrance of John's frequent allusions to his race had bitten deep.

"Yes, I guess we'd better be getting on, little Miss Business," he said at last. But he had resolved to tell her before they went back that he would not live in the same house with John any longer. If she would go away with him, he would be willing that she should have a child right away. He had not wanted her to have one so soon. He sensed how strong motherhood would become in her once she held in her arms a child of her own.

Later he faltered in his resolution over John. Would he lose Monny in setting such terms? To go away with him would seem to Monny deserting John. If she did it, she would be denying her natural compassion toward suffering. It was upon that compassion that Nate himself counted. No, that was not the way out. But how would he manage to live in the same house with John?

Charles, as he trudged toward the cabin, saw the splendid uninterrupted slope just behind it. "We could take it once before dark if we hurry," he said, turning to the girl at his side.

"Morning's time enough for me. I'm cold. Let's make the fire. The others will be here in a minute." She snuggled her mittened hand into his, wishing in a vague adolescent way that he should be especially nice to her.

Charles let her hand go, searched his pocket. "Look, here's

the key," he said. "You let the others in. I got to go." And with that he shouldered his skis and trudged up the steep slope.

"All right for you," she called after him.

But Charles never turned. It was almost dark when he reached the top, entirely so among the great pines. But the white slope glistened in the fading light. Then it was under his feet and his skis were carrying him down over its whiteness. He felt as if his heart would burst. It was the nearest Charles ever came to prayer, gliding down the gleaming white snow.

XLIII

ONICA, Nate and Charles had been gone two days. The only knowledge which Charlotte had that John was in the house was the sound of his crutch in the hall, on the stairs, its fainter sound on the porch steps outside her windows. Both evenings he had been away.

This morning she had asked the nurse to leave her door open, and as John went along the hall she called to him. He stood in the doorway asking, "Did you want me, Mother?" As she looked at his once straight shoulders, arched up now by the crutches, her heart almost failed her. Charlotte loved physical perfection almost as much as John did, and before his injury he had so nearly approached it.

She had done all she could this morning to make herself beautiful for him. She had had the nurse arrange her hair high on her head to show to the best advantage the classic lines of neck and chin. In her lovely well-set ears there were diamond earrings—André's gift to her at the time of John's birth. Both lips and cheeks were deftly tinted. Her negligee was in John's favorite color, a splendid deep red. The lace in its sleeves fell over her crippled hands.

For a moment John saw her as she wished him to see her. But as he drew nearer his habitual rebellion leaped up. There wasn't any sense in a world that allowed such a thing to happen to a woman like his mother.

"Mind if I sit down?" he asked, taking a chair far from her.

"Please do," she said, "for I have something important to say to you, John."

"Must you?" he asked. "I think I can guess what it will be."

"I'm afraid you can't," his mother answered him. "I wish

273

you could. John, I do not intend to discuss with you either what has happened to you or why. You are my son and I know something of the nature of your temptations."

John remained silent.

"You can blame me, or the hot blood of those before me, for your predicament," Charlotte went on, "or you can share that blame with your father's family if you wish. They're hot-blooded too. But you can't blame anybody but yourself for the present."

"Just what do you mean?" he asked.

"I mean," said Charlotte, her voice trembling, "that at present you are shirking."

John flushed. His fingers tightened on the chair arm. "You have no right to say that," he told her angrily.

"Yes, I have and I must, John—because it's true. And I am going to ask something of you, my son. It will be very hard for you to do. I want you to go away for a while, John —learn how to take what has happened to you without injuring other people."

John's voice broke. "You ought to know I can't get along without Monny's care any more than you can."

Charlotte saw fright come into his eyes, but she did not draw back. "It's partly because of Monny I'm asking you to do this. You're taking out your anger on her. And you're hurting Charles."

"So they mean more to you than I do." John's face set in bitter lines.

"I know what suffering can do to the human spirit," Charlotte said, not answering his accusation about her lack of love for him. "I know all the pitfalls, and I know you have to fight. It's a bitter draught that's been given you. Accept it, John."

John rose. "All you need to say is that you don't want me around."

"Very well," she answered, "if you prefer it that way. I have arranged a small bank account for you. It's not much.

We can't afford much just now. You'll have to work when that is spent."

"Okay," he answered, and without a word of farewell, he started toward the door.

"John," she cried in a last effort to reach him. "You know how much I have always loved you. You know——"

But John did not hear the end of the sentence. He had shut the door between his mother's voice and himself.

That afternoon Charlotte heard the commotion of luggage taken down the stairs. Perhaps for the last time she had listened to the knock of John's crutch as he went along the hall. If Charlotte had been able to enter John's room she would have found it as empty of him as if he had never inhabited it, except for a small crucifix which she had given him before her own sickness. It hung in its accustomed place over his bed.

It was evening now and André had come to sit with her. "Did John see you this afternoon?" she asked at last.

"No."

Charlotte could no longer keep back her sobs.

"What is it, my dear? Can I help?"

"André," she managed to gasp, "I have sent John away."

John drove north toward San Francisco. He had recently discovered that his lameness did not prevent him from driving a car. Just where he was going to go he didn't much care. But he meant to make money. There was one way he knew to make it.

The early winter darkness was settling over the Valley. Just below the crest of a hill he shot out from behind a truck. Suddenly there was the glare of headlights and the squeal of brakes. Then his car grazed the side of an oncoming car. He heard a familiar voice. "What do you think you're doing?" It was Andrew Fairon.

"What's the use trying to be a road hog?" shouted Andrew. "Can you pull back a bit?"

"Sorry," said John backing away. For a moment he saw Elizabeth's face at the window of Andrew's car. The light from his own headlights illumined her face. She was thinner than she was last summer but more beautiful, he thought.

"I guess there's not much damage done, except we both have smashed fenders," Andrew said coming around to John's side. "I suppose I'll see you tomorrow at the family dinner?"

"Not this year," John replied, starting his car. *Or any other year*, he added to himself.

"That was John," said Andrew, taking his seat beside Elizabeth.

"Yes, I saw him," she answered.

"Why didn't you speak to him?"

"He must have been driving seventy miles an hour," she answered, ignoring his question. "Now we'll have to lay up for two or three days at your mother's before we go on to Chicago."

"But we aren't in any hurry." Andrew secretly was glad for the excuse to stay a little longer in the San Joaquin Valley, to see more of his family before he and Elizabeth went east.

"No, I suppose not," she answered. "No, of course, we're not in any hurry." Her lightly spoken words covered the consternation she felt over seeing John again. Just before the cars had struck in the glare of the headlights, she had seen John's face, angry, sullen. Now a vivid sense of safety in Andrew, the quiet, good man, came over her. She moved closer to him.

"Are you cold, dear?"

"A little."

"Want my coat?"

"No, Andrew. Sitting close to you does it." If only she could always remember what this safety in Andrew meant to her.

XLIV

CHRISTMAS afternoon after the family dinner held this year at his father's house Andrew Fairon went off by himself, not asking Elizabeth to go with him. They were starting east in the morning and before he left there was a place he wanted to see. His horse took the path up the hill without much direction from him. The two of them had been there often in the years before Andrew's marriage. Close up to the foot of the hill crept the vineyards. Circling the horizon were the mountains, snow-covered on their peaks today. When they gained the top, Andrew tethered his horse.

Here's where the house was to stand, he said to himself, pacing the distance off. It would have been a nice house in which to bring up a family. He'd planned to level the hilltop to give the children a good place to run.

He walked back and forth in the wild grain which covered the hill, knee-high in some places, in others flattened to the ground in swaths of pale amber. *If I am to hold Elizabeth,* he thought, *I must make up my mind to move about a good deal, live in cities. She will never want to be quiet. She craves excitement.*

I could be lots of help in the business just now, according to Father. If we threw Elizabeth's share in with the others and managed the two places together, as we did when Grandfather was alive, it would be the way out for us all. I hate to tell Father we aren't going to do it. It's what we should do.

But it was not what Elizabeth wanted. What Elizabeth wanted he would do. Her cool touch left him with a growing hunger. To satisfy it he would sacrifice whatever she demanded.

The sky above the mountains had become a golden rim of light—the west a luminous afterglow, the east its luminous reflection. As the light faded, the mountains appeared to mount higher, forming walls of darkness which hemmed in the Valley. Up here on the hill, the wild unharvested grain was still visible. The frail husks emptied by the wind of their grain hung on the brittle yellow stems like small transparent cups. Andrew staring down at them felt a poignant emotional reaction to the empty husks. Bread and wine, the sacrificial fruits. Long ago on threshing floors close to their homes men had learned how to beat out the grain from the chaff. The beginning of man's settled living—bread and wine. Difficult attainment for a man and a woman to live and work together.

"You surely intend to settle down pretty soon, don't you?" his father asked Andrew later that evening. "Your money won't last very long if you carry out your plans. Besides I don't like to think of a son of mine idling."

"A year won't hurt him. He should get away for a little, see something of the world, Father," Elizabeth answered sitting on the arm of Andrew's chair.

Her soft nearness sent a shock through Andrew's senses. "Give us our fling before we settle down, Father," he said, but it hurt him to say it.

Elizabeth gave his shoulder a grateful pat, then rose and wandered over to her aunts, Isobel, Maria, and Martha, who sat in a group across the room. She could not meet the appeal in Isobel's eyes. She knew Andrew's mother did not want them to go away. She knew, too, that Andrew did not want to go. But some deep imperative drove her away from a quiet home life with Andrew.

Restlessly she wandered about the room, and over to the window where she stood with her back to her aunts. On that early morning in the summer when Andrew had declared his love for her it had seemed easy to love him. In the arrogance

of her ignorance she had willed it to be and therefore it would
be so. He was gentle, he was good. The escape from Henri's
furtive violence into the security of Andrew's gentleness had
given to her, for the time being, the emotional gratitude which
sanctuary always begets.

But once she was married Andrew had ceased to be sanctuary. Instead husband and lover. That he was gentle did
not make the sense of flight in her any less the convulsive,
demanding thing flight from Henri had been. Why did she
feel so toward Andrew whom she respected, whom she loved
in a curiously dispassionate way?

A flush crept up over Elizabeth's slim neck and into her
cheeks. If Andrew guessed why she had married him, he
would despise her. She could not bear to have him look at
her as she had seen him look at John the night he had bumped
into their car. *I couldn't bear to have him despise me.*

Andrew joined her, put his arm over her shoulder. "We'll
have fun, dear," he said, "wandering about together."

Something in his voice told Elizabeth the secret of his
hunger. Then she knew that she could do what she wanted
with Andrew. He would never despise her, even if she were
hard with him to get her way. She must see that they went
abroad and stayed there. She would not be bound by the re-
strictions of Philippe's will. She meant to free herself from
the family. Philippe's gift which he had meant should give
her independence had made her question even his intentions.
Did he too, like Aunt Martha, want to rule her?

XLV

WHEN the small sum of money Charlotte had placed in the bank for John was exhausted, he went to work for himself but not at the kind of work his mother had had in mind.

John was after easy money and he knew how to get it. Bootlegging in itself was too low-class business for a Rambeau to engage in openly. But he knew the Valley from end to end, and he knew those who were desperate and those who were weak. With a little sales talk he had persuaded the bootleggers, to whom he had sold wine from his father's winery the autumn after his accident, to give him a percentage of their returns for the information he would give them concerning the men of the Valley. He would tell them those who needed money and those who wanted easy money.

He even undertook to see some of the men himself, visiting the Valley at night, opening the way for the bootlegger's visit. Petucci was one of these. Not a good farmer at best, the sudden fall in grape prices the year before had wiped him out except for the money he took in supplying his neighbors with wine. He had a small family press for he had always liked to make his own wine. Petucci thought of wine as food. In Italy it had been so. To supply his neighbors he had never considered a breaking of the law. But when John suggested he sell to the bootleggers, Petucci was frightened.

"I no break-a da law. I get-a da trouble I break-a da law."

"You've already broken it," said John. "There's not much use drawing back now. All I'd have to do is to report you for selling to Bartolini down the road here and they'd have both you and Bartolini up."

Petucci's eyes grew big with terror. He waved his great hands about like the wings of a huge bird caught on the ground and unable to fly.

John laughed. "Don't look so scared, Petucci. I'm not reporting you. In fact, I am protecting you if you go along on this scheme. It's the little fellow that gets into trouble. You'd better be a big fellow. Then you can get away with it."

Petucci looked around the parlor where he had taken John for their talk. He was proud of his parlor. On one wall was a picture of Washington; on the wall opposite one of Lincoln. Hung on a forty-five degree angle the two great men leaned over Petucci from their frames, lending respectability and protection to John Rambeau's proposition. John Rambeau, too, stood to Petucci for respectability. He was not a little flattered that one of Philippe Rambeau's grandsons should come to see him. For a Rambeau to talk to him in the field in passing was one thing, but for him to come to his house to see him in the evening was quite another.

Still, Petucci was a good Italian and he wanted first to consult his wife and his priest. John Rambeau knew this would be the natural course for the childlike Petucci and he meant to bring him to a decision without such consultation.

"I can't wait for an answer, Petucci. The fellows are making out their routes tonight. I asked them as a favor to take you in. I knew it would help you out on a bad year. You haven't much to sell just now, but another year you could enlarge. See here, Petucci, what did you come to this country for? Wasn't it to get ahead? Why not take your chance when you have it?"

Petucci began to see a splendid picture of himself—rich and important among his fellow Italians, important, too, before his wife, who didn't think him very smart.

"They'll arrange everything," said John, watching the indecision growing in Petucci's eyes. "All you've got to do is to be around the night they come. You don't sign your name to anything."

"I do," said Petucci at last.

So it was arranged there in Petucci's good parlor with Washington and Lincoln looking down on him and John Rambeau sitting beside him.

For more than two years John sent no word home. Then on a spring night he drove his car along the road which led past his own home. At the far end of the long drive light shining from his mother's windows caught the downward sweep of a eucalyptus branch, making the glossy leaves glisten. What he had done to earn money would hurt his mother, if she knew. It gave him pleasure to think how much. This act was his farewell to the Valley. He was going to Mexico City and then farther away.

XLVI

LUIGI and Buz were no longer frightened as they had been at first. It was over two years since that day they had fled from Fresno. Time had at last dimmed their fear. In the beginning they had never stayed more than one night in a place. They had driven down into Mexico just as Buz had planned the day of Luigi's flight, then back into lower California—the no-man's land belonging to Mexico but holding the name of California. They had camped along the roadsides, and both Luigi and Buz had picked up any small jobs they could get. Sometimes for hours they felt perfectly safe. Then they remembered and tightened their precautions again. Twice they had changed their name.

At last they had gone back to California, hoping to find more settled work for Luigi. But after a time they had begun to be fearful again. Living by a kind of sixth sense of apprehension which the pursued soon come to rely upon to give them warning, they were certain that Luigi was being watched. A man in a store one day had asked him if he had ever lived in Fresno, and a man where he worked had laughed at his name. Johnson didn't sound real to him. "Aren't you an Eyetalian?" he had asked. That frightened Luigi.

Again they had started out.

Either one who could get work took it, and the other one looked after the baby. They did not complain over hard work. Camping along the road at night in an almost austere silence, they watched the darkness come down and felt awe at something too big for them to understand. Buz, through all their struggle, had been gentle with the baby and so had Luigi.

Their identical interest in finding safety for themselves

had welded them together. By some strange paradox fear had raised them both out of the commonplace. They had come near to living nobly those months, and they had shared the experience. They had forgotten the petty issues over which they used to quarrel.

Now after over two years of flight they had settled in Mexico City. Luigi had at last found a good job in the hotel garage. He had had one promotion. A sense of safety was beginning to take the place of their fear. It was as sweet as honey in their mouths. This they shared with each other, too.

Luigi was cleaning a car which had just come in from the dusty Mexican roads. He was humming to himself, not thinking much about anything, splashing the water and feeling good. *Guess Buz and him might step out tonight. The kid needed to have a little fun.*

"Hi there, big guy," the bellboy from the hotel sang out. "Don't you know your job? A fellow just come in his swanky roadster." His hands full of suitcases, the bellboy inclined his head in the direction of the front of the garage. "Get a move on. He ain't the kind to do no waiting."

"Cool off, Buttons, the guy will have to wait till I clean up a bit." Wiping his hands on a cloth, Luigi walked toward the handsome car standing just inside the garage. The sun shining through the entrance door blinded his eyes. Then as his vision cleared he saw a man getting out of the car. He had swung himself to the side, leaned over and picked up something. He was on his feet now by the side of the car—crutches, that is what he had reached for. Luigi waited a moment. *He'll not want me to notice. Give him a chance to get himself arranged first.*

"Hello, there," the man called out, "anybody around here ready to look after my car?" He turned. And in that moment Luigi recognized the voice and face of John Rambeau!

The car was between them. Luigi stopped, slipped to the side of a large truck just coming in the door. "See to you in a minute. Somebody here in a minute," he managed to say to the man in the truck. *He musn't seem to hurry.*

Two cars between him and John Rambeau now. Still he musn't hurry, not until he reached the door. No, even then he mustn't hurry. Not until he came to the corner of the street. He was outside now. The corner was only a few steps away, but it seemed he would never get there. Then he saw that the street ahead was full of people. He musn't run now, either. A block, two blocks, four.

His thoughts were mixed and tumbling around in his head. So he hadn't killed Rambeau. A weight rolled off Luigi. It was bad thinking he had killed a man. But he had hurt him. That made it worse in some ways. Rambeau was alive and would get his revenge. Rambeau would turn him over to the police. That was what he was here for.

Buz sat in the sun in the courtyard outside the shack they called home. She had her baby in her lap. She was enjoying herself. She didn't have anything to worry about. She wasn't ashamed of Luigi any more. And not being ashamed of him, she liked him, was proud of him. He was handsomer even than John Rambeau. They were getting on fine now. Another raise and they would move into a nice place.

She had been teaching the baby to walk. He had been slow about it. He was still unsteady on his feet. He had been quick in learning to talk. "Come, John," she coaxed, standing him against the wall, and backing off. "Come over here to me." He did it, tumbling into her arms at the last step. Taking him up, she cuddled him in her lap.

She and the child must have dozed, for when she opened her eyes Luigi was lifting John from her lap. "What you doing home this time a day, Luigi?" she asked sleepily.

"Come inside, Buz. I got something to tell you."

"You don't need to. I can see."

"Buz, John Rambeau ain't dead. He just drove into the garage. I guess he's after me. I lamed him."

"Did he see you?" Buz interrupted him to ask.

"I'm not sure."

"Then we got to hurry."

XLVII

Six years had passed since the reading of Philippe Rambeau's will at the end of that year of his great wealth. He would not have liked what had happened since in the valleys he so loved. Many of the vineyards had been left to die. Some of the good ones had been pulled up; in their place vines had been planted that old Philippe would not have had on his land. They bore grapes that shipped well, and reached the east coast in good condition for making homemade wine, but the wine made from them was flat and without character.

It was the Valley's effort to live.

Only Monica of all Philippe's grandchildren was at home. Elizabeth and Andrew had never returned, nor had John ever come back to the Valley since that night four years ago when he had driven by his mother's windows.

In the late autumn after the harvest a letter telling John of his mother's failing strength, after following him about for months, reached him in Vancouver. Even then he waited a few days to start. Perhaps he did not want to get there in time.

Only when he was in his car, driving toward California, did he know how much he wanted to see her again. Once he was out of the northern mountains of California and had entered the wide valleys he drove faster and faster. The dry hot air was good against his skin. At last he was in the wine country. In all his life he had not been so moved as when he saw the first familiar landmarks—the sign of the Italian Swiss colony, the green-domed church, the gray buildings of the winery, the undulating slope of the vineyards. He used to come here as a boy for the harvest festival. He remembered the year of the great prosperity, when the colony had built the huge underground tank and held their dance in it before its first filling. Mr. Rossi, the director of the colony, and his grandfather had been close friends. Each respected the knowledge of the other. Often Philippe Rambeau came to sit in the lovely Italian garden of his friend and in the years before John had gone overseas he had gone too. Philippe Rambeau had bowed before the greater knowledge of Mr. Rossi.

Yes, here was where the road narrowed and the trees shut away the road ahead. Scenes from his childhood passed through his mind—days spent in the comfortable hospitality of the Beringers, their German neighbors. Behind a gray lichen-covered wall stood the simple white house of one brother, the high-peaked, gabled house of the other. Against the hills, looking down upon the house, stood the stone winery. He laughed aloud, remembering a crowd of children riding the pomace down as it was emptied from the presses, the feel of the soft pulp under him, his mother's consternation when she came to fetch him and Monny and saw the seat of his trousers and Monny's panties stained a deep purple.

But before he reached the Beringers' he would be coming to the Rambeau land, his grandfather's northern vineyards, now belonging to Elizabeth. Now he could see the "pointed vineyards" as he and Monny had called the hillside vineyards, the rocky hillsides where the roots of the vines struck deep for moisture, where the grapes were small, the bunches meager, the wine made from them the best in the land. The muscles of his heart tightened. Before him was the brown old house where he had lived during the years his father was in charge. How often Monny and he had sat in the arbor and watched his mother coming down the steps toward them, strong and lithe.

The house was shuttered and empty. He would make the circuit of the drive. Slowly he drove through the gate along the half-circle of the roadway, stopped his car by the winery. There was no motion or life. The signs of neglect were everywhere; grass grew in the fine gravel of the paths. a shutter

hung loose on a window of the house, the doors of the winery
needed paint, a timber had rotted in the loading platform.
In the vineyards he could see here and there a vine was missing.

How could his grandfather have done this? Deliberately, it
seemed to John, old Philippe had surrendered the place to
someone who had despoiled what the two of them had so loved.
That year he was learning the art of wine making, Philippe's
mind and his had fused in understanding.

Through the winery door way just then came Diener. He
spread out his hands in a gesture of delight, crying, "It is good
to see a Rambeau! Come in. Come in."

"I can't!" John answered, roused from his bitter thoughts.
"I was just driving past. How are you getting on, Diener?"

The old man's face clouded and he made a gesture of help-
lessness with his hands; then he poured out his complaints.
"*Ach,* they don't send me money—only a leetle. I must make
it last. The inspectors they come, I hide the bad, show the
good. *Ach,* I cannot fool them always, and Andrew he play
around in Paris. Andrew should bring his woman home. And
the baby here it belong."

John lighted a cigarette, puffed angrily. These vineyards
he had wanted and would have cared for, going to ruin. Better
if his grandfather had wiped them from the earth! He put
in his clutch, shot down the drive, leaving old Diener gaping
after him in amazement. He drove faster, hurrying to reach
the last of the Rambeau land.

He was past house and vineyards now, out on the stretch
of road which passed that unfertile land given over to wild
grain, a menace to them always in the dry tinderlike air of
autumn. No strip had been plowed to protect the vineyards.
Neglect! Unpardonable neglect! Something snapped in his
mind. Suddenly the fear of fire to which he had been condi-
tioned all his life changed over into delight in fire.

A mad desire seized him. He stopped the car and deliberately tossed his cigarette into the dry stalks of wild barley
growing along the roadside, then sat and watched the tiny

triangle of fire with a crackling sound spread in a burst of flames.

Suddenly John realized what he had done. He grabbed his coat, lying on the seat beside him, climbed out of his car, hobbling along on his crutch. He could do nothing with a crutch. Throwing it to the ground, he dropped to his knees and beat at the fire with his coat. It leaped away from him. Blazing straws caught up here and there by the wind dropped farther out on the field, started new blazes. A hundred points of fire ahead of him, and around him the blackened stubble hot under his hands! Beating and sobbing he crawled over the ground.

A shrieking siren sounded over the valley. The first fire fighters dropped from trucks pulling up alongside the road. Quickly they spread over the field beating at the flames with wet blankets as they ran.

"Keep it off the vineyards!" John shouted. Already the wind had carried sparks to the dry grape leaves. And as if the fire fed the wind, it gained in volume, the gusts rising to a fury, fanning the burning leaves until the rough shredded bark of the trunks and then the slower burning trunks themselves were ignited.

"Hey, there!" the leader of the fire fighters called to John. "You can't do anything here. Get back to your car and take a message for me down to the next gas station. Tell them we've got to have a lot more men."

With the command John came to himself. What was he doing here, crawling over the ground like an animal? "Get me my crutch—it's around here somewhere," he commanded, "and I'll carry the message."

Fortunately nobody appeared to have recognized him. He'd get out before they did. Seeing Diener, bent and slow-moving, come out of the gate, he flung his crutch on the seat, sent the car leaping down the road, pulling up at the gas station only long enough to give the message. Then he was on his way again. Behind him the fire towered in a high column of flame. It must have reached the trees in the canyon that lay to the back of the vineyard.

Truckloads of fire fighters were passing him. The call had gone out to the near-by towns. *It will be all right now. Plenty of men. Vines don't burn very fast,* he kept assuring himself. Why, his hands were burned. Seeing a doctor's sign on a small frame house, he stopped.

"Come from the fire?" asked the doctor.

"Yes," said John.

"Hear it's going to do a lot of harm in the old Rambeau vineyards. Too bad. The Rambeaus have been hard hit these last years. Always got my supply of wine for medicinal uses from the old gentleman. Fine old gentleman. Did you ever know him?"

"Slightly," John answered.

"He'd feel pretty bad at what's happening today. Seems like his family don't show much interest in the vineyards any more. Diener, the old winemaker, is the only one I see around when I go there now. And he's getting too old to work. Better lay up for a day or two with those hands," the doctor ended. "You'll find it difficult to drive."

"I'm going south on urgent business. I can manage. But I wonder if I might change my clothes before I go?"

"Certainly. Let me get your bag."

Surely the man must know I'm a Rambeau, John thought as he dressed.

Soon he was on his way again, putting the car to its fastest possible speed, swinging around curves, darting down long stretches of straight road, ignoring town and state speed laws; only dimly conscious of the pain in his hands, his mind a jumble of emotions. There was the exultant sense of release which had come to him as he answered the violence which had so long surged up in him—done at last some deed commensurate with his bitter emotions; there was the terrifying aftermath of realization at the destruction he had brought to something he loved. Two men dwelt within him—one had exulted, one now grieved.

Darkness settled down. He was on the long straight road leading through the San Joaquin Valley now. His car seemed to be rushing through space, shot forward by the poignance of his remorse.

He left the main highway at last. The clock on the dashboard told him it was midnight. The house would be dark, his mother asleep. He slackened his pace when he turned into the drive leading to his father's house. The fast-growing eucalyptus trees had become very tall in his absence. They shaded his mother's windows. Then, as he drove up in front of the house, he saw there was a light in her room, the flickering light which candles give.

The front door stood open, but there was no one to greet him as he entered. He went across the familiar hall into the library where he might expect to find his father. The room was empty. The evening paper had not been opened. It lay neatly folded on the table by his father's chair, next the decanter of port. There was no sound. And then, far off in the depths of the house, a child's cry. He sank into a chair. He felt faint. He had not eaten since yesterday. The pain in his hands reached up along his arms.

The cold touch of a glass against his lips made him open his eyes. His father was leaning over him, supporting his head, holding the glass to his lips. The wine was cool and fresh. He felt life coming back into his exhausted body. He saw Monny kneeling at his side.

"Is she——?" he managed to ask, turning to her.

"An hour ago," was all Monica could say.

So he could never absolve himself, kneeling by his mother's bed with the touch of her hand on his head. Such easy settlement had been denied him even if he had wanted it, and he was not sure he did. Then suddenly he felt whole, the two men warring within him merged one into the other. It was a feeling so vivid he forgot to reach for his crutch as he rose, only to sink back in his chair. Yet the impression of his wholeness remained and coupled with it the knowledge that he had come back to the Valley to stay.

XLVIII

Ronald Fairon cabled his son in Paris of the burning of the Napa vineyards. Andrew felt grief akin to that he would have felt for the loss of some member of his family. These vineyards were to him the embodiment of his grandfather. With shame he thought of his long absence from the work old Philippe had evidently expected of him when he left the vineyards to Elizabeth.

The slow disintegration taking place in him stopped. He would no longer violate his own integrity. The edges of his identity, smudged in the years he had devoted purely to gratification of Elizabeth, sharpened. He would go home, live the life he was meant to live, bring up his son in the ways of his own people.

But when Elizabeth heard the news she said, "This decides the question. We must settle down here now. It will be far cheaper than living in California."

"I haven't told you before," Andrew answered, "that the money Grandfather left me is finished. So as things now stand we have only the income we can get out of the Napa vineyards. Cut in half as it now is, that is not enough to live on here. At home we have the old house and I can do a good deal of the work of restoring the vineyards. In time I can bring our income up to what it was before the fire. Probably the roots are still alive on the burned vines and we can regraft." Already Andrew's mind was busy with plans.

"Father would help us if we stayed here."

Andrew stood looking down at his young wife, a rich grace about her since the birth of the baby. She no longer seemed a girl. She had the assurance and knowledge of a

292

young matron. *She is lovelier than ever,* he thought. But then he had thought that just before the baby was born. Then pallor seemed to give her beauty, a delicacy her face lacked before. The Rambeaus' good looks were a strong virile sort of handsomeness. This new, more elusive loveliness of Elizabeth's had fascinated him. There was, he thought helplessly, no phase of Elizabeth's life that did not have its own peculiar charm. Sometimes he longed for the time when they would be old and he could take her for granted.

"Well?" questioned Elizabeth finally.

"Surely, Elizabeth, you would not ask me to let your father support us?"

"Lon would be glad to do it for us." Elizabeth's eyes fell before his steady gaze.

"I intend to take care of my own family," Andrew surprised himself by saying.

Elizabeth had a queer mixed feeling of anger and respect for him. With some uneasiness she remembered how once very early in their marriage she had thought, *I wouldn't want Andrew to lose faith in me.* And yet to go back—she remembered the intimacy of those months with Andrew when they had been there alone. In the five years they had wandered over the Continent it had seemed easy to live lightly on the surface—after she had learned how. And this last year, with Paris and the baby to distract her, had been all right too.

"I hear Phil." She jumped up and went into the next room. Soon she was back with the half-awake child in her arms. Sitting down she rumpled his curls and snuggled him close. "A little Frenchman, isn't he? Don't turn him into an immigrant. I've been to great trouble to get him for you." She smiled, stretched out her hand to take hold of Andrew's and pull him down to her and the baby.

This time I won't give in, Andrew resolved.

On the steamer, and on the train crossing his own country, Andrew was silent. Even for small Philippe he rarely had a smile. But a change came over him as they reached the high mountain pass which led down into California. It was dawn, and quietly, so as not to waken Elizabeth and small Philippe, he raised the blind in their compartment a few inches. It was November and snow lay among the trees and around the isolated houses. Then the train went swiftly down to the floor of the Valley. Andrew's heart seemed too large for his breast. In its mysterious winter renewal the land lay under its soft green covering.

Elizabeth was awake now and together they dressed Phil, both of them more than a little excited. Finally they were on the local train which would take them into their own valley. When it stopped at their station Andrew caught up his son. "Look, Elizabeth, there's Diener to meet us."

"*Ach!*" Diener exclaimed, with his eyes on the baby. "It ees goot, the leetle, big Philippe Rambeau." Phil soberly allowed himself to be taken from his father's arms. "So," said Diener, the tears running down his cheeks, "the old they die but they leave a leetle twig in their place."

Andrew laughed and almost hugged Diener in his delight. But he was silent when he saw their blackened vineyards, the charred stumps standing up out of the green of miner's lettuce and mustard which already had spread over the scorched earth. Immediately his practiced eyes took in the fact that no strip of land had been ploughed to protect the vineyards. Shame came over him that Diener had been obliged no doubt for lack of money to neglect such an essential precaution. With that telltale evidence of neglect the vineyards could even now be claimed by the state.

When they entered the long-closed house it was Elizabeth's time to fall silent. It had a musty smell that seemed to condemn her for its neglect. Old Philippe had given her his most cherished possession. But she did not want it.

For Andrew the rooms were filled with a thousand memories and traditions he wished to pass on to his son. Only he and John and Charles to preserve the name and the traditions for the next generation. Charles, he understood, had broken away, gone east after his mother's death and John's return. But John was going in with the men of his family, so Andrew's mother had written. *Now*, thought Andrew, *if Elizabeth is willing we could combine to the advantage of us all.*

But Elizabeth was not willing; neither was John. He had other plans.

XLIX

JOHN's vision of wholeness glimpsed the night of his mother's death meant to him no new heaven, no new earth. He was simply aware of an awakening of his old business instinct, lying dormant since his injury. He was tired of loafing. He wanted to get his teeth into work, the only kind of work he knew. He wanted to own a vineyard.

But he had lived luxuriously these years, and saved almost nothing. The banks, he felt certain, would not lend him money without his father's name as guarantor, and he did not wish to discuss his idea with André, who would urge him to come back into the Rambeau-Fairon business. John had never had a free hand, and he was anxious to see what he could do for himself. Besides, the Rambeau-Fairon business was run down. He didn't want to be a part of a half-going concern. He decided there was just one person to whom he could turn—Aunt Martha. Until the time of his accident they had always understood each other.

The next morning he drove over to see her. The grounds, he noticed, in contrast to those of his father's place, were as well kept as in his grandfather's time—the lawn close-clipped, the flower beds full of autumn bloom, the shrubbery trimmed, its leaves fresh from recent watering, the great oak newly cemented where it tended toward rot in the crotch, the tiled terraces washed free of dust. Pots of bright flowers stood as usual by the posts of the covered terrace. Aunt Martha was an expert gardener and the ancient art of gardening in pots had always been a hobby with her.

John pulled the bell, an antiquated contraption left over

from his grandfather's beginnings, and as of old he heard the soft shuffling of feet within.

"Well, hello, Chu!" John exclaimed in surprise when Chu opened the door. "I thought you'd gone back to your own country."

"Yes, I go," Chu answered him. "I come back. Missie need old Chu." Chu did not feel it necessary to explain that he had been lonely in his own country, that whatever harsh treatment he felt California had meted out to him and his people, he could not stay away from it. California was more home to him than China.

"And David?" asked John. "Where is he?"

"David very fine doctor velly soon. He live China side, San Francisco. He have one fine small boy." Chu grinned.

"Good for you," said John, "and now go and tell your missie I'm here. It's very important. You manage it, Chu. I must see her, so don't let her turn me down." He slipped a coin into the old man's hand. "For the fine small boy," he murmured.

"I fix," said Chu. "Master come inside."

Sitting in the central room, facing the great window, John had the opportunity to take stock of his aunt before she saw him. She was crossing the terrace in full sunlight. Her hair had turned snow-white. It seemed to give her height, and a kind of magnificence. Her face, he saw, held its old fierce vitality, but overlying it was a look which was new to him. A kind of resignation but not of her choosing. *It's because she has no power,* was his swift conclusion. Suppose he offered her power.

She had entered the room now, and her expression changed instantly to one of guarded brightness. "Oh, how do you do, John?" she said. She sat down some distance from him, omitting the family's customary salutation of a kiss on each cheek. "To what do I owe this honor?"

"Aunt Martha," John answered, "we've always understood each other, so there's no need to beat about the bush. I've a proposition to put up to you." He explained what he had in mind—a new brand of table grapes sold as a specialty in New York at top prices.

"There is a piece of property I've had my eye on for years that is just the spot," he told her. "It's high land, a little plateau, really, surrounded by hills. The frost comes a full month later there than it does down here. I've seen them picking grapes up there just before Christmas." He paused to let the idea sink in. Aunt Martha was business all through and would see the possibilities.

"And you thought?" Martha prompted him.

"The bank has had to take it over and they'll sell cheap. I've not money to buy it, and I thought maybe you'd like to go in with me."

"And why do you think so?"

"It would give you and me a chance to make money. . . . I'd let you boss me," he added with his old audacity, an audacity which had often won out with his aunt in the past. But he saw immediately that he had made a mistake.

Anger smoldered in Martha's eyes and she broke into a mirthless laugh. "You come to me! What money do you think I have, with this splendid management your father gives to the estate? I suppose you think we are all wealthy. If I were in charge, managing things as they should be managed, do you suppose, for one instant, you would dare come to me with such a proposition? You who have——"

"You don't need to say it, I'll save you the trouble. Who has disgraced the family."

"As you wish," said his aunt, rising.

He had meant to forestall her by rising before she did, but he had fumbled a moment in picking up his crutch, giving her the advantage. Without speaking again, he opened the french window and went out. His aunt had made him suddenly conscious that he no longer had any place among the Rambeaus, that the anger and hatred which he had dealt out to his family these last years were as tangible as brick and mortar.

No more than brick and mortar would disappear simply because he wished it, could his acts committed in anger be forgotten. He had created himself in an image that threatened them. Since his return he had seen a look of withdrawal in their eyes—in Nate's and Charles' before he left. Yes, he was certain that he had seen it in Monny's, too. Was she fearful that he would break up the even tenor of her family? Did she not want her two sons to come under his influence? The elder, five now, had liked John from the start. They could be good friends if Monny would allow it.

Aunt Martha's bitter statement had acted like acid, etching in clear lines the attitude of the family, only half realized until now. He sat down on one of the benches of the old garden. This garden from childhood he had taken for granted was part of him, just as all Rambeau things were a part of him. Only now, suddenly, they weren't. He was an interloper.

When his mother had sent him away from his home he had felt no sense of separation. She had not sent him away because she would be happier without him. He knew that there was not an hour in all the time he had been away when she had not longed to see him. But the rest of his family were happier and safer without him.

If he went away again he would not exist for them any more. They wanted to forget him. He rose and walked toward his car. The two-edged weapon of bitterness and anger he had wielded so long was now rending the fabric of his own life.

He had placed his crutch behind the seat and had slid himself under the wheel, when he heard Chu saying close at his elbow, "Meester John! You and the missie speak very loud. Old Chu hear."

"I see," said John falling in with Chu's explanation. He knew Chu's habit of listening at keyholes but he liked the old chap.

"Meester John, old Chu have leetle money. Old Chu think

scheme velly good. Meester John like partner? But more better Meester John be own boss." Chu threw back his head, laughing at his sly thrust at John for his inopportune remark to Martha about being the boss.

Sitting sidewise on the seat, his feet on the running board, John slapped his knee, laughed out loud with his old zest. What a revenge on Aunt Martha! It appealed to his peculiar sense of humor. "I think more better, too," he said.

"You wait." Chu shuffled away, taking the path to the servants' quarters. Presently he came back, a large bag in his hands. He placed it on the seat beside John. "Five thousand. And have got other bag, suppose Meester John must have," he said, slamming the door.

"We need you to help us," André said that evening to John. "It's been hard work living up to the terms of Father's will. In fact we had to sell Henri's land in order to save the rest. The Fairons have thrown in all they had, and Monica has invested her money in the business. Nate has worked hard. But your enterprise just now would help carry us through. We've only one more year to prove up on the property according to your grandfather's will."

A shadow of regret crossed John's mind. The business had been part of most of his life. Surprising what a hold it had on him. But he was glad that he had gone too far on his own arrangements to turn back.

"My enterprise hasn't been rated very high around here, Dad," he answered. "Why should it suddenly seem valuable to you? Grandfather definitely left me out and I think I'd better stay out."

"You ought not to hold a grudge like that, and you wouldn't if you understood." André was disappointed. He needed his son. Charlotte's going had left him bewildered and groping, lost in a world suddenly gone dark. He would have liked to lean on his son.

"I'm sorry if you really need me," John said, noticing the

tired droop to his father's shoulders. "I don't know that I'm holding a grudge. Just why I'm refusing perhaps I couldn't even explain to myself. I'm going to settle in the Valley though, if that's any comfort to you."

"You mean you're going in for yourself?"

"Yes."

"We've too many vineyards in the Valley right now." André was annoyed. "You'll only make it harder for the rest of us."

"I don't think so," John answered. "I'm going in for table grapes."

Chu's money was not enough to buy the land John wanted. With wisdom as shrewd as that of old Philippe he finally decided to buy a stretch of rather poor land—hardpan for the most part, but with good water rights. It was nearly as level as a floor, which would make irrigation almost automatic. Since he must save on labor, this would be a big advantage. Most of the vineyards would have to be pulled, for they had been neglected and the vines were infected with the deadly Phylloxera. But one plot of land had been planted to resistant stock, clean, fine plants ready for grafting. The place had a house and outbuildings, but all run down.

The tragic history of the industry was written upon these buildings—failure, discouragement, departure. The square, two-storied, finely built house must once have housed people of taste and refinement. Then as tenant after tenant had occupied it, it had received less and less care. Dirt and neglect had been allowed to mar its once dignified aspect. The paint had peeled away from the exposed parts of the house. Old clothes were stuffed into broken windows. The porch sagged on one corner; rusted screening was tacked on the window frames. No wonder he could get the ranch for a moderate down payment!

Chu proved to be no passive partner. When the time came for planting the new vines on the cleared land he complained to Martha of his health, asking for a vacation. But he found for Martha a capable substitute before he left her to join John in their undertaking.

He made himself a bunk in the lean-to of John's house. Chinese labor was almost at an end in California, but from some mysterious source known only to himself Chu gathered together a gang of Chinese laborers, housed them in an empty tool shed, led them into the fields at dawn, brought them back only when they could no longer distinguish between the dark soil and the dark night settling over the earth.

Late one evening the following spring John drove into the yard. "Here, Chu," he called, "come and get these bundles. They're cuttings for grafting. Damn that fellow at the nursery. He's put the price up on the kind of table grapes I wanted."

"What you get?" asked Chu fingering the bundles.

"A new kind—'Rebiers,' they call 'em. I've a hunch we can make a killing on them. Put out our own brand, sell 'em as a special."

On the precise and delicate job of grafting, John started the next morning. He was determined to do as much of it as he could himself. Years ago old Philippe had taught him the best method. There was no single task in the vineyards which John had liked so well. He made himself a low seat set on wheels which he could push from vine to vine.

Yes, today he could begin. The vines were in just the right condition to bring about union with the inserted canes. The heaviest flow of the sap from the sawed-off vines was over. Chu, with his race's natural aptitude for delicate work, soon equaled John in skill. They worked, silently, each absorbed in his task.

Good resistant stock in this vineyard, John thought. *Old Philippe would approve of it.* His grandfather always was careful in choosing the right stock for the right soil. "Regis St. George" he had used for the dry gravelly earth of the

Napa hill vineyards. The lower vineyard, along the roadside, which he had last seen swept by flames, had good roots, too. A good job of grafting could be done there. Remembering his part in the destruction of his grandfather's northern vineyards, he felt deep shame.

But as he took his sharp, thin chisel, split a cleft in the top of the first strong root, inserted the new bearing cane, he forgot his remorse. In its place came pleasure in the clean thrust of the chisel which seemed to satisfy the destructive instinct which had so long dominated him. His expert cut had made a cleft which fitted snugly around the graft. He slipped the new wood into place close up against the inner bark of the old wood, making a perfect union of the two green cambium layers. Delight in the finished work of his hands took possession of him.

Down the long aisles he went, repeating the rhythm of split and closed cleft. When he looked behind him and saw the growing lines of his vines, each new scion inserted into an old vine standing parallel with the grape post, just as old Philippe had taught him, he felt a strange new sense of harmony.

But on the evening the long, arduous task was completed the sense of harmony left him. Chu had gone back to his job with Martha. John was lonely and restless; never yet had he depended on himself for entertainment. He stood at his door looking out over his vineyard. The acres of T-shaped stakes led away in long aisles. Wherever he stood they converged around him in monotonous repetition. Where before had he seen that monotonous repetition of stakes? Suddenly he remembered. In the flat land of France. Acres of crosses, marking the graves of his comrades. Futility gripped him, as it had so often before.

He flung himself into his car, driving with the old clever recklessness. Why did he want to tie himself down to the monotonous job of a vineyard? Why did he want to tie himself down to anything? Where had he got the crazy idea that he ought to pay Elizabeth back for the burning of the vineyards? What did he owe her after all? What did he owe anyone?

The only responsibility he felt now was to Chu. Whatever else he might or might not do, he couldn't let Chu down. *The old son-of-a-gun!* he said to himself. Driving slowly back to his new home, he began planning to make the place pay dividends to himself and Chu.

John had always lived as he wanted to; he was living as he wanted to now. That one way was diametrically opposed to the other he never stopped to think. Some force, long lying idle in him, craved to be used. It seemed to him, in the months that followed, that he could not get enough of doing things with his hands. As soon as his vineyards were in order he began to work on his house. He tore off the old screening on the windows, felt angry when he saw the innumerable layers of tacks which had been hammered into the window frames. "The bastards!" he ejaculated to the empty air around him. "Destroying good stuff." It took days to pull the tacks, days more to putty the holes.

He hired a man to help put a new sill under the sagging porch. Then they painted the house. When they finished that, they repaired the outbuildings. John rose early; he worked late. There was a hunger in him he could not satisfy. When he was too tired to work any longer, he sat thinking about the work he had finished, as a man who has long gone without food, after his first good meal goes over in his mind the taste of meat and bread.

He saw little of his family. Occasionally he went to see them; occasionally Monny came to see him. She wanted to do over the interior of the house for him, but he would not have it. He wanted its walls bare, its space empty.

Something like Mother's room, Monny thought, as she sat by his open fire one winter's day. John had had the walls knocked out on two sides of the room and glass put in their place. A long table, a chair and a couch were the room's only furnishings. The floor Chu had covered for him with Chinese matting.

Something of their childhood relationship crept into these days when she came to see him. He no longer threatened Nate's happiness. Her husband and her two children secure, she dared reach out a little to include John. Little by little as the months went by Monny began to realize that the old bitterness was going from John, and the old restlessness too. Had he, she wondered, come to learn as her mother had how to accept his limitations? She dared not ask him. He never referred to his injury and he would not talk to her about their mother nor about the northern vineyards nor about old Philippe nor of Elizabeth and Andrew. It was as if he shut a door on the past, saving out of it only his love for her. Sometimes with rare tenderness he would draw her to him as if he were lonely. Then after a moment he would be all business again, absorbed in his one overpowering idea—the money he expected to make when his grapes came into bearing.

L

AFTER the day he saw John in Mexico, Luigi sought again to re-establish himself. If John Rambeau could follow him to Mexico, Luigi had reasoned, then they might just as well take their chances in California. The great vineyards and orchards represented home to him. Even if he could not go back to his mother's place, perhaps, if he worked hard, he could buy a square house like hers, with an arbor at the back and a few olive and fruit trees in front.

They had gone down into the Imperial Valley, where both he and Buz had picked lettuce, living in an old tent Luigi bought. Then when the season was over, he found a job in a garage in El Centro. With what he could save and Buz had made in the fields they had enough by the next year for a first payment on a house. It had been a trade, really, for the people who owned the house were willing to accept Luigi's car as part payment.

It took optimism to call it a house. It was little more than a roof and a floor. The sides, halfway up, had been enclosed with light lumber. On the upper half screens had been nailed and there were canvas shutters to be let down in the rainy winter months. There was not a single tree in the small space in front, but Buz and Luigi were vastly proud of their property.

Buz was to work in the fields just one more season.

"I ain't a-going to have my wife out with the pickers after that, and I don't want John growing up to that kind of life," Luigi told her. He loved the little boy with all the strength of his ardent Latin nature.

Buz loved him, too, but with a kind of hard unyielding

306

love, as if he had already demanded too much of her. "The young 'un won't be fit to live with, if you keep on acting the way you do, Luigi Griffanti," she often said.

Luigi would only grin. He had learned, during the years in which he had been hunted from place to place, of the softness which lay beneath Buz's brisk exterior.

Luigi could do things with a mouth organ. He'd been doing them for the last half-hour for John's entertainment. First John had sat very still watching him, then he had begun to dance in time to the music. He knew his parents were talking about him, and he began putting on little airs, shaking his black curls, looking up at Luigi from under his long black lashes. Finally he laughed outright, ran to Luigi and hugged his knees.

"Now, old man, you got to tell me your name," Luigi demanded, setting him on his knee.

John shook his head.

"Papa very mad." Luigi put his hands before his face. He could feel John's small fingers trying to pull his hands away.

Then very loud in Luigi's ear the child shouted, "John!" and drew off to see the effect.

"John what?" demanded Luigi, not removing his hands from his face.

"John Griffanti."

Luigi's hands came down then and he hugged his small son. Buz stood watching. This was the game they played together every evening when Luigi came home from work.

"You got a letter from your ma today, Luigi." Buz walked over and took John's hand. "It's behind the clock in the kitchen. I got to put John to bed. Then we eat."

The letter was a very fat one. Luigi would enjoy reading about all the things Simp and Antone and the girls were doing. His mother would tell him, too, about the trees and vines. It was only the last year he had dared to write to her and she to him. A letter was still a new and fearful delight.

But this began, "You better light out, Luigi, soon as you get this letter and you better burn what I say, Luigi, soon as you read what I say. And don't write home any more." A crime had been committed in the neighborhood of the ranch, so his mother wrote. Inquiries had been made of the Griffantis. Ever since Luigi had shot John Rambeau, they had been afraid of the law. They were doubly frightened now. "The policeman asked when you'd been home last, Luigi. Maybe they take you if they can find you."

Buz came into the kitchen to see Luigi burning the letter over the sink. He dropped it only when the flames reached his fingers.

"We got to go, Luigi?" she asked.

"I guess so," he answered dully.

"I don't see why they won't leave us alone!" Buz cried. "Ain't we been hurt enough? John Rambeau isn't dead. We'd live decent if they'd let us."

"It's not that. They want me for something else. They're trying to pin a murder on me, Ma says. You know, Buz, I been right here in El Centro all last summer."

Buz's voice sounded lifeless. "But who's to say we wasn't around Fresno?"

Again the hurried, furtive getting away, the story that Luigi's father had died suddenly, the selling of the house, the buying of a second-hand car, and then—once they were on the road—teaching John a new name. Buz had insisted before that it wasn't necessary to change the child's name. Now she agreed the old one wasn't safe.

"You gotta say it, old man, just as I tell you," Luigi commanded.

"John Griffanti!" The little boy laughed and moved closer to his father.

"Don't you ever say that again." Luigi shook him. "Say what I told you. Say it quick."

John's eyes grew big and his lip trembled. "Manuel Guiseppe."

He stumbled over the last name and Luigi made him repeat it. "Now remember. Don't ever say that other name, or I'll have to hit you."

"John hit too." There were pin points of anger in his black eyes and he struck Luigi on the arm with his fist.

Luigi paid no attention. Buz took Manuel Guiseppe into her arms, and gave his hands a smart little slap. "Your name is Manuel just as your papa told you," she said and then she cuddled him close. No unyielding love this passionate embrace of her son. The last remembrance of John Rambeau, to which she had been holding, was gone in the giving up of his name for her son. It is doubtful if Buz ever again thought of Manuel as John Rambeau's son—he was hers and Luigi's.

"We aren't a-going to monkey around in California any more," said Luigi. "We'll go far enough this time so nobody will ever know."

"Maybe we better go to Oklahoma," said Buz. "That's where Pa came from and he was always talking about how good it was there. Maybe we could buy a house and maybe we could have another baby. It would be good for "Man'l." "Man'l" was the way she pronounced the Italian name of Luigi's father.

LI

For Elizabeth and Andrew there had come no real satisfaction in the return to the Napa homestead. The grafting of the vineyard did not bring to Andrew the sense of harmony John had found in a like occupation, for he and Elizabeth were not happy together. And Elizabeth, as often as she could, fled from the old house. In this quiet country life Andrew's love seemed actually to invade her being.

On the third spring after their return Andrew stood one early morning on the veranda looking down into the arbor. The winter rains were over. There was no hint of cloud in the sky this morning, nor would there be again until after the harvest in the autumn. Sun and shadow lay in patterns of interlaced twigs, gnarled branches and new leaves, on the table and across the seat of old Philippe's chair standing in its accustomed place at the arbor's farther end.

In the three years of hard toil since his return from Europe Andrew had brought back the vineyards, if not to their former perfection, at least to excellent condition. He believed that the three inspectors appointed by his grandfather would give hearty approval on their next visit. He was grateful to them for their patience. It had exhausted him financially to restore the vineyards, but this year the vines which he had regrafted after the disastrous fire would bear for the first time. He liked to think old Philippe would be pleased with what he had done, but it troubled him that the family was not a total as it had been in his grandfather's lifetime, and as his grandfather had wanted it always to be, he believed. If Elizabeth's increased returns from altar wine and the money John would undoubtedly make from his table grapes this year could be thrown into the family business, it would ease things considerably for his father and Uncle André. He knew it had been hard going for them and since they had proved up on the inheritance they had been slipping a little in their care of the vineyards. He was sorry to see it happening.

The house was still and so was all the outdoors. It was daybreak, the air as yet cool—the best hour for sulphuring the vines. He strode off toward the outbuildings beyond the winery where the men were getting ready to go out with the hand dusters. He picked up his own, adjusted the strap over his shoulder, settling the tank against his hip. In a few moments he was walking down the rows, spraying the fine yellow dust over the small green grapes. For three hours he worked with the silent efficiency taught him by old Philippe.

Now the sun was far above the horizon and the wind had risen, keeping the grapes from catching and holding the tiny particles of sulphur. He must stop for today. He straightened his shoulders. *I'll have to go back to the house and be nice to those fancy friends of Elizabeth's*, he said to himself.

Unexpectedly Elizabeth had come from San Francisco the evening before, bringing several friends with her. Still a little soreness remained in Andrew, remembering how they had come in upon him and Phil, he in his work clothes, Phil in his nightgown. Elizabeth should have let him know. She had taken him at a disadvantage. He hadn't made her guests welcome. He had felt the intrusion and he had shown it. Later when they were alone, he had had words with Elizabeth. Only recently had they started quarreling. He hadn't attempted to explain why he was rude. Difficult to explain the sense of frustration in not having her to himself. She had been asleep when he left for his work this morning. Idle to attempt explanation anyway. *She is so beautiful*, he thought wistfully.

Now he raised his eyes and saw her coming toward him, Phil astride her hip. Her strong graceful body was scarcely thrown out of line by the boy's weight.

"Andrew darling, come and take him, please," she called.
He knew she wasn't tired. She was walking too easily.
She had come then to make it up between them.

As Andrew approached, Phil clung the tighter to his mother,
rubbing his hard little head against the soft round of her
breast, trying to encircle her waist with his arms. "Mummy,
please," he begged.

"Well then, let's sit down," said Elizabeth.

Andrew spread his coat on the ground. "Raleigh himself,"
Elizabeth rallied him, but she smiled up at him as she seated
herself.

"A dress like that won't stand very hard treatment," he
explained but a flush spread over his face. It was one of her
complaints that he never took her naturally, and his mistake
that he never could.

"Andrew, you're wearing yourself out. When are you
going to get through working the way you do?" Elizabeth
looked across the expanse of her land, her mouth set in rebellious lines.

"I've got to." Andrew picked up a stick, digging it back
and forth in the ground at his feet. Phil wriggled out of his
mother's lap and scuffed back and forth in the small trench
his father was making.

"I can't seem to make you understand, dear, that we'll lose
the property if we don't."

"Oh, I understand!" exclaimed Elizabeth. "I've always understood. But what you can't understand is that I should
not care if we did. All Grandfather thought about was his
precious grapevines. We're buried here. What does it matter
whether the Rambeaus furnish altar wine or not? Goodness!
Let's live."

"We haven't any money except what we get out of these
vineyards." Andrew spoke with a hint of impatience.

"Andrew, do throw away that stick," Elizabeth cried in
exasperation, "and talk to me! I can't understand you when
you mumble into the earth that way."

"I said—" Andrew tossed the stick away, turning toward her—"I said what these vineyards bring in is all the money we have to live on. We can't sell them and get any money out of them, at least not until the fourteen years are up. Besides, it's my home, and I love it."

"Oh, Andrew dear, I wish you weren't so bound up in this place. There's a way to get clear if you want to. You keep pouring money and your strength into these vineyards. If you stopped putting anything in and instead should take all you could out of the land for two years—and sell all the old stocks in the winery—we'd have money ahead, quite a lot. Then we could let the state take the land. We'd have had the best out of it."

"You mean do a thing like that to Grandfather's finest vineyards, after he left them to you?" It seemed to Andrew an appalling thing for Elizabeth to say.

Phil began to cry, frightened by the note of anger in his father's voice.

"Hush, Phil." Elizabeth took him back into her lap. She saw, now, Andrew never would be willing to part with the vineyards. "You never will let me know how we stand. How can you expect me to co-operate?" she demanded a little sharply.

"If I haven't, it's because I didn't want you to be worried. But I'll show you exactly where we are when we go back to the house." Then he, too, changed the subject. "Grandfather's trustees, when they made their last inspection, said they thought things were coming along very well now."

Elizabeth looked straight ahead. She held Phil's short fat legs just above the knee, raising one then the other. "See, Phil, you're walking in the air," she told him.

Andrew did not look at her as he rose. *I wonder if she wants to leave the place because she would like to get away from me,* he was thinking. He forced himself to speak cheerfully. "I've been up since daylight. I'm hungry. I'll knock off for the day. We could take your friends on a picnic and," he added after a pause, "I'll go over the books with you when we get back."

"Whom do you suppose I saw in San Francisco the other day?" Elizabeth asked, accepting the truce Andrew was offering her.

"I can't guess."

"Henri."

"Henri! Not really?" Andrew was indeed surprised. "He's given up living in Spain then. His old country not so loved, after all. Did you see him to speak to?"

"Yes. It seems he's been back several years."

"What is he doing? Mother has said nothing about his visiting Aunt Maria."

"No, he has not been south, he said. Doing something around Sacramento. Gone in for politics, I gathered."

All three of Andrew's sisters and their husbands came over from San Francisco for the week ends that summer, glad to get their children into the country. Monny and Nate came in July, bringing their two boys. Before they had left Andrew's parents arrived, bringing Aunt Maria. They had tried to get Martha to join them but she refused.

Elizabeth welcomed them all, glad of the excitement and activity. She had taken two good Italian girls to fill the place of Frau Diener after her death. They took most of the care of Phil. Phil didn't need her, she told herself, with all his young cousins to play with. Monny's children stayed all summer. Monny was going to have another child this autumn. She was not well and Andrew had begged her to leave her sons here at the northern home. "Grandfather would have liked to have them know the place as well as we knew it when we were children," he told her. "Besides Phil needs company and I like lots of children around."

Elizabeth, watching Andrew's absorption in the family, made herself believe he was perfectly content. It left her free for her own friends.

Monny's boys were several years older than Phil, and he regarded them as his heroes. But they wouldn't always let him play with them. Tiny Sue, his Aunt Suzanne's little girl, was the cousin he liked best, but she did not come often. She, like his mother, was always going away to a place called San Francisco. So, often Phil followed his father about. They had a game they played. They were brothers and Phil was as strong as Andrew. They both could do wonderful things that no one else could do.

When harvest time came Andrew worked at the winery from eight in the morning until six at night, relieving Diener of the care of the new-made wine. Diener was too old now to stand both day and night vigil. Each load of grapes coming in brought Andrew a greater assurance that the yield would be far heavier than last year. *I've made the grade*, he said to himself with no little sense of pride. *I've pulled us out of disaster. This year I can afford to do more for Elizabeth, devote myself to her; things will be all right between us then.*

Late one afternoon he went down to the house to change his clothes. As he finished dressing and stepped out on the veranda he saw a car circling the drive, followed by another. He heard voices, among them a voice he remembered. Henri! What vagary had possessed him to come here, and with a party of friends too? Andrew walked down through the arbor to meet his guests.

True to the tradition of hospitality old Philippe had established, Andrew invited them to spend the night. It was late to go back to town. Elizabeth, who had joined them, echoed the invitation. Even Henri was a diversion, and she wanted to hear from Madeleine any news she had of Lon and Mathilde.

Next day Henri rode the vineyards with Andrew. "It's been hard work," Andrew explained, "getting the vineyards back to the requirements set."

"Why do you worry about it?" asked Henri.

"Well, I have to," Andrew answered, "according to the terms of the will."

"Oh?" Henri's rising inflection indicated such interest that Andrew felt justified in explaining his problems.

"Well, I'm astounded," said Henri when Andrew had finished, "that a man like Philippe Rambeau would entrust such power to anyone on this earth. Where would he expect to find three men he could depend upon?"

"The men he chose are all right," said Andrew. "If anything, they're a little too conscientious."

"Would you think me impertinent if I asked who they are?"

"They're all men you know. Lake, Landis and Martin. All old neighbors of ours. Landis became one of them this year after the death of Ingram. Pretty good sort, you'll have to own."

Henri gave a low whistle. "Yes," he said, "pretty good."

"We'll be all right," Andrew went on, going back to his responsibility in the matter, "if disease doesn't get into the vines. In the last year or two I've had a case or two of this new Pierce disease."

"How do you recognize it?" asked Henri. "Never heard of it before. Must be something new that has come since I had anything to do with vineyards."

"Well, here's a sick vine," said Andrew. "The difficulty is it costs a lot to keep Pierce disease under control. Every vine should be pulled up the minute you detect any wilting."

The party was a boisterous one. On the last day of the visit Elizabeth arranged for a picnic in a grove of redwoods on the hilltop beyond the pointed vineyards—a spot which overlooked the pickers hard at work among the grapes. It took Madeleine's fancy to play at being a harvest hand. "Oh, lovely!" exclaimed one of the men. The women tied the gay picnic napkins over their heads, the men knotted them loosely around their necks. They ran down the hill, seeking out Andrew to ask for work. Andrew would have denied them because they knew nothing about the delicate process of picking wine grapes, but seeing Elizabeth's eager expectant face

among the guests, he hunted out knives for them. Laughing
and shouting they joined the pickers.

The novel experience of work pleased them. The sun was
hot against their backs as they bent to gather the clusters of
grapes. With noisy mirth they filled the lug boxes and
carried them to the vineyards' edge. There a young Italian
loaded them onto the wagon drawn by white horses. Andrew
held to his grandfather's customs. White horses had always
drawn the grapes down from the hill vineyard.

It was a bright picture: the white horses, the mounds of
purple and amber grapes filling the wagon box, the gaily
clad pickers, the deep green of the vines, the periwinkle blue
sky, the dark mass of the mountains.

Whether it was because of the beauty of the scene or because of some ancient inherited sense of the mysteries of the
vintage—man's long association of the fruit of the vine with
his undying sense of deity—these carefully reared men and
women, sons and daughters of the peasants of Europe, after
a time grew quiet as they toiled. The sun beat down upon
them, the sweat ran down their backs and breasts. They were
pushed beyond the trivialities of their ordinary speech into
silence. Urgings of both body and spirit took possession of
them.

When the party returned to the house for a country supper,
the Italian girls set out on the arbor table a huge dish of spaghetti and another of ravioli. Andrew brought red wine from
the winery, some of old Philippe's best.

Instead of taking his seat with the others on the benches,
Henri pulled up Philippe's great chair and placed it at the
end of the table. This was not a bad place to live in the summer. He had had a profitable visit—gained information from
Andrew, enjoyed Elizabeth, and above all, made Madeleine
unhappy. Henri specialized in the little cruelties in his handling of his wife to shape her to his own wishes. To inflict
jealousy on her was one of them.

Elizabeth frowned. She did not like to see Henri sitting

in Philippe's place. Henri had taken too many liberties today. She looked up at the great vine. The once slender branches, which had wound themselves around the parent trunk for support, were now as strong and thick as the trunk itself, hardly distinguishable from it until upon the trellised roof of the arbor they fanned themselves out, tunneling in and around the thick mat their own leaves made. The lights on the table threw into relief the gray underside of the leaves. The sturdy vine always gave her a strange sense of Philippe. She shifted her position. She had an uneasy feeling that he was not pleased with her.

Andrew was weary, not with one day's toil but with the accumulated weariness of years of effort and worry. But he had saved the property for Elizabeth. Now he sat silent among his guests, his silence not noticeable, for tonight there was no boisterous chatter. All were content to eat as hungry peasants eat.

He looked across at Elizabeth. Her cheeks were flushed from the day in the sun, her eyes a deep lustrous blue as they always were when she had friends gathered about her. Only when she was alone with him did her eyes go flat and colorless. *Strange,* he thought, *how her eyes give her away.* Suddenly he was angry. Why should he work as he had for her and receive so little in return? Immediately he knew the answer. He wanted Elizabeth on any terms. *If I can't have the kernel,* he said to himself bitterly, *I'll keep the husk.*

That night, when they were alone, he demanded, "What have I ever had out of our marriage? I've done your bidding since the very first. I wanted a home. I've had none."

"How about these last three years since we came back from France?" Elizabeth asked.

"A home!" he laughed bitterly. "I've had the job of managing your property. I want a wife."

Her eyes were as blue as Andrew could wish now. Her world was crumbling around her. Andrew's gentleness, An drew's patience! She had drawn upon them for years. There was nothing left if such firm foundations could be swept away.

Andrew enjoyed the look of consternation which passed over her face. Some harsh element he did not know he had in his nature took possession of him. He was worn from within in a struggle too long maintained. He, the least acquisitive of Philippe's offspring, of all of them the most moved by the spirit, would this night take all he could get.

LII

SINCE that night Elizabeth had rarely been at
home. It was December now. She had come back a few days
ago for Phil. She wanted to buy clothes for him in San Francisco. Before she left Andrew had shown her an estimate of
the returns from this year's harvest.

"After all, this property is yours," he said. "You should
decide now whether you want to go on with the place or
whether you want to abandon it. You must tell me soon before I invest more money in the fall work. If we are to go
on, I must do something about Pierce disease, which is getting
a hold in the lower vineyards. If we are not to go on, then
I must get ready to sell out our old stock of wine as soon as
Repeal comes in. You can sell the wine for a very good price."

"Wait until Phil and I get back, then we can decide," she
had answered.

This afternoon a soft gray haze had crept over the sun and
the sky. It was very still. Every bird, every insect,had hushed
its cry. Andrew, unable to work, went down to the house.
But the house was still, too, with Phil and Elizabeth gone
away. Finally he walked up to the grove where they had held
their last picnic. As he looked down on the vineyards, he
saw that the color which had been so brilliant only a few
weeks before had gone from the leaves. Here and there a
bunch of grapes missed by the pickers showed, shriveled and
black, against the now all but denuded vines. The place
seemed desolate.

The soft haze thickened and spread itself out over the sky
like a pall. The earth seemed dead beneath his feet. Denied

rain for many months now, the trees and vines, thrusting their roots deeper and deeper, had taken the earth's reservoirs of water to perfect their own fruits. Lower pressed the gray sky and the stillness. One bird somewhere cheeped as if it could no longer bear such stillness. He went back down the road to his house.

The stillness followed him in. He could not forget how that night at the end of the harvest Elizabeth had stiffened under his caresses. His love was distasteful to her. There was no doubt in his mind that he ought to free her. *Well, why should you?* a voice spoke within him. *She is the one who has injured you. She had no right to take your love and use it to save herself from Henri.* He knew Elizabeth would live up to her bargain if he insisted. She was too honest not to do that.

I should go away. But I cannot. I will not leave everything I love. If I go, I should go now while they are both gone. Then Elizabeth will not guess until it is done. I must not let her know where I am or she will think she should ask me to come back. I must be dead to her. So his thoughts beat about in his mind.

It was late when he went to the telephone and called Elizabeth.

"Is that you, my dear?" her voice reached him over the 'phone. "Why ever are you calling at this hour? Isn't everything all right?"

"Yes, but I thought as you are away and it's between seasons, I'd go down to see Mother for a few days."

"Oh, yes, do, Andrew. You ought to have a change." The ease with which she accepted his going stabbed him. Had he hoped then, still hoped, she might be wanting him?

"Good-by then. I'll be off in the morning," he heard himself saying. "And kiss Phil for me." It was done. He would go to his mother's for a few days, then tell her he was coming home, and then just disappear.

Not much to take. How little in a home really belonged

to a man personally—a few keepsakes, some clothes. Their pictures? No. He must not put so great a temptation to return in his way.

He opened the door, went down into the arbor, jet-black under the impenetrable mass of leaves and branches. The first difficult drops of rain were falling. Again that exhausted stillness. Finally a sudden quick bombardment of huge drops on the steps, the leaves, the earth. Again the stillness. Then a sharp burst of rain. From the ground around him there rose a strong odor of the fecund earth. It stirred his senses. *Must I go away?* he begged of himself. He stretched his arms across the table, laid his head on them and wept.

A day or two of Isobel's ministrations lessened his terrible aloneness. Then it was increased for he need not worry any longer about Elizabeth's finances. She would not need his help. Repeal, which they had been expecting, was an accomplished fact. Wine, now legal, would be in quick demand, and Elizabeth had plenty, aged and ready for use. She had only to carry out her plan, sell out her stock at a large profit, neglect the treasured vineyards, let them go to the state.

Andrew lingered for a last celebration with his family. The day the Government released the stores of wine in the San Joaquin winery the family had asked in the name of old Philippe that every man, woman, and child who had ever worked for them should help them celebrate. The day was warm and sunny. At noon there was to be a barbecue. Early in the morning fires were started in the pits and the laden spits started turning. There was to be a dance in the evening. Chinese lanterns, Chu insisted, should be strung over the wooden platform erected for dancing.

The Rambeaus gathered once again at the family home and walked together down the road that led through the vineyards to the winery. In front of it they saw their guests already gathered to greet them—Italian, Russian, Armenian, German, Spanish. Suspicions and hatreds were forgotten in

the general new optimism sprung up. In Repeal everyone saw
the end of difficulties. Because the old were touched with
nostalgia and wanted to remember just for a day lands they
would never see again, and because both young and old shared
the gala mood, the crowd was dressed in the bright costumes
of Europe. When André Rambeau gave the signal they rushed
into the winery and rolled out kegs and barrels. Singing, they
bore the wine to the long tables.

In the evening, when the dancing was in full swing and
even the old stone building resounded to the rhythmic beat
of half-forgotten peasant dances, the Rambeaus gathered together in the sampling room. *If Elizabeth were only here,
then we'd be all together,* automatically Andrew found himself thinking, forgetting for the moment that they would
never be together again. Neither would he see his family again.
He studied them closely to fix upon his memory their well-
loved faces. Andrew could hold in his memory a gesture or
a way of speech, but faces eluded him. It was to be a tragedy
to him in the days to come.

He concentrated his mind now on his mother, standing
with her two sisters. Aunt Martha dominated the group.
She looked almost theatrical with her snow-white hair beautifully waved. Her heavy eyebrows all but meeting at the
narrow bridge of her nose were like lifted wings above her
smoldering black eyes. Maria, on one side of her, made little
ineffectual movements, her gaze blank. His mother's eyes
were as black as Martha's but touched with a soft light of contentment. He it was who would change that expression into
one of suffering.

He turned toward Monny. Nate stood at her side. Here
was that mysterious accord in marriage he had hoped might
be his. Again he turned away. There were the men standing
together, his uncles, André Rambeau and Francis Fairon, and
his father, Ronald Fairon. And behind them stood John, his
back toward them. Andrew saw him reach up and take one
of the goblets from its place on the wall.

André lifted the first bottle of wine from the basket, gave it to Chu to pass. Chu, bent, wrinkled and smiling, filled the glasses, then stopped before John, uncertain.

"Here, Chu, you can fill this for me." John thrust forth the ancient goblet.

André stood looking at his son, not giving the toast. From John's expression no one could tell whether he meant to honor his grandfather or was twisting the moment to emphasize the injustice of his position among them.

Suddenly Martha stepped away from her sisters, pushed her brother André aside. "I am the oldest," she said in a harsh voice. "I will give the toast. Our father, Philippe Rambeau!"

They drank in silence, John among them.

LIII

THE December day was a succession of quick showers and sudden bursts of sunlight. Elizabeth, when she wakened, decided she would take Phil home. He was just too difficult to manage in a big city. She was not used to caring for him without Andrew's help.

Undoubtedly by this time Andrew would be back.

Now that Repeal was an accomplished fact, he would rush home to the Napa winery as soon as he heard the news. He had been talking for months about the rush of business once wine was again legal.

There was another reason for going home. The doctor had confirmed what she knew herself. She was to have another child. And he had told her she needed more rest than she was getting.

I didn't want another baby, Elizabeth thought, as she drove out of the city and took the road leading into the hills, *not the way things are between Andrew and me. I shan't tell him until I have to. He'd just fuss over me. What does all his care of me mean after all? I've learned now.* Elizabeth's eyes were scornful and her lips tight closed. She drove faster, to rid herself of her depression. Phil, with no chance to brace his short legs, fell against her as she swung around a curve, righted himself only to topple in the other direction. He was indignant with her.

"Mummy, I don't like you to knock me about."

"My poor darling, it shan't be knocked about any more." She patted his hand and slowed the car. After all what was she hurrying for?

When she reached the house and only the two Italian girls

325

came to take her luggage and help her with Phil, she felt annoyed.

"Isn't Mr. Fairon here?" she asked. No, they told her, Fritz Diener said sure he'd come today but he hasn't yet.

"He is too here," said Phil.

"And what do you know about it, little All-Wise?" Rose Marie, the gay one of the two girls, asked him, poking him gently in the ribs.

" 'Cause he always is," Phil replied, refusing to enter into her game. He trudged up the steps into the house, going from room to room to hunt for his father. When he did not find him, he walked toward the door that led to the arbor and the winery beyond. Elizabeth found him straining to turn the knob, his small hands locked around it.

"Where do you want to go, Phil?" she asked.

"I want to find Andrew."

"He's not at home, darling. Rose Marie told you and you wouldn't believe her. But he'll be back soon."

"I want him now."

"But you can't have him, dear."

"Why can't I?"

"Because he isn't here."

"Why isn't he here?" the child persisted.

"He's gone for a visit, just the way you and I went to the city."

"We came back."

"So will he."

"Tell Andrew to come now." Phil pulled at her hand, trying to lead her to the telephone.

"We'll talk to him in the morning, Phil. Mummy's tired now and wants to rest. Why did you call him Andrew just now? That's my name for him. Yours is——"

"I like to call him Andrew," Phil said, "and he likes it, too, when you go away."

It was revealing to Elizabeth to realize this companionship

between her husband and son. She knew that Andrew was unconsciously seeking to gain from it compensation for what he had missed in his marriage. It set her thinking. She was glad now to have this quiet time before Andrew returned to put herself right. All day long she delayed calling his mother's house.

The next morning she received Andrew's letter. "Why, it's postmarked Chicago!" she exclaimed, turning it over and over in her hand. "Repeal will make no difference with the sale of sacramental wine; it's here he is needed." She turned to Phil. "I suppose if I read it I'll find out, won't I? It's from your daddy."

"What does he say to me?" Phil asked as Elizabeth opened the letter.

"Well, it begins with you, Phil. It says you are to take good care of me."

"Is that all?" asked Phil in disappointment.

She did not answer. Suddenly she realized Andrew was trying to tell her something he found hard to say, something about going away and not returning.

"Look, Phil," she said taking the child by the shoulder and leading him to the door, "go out and find Fritz."

Once he was gone Elizabeth locked the door of her room and read on. Andrew was speaking frankly, as they never had spoken to each other in all the years of their marriage.

"I have always known, Elizabeth, since that first night when we went away together, that you did not love me—not in the way I love you. I thought at first you might come to love me. But I've known lately that you never could. Still I have held you to your promise. I can no longer do this, Elizabeth. For my own sake, too, I must go away. It does not make a man of anyone to live as I have been living."

The letter fell from Elizabeth's hand.

Her first impulse was to get in touch with Andrew as quickly as she could. Of course he must come back. And then, slowly, a sense of relief came over her. "I am free," she whispered to herself. She bowed her head in her arms, whispering between her sobs, "He's let me go free."

She went for her coat and hat. In a kind of dream she walked down the steps, through the arbor, out past the winery. She was almost to the tree where she and Andrew had kissed that early summer morning. *Not there,* she thought. She turned, walked along the drive, and then with a quick swerve slipped through the hedge of oleanders. Hidden from the house, she stood looking over the fields with their faint green cover brought by the first rain. "My fields," she said. "I've never thought of them as mine before. I've always thought of them as Andrew's because he looked after them. I can get rid of them now if I like. I can do with myself what I like."

Little by little the extent of Andrew's sacrifice began to temper her joy. Andrew without his home would be completely lost. Why, care for this land and his family were his sole interests. Andrew without Phil, Andrew without her and this old house! She could not accept so great a sacrifice. She *must* find him. Perhaps now that things had been expressed between them they could work out some way of life acceptable to both. At least she must try.

But when she took out Andrew's letter she saw it bore no address. Certainly he'd leave one with his mother. She could not believe he had cut himself off entirely from his family. All at once suspicion took possession of her. Andrew had left a loophole by which she might trace him. He had not really set her free.

She went to the telephone and called his mother. "Where can I reach Andrew?" she asked.

"Why, isn't he with you?" Isobel's voice held alarm. "He's been gone several days. Do you suppose there's been an accident?"

"Oh no, don't worry, Mother. I've a letter from him from Chicago, saying he has gone east to straighten out some affairs, but he neglected to tell me where he was staying. He's probably on his way home now."

I am free, thought Elizabeth. *He has made it a clean break.* It was only then she remembered that she was going to bear him a second child in the spring.

A strange kind of freedom, the responsibility of two children, the responsibility of making a living! And yet the feeling of freedom persisted. Never since her father had returned from the war and had asked her, a little girl, to be a woman, had she been free to be herself. An odd smile twisted her lips. *I wonder what I'll make of it,* she thought.

And then she was angry with Andrew. *It's Andrew again, taking everything into his own hands. He's given me no choice. It's he who has made my decision without consulting me. It's not simple for me, the way he has planned things. How shall I explain to his mother and father? What shall I tell Diener? And what shall I tell Phil?*

She heard Philippe running along the hall toward her room. Again she locked the door against him. When the knob did not yield to his clasp, he cried in alarm, "Mummy, Mummy, where are you?" She could hear him sobbing as he threw his weight against the unyielding door.

"I'm here, dear." Quickly she opened the door. "You mustn't be afraid, darling, the minute you can't find me." She took the sobbing child on her lap. "I want you to look at me, Philippe. You must learn to be strong and help Mother. You didn't used to be afraid like this. You didn't used to cry."

"But Andrew was here then. I want Andrew!"

Why did the child persist in calling him Andrew? "Look at me, Phil," she said, and put her hand under his chin, raising his head so that she could look into his eyes. "Your daddy isn't coming back for a long time. You must be a big boy and help Mother."

"Isn't ever?" Phil stopped his crying. His blue eyes, a startling as her own against his olive skin, searched her face.

"I didn't say never, Phil. I said not for a long time."

Philippe slid slowly down from her knee. "I guess I'll go now."

She found him in the farthest corner of his room, making little hitching movements as if trying to get deeper into the corner. "Come, darling," she said, very gently. "Let Mother put you to bed. It's late. She'd like to talk to you."

He did not move. "I'll put myself to bed." It was a sturdy little voice, only it broke at the end. "But perhaps I could sleep with you?"

Late in the night she crept in beside him, pushing the sprawled, angular boy's body over enough to make room for herself. Elizabeth had made her resolve. The strands of Andrew's life and her own were too intricately interwoven to separate without harm—certainly to little Philippe. She would conquer her pride, go to Andrew's mother, tell her just how things stood. Surely Isobel would have some clue to Andrew's whereabouts.

LIV

I<small>T WAS</small> late the next afternoon when she reached her mother-in-law's house. The short December day, further shortened by the gray sky and the falling rain, had come to an end. The lights were already on but the curtains had not been drawn. She could see her parents-in-law sitting one on either side of the fireplace. They were talking. Occasionally the fire leaped up and the light played over their faces. They looked serene and content. For a moment she hesitated. Then she pulled the knocker on the door.

Dinner was over at last and Elizabeth knew she could not wait longer to explain her sudden visit. When they were in the drawing room once more, she went over to the open fire and held out her hands, for they were cold.

Isobel watched her. Apprehension had been slowly gathering in her ever since Elizabeth's arrival. Her coming had something to do with Andrew although Elizabeth had said he was well.

"You must still be chilled from the long ride." Isobel Fairon rose. "I'll ring and have the fire mended."

"No, don't." Elizabeth whirled around. "I need your help, Mother—and Father's, too."

Ronald Fairon lowered his paper. Isobel stood, one hand reached out toward the bell.

"It's about Andrew. He is well, just as I said, but——" Elizabeth hesitated a moment, then plunged ahead and told them all that seemed necessary to enlist their help in finding him.

"He said nothing of this when he was here." Ronald Fairon was puzzled over the private lives of these two, who had so

331

much to give each other and, somehow, had failed to do it.

"I'll do what I can, Elizabeth," he said. "But if Andrew has decided on a clean break I think he is too clever to make it an easy matter to find him." He said no more. After a little he went out. The two women heard his car going down the drive.

For Ronald Fairon life seemed to have come to an abrupt end. These last years he had pinched and denied himself that Andrew might some day have his share in the great southern vineyards. Andrew and Elizabeth together would bring again the coalition of the two properties. He wanted his son who bore the Fairon name one day to occupy the proud place Philippe Rambeau had once occupied. He wanted his son near him. Only later, when his first sorrow was over, did he realize the new burden placed upon him. He would have to take over the care of the northern vineyard. Elizabeth couldn't run it. A heavy load for him. Well, he'd have to talk to Elizabeth in the morning about it.

Once Ronald Fairon had left the room, the young woman and the old one confronted each other. They could speak now without reserve. They were Rambeau women; Isobel would give no quarter, and Elizabeth would ask none.

"A man like Andrew does not leave his home without good reason. What is it?" Isobel demanded.

"Because he thinks I don't love him," Elizabeth answered. "Is he right?"

"He has every reason to believe he is."

"*Is he?* I asked."

"I don't know."

"Have you ever known? You had no right to do it, to marry him as you did and spoil his life."

"I know that now, Mother!" cried Elizabeth. "But I was so young. . . . But that is no excuse," she added after a pause.

"Well, it's done now anyway," said Isobel coldly.

"We must get him home, Mother." When Isobel did not answer, Elizabeth went to the hall for her coat and hat. "I want to get back to Phil. I'll go as far as I can tonight and be at home before he's up in the morning," she said as she re-entered the room.

"Nonsense, you can't start out at this hour." Isobel found it impossible just now to be gracious.

"I'll have to take over the business," Elizabeth went on. "I'd better begin in the morning."

"You ought to wait and talk to the men of the family about that. You can't do it alone," Isobel answered.

"Maybe not, Mother, but I mean to try, and I think I'll succeed."

I've six months to work, Elizabeth estimated, driving through the rain and the dark, *then a month when I shan't be able to do anything. Then a baby to take care of and more work.*

But I've Diener to help me, one of the best winemakers in the country even if he is getting old. . . . He might resent me. . . . He was devoted to Andrew. She drew back from the explanation which must be given to Diener. Why not carry out her first idea and give the place up? And then quite definitely she knew that she wanted to keep it. She intended Andrew should come back—and the vineyards were part of Andrew.

Once she was at home again she went directly to the office of the winery, unlocked Andrew's desk and the files. Everything was in order.

A young Italian came into the office, glanced around and was about to go out. "Are you looking for someone?" Elizabeth asked him.

"Why, yes," he said. "I was hoping Mr. Fairon would be around this morning. The orders coming in plus the big ones sent in as soon as folks knew there was going to be Repeal are swamping us. He said when he left he'd be here to handle the rush of business after Repeal."

"I am here in his place," said Elizabeth. "We must get

along without Mr. Fairon for a time. He's been detained.
You are——"

"My name is Peter."

"Peter what?"

"Oh, just Peter," he said nonchalantly.

"Are you in charge of the shipping?"

"Yes," he said, looking at her a little doubtfully and wondering, she imagined, how she would be able to help him.

Diener entered the room now, wildly gesticulating. "When's
Andrew coming? I got to talk to him."

"Not right away, Fritz," Elizabeth answered. "I'm taking
over in his absence."

"Suppose I got to manage everything myself then." He
turned to go out.

"Come back, Fritz." There was a note in Elizabeth's voice
that made Diener pause. All these Rambeaus were just alike—
commanding in their ways, he grumbled to himself, and
walked over to the desk where Elizabeth had seated herself.

"I take it," Elizabeth said, surveying the two men, "that we
have an emergency due to a sudden demand for wine."

"That's about it," agreed the Italian.

Diener began gesticulating again. "Peter here vants us to
sell our new wines."

"Well, we got the orders. What we going to do if we
don't?"

"Do!" shouted Diener. "Tell 'em wine iss not ready."

"Aw, shucks." Peter softened his expletive to fit the
feminine company, but he felt it weakened his position with
Diener.

"What would Andrew do, Fritz, if he were here?" Elizabeth asked.

"He'd do same as Philippe Rambeau."

"And what would that be?" asked Elizabeth.

"He tell 'em go to hell."

"You have your answer, Peter." Elizabeth turned back to
her desk.

It was only later, when she knew more about the business, that she realized how disastrous to her it would have been if she had allowed raw wine to go out under the proud name of "Rambeau Vineyards." But one thing she grasped immediately—she must gain Diener's loyalty. To do so, she must explain to him her position.

When she had made her explanation, Fritz's old eyes studied her for a little. "The young I do not understand," he said. "Only wine I understand." His look was hostile. Elizabeth was aware that he blamed her and was on the point of leaving.

"My grandfather willed these vineyards to me," Elizabeth went on. "If I can't care for them you know they go to the state."

"The state!" Diener snorted. "What will the state do with them? How does the state know about wine? Mees Elizabeth, I am an old man. Today you begin. You must know everything I know. Come, you got to begin right away." He took her into the cellars.

"Two months ago everything bustle. Things doing." Fritz dropped unconsciously into the slang of his adopted country. "The sugar she change. Then—— Ach, so much to teach you! Now peace, quiet—the wine she breathe quiet, she mellow in these leetle casks and puncheons. And here in the bottles she grow beautiful."

Elizabeth had taken a cigarette from her case. Diener, walking ahead, heard the sudden scratch of a match. He wheeled, knocked the cigarette from her hand, trod on it.

Elizabeth stood for a moment, confronting him in bewilderment. His eyes, usually watery with age, were bright with angry light.

"You do not know anything. You are dumb. Wine iss— how shall I say? I tell you it iss living. It takes a breath. You smoke. It breathes in the smoke."

"I am sorry," murmured Elizabeth. "I will not offend again."

The incident fixed itself in Elizabeth's mind. Fritz, old Philippe, and Andrew, too, did not see these rare dry wines just as a commodity out of which to make money. Until now she had seen them only commercially. With a humility not known to her before, she followed Diener, listening to all he said.

For weeks, Elizabeth had no time to think about herself, whether she was happy or unhappy. If she were to make a success of the winery she must learn down to the last detail the whole delicate process of winemaking, learn it while Diener was able to teach her. He was a very old man, too old even now to be working as he did, and he could not live long.

In the cellars cut deep into the hillside she worked with him, bringing to perfection the wines Andrew had started in the fall. Three rackings they made, slowly drawing off the wine from the sediment—each time the careful analysis, each time greater clarity. At last they stored it in small casks and placed it in the coolest part of the cellar for aging.

Wine of two and three seasons ago, now sufficiently aged, was carefully run into bottles which were placed on their sides in the racks, left slowly to mellow, slowly to take on brilliance, bouquet. Holding bottle after bottle of finished wine to the light, Elizabeth looked into its glistening purple or amber depths, learning to detect the slightest cloudiness, the slightest sediment.

Diener showed her the glasses for wine tasting—tulip shaped, narrow brimmed to concentrate the aroma of wine, thin walled to display its color.

Still Fritz was not content. "Every vine you must know as Philippe Rambeau knew them. He vould vant you to know them like dat," he insisted.

The vines were ready for pruning now. "Ve go to de high vineyards where I teach you. Dat is where the great Philippe get his finest wine. He do not blend the wines. He blend the grape. Philippe was an artist. Here, on this hillside, he haf different kinds grow together side by side. Ve pick them as they come and haf the fine blend."

A sense of excitement took hold of Elizabeth. She had seen the diagram of this blend. Locked in an inner drawer of the desk was a paper she had not understood. A mosaic of lines and crosses and at the foot of the paper names against the crosses, the names of the varieties her grandfather sought to blend.

"And now I teach you how to prune. Some day ven old Fritz iss dead you boss dese men."

Into her hand he put the pruning knife. He showed her how to hold it and how to make a clean cut without crushing the cane. "Ve call the vay this vine have been pruned head-training. Long ago ve cut this vine, make it a leetle tree with three arms at the top to hold the canes. Ve leave only four new buds. Then at the top the foliage droop down like an umbrella next summer."

To bend over the squat vines Elizabeth found very difficult. The weight of the child dragged at her back. At the end of the row she straightened her shoulders, looked around for a place to sit and rest. Old Diener stood looking at her. *"Ach,"* he said at last, "ve must take more care."

Elizabeth felt the tears hot against her eyelids. She wanted the comfort, the protection Andrew had given her when she was carrying Phil. "I'll rest here for a while," she told Diener. After he had gone she walked around the slope to a spot where she could look out over the Valley. Had she known it, this was the place where Andrew had come in his despair just before he went away, and where old Philippe had stood when he first dreamed of the vineyard he would plant on these slopes. She was lonely.

When at last she went down the hill she stopped for a moment at the winery to close her desk and sign the day's letters. Peter would take them to the post office on his way home. Then she went to find Fritz. He had placed a memorandum on her desk about stocks to be sent to Kansas City.

"He's in the caves," Peter told her.

As she entered her attention was caught by small flickering flames among the oaken casks. She was frightened, fearing fire had broken out in this inner room. Then she saw the flames were lighted candles which children were carrying. She recognized a neighbor child and then Phil. Elizabeth hurried forward. "Philippe, oh Philippe," she called, "bring the children out of here. Fritz will be angry with you."

"Na, na," came a voice close at her side. "His father played so. Let him grow up to luf de place."

"But Fritz," she protested, "it's dangerous. They might set fire to their clothes."

"Na, na. I watch, but it iss the game to carry the candle very straight. The candle must not go out. If it does, you are it."

"One, two, three, four, five, six, I'm coming," shouted Rose Marie's little girl, beginning the search.

Elizabeth saw Phil steal out from behind a fat-bellied cask, carrying his candle carefully, its flame shining up into his face. "One, two, three, for me," he cried, pounding on the old puncheon that was the goal.

Elizabeth left them and went on to the house. Suddenly she knew what she had done to Andrew. *Oh, Andrew,* she thought, *if I had left you alone you would have married someone who would have lived a quiet life among the things you love. Simple things nourished you. Everything was resolved for you except your marriage. And I, craving security, robbed you of your security.*

As the growing weight of her child made work more and more difficult, Elizabeth went often to sit at the edge of the lower vineyard on a bench old Philippe had placed there. When she first went to sit near her vines, their buds were covered with two dark, hard scales, then as spring advanced the two scales loosened, and delicate shoots appeared. One morning every node on her vines, as far as she could see, was tipped with a young leaf fresh and delicate. She could see the pattern of Philippe's planting. According to their kind the young leaves were a pale mossy green, or bright carmine, or green edged with cream or carmine with gray. Some were covered with down and some were glossy.

Now Elizabeth came to love Philippe's gift to her. Absorbed, she watched the growing tips unfold—more leaves, then a leaf and a tendril, then a leaf and a grapelike cluster of infinitesimal flowers. The first burst of the vine's growth was done.

One afternoon in the very early summer Elizabeth left the winery in haste, realizing that she had waited overlong to reach San Francisco. As she packed, the first pains took her. The intervals between the pains were surprisingly short. Why had she not remembered how quickly Phil had come? Well, her child would have to be born at home. *I think I'm glad,* she thought, calling Rose to send for the local doctor. She lay down on the great bed where her grandmother, Marie Rambeau, had born three of her five children. From the window Elizabeth could see her vines, the leaves almost mature now; the tendrils, once groping, were beginning to grab.

Before the sun had set Elizabeth gave birth to a son, easily, as she had her first. But he was a bigger, stronger baby than Phil had been. The doctor did not have to slap him to make him cry. He let out a lusty wail and his arms and legs, folded in the womb against his chest, at birth were immediately thrust out. The first time he was put to her breast he took hold with evident satisfaction and dropped off to sleep when he had had enough. In his bath he fanned himself out as he had at birth and with equal gusto.

"There'll never be any doubt what *he* wants," Elizabeth said to Isobel who had arrived a few days after the child was born.

Isobel was holding the baby and studying his small vigorous countenance. "He's just like Father."

"Do you think so?"

"He has his mouth and his eyes."

Phil came running into the room. He seemed at last to have forgotten about his father in the excitement of the new baby. "What do you want him called, Phil?" his mother asked.

"Andrew," Phil answered, slipping his finger into the baby's fist. Elizabeth suddenly lay back against her pillows, her head turned away, but Isobel could see that her lips were trembling. Isobel felt a sudden hope that Elizabeth had come to love Andrew. If so they might get him home. *I wonder if she is strong enough to tell her we have found him.*

"The baby's name shall be Andrew," said Elizabeth at last, "only changed to the French. Yes, I shall call him André."

Isobel leaned forward, laying her hand over Elizabeth's. "I don't want to hold out too much hope, my dear, but we think we've found trace of Andrew. If he's there yet this address will reach him." She took out of her bag a folded paper.

"Spain!" cried Elizabeth. "He has no friends or family in Spain. I wonder why he chose Spain. We must hurry and get him home." She fell silent. She had guessed why he had gone to Spain. It was a country they had not visited together. Too painful for him to go to France where they had been together. Her fingers twitched under Isobel's hand. Isobel's clasp tightened. No further word was spoken of Andrew but the barrier which had existed between the two women since the day Elizabeth had eloped with Andrew was broken down.

In her letter to Andrew Elizabeth told him that he had another son, that Phil asked for him, that Repeal had brought its own problems. "The trustees are coming again in the autumn when we are making wine. I don't know whether we can satisfy them or not. They act as if they didn't want us to make good. I don't know whether I can handle them. I need you, Andrew."

Her needs would bring him back if anything would, she thought. At the end of the letter she wrote, "I've not been happy without you, Andrew. Let us start again, my dear. I've learned many things in your absence."

But the way back into Andrew's trust, Elizabeth learned, was not easy. Spring lengthened into summer and summer into autumn and Andrew did not come.

A weariness had set in which Andrew found impossible to throw off. He had not known until he left Elizabeth how hard he had worked to win her, how often she had given him new hope only to snatch it away again. What was there to guarantee that this was not another false hope?

The only chance there seemed now for him to work out a way of life for himself was to serve in a religious community. He could not now study for the priesthood as he had once thought of doing. His marriage precluded that; but working among the priests in whatever humble capacity they saw fit to place him, he might lose that weariness of spirit which paralyzed him against action. An austere order in northern Spain appealed to him as a retreat. But with Elizabeth's letter before him he found himself unable to decide upon this step. He drifted from city to city in Spain, then into France, then back again to Spain. Finally he wrote Elizabeth telling her what he was thinking of doing.

LV

IN THE autumn John Rambeau's table grapes came into bearing and made for him a small fortune. Large as walnuts, black and velvety, in bunches too large to hold on the palm of a man's hand, they took the fancy of the luxury trade.

John had gone east and had seen to it himself that wherever his grapes were displayed the name went with them. Crowning the great clusters, their rounded surfaces like velvet pile, in bold letters were the words, "Black Brocades."

In golden America even in the hard years of nineteen hundred and thirty-four there were men used to providing themselves and their families with the choicest foods from all over the world and its best wines. For them there was little more to anticipate in the way of new sensations for the palate or the eye. But John's Black Brocades in their grandiose elegance did just that.

John meant to use his money to fulfill a dream he had until recently believed never would be gratified. Years ago had not his grandfather told him that of all his family he, John, had a flair as rare as the old man's own for the making of fine wine? He had never forgotten that remark. It had raised in him the ambition to use his unique ability. First had come the war, then Prohibition, then his grandfather's anger, to thwart that ambition. Now he was in a position to fulfill it for himself.

One of the rarest vineyards in the state—comparable to old Philippe's Napa vineyard—had been offered for sale. In the Livermore Valley, cupped in the foothills, on gray stony soil old vines grew, producing small, stringy bunches of grapes

342

whose sparse return of juice matured into wine fit for a connoisseur. The owner was selling the vineyard at a sacrifice. He wanted only to get enough money to care for himself during the few years left to him.

So many years had the work of his hands been considered the work of an outlaw, so many years had his winery been closed (for he had not been among the fortunate ones to supply sacramental wine), so many years had he been under bond not to draw off so much as a pint of wine, watched by the inspectors, suspected by them if the shrinkage seemed excessive, that he had grown to think of himself as disgraced, a man to be classed with bootleggers. Now, facing the long process of putting his wines on the market again, he had suddenly sickened of the whole affair. He wanted to live out the remaining years of his life in a cottage, in some remote spot where no one knew him.

John Rambeau knew of the vineyard by reputation, but had never visited it. When he came to it the day after he learned it was for sale, he was swept with emotion—a thing rare for John. Its gray gravel thrilled him as nuggets of gold would not have. France on such soil as this had produced her finest vineyards. On the steep banks of the Rhine, the sun-baked slopes of the Rhone, as here, the vines led a stubborn and fruitful existence. These vines, like those in the valleys of France, would have great episodes of growth and bearing.

The old man, answering John's intelligent questions, said at last, "If I had a son like you I wouldn't have to give up my vines."

Walking through the vineyards, studying the vines, John was aware of the skillful grafting. "There is nothing here," he thought, "that I would have done differently." The strong resistant roots had been cut and grafted correctly. They threw out few wild shoots to take the strength from the bearing vines.

There was no irrigation ditch here. During the long period when the grapes were slowly maturing—the content of sugar growing—the vines must thrust deep for their nutrition. The yield would not be large, but the wines would be rich in both flavor and aroma.

In the small but good winery placed close to the vineyards the grapes could be crushed almost as soon as they were picked.

John wanted these fields as he had wanted nothing else in his life—except the Napa Valley vineyards.

"There are others who would buy," the old man replied when John offered him a price. "Some to get hold of this land would be willing to pay me a good deal more than you offer." He gave John a scrutinizing look. "In fact, you've offered me the lowest price of anyone. You know this land is worth more than you offer. You're too smart not to know that."

"I've set my price," said John.

The old man smiled. "I knew your grandfather, so I guess when you say you've set your price you have. I'm going to let you have the vineyards. I don't want my wines to lose their reputation. You'd see to it that they didn't."

As soon as John reached Fresno he arranged with his lawyer to go over the deeds and see that everything was in order. "I'd like you to let me know as soon as possible," John told him. He felt he could not wait until he had the land.

He was sitting in the hotel eating his dinner when he was called to the telephone. Monica's voice came through to him as he picked up the receiver. "John, is this you? I've been searching for you all day. Father died this morning, suddenly—in the office, from a stroke."

John was stricken. His family was suddenly important to him. The purchase of the vineyard seemed robbed, now, of some of its significance.

When André Rambeau's will was read there was a surprising clause in it. "The winery I leave to my son, John, at the express wish of my father, Jean-Philippe Rambeau, who left it to me only in trust for his grandson, John Philippe Rambeau." André had kept the secret well. To no one had he ever spoken of the conference he had had with old Philippe just before his death when Philippe had explained the terms of his will to him. "When John has learned to work instead of to scheme he will be ready for his inheritance," the old man had ended.

John had an almost uncontrollable desire to laugh. Of all the tricks life had played him this was the most complete. He knew how pressed his family had been to maintain the San Joaquin properties. For him, now, the Livermore vineyard was a luxury he could not afford. Every extra cent he had would have to go into the family vineyards.

He can't let go his piece of earth, he said to himself thinking of his grandfather. *And along with himself he's bound me to it. I'll just kick over the traces, buy the Livermore land, let the family struggle along as they have been doing. I don't want to make wine for the general trade.* But he knew he would not kick over the traces. *Why? That's what I'd like to know,* he asked himself.

It was hard giving up the Livermore property. It was not John's habit to give up anything he wanted.

In December John took his father's place in the winery.

The financial burden he faced was large. The crowd of vineyardists who had gathered the year before at the Rambeaus' to celebrate Repeal, like all the others in the industry, had not seen that they faced difficulties equal to those of Prohibition years.

In the excitement of the first months after Repeal the whole nation had clamored for wine. But there was only that limited supply carried over in the old wineries, well aged and mellowed. While it lasted the returns were fabulous, but in a few months it was exhausted.

Then the growers found that almost overnight the industry must expand from its diminished state into an industry large enough to supply a legalized market. Wineries had to be rebuilt and modernized, new and expensive equipment had to be installed, great quantities of new tanks had to be erected. There were license fees and taxes to pay, distributing organizations to set up, bottles, labels, shipping cartons to buy, advertising to pay for. The industry had to have both fixed and working capital. Little and large growers besieged the lending agencies. The industry was mortgaged almost to the last drop of wine in the wineries and the last grape in the vineyards when suddenly California faced a crisis.

Men pressed both by greed and necessity had shipped wine made from the immediate harvest. It was raw, sharp stuff over which the public grimaced. Dealers began looking again to Europe for fine wines. For America's winegrowers the post-Repeal honeymoon was over. All up and down the state the signs of disaster were evident. As far north as Lake County, where the vineyards began to thin out, and south to the old Spanish vineyards, the necessity of meeting operating costs and payments on borrowed money strained the growers to the limit.

In the San Joaquin Valley the dreams of wealth the men of the Old World had brought over with them in the eighties and nineties were vanishing. Gradually the kingdoms they had built for themselves had crumbled. Only the bare bones of the estates now remained, the avenues of palms and eucalyptus that led to the once magnificent houses. Philippe Rambeau's fear, expressed years ago on that last drive with Francis Fairon, his son-in-law, was coming to fulfillment. Much of the land they had looked out upon that day, rich and cultivated then, was now run-out land which could be brought back to fruitful bearing only by years of arduous toil and much expenditure of money. Some of the vineyards and orchards already had been given over to Johnson grass.

Between the neglected lands there were stretches of carefully tended vineyards and orchards, for the most part little holdings. A horde of new dreamers had come to the Valley—all land-hungry, some freedom-loving men—from Armenia, from Greece, from Portugal, from Russia, they had come.

There were second-generation Japanese, poverty-stricken Americans, leaving the crowded Eastern coast, seeking out unused land free of disease and rich in the minerals that would produce healthy crops. They had brought under cultivation vast tracts of land, overproducing for already glutted markets, further increasing the problem of the older settlers.

The autumn after John Rambeau came into his inheritance California had the hugest grape crop it had ever known— and its wines had no adequate market! Men were disappointed, confused, discouraged. Among them the Rambeau-Fairon men. Not only had they had to let go Henri's vineyards, but when the seven years of probation were over they had sold some of their own land in order to live as they were accustomed. That prosperity had come to their neighbors, Petucci and Dietrick, was a bitter reminder of their losses.

There had been a great deal of talk at first about the means Petucci and Dietrick had employed to get their money. Everyone whispered that they were in with the bootleggers, but after Repeal the prestige of their money began to silence the talk. Petucci built himself a large square house and a splendid winery on the Don's land, much of which he had quietly bought. Dietrick had bought some of the original Rambeau property.

John, in taking his father's place, found that the psychological burden was even greater than the financial. Ronald and Francis Fairon had aged these last years, each of them disintegrating under his own secret trouble and the slow disintegration of their wealth. They wanted no improvements, no changes made. Added to their opposition, John suspected that Nate resented his return.

It was true. Years had covered over the antagonism between the two men, but the old hurt lay deep in Nate's mind. He felt, too, that he had been duped. Monny's money, his own hard work had gone into the business—and, yet unknown to him, John, who had lived as he pleased, had been destined to reap the fruit of their efforts. A hard moment for any man, it was harder for Nate who had never been entirely certain that his racial background was not resented by the family. But never should John know that he had expected sometime to be head of the business. That would make his position intolerable.

From the first Nate had to grant two things. John was a worker, and he did not attempt to override Nate's established place in the business.

Furthermore, John immediately used his own money, even mortgaging his vineyard of Black Brocades to buy the new and expensive equipment necessary if they were to produce a good quality of wine and sell it at a price which the ordinary customer could afford to pay. It was on sweet wine that Philippe Rambeau had made his fortune here in the San Joaquin Valley. This market, despite the competition of larger wineries better equipped for volume output, John planned to recapture.

At the first annual meeting of the Rambeau-Fairons after his re-entry into the firm, John asked that for the coming year they each accept a smaller amount for personal expenditures. John explained the need for certain improvements.

The meeting, according to a custom established by old Philippe, was held in the sampling room at five after the winery was closed for the day. Martha was sitting opposite John. In the fading light he could not see her face clearly when he made his request, but he judged she was against it for he heard her short, sharp laugh.

It roused him to do battle with her. The greatest single obstacle to putting the business on its feet lay in her extravagances. And no one had had the courage to check her. He intended to do it now.

He rose, switching on the electric light so he could see her clearly. Then he returned to his seat and, looking straight at her, said, "We either maintain the standard set by Philippe Rambeau or we become an inferior concern. I will begin with Aunt Martha. What is your wish in the matter?"

Their eyes met like swords clashing together.

Suddenly Martha gave way. "I will do whatever is necessary to maintain Father's reputation, of course." Only John suspected that until now she had been purposely extravagant, exerting her living will over Philippe's dead one.

LVI

In the midst of the third harvest after Andrew had left, Fritz Diener died. Elizabeth had to have a wine-master immediately. She ought to have talked over such a possibility with Diener, she realized now, finding out from him a man he considered worthy to succeed him. *I suppose,* she thought, *Diener had lived here so long he could not think of anyone else tending the wines, or else he would certainly have made known to me in some way his wish in the matter.* She was on the point of writing her father-in-law, Ronald Fairon, asking if he could recommend someone, when Peter came into the office and asked for the job.

"But, Peter, do you know enough about winemaking?" Her tone was anxious.

"That's what I was brought here for, wasn't I? To learn the business. Diener always said so."

"You and Fritz didn't get on very well," Elizabeth answered. "I don't know whether he has taught you enough or not."

"I never let it interfere with my learning things—my not liking him. I'd have been a sap to do that, wouldn't I?"

"Yes, I suppose you would," said Elizabeth a little doubtfully. "You were the one, though, who would have got us into the predicament of selling raw wine, Peter."

"Look, Mrs. Fairon," Peter protested, "you oughtn't to hold one mistake up against me. Everybody pretty near was doing that at first. I've learned a lot since then."

"I suppose you are right. I suppose you are entitled to a trial. But, Peter, you know I must not fail—not even once—with my wines."

350

"I'll see you aren't ever sorry you gave me the job," said Peter. "Thanks." His bead-black eyes shone with pleasure as he went out.

Elizabeth had not meant him to interpret her remark as an offer. She was astonished at his quick assumption that the matter was settled. *But perhaps it's the best I can do—and I'll keep a pretty close supervision over him until I'm certain he's really good,* she thought. *The point is, do I know enough myself? Although I've learned a good deal in these years I have depended on Diener in a great many expert matters, devoting my time to Phil and André. I guess, too, I have been counting on Andrew's coming back and taking charge.* She was unable to believe that Andrew did not want to come home. *I must try again to make him understand.*

Andrew's answer was definite this time. "I've a place here," he wrote. "This civil war in Spain may not seem important to you in America, but it is. Right here the eventual safety of America is being fought out."

When Elizabeth received this letter she was stricken. She knew at last how much she had injured Andrew, injured him seemingly past any recovery. She could not break through his obsession that he was of no use in his own home. Only could he serve her by doing such a crazy thing as to fight in Spain, a country which had no hold on him. *I should have gone to him, worked it out with him face to face.* Why had she not gone to Europe when she first found out where he was? Had she drawn back at joining herself to him again? *Now it is too late. I can only wait and see what war does to him.*

LVII

THE problems of the San Joaquin winery were so many and so absorbing that John forgot every other interest. At the end of the second year after he took over, the Black Brocades no longer had to be the backlog for the winery. Both his own and the Rambeau-Fairon business prospered although he still carried a heavy mortgage. He gave little thought to the hard-pressed condition of the industry as a whole.

One morning in the early spring he rode his horse out to see the newly cultivated fields. Recently he had found that, given help in mounting, he could ride with ease and pleasure. While he was on his horse he lost the sense of any handicap, felt, instead, his old delight in the perfection of his body. This had led him to take over much of the supervision of the vineyards, leaving the office work to Nate. He was pleased with what he saw this morning. The Filipinos he was hiring this year for the field labor had done a splendid job. Not a sprig of grass could be seen in all the long aisles, and from around each vine the weeds had been carefully hoed.

Riding back from his inspection, John noticed a man coming toward him. *Looks like an agent*, he thought. *They are locusts over the land, devouring the farmer's resources, selling him machines he doesn't need, fertilizer his fields don't need.* That was the kind who came out to hunt you, determined to run you down.

"Good morning. What can I do for you?" he asked. His tone was cold, his manner forbidding.

"You are Mr. Rambeau, aren't you? Your name was given to me as a man who could be of special value——"

John interrupted him. "Just what is your business?" he

352

asked. He particularly disliked the way these agents tried to flatter you by their assumption that you, of all men, were the most important.

"My name is Ritter, Galen Ritter. There are a group of men, some of them you know, who are trying to form a trade association to help the wine producers."

"I'm not interested," John answered. "I've been burned twice on associations of one sort and another. They do more evil than they do good." His mind jumped back to the efforts he had made to pledge the men to the raisin-growing program. That had cost him old Philippe's respect. And his effort to get Dietrick to go in on a car-control agreement had cost him a leg.

"Would you mind explaining the kind of trouble you think grows out of them?" Ritter asked.

The man's manner was mild, but John detected a bulldog determination in the set of his jaw. If he gave him half a chance he'd spend the rest of the morning arguing.

"I simply think a man is better off on his own," John answered. "It may be a grand idea but it never works. There are always a few chiselers to spoil the setup."

"Suppose you had a stick strong enough to get after the chiselers?"

"There is no use arguing with me." John, sitting his horse, looked straight into Ritter's eyes. Intelligent brown eyes, keen too. *He is nobody's fool,* John grudgingly acknowledged to himself. Aloud he said, "I did my best to help in the raisin setup."

"That sort of thing isn't what I'm talking about. I understand you tried to force men to an agreement on that deal. You can't drive people into things like that. It runs you into trouble."

Ritter looked squarely at John as he said this. He had a feeling Rambeau might well have been one of the night riders. Hefty fellow, and with a jaw that indicated he wouldn't stand any fooling. *He is shrewd and hard but he is also——* Ritter could not analyze just what it was in Rambeau's face that made him covet him for the new organization. Ritter had been a reporter covering the docks of San Francisco just before he took this job. He understood men, and his intuition told him that Rambeau would be a power in the organization if he could get him.

"Look here," he said, "I'm not promoting anything for my own benefit. I don't think we're going to bring a millennium on earth as a lot of men do with such setups, but I think we've got a chance to put the wine industry on its feet, and God knows it needs to be! It's about the lamest thing I ever got myself connected with."

"It's all of that," John answered him, "and then some. But I still think I'll do my own resuscitation job."

"I wish you'd let me come along to your office and show you what we're after in the way of advertising and publicity. We don't want to curtail production, we don't want to uproot vineyards. We want to go after markets, make the American people proud of their nation's wines."

"You're on the right track there," John answered. Ritter had struck a responsive chord in him when he spoke of making America proud of its wines. Some such national promotion for wines would be smart. Even the wine men themselves needed to have their pride strengthened. There was old Philippe, who puffed out his cheeks and let out his breath like a fire-spouting dragon if anyone hinted his wines weren't as good as European wines, and yet put on that stunt of pretending he was serving French wines.

"Come along to the office," he said, reaching a quick decision, "and I'll see if there's anything in this idea of yours."

Plodding along on the soft ground behind Rambeau's horse Ritter wondered why the fellow didn't get off and walk, too. High-hat maybe, being one of the big owners. But when they reached the door of the winery and a workman came out to help John down from his horse, Ritter saw with a shock how helpless this man of magnificent physique really was. It must

be particularly hard for a person of that type, he thought,
turning away with a show of interest in the building. He had
heard of its beautiful stonework. He strolled beyond the of-
fices, looking at the fine Gothic arches that supported the
roof of the wine cellars.

As the two talked, bit by bit John became interested in
what evidently was a cherished dream to Ritter, a man as
strong and powerful by nature as he was himself. *I might
have called it idealistic rot if he weren't such a he-man,* John
thought, looking at the short, stockily built Ritter with his
bulldog jaw.

"So you think," said John, "that five hundred or more separate concerns, representing fifty-odd nations, now in competition with one another, can be made to sit down, the lambs
with the wolves, and lick each other's wounds?"

"Something like that," Ritter said with a laugh.

"Well, I tell you," said John at last, "when you get ninety
per cent of the growers lined up, come back and I'll put my
name on the dotted line and accept my proportion of the
expenses."

"You don't think I can do it, but I can," Ritter replied.
He had not missed the note of incredulity in John's voice
which changed what sounded like a promise into a refusal.

John looked at his watch. "It's about noon. I'd like you
to meet the rest of the men. You might like to tell them
what you're after. We have a custom started by my grandfather of having a glass of wine together at noon. . . . Here
we are." As he spoke he opened a door and ushered Ritter
into the sampling room.

Ah, thought Ritter with no little excitement, *this is what
I'm always coming up against. These wine men talk as if they
hadn't any of the Old World's feeling of the artist in them—
then they spring something like this on you!*

A loving hand had planned this room with its leaded windows, its old French tavern furniture, and its lovely drinking
goblets—someone who believed in the work of his hands. And

the man, who, half an hour ago, had been saying to him, "All we want of an organization such as you propose is the dollars we can get out of it and as fast as we can get them; wine has been red ink for years and for most of us it's still just that and nothing more," was now saying, "Here's a fine old wine my grandfather made in 1890."

Three men had come into the room. "I'd like you to meet my uncles—Fairons, both of them—and my brother-in-law Frostner." John Rambeau turned to the younger man. "Ritter has a scheme I imagine would appeal to you. In fact I've heard you express ideas not unlike his."

Ritter noticed the slightly Jewish cast of Frostner's face. *The idealistic type,* he thought. The kind that would die for an ideal.

"To your association, or institute, whatever it is." John raised his glass.

LVIII

IT WAS another year before John was called upon to make good his promise. Reluctantly he joined the organization, reluctantly he consented to attend the first general meeting. The banquet which had been planned seemed to him a doubtful undertaking. Certainly the vineyardists would not journey from all over the state on what appeared to be little more than a good-will gathering. Nate liked the idea; the Fairons didn't. But not even Nate wanted to take part in the great gathering to be held at the biggest winery in the state, a building newly built, newly equipped; a mushroom growth since Repeal.

Alone, John entered the vast bottling room of the plant. He noticed first the great size of the room. *Our whole winery could be put into it*, he thought. It was as immaculate as his own. That pleased him, but not the concrete tanks above him on the mezzanine. John believed in wood for holding wine.

Next, he noticed a small group of men standing under the runway which carried the boxes filled with bottles to the packing platform. They seemed a small group in the vast space. About the size of crowd he had expected Ritter would be able to get, was John's conclusion, as he made his way across the room to join them.

"Hello, Rambeau." Ritter came toward him. "Have to eat your words. Couple a hundred here already and more coming all the time. Here, I want you to meet the board of directors."

They were all wine men, but John knew only a few of them, although he knew their names as brands that competed with his own.

Looking around at the crowd on the edge of which he stood, he saw it was made of little islands of men, each island a nationality. He wished he'd insisted that one of the Fairons come with him. Then he would not be the only Frenchman here. The other French winery in the state wasn't in on this, evidently. *By gad, it is!* A member of the family was coming in at the door that very minute.

The door opened again to admit a woman. *It must be Elizabeth,* John thought. *She is the one woman owner in the state.* He stepped back a little into the crowd, not wishing to speak to her.

Feeling a touch on his elbow, he turned to face Ritter. "Rambeau, I'm going to put Mrs. Fairon in your care. Let me introduce her, if you don't already know each other." Ritter, the introduction over, left them to welcome a new group just coming in.

Damn Ritter! He ought to know they were cousins and either liked each other, John fumed to himself, or didn't like each other. It was Ritter's business to know such things. What use would he be in a publicity campaign for wine if he wasn't any more aware than that of people's feelings?

Elizabeth was holding out her hand, "I'm so glad you're here, John. I'm frightened among so many men."

"I must say you don't look it," John answered, appraising with considerable interest his well-poised, well-gowned cousin.

Suddenly he remembered their first meeting. They were so young when they had sat beside each other at Aunt Martha's dinner table! There was that other dinner from which she had run away with Andrew. And the time at Monny's wedding when he had seen her and wished bitterly for the defeat of her marriage. His wish had apparently been fulfilled. Evidently Andrew and she had decided to part. It was nearly five years since Andrew had gone away.

Ritter, speaking through a megaphone to the crowd now scattered over the room, was urging them to take their seats at the tables placed under the overhanging mezzanine. John

saw he was definitely caught. Elizabeth would have to see that
labored effort of his to seat himself.

As he held to the back of the chair, making an effort to seat
himself and lower his crutch to the floor, she said, "Give your
crutch to me." He was so angry with her he could not speak.
Everybody else had the decency to look away, at least pretend
they didn't notice his disability.

"Now we can talk." Elizabeth smiled as she took the seat
beside him, seemingly no more conscious of his handicap than
if it had been something common to the roomful of men. His
embarrassment and anger left him.

"Is there anything in Ritter's idea, John? I need all the help
I can get. I'm not ignoring a single trick. I'm worried about
my business."

"You shouldn't have any trouble," was John's response.
"You're in a kind of class to yourself."

"Oh, am I?"

"Should be." John looked across the table. "There's Petucci," he said, changing the subject, "all dressed up like a
plush horse."

Elizabeth smiled, enjoying the sight of Petucci's childlike
delight in his dinner coat and white boutonnière. "Yes, flower
in his buttonhole and all."

"He's one of the big fellows now, you know." John gave a
short laugh.

Elizabeth glanced at him, wondering if there were some
point about Petucci's prosperity which she had missed. "And
farther down, there's Dietrick. Is he prosperous, too?" Elizabeth asked.

"Yes, he is. He owns some of the Rambeaus' finest vineyards now, you know."

Elizabeth did not answer. The recognition of Dietrick had
brought them nearer than either meant to come to the past.
Each had determined to make the evening a casual affair, but
instead both found themselves probing for the measure of
change in the other.

John was thinking, *She is not so beautiful as she was.* But when he looked at her more carefully he wasn't sure. *She's too thin and she looks tired. But she's a lot nicer than she used to be.* Something friendly about her made him feel less lonely than he had felt for a long time. She seemed more at home with him than his own family had of late. Even Monny, since his return to the business, had changed. He had taken it for granted Monny would ask him to join her family at noon every day. But she hadn't. He carried his lunch with him, ate it in his office while the others were at their homes, if he was too busy to drive to his own house.

Ritter had risen and was rapping for order. The conversation died away in waves with the last clatter of dishes. "Wine is a curious industry," Ritter began. "It's the industry in California which has been lifted the highest and brought the lowest."

"I'll say it's been brought low," a man across from John and Elizabeth said in an angry undertone.

"I said low and high. Wine," Ritter raised his voice, "is a part of the history of mankind."

Someone gave a cynical laugh.

Ritter's eyes behind his heavy glasses began to shine. John knew that expression. Ritter was ready to do battle. "Wine has been made to stand for both evil and good in the world. In Europe they know wine as a food. And both kings and common men have used it at their banquets and feasts to welcome their guests, and to express the association of men." Ritter paused a moment, then very quietly added, "Man has always, as far back as we have any record, used wine as a symbol through which to pass on his spiritual knowledge from generation to generation."

A murmur of uneasiness spread among the younger men at the table at this frank reference to the spiritual significance of wine, but one or two of the older men, born in Europe, were seen to cross themselves.

"It is well for us to remember these things and forget that

we have ever been classed as outlaws," Ritter ended. He raised his glass: "To our very good selves."

Elizabeth was only half listening. Her chair, turned toward the speaker, brought her a little to the side of John. She could study him without his knowing it. *His face contradicts itself,* she was thinking. *There is the old expression of will and animal strength, even violence. But there's something else. He looks as if he had submitted to something greater than himself.*

I'm going to ask his advice, she decided on a sudden impulse, as they rose at last from the table and John suggested he take her back to her hotel. Once they were out on the street Elizabeth burst out, "I'm worried, John." Then she stopped. Why on earth was she telling him? Well, she needed a man's advice and he seemed to be capable of advising her.

"I don't know whether I can keep the property or not," she hurried on. "The committee Grandfather appointed seems lately almost to *want* me to lose it. Last year when they came, Henri and Madeleine dropped down upon me suddenly. Henri offered to go with us on the inspection. He called their attention to some vines which he said were interesting because they showed signs of a new disease. They acted very shocked to find any diseased vines at all and yet I know we had one outbreak of the disease before Andrew left. He mentioned it to me. Andrew always said the committee was very understanding. There's been a change in one member only. You probably know Mr. Ingram died and the next man Grandfather named took his place—Mr. Landis—you probably know him. I don't know whether that has made any difference in their attitude or not. I've only until Fall to prove up on the property. I can't bear to lose it now."

"What's the disease?" John asked.

"Pierce disease."

John gave a low whistle. "That's bad, Elizabeth. Grandfather always dreaded a possible appearance in his vineyards of Pierce disease. It wasn't much known in his day around here. But it had wiped out a whole district in Southern California. He said if it got started it might take all the vineyards of the state. The wine men are all worried about it. Henri has kind of got you if it's Pierce disease. It's difficult to get rid of."

"Why do you say 'Henri' as if he had anything to do with it?"

"Because my guess would be that Henri plans to have the state take over the vineyards—and later get hold of them himself. There's no clause, unfortunately, in Grandfather's will which would prohibit the state from selling the property. I'm only surprised from what you tell me that you haven't lost it already. Probably because Henri hasn't until now had enough influence with the committee."

"What can I do, John?" Elizabeth was alarmed.

John drew a deep breath. He would like to close in on that rat Henri more than anything else in the world. "Suppose you let me come up and go over your vineyards and see if they've any grounds for condemning them. Then we'll know how to fight Henri."

"I'd be awfully grateful if you would. I couldn't bear to have Andrew come home and find the vineyards gone."

It surprised him to have her speak of Andrew's return. Why did she? Was she, then, a little fearful, trying to tell him that her appeal to him was purely a business one? And did she really expect Andrew back after all this time?

"Will it be all right for me to come up next week?" he asked.

Along the road past his grandfather's old vineyards John drove with mixed emotions. The fire which he had set with his own hands and which he had seen ravage the vineyard was as if it had never been. The new vines were as sturdy as the old.

He turned his car into the familiar drive. Immediately he noted changes. The house had been freshly painted and the shrubbery trimmed. But at the back of the house everything was the same. The arbor, this early spring day, was bursting into leaf. As always before, the vine had been trimmed just enough to give a glimpse of the green paneled winery door.

The maid who answered his knock said Mrs. Fairon had gone out with the boys. While he was waiting for her John decided to take a look at the winery. He'd like to see what was going on there. He had been making some investigations since his talk with Elizabeth. Rumor had it that some of the Rambeau wine had not been up to reputation of late. He would ask for the winemaker, see if he could find out what was the trouble. It might be simply a story Henri had started to serve his purpose in closing in on Elizabeth.

At the winery no one seemed to be about except the girls in the packing room. He went on into the "bottling chamber" as his grandfather always called the alcove cut in the rock where the wine was bottled. This small neat space thrilled John, the artist, as the great bottling space of the large winery where the Association had met had failed to do. A young fellow sat at a small eight-spouted machine. John had often sat there himself, carefully filling and quickly corking the bottles before any foreign yeasts floating in the air could enter the wine. But this young fellow was leaving the bottles uncorked!

"What are you doing letting wine stand open?" John snapped.

The boy looked up, saw the stranger. "What's it to you?" he asked.

John spared himself an answer. If one thing was wrong there would probably be another. He took a bottle from under the boy's hand, lifted it to his lips, tasted the contents. With an oath he spit it out. "Go and get the winemaster and bring him here at once."

All the glibness was gone from the boy. This must be some Government official he didn't know about. "Gee, how would I know? Why didn't he say who he was?" he told Peter when he found him.

Peter hurried in, knowing no Government official had that

kind of jurisdiction over him. "I've got to ask you, sir," he said, confronting John, "to get out of this part of the winery. We don't allow strangers in here. Any business you have is with the office."

"It's you who will get to hell out of here." John in his anger didn't bother to mention who he was. "What do you mean letting raw wine go out of the Rambeau winery bottled as vintage wine?"

"Just who do you think you are?" Peter took a step nearer. He didn't need to put up with a man who had to dangle himself on a crutch. "I'm the master here."

John's anger leaped up white-hot within him: anger against this impostor, and against old Philippe for his silly will, and against the inefficiency of Elizabeth, and against Andrew for leaving her to manage. He let out with his right arm, landing a blow on the point of Peter's chin. The man spun halfway about in a kind of fantastic dance, then went down in a heap in the midst of the bottles. The bottles danced their own jig, then tumbled over, too, the wine trickling over the fallen man and onto the gray floor.

John let out a howl of delight. "Bastard!" he shouted, picking up the last bottle and throwing it into the heap around Peter.

"John!"

Pivoting on his crutch, John swung round to face Elizabeth. A tall boy on one side of her was staring up at him with fright in his blue eyes. The little one, a step ahead of her, was looking down at Peter with vivid interest but Elizabeth kept his hand tightly in hers, as if to hold him back.

"André, Phil, run in to Rose," Elizabeth commanded. As she loosened her grasp on the smaller boy, his foot shot forward and he kicked the fallen man. "I don't like him," he said, then followed his brother who had turned obediently and without looking back was running out of the room.

Peter slowly got up, wiping the wine out of his hair and

eyes. "Get out of here or I'll knock you down again." John's eyes were blazing and he paid not the slightest heed to Elizabeth.

"Peter, go into the office," Elizabeth commanded. Only when Peter had gone did she speak again to John. "After all," she said, "this happens to be my winery."

"I don't care whether it's your winery or not. You haven't any business to disgrace the Rambeau name."

"Really, John," Elizabeth protested. "I didn't ask you to come here and play the brute." She was as angry as John now.

John would have turned and left her had he been thinking only of his own pleasure, but he wasn't going to see all old Philippe had built destroyed because of a silly woman and a lying, cheating underling. "I'm sorry, Elizabeth," he said swallowing his anger, "but this fellow you've got deserves all I gave him. He's putting out wines here that are a disgrace to any house, let alone the house of Rambeau. This wine he's bottling can't have been aged a year, and I'll bet it's not registered on your books. Runs it through between times, probably, using your name and taking the profits himself. I've heard rumors lately about the wine here not being up to standard."

Elizabeth was only half believing at first, and yet she knew it was the kind of thing Peter would do. But she was angry and did not like the idea of giving in to John. Finally she made herself say, "I shouldn't have spoken as I did, but you are altogether too highhanded. We've always fought with each other, haven't we?" Then all at once she capitulated. "Tell me what to do, John. I know I'm trying to carry on a business I don't know too much about."

"Yes, that's true," John answered. "First go in and fire that fellow—but perhaps you'd like me to do it for you."

"No, I'll do it myself."

"Come to think of it, you'd better let me take care of this." John's tone was quieter than it had been. "I've got to find out where he's placing this phony stock. He probably wouldn't tell you. What I mean," he added, "is that he may have to be knocked down again."

"No," said Elizabeth, "you can't do that again. You won't need to. I think he'll tell you anything you want to know."

As soon as John had his information and had seen Peter off the place, he climbed into his car and started for the vineyards. When he returned, he seated himself by Elizabeth in the office. "The inspectors are right," he told her. "The lower vineyards are pretty well honeycombed with Pierce disease and there's some in the hill vineyard. You will have to destroy every vine that shows the slightest sign of wilt—and there are a lot of them."

"What I have to do first, John, is find a new winemaster. Our orders must go out on time."

"I think I know of a trustworthy man you can get and who understands his job. I'll tend to that tomorrow on my way home, but now I must make you realize the necessity of getting after your vineyards."

"It's all right for you to talk, John," Elizabeth answered, "but I haven't the money to do it."

"What would you think of running the two wineries together as we used to? I imagine that's what Grandfather had in mind when he made his will."

"You're saying that to help me out. Besides——"

"Besides what?"

"Besides I want to succeed on my own."

"Well, let me lend you some money then. You simply must take care of your vines or you'll lose your vineyards and jeopardize all the vineyards around here."

"I don't believe you'd consider me a very good risk after all you've seen this afternoon. No, lending me money is out, John."

John was silent so long that finally Elizabeth said, "Look here, John, you don't need to bother. I'll come through somehow. I always do."

John could feel the sweat running down under his shirt,
and the palms of his hands were moist and cold. If she weren't
so stubborn he would not have to tell her. "I owe you some
money," he said at last and his mouth was dry so the words
were hard to speak.

Elizabeth was touched. "I'm grateful, John, but even I
can't be made to believe that. I'm not that simple."

"It's true." He was angry with her again. "If you weren't
so stubborn you'd take the money and I'd not have to tell you
why I'm offering it to you."

"Look here, John," Elizabeth answered him. "I won't let
you bully me into taking care of my vines."

"Well, I'll let you have it then." John's eyes were defiant.
"Your vineyards weren't burned by accident as everyone
thought. I burned them. Deliberately threw a match into
that stubble. Now put me out if you want to, but I'll send
you the money."

Elizabeth sat back in her chair, too astonished, too confused
to speak. It was that fire which had brought them home
from France. It was why she was sitting here now, trying to
do something she didn't know how to do.

"Why?" she asked at last.

"To hurt you," John answered coolly. He didn't intend to
go out for her sympathy. He had never come to any understanding with himself, really, for his violent act. It was none
of her business.

"You must have wanted awfully to hurt me to hurt the
vineyards. And why do you want to pay me back now? You
didn't seem to worry much about what you owed me until
you met me the other day. You must have known things
would be hard these last years with Andrew gone."

"I've wanted to pay you for a long time, ever since—well,
ever since I started to do things, after my injury."

"That's several years. You seem to have been able to control the desire pretty well."

"We're not so different, Elizabeth," John answered. "We're

from the same stock. Would you find it easy to tell a thing like this? But that's beside the point; the thing is there is money rightfully yours to put the vineyards in shape."

Elizabeth rose and walked over to the window. Finally she came back, stood leaning against the side of the desk. "I'm the last one really to condemn you. You might as well know I've hurt Andrew a lot worse than you've ever hurt me. I accept your offer. Now suppose we go and have some dinner."

"Good. Now we can plan how to beat Henri." John was glad to be back on the safe ground of everyday matters.

When he entered the house he had a sense of coming home. In general the rooms were as they had been through all his childhood and young manhood. Any changes Elizabeth had made seemed only to emphasize their original character. His grandfather's desk occupied a more important place than it used to. So did his easy chair, reupholstered in a faded-looking stuff that did not suggest change, but did do away with the actual rags of the tattered covering. Old Philippe had refused to have it touched in his lifetime, saying it was comfortable and he was used to the chair's hollows. John noticed that everything connected with the old man Elizabeth had preserved.

The two boys came in for dinner. John saw he was a hero in André's eyes, but knocking Peter down had not, he feared, got him anywhere with Phil.

Elizabeth and he spent the evening going over her accounts, invoices and orders, estimating, valuating. It was late when they finished.

"I had Rose prepare your old room for you. I thought maybe you would prefer it to any other," she said.

So she hadn't expected him to go on tonight. It would have seemed a rejection in more ways than one if at this hour of the night he had felt he must leave this house, so much connected in his mind was it with his childhood's security. All the evening the idea had not left him that he would feel cast out when the moment came for him to leave. However un-reasonable it might be, going out tonight would seem to place finality on his separateness from his family. Both Monny's and Elizabeth's houses closed against him—in neither a member of the household.

When he had stretched himself out between the cool sheets of the bed in his old room, his relief over setting things right with Elizabeth flooded over him. He felt clean and whole again. He lay there contentedly, listening to the wind brushing a branch against the house wall. The illusion was perfect that his mother and old Philippe were alive in this house.

That this lovely bit of land should fall into Henri's hands was a thing John could not stomach. He knew he could not save the vineyards from Henri's grasp simply by bringing them back to their old standard. There was no such thing as perfection in growing things. If there was a plan afoot to condemn the vineyards, some flaw could be found to make the condemnation seem reasonable.

John meant to find out where Henri's power lay. He knew that for some time Henri had been mixed up in the most unsavory politics of the state. Just where did Henri get his influence over the men Philippe had trusted? His grandfather did not often make mistakes in his valuation of men. All the men whom he had appointed were trusted men in the community.

He would have to fight Henri on his own ground, ferret him out in the labyrinth of crooked politics, make him loosen the hold he had on one or all of this board of three. Was it some sense of fright, real or imaginary, or some desire for profit, that made them betray their own integrity? John had some knowledge of that world beneath a world. In those years he had lived by helping the bootleggers, he had touched the outside strands of the closely interwoven skein of intrigue and subterfuge—gossamer threads so fragile a man hardly realized he touched them until they were wound about him.

He meant to send out along those interwoven strands, sensitive as telephone wires, a whisper of warning. Petucci was a powerful man now in the state. John believed that through Petucci he might save the property for Elizabeth.

Petucci had long ago ceased to worry about how he "fool-a da Government." During those years when he was building himself a fortune, he had been associated with strong, powerful men and they had protected him. Year by year he had undertaken more and more important work for them. He rarely thought of the clear and sunny world free of intrigue in which he once had lived, rarely and then only as a world which he wanted his family to occupy.

John came directly to the point when he went to see him. "Petucci," he said, "this little affair of ours, years ago, seems to have borne fruit."

"What you mean?" Petucci's countenance was one of bland ignorance.

"No use trying that stuff on me," said John. "There's something I want you to do."

"I dunno," Petucci began. "Petucci vera ordinary man. No man listen Petucci."

"I'm not going to ask you to do anything crooked—I'm sorry I ever started you on such a course. I never expected you to get in so deep—but you *are* in deep and you may as well use your influence to do something good."

"What you want-a done, Meester Rambeau?"

John explained.

Petucci's face grew black with the sudden anger that rose so easily in him. "I make-a da try, Meester Rambeau. I very fond of Philippe Rambeau. He vera good man. No man have a right to steal-a da land from Philippe Rambeau." He spoke as if Philippe Rambeau would personally lose the land.

John rose to go. "My sister Monny tells me you have a very beautiful daughter, Petucci. I think Monny would like to invite her to meet some of her friends."

Petucci's smile broke out like sunshine. "My girl vera nice."

LIX

JOHN put forth every effort to bring the vineyards into condition in time for the next inspection. He superintended the pulling of the diseased vines. He wanted to be sure that no single infested vine was left to spread infection.

Elizabeth grew used to having him drop in unannounced, for even after the infected vines were out he allowed few days to pass without a careful going over of the remaining vines. There was no way to detect the disease until it had taken possession of a vine. The germ could not be seen even with a microscope. Only with an ultraviolet ray could it be photographed. All John could do was to go over and over the vineyards, time after time, until not one wilted vine remained.

There was much sharp argument between Elizabeth and John. Barely a conference passed without one of them vigorously opposing the other. Elizabeth found the encounters stimulating, but sometimes, as hot-tempered as he, she rebelled against his mandates. "You think you know more than anyone else in the world, John Rambeau," she told him once.

"Well, I do when it comes to grapes. I learned, as you know, under Grandfather." He looked very handsome and proud sitting in old Philippe's armchair, his head thrown back. Elizabeth felt a sudden surge of happiness.

As the weeks went by she found she was waiting for his coming. She told herself it was because she needed his help so much. He was good for the boys, too. She had thought until he came that she ought to send them away to school. No woman alone could manage André. And Phil clung to her far too much.

The days when John was not with them were sometimes hard days for all three of them. Such times made Elizabeth

371

aware of the vacancy in their lives, made her fearful that she might grow to need John too much. On one such day, she wrote Andrew a letter begging him to return.

For months Andrew had lain in a hospital with no will to get well. He had been injured internally. To die was the thing for which he had come to Spain, and he wanted it to be over with quickly. But, although he was a Fairon in name and character, he had the Rambeau vitality and it gave ground slowly against shock, injury, and unhappiness.

Elizabeth's letter fell from his hand. Could it be that he had misunderstood her before? There was unmistakable longing in the tone of this one. He must see her. And his boys—Why, he must go home. He must see the Valley where he had been born. It became an obsession with him to see all the valleys that lay between the great Sierra and the Coast Range—the San Joaquin, the Sacramento, the Napa Valley. He saw them always with the sun shining down upon their peace and plenty.

For several weeks Elizabeth did not see John. Then one afternoon in the late summer he came again. There was a loud shout from André and Phil when they saw his car drive in.

"Uncle John can't ever go away," cried André running out to the car and climbing in beside John.

"May I stay for a few days?" asked John of Elizabeth, who, hearing the commotion, had come down from her office in the winery to greet him. "I need to make sure the vineyards are all right. May I stay?" His question was hardly a question, so confident was he of welcome.

After dinner, he sat down at his grandfather's desk. "I'd like to go over a few things we ought to do before the inspectors' visit. It's important we don't miss a trick if we hope to win out."

Elizabeth was standing beside him, but she was giving scant

attention to what he was saying. How strong and lean his hands were. All at once she was conscious that John had ceased his explanations and was looking up at her—there was no mistaking the look in his eyes. "Elizabeth," he said at last, "we belong to each other. We've always belonged to each other."

"Oh, my dear—" Elizabeth's tone was full of anguish—"it's too late."

"Nonsense!" exclaimed John with his old impatience. "Your life isn't half over."

"I can't run the risk of hurting Andrew. I've spoiled his life, John. I can't do anything more to harm him."

"He's been gone for years. Surely——"

"I've had a letter from him in answer to one of mine. He's sick. He's coming home, John."

John reached out and with a fierce gesture drew her to him. "I can't give you up, Elizabeth!" he cried. Then he let her go and sat staring straight before him.

Elizabeth drew him to her, stroking his hair as his head lay against her. Then she left him but she could not forget how the strong firm cords in his neck, the beautiful curve of his head, had felt under her hand.

LX

PHILIPPE and André walked up and down the porch. Phil was tall for his age and slender; André, a stout, firm little boy. Phil had on his first long trousers. He felt very grown up beside André, who still wore socks and short trousers and was only five. Besides, had he not seen Father who was returning today, and André hadn't?

"I called him Andrew. He liked me to say it. He practically never did anything without me," Phil said.

André looked at his brother, awed, but only for a moment. "He'll like a new boy better'n one he's seen a hundred times," he said and stuck out his small fat chest.

"He won't."

"How do you know?"

"Because Uncle John likes me best."

"I don't care if he does. Mother doesn't."

"She does, too." They had squared off now with some idea of fighting when they heard a long blast of a motor horn followed by two short ones, the signal Elizabeth always gave when her car reached the gate. Around the veranda to the back of the house they raced—Phil ahead because his legs were longer—down the three steps and through the arbor. Phil was there first but André pulled up just as the car stopped.

Suddenly they were overtaken with shyness as they watched a strange man get out. Both of them had pictured their father as a man like Uncle John, only without a crutch. This man was very thin and quiet and as shy as they were.

"Hello," he said a little awkwardly. "Phil, you've grown a lot. I wouldn't have known you. André, I'd have known you

374

anywhere." He looked at Elizabeth. "He's like Grandfather, isn't he? A true Rambeau."

"We're Fairons, both of us," said André. Then, executing a rapid run through the arbor and back, he mounted the steps to the veranda ahead of them.

Quietly Elizabeth and Andrew followed. Andrew placed his hand on Phil's shoulder and leaned on him. Phil's heart jumped up within him. *I'll call him Andrew when we're alone*, he said to himself.

Andrew turned when he reached the top step. The sun burst through the high fog which until now had obscured the mountains. The Valley was alight just as he had pictured it so often in times of terror and desperation. There was the arbor below him—just as he had dreamed of it—the great vine throwing its design of leaves and branches onto the gray gravel beneath. Beyond the circling driveway through the trees he could see a bit of gray stone masonry. The blue-black masses of the mountains were firm strong barriers standing between him and the world of chaos from which he had come.

He reached out for Elizabeth and their hands clasped.

Once they were within the house Andrew wandered from window to window. One looked out across the vineyards. From another he could see the shining green of the live oak under whose branches he had first kissed Elizabeth, from another the mountains on the far side of the Valley which shut them in from the long coast of California and the Pacific. "It looks so safe," he said at last.

John and I have kept his home for him, thought Elizabeth. *He must never know our possession of it is threatened. I must work hard.*

Finally, Andrew pushed a chair into the bay that jutted out at the end of the living room. From here he could look in both directions and see the protecting hills. There, day after day, he sat waiting for the strength that did not come to him.

There John found him on his next visit. John had been in doubt whether to come at all. He did not wish to see Elizabeth and Andrew together. It angered him that Andrew should think he had a claim on Elizabeth after all these years. And he was a little angry with Elizabeth. Then he knew if he didn't finish what he had begun Elizabeth would lose the land.

She came out to meet him and together they went in to Andrew. Elizabeth told him she had not explained to Andrew the threat to the vineyards. "Not until he's better able to bear the uncertainty," she had said.

"What, then, will he think of my interference?" John asked.

But Andrew seemed not to question the arrangement. *Whatever troubles him, and something does, it's not that,* was John's conclusion. He had never understood Andrew and he did not now. "If we armed those mountains, we'd make them impregnable," he said to John. "I haven't wanted to say anything to Elizabeth, but it ought to be done."

"What do you mean?" John asked in astonishment. "You certainly don't think this pint war or revolution or whatever you call it in Spain threatens us here?"

"Well, I don't know. It's hard to explain. You see I've seen valleys look peaceful like this and then——"

"Look here, Andrew," John broke in, "you get well and you won't be having such gloomy ideas." And to himself he said as he rode away, *I'll be damned. Fighting a mythical battle like that while Elizabeth and I fight the real one!*

Elizabeth was fighting now, but for more than the vineyards. She was fighting for Andrew's recovery. With horror she had realized the first night of his return that he was injured in mind as well as body. As darkness had closed them in, he had grown restless. He kept asking if they'd had much fog this year and if Elizabeth thought the sun would be shining in the morning. He seemed worried because it had been gray and cold in San Francisco when he arrived. He would not undress. Instead all night he kept watch. Only when the sun came over the mountains did he seem like himself again. Night after night it had been the same.

If he should have to move from his home, there would be no hope that he would ever get well. She wished she could tell John how important it was that they hold the vineyards. She knew John was doing everything he could, but if he shared her anxiety it seemed to her that in some mysterious way their chance to win through would be greater. Yet some loyalty to Andrew kept her from betraying his secret. *There isn't any more John could do even if he did know,* she kept reassuring herself.

John was delighted with the way Elizabeth began to take hold of the work. What Diener's and John's instructions had not accomplished Elizabeth's own good brain accomplished, now that her emotions gave her the incentive. There was not a detail of the business that she did not master. She learned to be as firm with her winemaster as even John could wish. "She really has executive ability," John decided, "and an understanding of wine. Even Aunt Martha never came near Elizabeth in her knowledge, and Aunt Martha was good."

Through all the hours of the day and night Elizabeth had but one object in mind: to surround Andrew with security. If he could just once feel he was safe. She learned never to be impatient with him as she sometimes was with John or the boys.

It was not easy for her always to be serene, but for Andrew's sake she mastered the technique until finally she built between them a bridge of confidence. He began to tell her a few things out of those years when he had been away. She came to know that he had received some shock, the terror of which he could not yet face. If he slept and wakened suddenly in the dark it mastered him. Then she would put her arm under him, draw him close, fold his trembling hands together and placing them against her breast wait for the paroxysm of pain or grief or terror, whichever it was, to pass.

She had a long chair placed for him in the arbor, and there she would find him when she came in from her work, sleeping quietly, with the sun lying across his face.

The summer passed in a succession of bright days and slowly Elizabeth could see Andrew gaining. The sun turned his skin to a rich brown. He was beginning to sleep at night. And when he did not, the day seemed so soon to come with the sun pushing itself up over the mountain that the night lost something of its terror. He would lie close to Elizabeth. He was almost safe with her so near.

If only we can win out and keep the property he will get well, she assured herself. But it would be disastrous to have anything happen now, she thought, finding it harder and harder not to show anxiety before him.

There was no way she could keep from him that this fall the inspectors were to make their final visit. He knew the date as well as she, but he did not appear to be disturbed as the day drew near. He simply took it for granted that she would meet the requirements and the property would be theirs. She was thankful for his unconcern, and for the fact that he took no interest in the work going on around him. He had never once asked to be driven through the vineyards, so he knew nothing of the toll disease had taken of the vines.

On a late day in autumn just at noon the three trustees arrived. It was one of Andrew's least apprehensive days. He was sitting in the arbor when the car drew up, and he went himself to welcome the men. "I hope you will excuse me not going with you into the vineyards," he said after wine had been passed. "I've not been well."

"Oh, certainly," they answered almost in chorus. "John here can show us about." They turned with evident relief to John Rambeau. All three were competent men. They possessed solid fortunes and positions, and they eyed Andrew with considerable distrust. The mildest judgment passed on him was by Chairman Martin. Erratic and unreliable, neglecting his family to fight another country's war, was Mr. Martin's estimate of him. If it had not been for Fairon's wife Elizabeth and for John, Martin would have felt that Philippe Rambeau would be better served with his vineyards in the hands of the state.

Not much was said as John drove the three about the vineyards. John was watching to see what was the reaction of each to the improved conditions. He had had word from Petucci that all had been done that could be done. How much that might mean he could not guess. He meant to find out which man or men had been reached by Henri. The inspection of such a one or ones would be purely perfunctory. The others would study the vines conscientiously. He wanted to know who were the dishonest ones. If the decision went against them possibly he might expose the guilty ones and yet save the vineyards.

Martin, the spokesman of the group, John had always liked. He used to come to the winery a great deal in old Philippe's day. He was a man with a deep knowledge of the industry, and an equally deep knowledge of California. He had been a wine taster now for many years, but at one time he had had his own vineyards. John was pretty certain of his sincerity, and he was not to be disappointed. It was a pleasure to see a man go so intelligently about his task as Martin did. He was small and neat, with quick darting eyes. He walked between the rows studying, estimating, evaluating. No doubt that Martin would make an honest decision.

Of the other two men John was not so certain. Lake had been involved in a water suit for several years now—the irrigation rights on a strip of grape land he owned. It might be expedient for him to stand in with a politician like Henri. Such a temptation to an honest man, evidently old Philippe had not foreseen.

Landis, the third appraiser, the new member of the board, was one of the wealthiest men in the San Joaquin Valley, but he had been only moderately wealthy at the time of Philippe's death. John knew he now entertained social and political ambitions. He, too, might have been reached by Henri.

It was toward the end of the inspection in the high vineyards that Landis' interest flagged. The dapper little Martin was ahead, exclaiming in excited approval over the improvement in the vineyard since their last visit. "I'll go around the brow of the hill here," he called out to Landis and Lake. "Each of you take a section below me."

It was warm on this southern slope, and Landis was a stout man. Once the other men were out of sight he made no pretense of inspecting the vines. He walked over to John saying, "I'm willing to pass the vineyards on your say-so, Rambeau. All I've seen looks pretty good to me." Abruptly he changed the subject. "Petucci is one of our coming men in the state, don't you think?"

That was enough. John understood that Landis was informing him of a service rendered. So Petucci had talked as to whom Landis was benefiting. Petucci had told Landis that he would be doing John a favor. He had not expected Petucci to mention his name. There might be a price to pay later to Landis. Well, anyway, he had made things safe for Elizabeth.

The inspectors had given their verdict and gone. John had driven away soon after. Elizabeth and Andrew had deserted the arbor for the house.

What a fight it's been, Elizabeth was thinking. *But we are safe at last.* The years she had served for the vineyards were over. She glanced at Andrew, noticing with compassion the fragile look of both body and face.

There was a loud banging of doors, books dropped with a thud on the table, the voices of Phil and André raised in delight over a jar of cookies they found set out for them. Then another banging of doors and then whoops of delight growing fainter as they ran toward the gate and freedom. Through Elizabeth flooded the exquisite sense that the safety of her husband and children lay in her keeping. *I guess I've grown up,* she thought. *I never wanted to before but it's nice.*

Andrew thought, *How beautiful she is!* Today he could enjoy her beauty without hurt.

LXI

John had found a friend in Ritter. They liked each other. Whenever Ritter was in the valley he stopped in to see John, often asking his advice about some plan he had on foot. John's shrewd mind cut into a problem, shearing it of any superficialities. He seemed to know, too, all the little crotchets of the wine men. But when it came to the great advertising campaign planned to benefit the industry, John began calling Ritter by long-distance offering suggestions.

"What do you mean?" Ritter would ask eagerly.

John was excited over the growing demand for good wine and his own answer to that demand. He took pride especially in what he had done in bringing back old Philippe's northern vineyards. He was beginning to take pride in the Association too.

One morning John went into the sampling room and shut the door. No one came there at this time of day. He was developing a habit old Philippe had had of making it a retreat when he had a particularly knotty problem to solve. There was something about the room that gave him some sort of special control of himself.

Petucci and Landis had just left. *So that is what the price is,* John thought, walking up and down. He had never kidded himself into thinking that Landis would not exact some favor from him—that was to be expected. The laws of the world of special privileges were inexorable and unbreakable. You received and you gave in return.

It had all seemed legitimate to John before. Night raids, control of railway cars, bootlegging, using a man like Petucci to manipulate men for him, not asking what tricks were used to do it. All a part of man keeping his place in a not too pretty business world.

But this thing Petucci and Landis had asked of him sickened him. He could not go back on Lake, the man who had risked his own safety to give an honest estimate on Elizabeth's vineyards. And yet that was exactly what Landis was asking him to do. Landis had just informed John that he owned the property next to Lake's—a blind ownership as yet. Many men had bought bits for him. It was he who, behind the scenes, was fighting Lake over his water rights. The state engineers refused to let Landis put down more wells. Water surveys showed that if he did he'd take the water from Lake's land. The surveys indicated the water table had been falling of late years. Landis had a big scheme on. Heavy irrigation would make his land some of the most productive in the state. But he was completely blocked now by the engineers, unless he could get hold of Lake's land. Lake's property was heavily mortgaged due to his long fight over water rights. With a little maneuvering with the right men the mortgage could be called. John Rambeau, Landis understood, had influence with some of the "right" men.

John could refuse. He'd felt like kicking Petucci and Landis out of his office. But if he refused they'd get even with him. The world of special privilege would be set against him. You were supposed to decide for your group, you didn't get soft with pity for a fellow outside it. If you did, you got yours, and it might be plenty seeing John was a man of position and wealth, potential if not yet actual.

Perhaps I wouldn't care very much. I haven't any family they can hurt, he thought. But hadn't he? They could strike at the whole Rambeau-Fairon outfit through him. After all they, like Lake, were pretty heavily mortgaged.

The door opened. "Oh, hello, John! Didn't know you were in here. Thought you went out with Petucci and Landis." Nate hesitated, seeing no one else in the room.

"I didn't realize it was noon," said John. "I came in here to do a little thinking and forgot all about the time."

Immediately Nate's sensitive lips tightened. *The crazy guy thinks I meant he'd disturb me if I stayed in my office,* thought John. *He feels he's being discriminated against. Thinks we would like to get rid of him. I believe he takes all this Jewish business over in Europe personally. I've even thought sometimes the way he looks at Monny he isn't sure of her.*

John took his problem home with him that evening, carefully, laboriously working through all the angles. He had never been up against himself like this before. He was caught on the horns of a dilemma—either he must injure Lake, a man who had honorably performed his duty to old Philippe in the inspection of the property, or he must jeopardize the security of his own family—Monny and her kids, and the Fairons, even Elizabeth and her boys. The sweat stood on John's forehead. A struggle like this was physical labor for him.

He might even stomach doing the thing against Lake, if that were the end—but it would be only the beginning. From now on, whenever he was needed, he would be asked to dip his fingers into all kinds of sticky politics. Nobody knew better than John the many fantastic angles of California's politics. He had committed himself, now that he had once accepted a favor of men who manipulated others in that world. They had risked going against Henri to help him. In return they would expect him to take risks for them.

Suppose he placed himself where he would not fear to be honest? Why not sell out to Nate? Things weren't going to improve between him and Nate. It would cut a lot of crossed wires if he got out of the Rambeau-Fairon business.

He rather liked the idea. He was finding, after being on his own for so many years, that managing two old men and a sensitive brother-in-law had its drawbacks. Shucks, though, he knew he liked it. He'd always liked to manipulate his family. He was always one lap ahead of them when it came to business. They'd probably get themselves into an awful muddle without him. Still, he might sound out Francis Fairon in the morning, see how he would react to having Nate in charge. Down in his heart John knew that if Nate were given a break he would make good.

Francis was not in his office the next morning. Toward noon he called to ask if John would come over. "Your Aunt Martha wants to see you."

"Four o'clock be all right? I'm working with Ritter just now over some new advertising. Wish you were here, Fran, to see the setup. They've caught the very color of our best port. It glows. It actually has aroma in the picture." He laughed delightedly.

"I'm afraid she can't wait, John. Could you come now? I'm afraid . . . I'm afraid you might be too late this afternoon. Your aunt may not last out the day, John."

"Of course," said John, shocked over his uncle's words but puzzled that Martha should ask for him. His aunt had not spoken to him directly since the day he had thwarted her in that extravagant use of money which had jeopardized the business. Never since then had he been invited to his grandfather's old home. What could she want of him now when it had come time for her to die?

Francis came to the door. "She's heard your car and she won't wait a moment. I want you to know before you go in that she's dying, John. She's been sick for a long time but she's never let anyone speak of it. I've known it only because I have heard her groaning sometimes at night, but I dared not go to her or in any way suggest that I knew. She would not have the doctor until a week ago. It's a matter of a very short time now."

John knocked on the door of his aunt's room.

"Come in." It was Martha's voice, weak but imperative as ever. The nurse was adjusting a pillow as he entered so that Martha could appear to sit erect.

She looks like a sick old eagle, John thought. Her once white hair, cut short, rose in a kind of faded crest when she slowly pushed it back out of her eyes. Her face was thin, her cheekbones stood out from the hollows of her cheeks, her nose, a little too prominent always for beauty, seemed arched and sharpened, and her eyes, fierce and rebellious, were narrowed under drooping lids.

"I've got to die," she said without preamble. "I don't like it but I want less to live. It doesn't offer anything—life, I mean. It's not much of a world as I see it, today, but there's one thing in it I want kept the way it has always been—and I guess you're about the only one in this family that can do it."

She paused, exhausted. John started to speak but she forestalled him, saying, "Don't talk, please."

After a few minutes she went on. "Don't think what I'm doing is out of love for you. I don't like you, but I respect your abilities. You've got Father's mind-for business."

John bowed his head in recognition of her unwilling compliment.

"I've been watching you. You've brought Elizabeth into line, Lord knows how. Nate you have under your thumb and the two old Fairons. You evidently have sense. This house now. It must go to a Rambeau. I'm leaving it to you, but you've got to say that you'll keep it just the way Father, and I after him, kept it."

John did not answer her. He was thinking that wealth is something you don't run away from easily once you have it. Just as he planned to minimize the influence his money gave him, more money came his way. His eyes wandered over the elegant appointments of the room. Curiously feminine it seemed to him for a woman like Martha. The rich damask of the curtains was pale rose. The upholstered headboard of the bed was a pattern of delicate grays and pinks. The carpet was oyster gray. For this house she had probably spent a fortune in antiques alone. He thought of his bachelor's quarters with a feeling of relief.

"Come," said Martha, "I haven't much more strength. There was a time when you wouldn't have hesitated—that day you came to me for help and I wouldn't give it."

"That time is past." John met her bullying gaze with a look as determined as her own. "I'll accept the responsibility, Aunt Martha, but only on my own terms. I'll not promise you how I'll fulfill the responsibility. You can't control the world after you're gone."

"Father has. Come, give me your promise. I'm waiting."

John wondered what she would say if he were to tell her how near old Philippe's plans had brought them to the loss of his choicest vineyards. Anyway, his grandfather's control after death was one thing, Aunt Martha's was another. "I am the one that is waiting," he answered. "I've given you my answer." The room was very still as their two wills battled for the last time.

Finally with a tired sigh she closed her eyes. "Very well. Have it your own way."

Then John did a strange thing for him. He reached over and laid his hand on hers. "As far as I can, I'll keep the place as it is and for the same reason you have."

"Which is?"

"Because I love it."

A wry twist that might have been interpreted as a smile played about Martha's lips before they were pressed together in a grimace of pain. Then her hand turned under his and she clutched his fingers.

"See me through it, John," she whispered.

John walked across the lawn to his grandfather's wing of the house. Old Philippe's camp chair stood in the protected angle just where it had always stood when he was alive. John sat down on it, wiped his forehead of the drops of sweat that stood on it, straightened his shoulders. Yes, he had seen her through as she had asked him to do the day of their talk over the old home, he had not shirked this time in the face of suffering. And during that hour he had decided on his future course. He intended now to work out the details of his plan.

His vineyard of Black Brocades he would sell, and take up the mortgage on the Rambeau-Fairon property. Let Nate pay him in small yearly installments. He believed Nate, once given authority, would prove a good business man. It was in his race to be so. That yearly payment would be enough to keep up this house and the grounds if he could get Nate and Monny to live here and help him with the expenses. That wouldn't exactly be Aunt Martha's idea, but the place would be kept up and in a way Grandfather would have liked.

John's mind moved cautiously, surveying the various aspects of his plan. He was certain it would work. But he wanted to be sure each little bit of it fitted into every other bit. For himself he had a plan he wanted to talk over with his friend Ritter.

"What's the chance that you could use me?" he asked, dropping in at his office a few days later. "You come to me for a lot of advice. Why not pay me for it?"

Ritter sat back in his swivel chair trying to collect his wits. This was about the last thing he had ever expected—John Rambeau wanting to live on a salary and do a job without large returns. Somehow he had always thought of Rambeau as after money.

"Well, we could certainly use your brains," he said, "for the good of the industry, but you'd have definitely to get out of business for yourself, or our assorted members wouldn't trust you. You know there are bound to be jealousies in a setup that draws in as many people and nationalities as this one."

"That's understood," said John. "The question is, have you a job for me and could you make your constituency believe I was not out to benefit myself?"

"If you're really not in business for yourself, I think I could present you to the directors in such a way that they'd approve of your appointment."

"Meaning?"

"I want proofs that you have no further connections with the wine industry."

"So you don't trust me." John's tone had an edge to it.

"Don't be a fool, Rambeau." Ritter swung his chair around to face John. "It's the good of the whole organization I'm after, and I want to be able to spike any suspicions. As far as I'm concerned, you're a kind of answer to a maiden's prayer. None of us in the office has been trained directly in business. You have. You've got a nose for it. We need you. But you come from a money-making family. Money seems to stick to you somehow. It isn't going to be easy to make people believe you've suddenly turned altruistic. I'll be damned myself if I see why you're doing it."

"Altruism, your grandmother! Why do you think I'd be monkeying around with that kind of stuff?"

Ritter laughed. He had to at the look of dismay on John's face.

"Now get this into your wooden head, Ritter. I'm no philanthropist. The job is something I'd like and I don't like being the head of a family business. Other than that it's nobody's concern as I see it. If you say you'll take me on, I'll go ahead. But I don't want to be out on a limb without any work to do."

"I do the hiring and firing here," Ritter answered, "and that means you're hired. I tell you, Rambeau, you're the man to help me put through a big thing we've got on. You know the raisin business."

"Yes."

"Well, I've an idea that before we get through with it we'll have to turn every grape in these valleys that we can into raisins, to feed Europe. Sure as I'm sitting here Europe is going to be starving in another year. Then the government will be asking for all kinds of concentrated foods. We'll need an expert like you to help on plans then."

"All right," John answered. "I'm your man."

John decided to sound out Francis Fairon next. A trifle tough to inundate him with a family as large as Monny's unless he wanted it. Nate and he always seemed to get along, but there were four children and another one coming. The two eldest were away at school but there were vacations to think about when they'd all be around the house, and Francis was used to quiet and order—a thing not found with a pack of children in and out.

A few days after Martha's funeral John went to see Francis. A strange look crossed Francis Fairon's face when John told him his plan and then he made an even stranger remark. "I wish your mother could have known that Monny and her family were to live with me."

It seemed an irrelevant answer. John wondered if Francis were trying to evade stating his own preferences. "But what about you? That's the important thing, sir. You've never had a lot of kids around. Do you think you could stand them?" he asked.

"I'd be delighted. As a matter of fact it's been lonely in the house ever since Elizabeth went away." Then Francis turned and walked hastily out of the room.

Everything was going smoothly, too smoothly, thought John. There was bound to be a hitch somewhere. It might come with Monny. Monny might not want to leave the house where she was born. She clung to the things she was accustomed to.

He found her out by the swimming pool with her two youngest. There had been a space of several years between her older boys, born in quick succession in the first years of her marriage, and this boy and girl ten and eight. Now after a second and longer wait there was to be another. *There isn't a Rambeau look or trait about them,* he was thinking, watching the boy and girl at play in the pool. *They look like Nate.*

Monica seemed entirely absorbed in her sewing. How remote from him she seemed. Of late years he always felt lonely when he was with Monny and her family. Her happiness was so complete that it didn't seem to have room in it for anyone but Nate and her children. The days when Monny had mothered him seemed to belong to some other existence. He doubted if she even remembered them.

"I came to talk something over with you, Monny," he began, "something I want you to do for me."

"Why, yes, John, of course," she said. "I'll do anything for you I can," she added.

She means, thought John, *she will do it if it doesn't interfere with her plans for Nate and the children.* "You can do this," he assured her. "Of course you know that Aunt Martha left me the old home."

"Yes," she answered, a little wistfully.

"We don't need to keep up two houses. We ought to consolidate. Two big houses are too expensive the way our business is going. Future prospects don't warrant it either. I want you to move over into the old home."

Monny looked up now, leaving the needle stuck in her work. John couldn't tell from her expression what she was thinking and he was afraid she might refuse him, so he hurried on. "I don't mean that you'd have to take me in. It would mean having Uncle Fran there. But you wouldn't have to put up with me very much."

He thought a look of gentle stubbornness crossed her face. So she *was* afraid of having him around. "I do want to keep for myself Grandfather's wing of the house," he went on. "But I needn't interfere with you—and as I said I wouldn't be there much. I hadn't meant to tell you until I had talked it over with Nate but I am planning to get out of the firm." There was no doubt now of the look of relief in her face. "I am getting out of the business. I don't think I belong there. That is, I am getting out if Nate will take over. I had meant to talk that over with him first—and of course with the Fairons. Nate is just the man to head it up."

Then suddenly he saw whatever it was that had kept Monny and himself apart these last years was gone.

"J. G.," she called out to her son floating on his back in the pool, "you and Sister must come out now."

"Oh, Mom."

Once the children were out of earshot, Monny began pouring out what she had to say almost incoherently. Finally she stopped, crowning her words with a burst of tears.

John neither spoke nor moved. He understood now how Monny had lost herself in this man she cared for so deeply, how she had protected him, yet not softened him—instead had kept his spirit vitalized; how she had taken the sensitive but inexperienced boy and welded him into a man of ability and courage. But of late, Monny told him, her fight seemed to have been against an adversary too mighty. She had succeeded in making Nate see that John's return to the firm had not been meant as a slight to him, but the slow torture of his race's suffering had crept behind even her guards.

"Position and authority—I'm sure they're what Nate needs. You can't know what it will mean to him," she said.

John had a sudden sense of what it would have meant to have had Elizabeth close to him all these years as Monny had been to Nate. He had seen Elizabeth only occasionally since the clearing of her property two years ago. He felt suddenly very much alone.

Nate did not display any very great joy when John talked to him. "It's very noble of you, John, helping the down-trodden race within your gates, but I'm quite reconciled to going on as your pensioner." Nate's tone was bitter and sarcastic.

For a moment John was so angry he could have thrashed him. Then he felt himself cooling off. "Don't be a damn fool," he said. "You don't suppose I'd get out if I didn't have something else I wanted to do more, do you? Nor," he added, "unless I thought you could do the job. I'm not the heroic kind."

Then John came as near as he had ever come in his life to

making an apology to any man. "I know you have reason to distrust me," he said. "I had been hurt and I wanted to hurt somebody just after your marriage. You happened to be in my path."

Nate's guarded expression changed for a moment. "Of course I'd like the job," he managed to say before his defenses went up again.

John hitched his collar, straightened his cuffs, picked up his crutch and got himself out of the office. These confidential tête-à-têtes with his family just weren't his dish. Well, everything was arranged now.

It took him a few days to straighten out his papers and turn matters over to Nate. Once he was through he had intended to go directly to San Francisco. He would see Chu, then report to Ritter. David's wife had written saying Chu asked to see him. Chu was a very old man now, living out his last days with David's family in Chinatown. David was in his own country now. Chu lived there in spirit. Long hours each day he spent picking out on his Chinese violin the new songs of China—the song of the co-operatives, the song of the farmers, the song of the soldiers. Probably what Chu wanted was to arrange to send some more money to David.

A letter from Elizabeth made John decide to stop to see her on his way north. She was distressed about Lon and Mathilde. "We've heard nothing from them," she said, "since the spring —just before France fell. I don't dare talk to Andrew about it for fear the news will make him worse. Could you help me, John?"

LXII

He ENJOYED the long ride up through the hot valleys. The grapes were beginning to move. He passed great loads of them, with men in their clean rubber boots standing knee-deep in the fruit.

Deep content settled over John. Never probably had old Philippe ridden through the valleys in such perfect contentment. His dream of the consecration of his wine to the church had always contended with his consecration to wealth. John had the contentment come of singleness of purpose.

His idea of his future job was growing. Nate had set him to thinking. If men like Nate could come to feel themselves welcomed in the larger association of men, the valleys would be a lot better off. *I suppose that's what Ritter, the old fox, has been after all the time—make men of different racial strains pull together in a co-operative effort.*

All through the valleys he rejoiced in the signs of the vintage. Old jalopies, the cars of the pickers, stood in the vineyards. Great trucks passed him, loaded so high that bunches of grapes hung over the side. He could hear the rumbling of the trucks through the canyonlike street of the town where he stopped for the night. He had started late and had decided to break his journey.

It was noon the next day before he turned in at Elizabeth's gate. A truck stood by the unloading platform. In a steady gold and purple stream the grapes were traveling along the conveyor that led to the crushers, and in the air was the clean, fragrant smell of the crushed fruit.

"Hi!" he called out to the young winemaster. "The Missus around?"

"They're all picking the upper vineyards. They took their lunch—staying the day."

As John came around the bend so dear to all the Rambeaus, he looked down upon the Valley spread out before him, saw the bright shimmery lines of village streets, bordered by little homes. Scattered over the Valley were windmills and white houses and trees. Each time he stopped to look, there seemed to be a new house or a new windmill. He raised his eyes to the first and second line of mountains. The light between the ranges meant other valleys.

André ran down the slope. "Hi, John. We won't have to pick any more now you've come."

"Where are you working?"

"Just over there. See Dad lying on some grass." He put his warm moist hands into John's and pulled him forward. Hidden by the wagon and the white horses standing in the road, John saw Elizabeth before she saw him. She had a bright kerchief over her head. Her blue cotton shirt clung to her. He could see the curve of her cheek, the curve of her breast, and the curve of her arm as she drew a dozen clusters toward her and cut the bunches loose with the grape knife fastened to her finger. He heard the soft thud of the fruit as it dropped to the lug box beneath.

"Mom," shouted André, "it's John." She was caught off guard and he could see a light come into her face. He must shut his heart against the knowledge of their love for each other.

"I'm so glad to see you, John!" Elizabeth said, getting up from her knees. "I've had news from Lon. They've left France. The letter has been delayed. I can't quite make out just when they will arrive. But I think tomorrow or the next day. Could you meet them? I can't leave Andrew. He's not been so well lately."

"Mom, Mom," André broke in, "can't we eat now?"

"If your father is awake."

"Yes, he is."

Elizabeth took André's chin in her hand and lifted his face so that she could look into his eyes. "You didn't wake him, did you, André?"

His big black eyes looked straight into hers. "It was time." Then he wriggled loose and ran up the slope to the grove of redwoods. Just out of their shadow a blanket had been stretched. Full length upon it lay Andrew, idly toying with the stalks of wild oats at its edge, shaking the kernels out of the chaff. His hand looked as thin as the empty husks. Phil was beside him, laying out bread and wine from a basket.

At the end of the day Phil and André rode in on the load. Elizabeth and Andrew followed in John's car.

"I like this coming down to the house, John, from this hill. You can just see the roof and the top of the arbor and the half-circle of the drive. It's so locked into peace," Andrew said. Elizabeth's heart gave a leap. He had never spoken of peace before.

"There's a car turning in at the gate," Elizabeth said. They had reached the winery now and looking down, they could see a man and a woman walking toward the house—strangely familiar figures.

"Why, it's Lon!" cried Elizabeth. She hurried down and met Lon and Mathilde at the steps that led from the arbor to the house.

"My little," exclaimed Lon holding out his arms to Elizabeth, "we must cast ourselves on your mercy." His voice broke on the last word.

Elizabeth kissed him first on one cheek, then the other. "You're in your father's house, Lon." She felt herself standing in the place of old Philippe guarding the family. Phil and André appeared. She drew them forward. "Your *grand père*— and *grand mère*."

"It's just as I dreamed it would be," Mathilde murmured. "Fat little boys like this." She put her hand on André's shoulder, warm and moist from his hours in the sun.

"We must make you understand," said Lon as they sat at dinner that evening in the quiet arbor, "what it's like."

"Lon dear," Elizabeth broke in, "you must forget, as Andrew has." It was weeks since Andrew had clung to her in panic as he had for so many nights after his return. He was listening now to the twilight sounds of the valley: a bird settling itself comfortably in its nest in the arbor over his head, the dry rustle of old leaves in the fitful night breeze.

Lon began again. "I must make you understand."

What could she do? Elizabeth did not want Andrew to hear, and she wished she could get the boys away. But Phil was too old for bed at this hour and André was willful. It was too soon after dinner to send them to the pool.

Mathilde leaned forward, her eyes mournful and frightened. "Look," she cried, flinging down on the table a paper she had been holding in her hand, "you must look so you'll see what it's like. What is happening. This is Europe. There is no mercy there. Don't let it be like that here."

In the fading light John, sitting the farthest away, saw only a crude mass of blues, reds, and yellows, the figure of a stalwart man throwing refuse from a wheelbarrow onto a dung heap. Noticing the look of horror on Elizabeth's face he leaned forward to get a closer view. Now he saw the picture in all its detail. The refuse dumped from the barrow took shape—a man. He saw the thorn-crowned head, pierced hands and feet. Hurled after Him into the pit the cup and the loaf. All around rose man's creations, tall buildings, factories, mammoth machines. Below were the words, "The Exaltation of Man."

A sudden sob escaped from Andrew's throat. John looked at the boys. He saw fright in Phil's eyes, fascination in André's, before Elizabeth gently laid the folds of her napkin over the picture. John was not a religious man, but he was shaken.

"Is blackness to come over all the earth?" Mathilde's mournful eyes searched the faces around her.

"Only until the ninth hour," said Elizabeth resolutely. "Come, Andrew, it's getting cool. Phil and André, I want you to come in, too."

When Mathilde and Lon had gone in also, John went up the road that circled the house. He stood for a long time in front of the winery. One by one the lights in the house went out, except the light in Andrew's room.

"Only a damned silly fool would make a picture like that," John said aloud. But he could not dismiss it so easily. The words under the picture haunted him, "The Exaltation of Man." There *was* exaltation in violence. John remembered his own violences and their exaltations. That sense of the super-human in him when he had kicked Mamoulian, when he took Buz, and when he burned the vineyards. Other deeds. And now, because of the violence he himself had brought about, he was useless to defend the things he loved. Beyond the coastal range sheltering these quiet valleys lay the Pacific and Japan. Beyond the Sierra to the east lay Europe where men, ruled by violence, sought to destroy all that the Christian world had attained.

A light went on behind him in the winery, casting a bright square from its open door. The winemaster was going his rounds.

Mechanically John entered the building and went with the young Italian up the flight of steps to look down into the vats, filled with the new crush boiling and seething in first fermentation.

The familiar routines quieted him. In an alcove off the bottling chamber stood a small table and chairs. Old Philippe had used the place when tasting wine. John took from a shelf, cut in the rock, one of the tulip-shaped glasses—narrow lipped, crystal clear—held it in his hand. It was beautiful in its functional simplicity. He thought of the ancient goblets old Philippe had left him to be passed down in the family. In the tombs of the Egyptians cups had been found. Cups were traced in the margins of sacred books. He thought of the mystical, sacrificial cup which Christ had offered man—God in man dying and living again.

The winemaster had come into the room. "It's midnight," he explained as he laid out a loaf and cheese and wine. Silently the two men munched the bread, drank the wine.

LXIII

Two years, and over the valleys of California to the mountains that shut them in, warplanes guarding the valleys droned during the day and during the night.

On the high Donner Pass, named in remembrance of the men who had starved in the snow on the march to California with its gold fields, its rich valleys, stood a gas station. In front of it a boy of eighteen worked. He was tall and powerfully built. His work shirt, made to fit the average man, was stretched tight across his chest. Occasionally he stopped work on the tire he was mending to look up at the planes overhead. The words of the song he was singing, clear and strong when he looked up, were muffled when he stooped to his work.

> "Lots of folks back east is sage leavin' home . . .
> Cross the desert sands they roll,
> Gittin' out of that old dust bowl.
> They think they're goin' to a sugar bowl;
> But here's what they find:
> Now, the police at the port of entry say,
> 'You're number fourteen thousand fer today.'
> Oh, if you ain't got the do-re-mi, folks,
> If you ain't got the do-re-mi,
> Why you'd better go back . . ."

"Somebody's got to do it," he said stubbornly to himself. "Somebody's got to stop all this here killing. Somebody's just got to lick the pants off 'em. Keep 'em out of this country." He began singing again, still watching the sky.

"California is a garden of Eden,
A paradise to live in or see,
But believe it or not, you won't find it so hot
If you ain't got——"

The song was suddenly clipped off short. "I guess one of 'em has got to be me," he said with some surprise.

"Man'l—Man'l," a woman called from an upstairs window.

"That's me, Emanuel Guiseppe." He struck his chest with his hand. "Protector of California." He grinned.

"California is a garden of Eden,
A paradise to live in or see,
But believe it or not, you won't find it so hot
If you ain't got the do-re-mi."

So did Jean-Philippe Rambeau, immigrant, live on in his children.

THE END